Copyright ©2022 by H

All rights reserved. No part of this book may be reproduced in any form by any electronic or mechanical means, including information storage and retrieval systems, without permission in writing from the copyright owner, except by a reviewer who may quote brief passages in a review.

The moral rights of the author have been asserted.

Also by Hamish Brown

The Hunt for the Treasure of Demarco

Utter Madness

This book is dedicated to my brother because he let me use his much better computer for the formatting stages. So yeah cheers for that Ross. Dickhead.

Grit and Magic

Chapter 1

Lakeitha was not a sadistic woman, although she had ended thousands of lives, she had enjoyed no more than ten, no, twenty of the killings. But she knew that when she finally killed this monster, it would be one of the great sensual experiences of her life, like her first orgasm and the best meal she ever ate.

She had five blades on her. In her right hand she held her sword, it was a lightweight double edged straight sword with no crossguard and no groove down the centre, three feet long and made of a near unbreakable crimson metal from an unknown world. She had a big curved knife also made from an alien metal, the blade black as sin. She kept it on her left hip. She had a smaller set of twin stilettos that she kept in sheathes on her thighs. These were made of steel as was her fifth blade, a little boot knife that she kept hidden by her right ankle.

As well as her blades she also had big metal studs over the knuckles on her gloves, ensuring that her already powerful punches would be even more devastating. Last of all, she had a World Saver Hand Cannon holstered at her hip on her right side. It was loaded with two metal cylinders the size of a man's fist; these bullets were wrapped in barbed wire so that they couldn't be removed from a wound and they were soaked in an extremely potent contact poison.

Lakeitha was armed to the fucking teeth, but her many weapons had barely tasted blood today. The monster she fought was fast and intelligent, its hard skin camouflaged against the dense trees and undergrowth. She could hear it rustling around her, but she rarely spotted it until it attacked. It felt like she'd been locked in a deadly battle of focus for hours now. It could be anywhere around her and the moment she let her guard down it would attack.

Her bicep still hurt from when it had swiped at her from behind, scraping its talons into her hardened leather armour. It was her own fault, she had tried to make a run for it. She'd lowered her sword and turned tail and made a run in the vague direction of safety. She didn't cover ten meters before it was on her, scratching her and flapping its massive bat-like wings. It had pulled her off the ground, taking away her leverage.

She'd managed to break free but she knew that she didn't deserve to still be alive. She should be dead right now; she'd made two mistakes in quick succession and out here, a single error was lethal. She had tried to run and when it was on her, she had been shocked by its horrible beady bug eyes, massive mouth full of sharp teeth and the piercing shrieking noise that it made as it attacked. For seconds she had been stunned, incapacitated by fear and revulsion and the pain in her arm. In those seconds it should have killed her, but it didn't, it wounded her instead of finishing the job. When she got her chance, she wouldn't make the same mistake. And she knew her moment would come, her focus would not waver, her guard would not drop, she was going to pin it done, cut and stab and tear into it and she wouldn't need as long an opening as the one her enemy, no, her prey had squandered.

It was the hottest, brightest time of day, but it was dim on the ground where the battle was being fought; there in amongst the leaves, thorns, thistles and weeds, weaving between the massive trunks of the two hundred metre tall trees that kissed the sky with their thick branches and greedy leaves that stole most of the sunlight. Lakeitha and the monster were the two biggest creatures in the area, but there were many thousands of living things around them. Countless species of bugs, birds, strange mutated flying rodents, harmless floating spores the size of fists that bounced aimlessly through the jungle, occasionally draining trees of their sap. The canopies above them were teaming with life. All these creatures produced constant noise, an endless chattering orchestra of competing volumes and pitches. Chirping, squawking, squealing, chewing, running, climbing, screwing, howling, crying. Noise so unceasing and imprecise that it was impossible to tell where any individual sound was coming from.

There was movement all around her, but nothing big. It was watching her, she knew it was blended in with a tree trunk or a giant leaf or a bush or maybe it was perched on the side of the thirty foot tall ant hill. She had no way to tell, until it gave itself away. It could be standing behind her, in the tree branch above her, staring down at her, building up the nerve to pounce onto her back and tear through her skull.

The ground squelched under her foot, she took another step back and her boot sunk even deeper into the mud. She hesitated, she couldn't keep backing up, standing in mud would fuck her balance, she wouldn't stand a chance. She flushed with panic, she was vulnerable here, if it came at her head on then she'd be unable to back up with the mud behind her, and if it came at her from behind then it would have the high ground, it would be able to push her down this slope. She took a few wary steps forward, squeezing the sword tightly with both hands. She caught movement to her right, turned to it, saw it darting through the trees with terrible speed. It flapped its wings to propel it forward, latching onto and then pushing off tree trunk after tree trunk.

She couldn't take the hit, not with her arm like this, standing on this uneven ground, how the fuck had she allowed herself to end up in this position. Trying to focus for hours on end, it couldn't be done; she'd missed it, she had lost track of the ground she stood on.

She dropped her sword and ducked down as it lunged at her. She grabbed her ankle knife, drew her arm back and raised her head. She threw the knife at the monster, the moment it left her grasp she rolled downhill. She felt a woosh as it passed by her and heard a satisfying screech when the knife hit home.

She tumbled down the slope head in her hands, rolling through the mud. She dug in her heels and grabbed at the ground. She rolled a few more times, tearing out clumps of mud in her hands. As soon as she stopped, she got up into a low ready crouch, with her biggest knife in her right hand. She couldn't see it but she heard it. She heard it moaning and hissing at its new wound. Her heart was racing, she loved the sounds of its pain, she fed off them and she wanted more. She had this thing, she'd weakened it and now she was going to find it as it wallowed in agony and she was going to tear its throat open.

She stood, holding her knife in front of her at chest height and advanced towards the sounds. There were little streaks of red blood on some of the tree trunks and on the ground. Enough blood to create a trail. The sounds of pain got quieter and harder to locate. She kept following the trail, she knew its fate was already sealed, she could hear the life draining from it as its desperate noises faded away. The trail took a sharp turn around a large tree trunk, and she followed it. She knew how quickly this thing moved and wondered how far it had run before it lost the strength to keep going. The drops of blood on the dead leaves and dirt reached the roots of a tree and climbed up it, then the trail curved around the tree trunk and led back onto the ground.

She followed it further, until it led her back to a different part of the bloody trail. This was no accident; she went a little further, the trail wound and turned and backed up on itself in a random mess that led inwards and outwards in every direction. She'd completely lost it and knew it wasn't dying just yet. This thing was smarter than she'd thought.

The freakish creature had eluded her, but she knew it hadn't given up on the fight. She knew that neither of them were going to back down from this. It wasn't an option anymore. They'd locked themselves into a mortal dual, this had to end with one or both of them dead.

She heard a rustling at her feet and looked down as the jaw of the big bat-like insect clamped down around her leg. Its massive two top teeth pierced the material protecting her shin and sunk into her. Its smaller four bottom teeth hurt her but failed to tear through her armour. The pain was so extreme that she felt paralysed for a moment, then it flapped its wings and lifted her legs off the ground. She fell, her back landing on a jagged little tree stump. She felt like she'd been stabbed between her shoulder blades.

The creature released her leg and jumped on top of her, it opened its mouth, the big fleshy sack below its neck bulged to the point of bursting and it spat acid onto her face. She screeched and shut her eyes as her skin burned. She tried wiping it off her face with her left hand as she stabbed blindly at the monster with her right. She imagined all her skin dissolving and her eyes never seeing again. She was scared and panicking and in so much pain, her leg was bleeding, her arm was bleeding, her back was practically impaled and she was losing, like a pathetic little bitch. She wasn't going to die like this. She paid no mind to which limbs were injured and which were not, she had to use everything that she had, or in a few seconds she'd have nothing.

She kept swinging her knife but she didn't hit anything, she felt it jump off her and heard the flap of its wings as it backed up. She kicked upwards blindly and caught it with the steel toe of her boot, making it back off even more. She put her left hand down onto the ground and pushed hard, kicking the ground to add to the thrust. She launched herself from the narrow tree stump and rolled to her right. She rolled twice, then jumped to her feet, stumbling but not falling, and started swinging frenziedly, yelling out with each strike, she sounded scared and this made her angry, made her swing harder and shout louder, until she sounded like a wild animal that wasn't scared of anything. She clattered into a tree, turned and headed in the opposite direction, "Raaghhh!" She roared, "Come on! Come on you fucker!" She shouted as she stabbed at thin air.

The monster smacked hard into her back, the force of the impact sending her flying into another tree. She hit it chin first. It hurt, the way only a heavy blow to the chin hurts. Made her head fuzzy, made her chin feel as if it was made of cracked porcelain. She spun round and stabbed, feeling the blade cut deep into something. Instantly more acid was gushing onto her chest and down her torso, but thankfully it didn't burn through her armoured clothing. The monster gave a head splitting screech. She couldn't see a thing, but the wretched noise it made and the feeling of its flapping wings moving the air, told her exactly where it was. She took six quick steps and stabbed.

She missed and its wing knocked into her side, sending her stumbling. She swung again and the blade hit a tree branch. She tried to pull it free but it wouldn't budge. The monster flew into her, leading with its foot claws, which stabbed her gut, but didn't cut through her clothes. She was lifted off her feet and experienced a very precious moment of ignorance that she didn't appreciate until immediately after it ended. This moment lasted from when she got knocked off her feet, until when she realised that she should already have hit the ground. She kept falling, picking up speed and felt immense dread that she'd been knocked off a cliff. She opened her eyes, she couldn't help it. They stung a little but it wasn't too bad. There was a lot of blood in her eyes; everything was red. Before she hit the ground, she had just enough time to register the ridge above her and the blood soaked monster with a slashed acid sack, diving after her.

She landed on her back. She couldn't breathe and she couldn't move, her body was paralysed.

It came down, grabbed her and started flapping its wings. She was surprised that it didn't kill her on the spot. Her injured body being dragged up into the air made every bone in her back feel as if they were about to break.

It wasn't gaining height very quickly, she was only a few feet above the ground. Now was the time to make her move, before it climbed to a lethal height. She couldn't bear the idea of another serious fall. She knew what to do. She still had two knives on her, and right now it was vulnerable, its head pointed upwards, its body, its neck, its slashed acid sack, all of them were exposed and within an arm's length of her. But she couldn't do it. Her arms were limp, she couldn't lift them to save her own life. They were getting higher, it flapped its bleeding wings furiously.

She had to act now. She stopped thinking about it, shut out all the pain, ignored time bleeding through her fingers and just did it. She raised her right hand and grasped onto the handle of one of her knives. Her grip was frail and her arms weak, she started pulling it from the scabbard on her leg. She got it halfway out; then she pulled it loose and held it in her hand. She pushed through her paralysis and thrust the blade upwards, it meekly bounced off the monster's torso without cutting into it at all, the impact breaking her pathetic grip. The knife fell out of her hand, a few seconds later she heard it hit the ground. That was it, she needed more time to recover from her fall. Not long, but more than a few seconds. So she just let it carry her higher.

She couldn't fight her way out and she'd missed her moment anyway. She'd lost, it had her, when it dropped her, she'd die, it was only a matter of time. Ten seconds or so passed, they got higher and higher, it still hadn't dropped her. Was it taking her somewhere. A nest, a den, a hovel, a cave. There could be a thousand of them waiting, hanging upside down on the ceiling.

It started to carry her off to the left, away from the ditch far below them. The thing was struggling with her weight, it was hissing and their ascent was slowing. It carried her further, there was hardly any wind, everything around them was still and open. Beneath them, far below was the ground, they were so high up and the thing that carried her was so shaky and unstable that Lakeitha started feeling terrible vertigo. She would've vomited if there wasn't so much raw adrenaline coursing through her. Far below her were rocks that would crack her open when she landed on them and creatures of all descriptions that would gorge on her corpse.

They hovered above some much shorter treetops, compared to the two hundred metre behemoths that they had been surrounded by. It was definitely trying to take her somewhere but it was also struggling, its gasps and hisses got louder and the flaps of its wings got weaker.

They started dropping in the space between flaps. Then the flaps stopped lifting them higher. It let out a worried yelp and started flapping even harder, trying to keep them in the air but they slowly dropped closer to the treetops beneath. There was no way that it could keep this up, she was too heavy. She knew what was coming. She glanced down, those trees would probably kill her before she even hit the ground.

Something came over her, she experienced a burst of primal strength, released from somewhere inside of her that had been locked off until this moment. She reached up and grabbed ahold of the monster's leg just as its claws released her.

It screeched its alarm as it realised that Lakeitha was holding onto it. She pulled out her last remaining knife and used it to hack at the monster's other leg before it thought to claw at her face. She hit it again and again, drawing screams from the thing that held her precariously in the air. She held on tighter, her grip was the only thing that kept her alive. She hacked straight through the monster's leg and the claw fell in a squirt of blood.

Despite what she'd just done, the monster had no choice but to keep flapping its wings, or they'd both die. It stopped flapping.

After a moment of weightlessness, they started racing towards the treetops below. The monster had its head pointed down and its wings tucked in, making the fall even faster. Lakeitha flailed around gracelessly, the wind shrieking in her ears, but she didn't let go of the monster's leg. As long as she didn't let go she still had a glimmer of control, her hand on the monster's leg was the centrepoint of her existence, it was all that mattered. But this control was all an illusion, either way she was still falling through the sky and the only one with a shred of control was her enemy.

Just before they hit the trees the monster unfurled its wings and flapped hard, stopping their fall and sending a terrible jolt through Lakeitha's shoulder. It lowered her into the tallest treetops and dragged her through them, her arm feeling like it was going to be ripped from her body at any moment. She smashed into treetop after treetop. She was battered by big branches and scratched by small branches. Through all of it, all she focused on was that she could not let go.

They stopped moving forward when her entire body hit an especially tall and sturdy treetop. It kept dragging her against the tree, she kicked against it, trying to push herself away, then her legs slipped and her head cracked against it, hard. Everything went black. She thought she was dead, then she realised that she wasn't dead, she was blind, then she remembered that she could not let go of this sneaky fucker's leg or she would find herself dead imminently. She was flung against the treetop again, she just had to take the hit. She couldn't see a thing, couldn't even make out any shapes. She felt her body being moved and heard the monster flapping its wings even more aggressively. She braced herself for another hit, but instead felt herself being lifted higher into the air.

The creature stopped flapping and she went back into freefall. This time she knew what was coming and braced herself before the monster flapped its wings again. As she stopped falling and her arm once again took the brunt of gravity's displeasure, her sight suddenly came back. It wasn't perfect, everything was still very fuzzy, but she could see, so she was back in the fight.

The monster was flapping its wings hard, struggling with the effort of lifting her higher again. She could feel how much this tactic was taking out of it. Remarkably, she still had her last knife in her hand, she readied herself to use it just as she felt the monster about to start another free fall. In that breath moment of anticipation, Lakeitha pulled herself up towards the monster, using only the strength in her injured right arm, and she plunged the blade into the monster's wing and held it there, using the purchase to wrap her legs around the monsters back and tuck her knees against the ridge of its spine. They started falling.

She held onto it as it struggled, the two of them stuck together, spinning around, neither one of them in control. They fell clumsily from the sky. The drop towards the trees lasted an eternity in two seconds. As luck would have it, she was on top when they hit the first tree branches and the monster took most of the impact as thick and thin branches alike snapped underneath them. Shards of wood filled the air and her screams got louder as the screams of the monster were silenced. They hit a tree trunk, it felt like they'd been struck by a giant's bat. They were sent spinning into more branches, both of them being stabbed all over their bodies, as they fell, they were grated against the trees like cheese.

Somewhere along the line Lakeitha had let go of the monster to use her hands to shield her face. The endless impacts had jarred them apart and now they each had to take every hit on the way down.

The back of her head felt as if it was being carved up with a dull knife. A thick branch hit her face and her hands made no difference, her head was snapped back so hard that it was a wonder she wasn't decapitated. Her whole body flipped back and for a fraction of a second, she fell horizontally facing upwards at the unsettled branches she'd left behind and the sky above. In that brief moment she thought, *falling from the sky, what a way to…* Her thought was interrupted when the backs of her legs hit another branch, which flipped her over and sent her face down again until she landed gut first on a strong branch, stopping her fall and knocking the air out of her lungs.

She teetered for a moment on that branch, gasping for air, gravity threatening to pull her in either direction. A lot of blood was leaking out of her nostrils.

She started slipping backwards. Her hips tipped over, her belly slid down it and her breasts followed, she let out a desperate snivel as her head dropped beneath it and she grasped her hands around the branch. The weight of her body was torturous on her damaged hands. She was sure that a few fingers were broken inside those gloves and every muscle in her arms and shoulders felt spent and ruined. She was amazed that she was even capable of holding on. But holding on was all she had.

All those thousands of pull ups that she'd done in training and when she really needed to do one, she was just too fucking tired. Typical.

She looked down; she was maybe fifteen meters above the ground, there were a few large branches beneath her but not many, and there were none for the bottom five meters or so. She'd probably break both legs but survive. She'd pass out quickly and then either blood loss, organ failure or some creature in the area would finish the job. But before any of that could happen, first she'd have to let go of the branch. She held on and thought about her brother. If she died here today, then Mikey would be alone and he'd have no one to take care of him and if that happened, he'd be dead within a month. Her brother was strong, he had a resolve, a strength in his soul that kept him alive when most people would have died long ago, but she was really all he had left to live for, and he was all she had to live for.

She gritted her teeth. She was strong like Mikey, stronger than anything this world had to throw at her and she would not let go.

She heard a noise that broke her focus. To her it was unmistakable, the determined hiss of the monster that she'd been fighting for an achingly long time.

She looked around her, acutely aware that she didn't have a single blade left on her. She still had her World Saver strapped to her back, but it would be no use in this situation. She heard a rustling behind her, something big was moving between the trees. Then she heard another hiss, it was so loud, it was a noise that a creature ten times its size would make.

She was completely exposed like this, with her back to it, hanging from the tree branch like a hunk of meat on a butcher's hook. She heard it coming closer, a creature with a natural talent for stealth so beaten and battered that it couldn't even sneak up behind her without buckling branches and wailing in agony.

She had an idea. She hated the idea, it would probably go wrong and even if it didn't, just the thought of performing the act made her want to cry. But she had no choice in the matter.

She let go of the branch with her right hand and wrapped it around the other side just as her left hand slipped, unable to hold her full weight. She held on with her right hand, as her body turned to face the monster. She swayed from side to side, trying to reach up to the branch with her left hand, feeling herself about to slip. She kept her eyes on her enemy; it was perched on a branch on another tree about ten meters away from her and about a metre below her. It was ragged, covered in blood and had numerous brand new gashes and tears in its skin. She could see that it was preparing to make the last leap across the gap between them, from the way that it leaned forward, moving its pointed shoulder blades and baring its fangs. She reckoned it was probably so badly beaten up that it couldn't activate its near perfect camouflage, but looking at it, she was sure it could at least make the jump.

Her dangling slowed and with great effort she swung her left hand up and grabbed back ahold of the branch. She felt like her belly was exposed, especially to an attack from below. She was very aware of how fast this thing could strike.

She started swinging her legs backwards and forwards, backwards and forwards, building up momentum. This fucking disease had been after her for hours, had chipped away at her, draining her energy, her focus, her strength, like a leech, but she was not going to let it win. Even if she did die, she was going to make sure that it died first. She was a fucking animal, the most dangerous thing alive and she would not lose. Rage and determination fuelled her swings and reinforced her grip and when the monster made its leap for her, she was ready.

She let go before the peak of her up swing and dived through the air to meet it, leading with her feet in their big, solid boots. She kicked it in mid-air, her feet smacking into its open mouth, and reversing its momentum, sending both of them into the tree it had jumped from. They bounced off of the tree trunk and her feet were dislodged. They fell straight down. It hit the ground first and she landed on top of it, with the sound of snapping bones.

After a moment's pause they both started screaming, loud guttural noises that merged together, creating an agonised duet.

Her scream ended and she cried, crying in pain and exhaustion and anger, crying without tears and making a lot of noise. She really hated this thing. She slumped on top of it, pinning it down with her knees. Even sitting up straight took a lot of effort. She wanted to collapse and cry herself to sleep on the ground, but more than that she wanted to kill this thing and the noises it made were a powerful reminder that she hadn't accomplished that yet.

She balled up her hands into fists and punched down on it, the big metal studs digging into its beady eye. She hit it again, harder and again, raining down punch after punch, feeling immense pleasure with each strike and the sound of its screams and the feeling of it squirming beneath her. She punched its massive fangs, hitting them, watching chips break off until she punched one of them and half of it snapped off. She punched it until she felt its skull start to cave in and the squirming stopped and it was completely dead. She let her bloody fists hang by her sides, panting hard, her upper body swelling up with each heavy breath of air. She let out a triumphant roar, her anger gone and her bloodlust satisfied.

She crawled over to the tree trunk and rested her back against it. She wanted to fall asleep right there and then, but if she did, she'd probably never wake up. She checked her limbs; none broken but they'd all come close. She looked over at the monster, just making sure that it was definitely dead. Yup.

Chapter 2

It took her almost an hour to find all five of her blades again. Unless her life absolutely depended on it, she would never abandon any of them. She carried five for a reason. Because out here, four simply wasn't enough.

Then she walked around, warily monitoring how much daylight she had left. She never spent a night outside if she could help it. She was a little bit lost, she knew roughly where she was, roughly six miles away from Dantez, but she hadn't been to this particular area in years and she wasn't quite sure which direction she came from.

After a while spent limping around, she found a spot she knew well. Where the soil turned from brown to bright pink, where the trees were white with purple leaves, where massive harmless flowers bloomed in many different patterns and colours. She spat blood on the pink soil and leaned her back against a white tree as she took a piss. She remembered which direction to walk in and set off, holding her sword in her hand, constantly worried that she was about to pass out and become an easy meal for whatever found her first.

She walked for two hours before she reached The Passage, joining it a little over a mile away from the gates of Dantez.

The Passage was the only road left on planet earth. It was three hundred meters wide and a little over 40 miles long. It connected the only two remaining cities on planet earth; Dantez and Alcraze. Being so close to the gates of Dantez, Lakeitha was walking on cracked tarmac but further along The Passage was unpaved. The further away from the cities, the more exposed that part of The Passage would be. It wasn't safe to have crews of Grand Scrapers crawling their way along the road for several weeks. They'd all be dead before the job was done. They were quick to find a solution in order to prevent the jungle from spreading over The Passage and cutting them off. The two cities shared responsibilities poisoning the ground every few months. Nothing ever grew there and it took a fraction of the time that paving the road did. Trying to cross the passage was still a perilous journey.

There were open camps in the jungle beside the passage every six kilometres but the only truly safe place to spend the night was at The Keep, a fortress which sat halfway between Dantez and Alcraze. Lakeitha always thought people who were afraid to sleep anywhere except The Keep were pussies. She had spent over a hundred nights in camps far more isolated than the ones by The Passage, and hundreds more without any camp at all, sleeping light, alert to every sound around her with a weapon in her hand.

She staggered towards the gate, her face felt numb in places and in other places it was on fire. Her vision in her right eye was going blurry and she wasn't going to be able to stay on her feet much longer. Being so close to Dantez was tantalizing, soon she would be safe and she could sleep and she could let the doctors take care of her.

She was always happy to see the gates, they were almost one hundred feet tall, made of six foot thick steel. On top of the battlements were hundreds of soldiers who manned the weapons and Grand Scrapers who maintained the wall and the traps. The huge concrete wall around Dantez was practically impregnable and the people who defended it were just as solid. She was close but she couldn't relax, not until she was inside. People still died when they were this near to the gate, even though the jungle stopped a hundred meters away from the wall on all sides and the space between was filled with booby traps both mechanical and magical. There was no risk of a booby trap catching her, as long as she didn't divert from a direct course to the gate.

She knew there were a dozen sets of binoculars and scopes watching her right now. She doubted any of them would feel sorry for her. She stopped in front of the gate and waited for a minute or so before she heard the loud turning of the mechanisms that opened the gate, just a crack. Two doctors and ten soldiers ran out to meet her. The doctors greeted her by name and she started listing her injuries while the soldiers covered their backs. No one ever relaxed until they were inside.

Chapter 3

Luther batted down his opponent's forearm, the weak block folding with no resistance and leaving his face wide open. Luther hit him with the right and then the left. He battered the head with punch after punch, each blow yielding a loud pop or crunch that made the crowd roar and squirm. It was like this guy wasn't even trying to fight back anymore, he couldn't move out of the way, couldn't defend himself. Like hitting a punching bag. He shot an uppercut into the man's ribs. He heard them break. Luther was fighting like an animal, so filled with anger and a need to hurt, each hit bringing a moment's ecstasy. He'd reached a state of controlled frenzy, his technique was perfect, his body fighting for itself, relying on its well-honed muscle memory to channel his savagery.

It was time to finish the fight. He stepped in, tucked his right leg behind his feet and shoved his upper body with all his immense strength. The fighter fell gracelessly, hit the ground hard and Luther jumped on him, leading with his elbow, smashing it down on his bare chest. Before the gasp of the crowd had finished, he had already put on a triangle choke. Immobilising his right arm and wrapping both his legs around the man's neck.

Bane watched the fight and admired Luther's grace, impressive for a man his size. He was rippling with muscle and his form was perfect, he cornered his opponent, dismantled his blocks and never let up the attack. He took the poor bastard down to the ground and quickly trapped him in a triangle choke. The other fighter pointlessly kicked his legs in the air and stamped on the floor, but he abandoned this effort after a couple of seconds and tapped out.

Joe turned to him grinning, "Well?" He said with such smugness that you would have thought he'd personally won the fight. Bane shrugged, watching Luther pacing back and forth in the cage, shouting to the feverishly applauding crowd. "He's a bit showy isn't he." "Of course, he's the champ." Replied Joe, "Well, he won't be the champ out there. He'll be just like everything else, always one mistake away from death. If we send him out cocky, then he won't come back. You think he can get his head around that?" Joe shrugged. "I honestly don't know. I can't tell you that he hasn't got an ego. Because he does, big time. He knows he's the best fighter around, he has been for a while now and as you can see, he enjoys it. But he wants more. He wants a new, bigger challenge." Bane had dealt with a lot of people like that over the years. In a world with less than two hundred thousand people left, very few of them were willing to work as Hell Hunters. And a lot of them wanted to do it to prove that they were the toughest and the best. All Hell Hunters were ambitious and a little crazy, but too much ambition got people killed.

They watched Luther wiping blood from his knuckles and amping himself up for the next fight. "He's a very big guy. That could hurt his stamina." Joe shook his head, "Don't worry about it, I've had him do three fights in one night." "If this guy can't walk the length of The Passage in a single day, then I won't take him on, that's a deal breaking." "Trust me, he can do it."

Luther watched two fighters step into the cage. Both were a little shorter than him, muscular but not as broad as he was and had shaved heads. Luther liked to keep a little bit of hair on his head. He had to keep it short, so that other fighters couldn't grab it, but he didn't want to be bald. He knew them both of course, he knew every cage fighter in Dantez and most in Alcraze. He'd fought one of them before. He'd been good, a little better than the guy he just battered. His name was Eric, the other was called Devon.

They spread out to different sides of the cage, Eric going right and Devon going left.

"Two at once huh." commented Bane, "I know right, he didn't bat an eyelid." "He needs some fear in him if he's gonna survive." "Right now, he's a big fish in a small pond, he has no reason to be afraid." "These guys good?" "Best I could get for tonight."

The bell rang and Eric came for him, moving fast and Luther went to meet him. Eric started swinging a right hook and Luther cut him off with his right palm, jamming it against Eric's wrist, then popping his right elbow up into

Eric's nose. He turned and caught him with a left jab in the face, then dropped low and fired three quick jabs into his stomach. Luther backed up, turning to face Devon as he approached. Eric backed away, dazed and needing time to recover.

Devon came at him with flying fists. Sending two punches to Luther's head, fast as he'd ever seen. He blocked both punches and while he was covering up Devon snuck a low blow to his exposed right side. Luther grunted and replied with a right hook to Devon's face, but Devon sidestepped him and kicked high, catching him on the right side of his head. This sent Luther stumbling, thrown off balance, he barely even saw the foot coming before it hit him. He managed to get away from Devon as he regained his bearings.

Through the fog he saw Eric coming straight at him, fists high, ready to box and Luther ran at him, dived low and tackled him above the ankles. Eric toppled over and Luther was up and on him in no time, knees pinning his shoulders, raining punches down on his face. One, two, three.

He turned, seeing Devon coming towards him out of his peripheral vision. He crossed his forearms into an x and blocked the kick that Devon had aimed at his chin. He pushed his arms down, repelling the foot and then he pushed himself up and kicked at Devon's stomach, but Devon backed out of range. Devon sent another kick to Luther's head, which Luther blocked and then grabbed a hold of Devon's leg before he could pull back. He held Devon off balance and then drove forwards, pushing him off his remaining foot. He fell halfway before his shoulders and head rammed against the cage. Luther dropped the leg and punched downwards as Devon was already attempting to get up. He caught Devon perfectly in the face, he practically set himself up for the most devastating punch possible.

Even Bane winced a little when he saw Luther flip the guy off his feet and smash him against the cage. The whole crowd went wild. "Very quick reflexes." said Joe. Bane was liking what he saw, Luther was a formidable cage fighter, which itself deserved respect.

Luther hit Devon a second time going for the knockout, but then Eric barged into him, pushing him away from Devon. Eric hit him hard in the ribs, then across the face and then went for his chin but Luther blocked it and grabbed ahold of Eric's ear. He held him in place and headbutted him, hard. He headbutted him again, then kneed him in the stomach. Eric dropped to his knees, swaying like he was drunk. Luther was practically holding him up by the ears. He could have kneed him in the face right there and then, that probably would have knocked him out, or at least made it much easier to finish him off, but that would have been cheating. Hitting a man when he was down was one thing, when he was on the ground he could still fight back, still posed a threat, but this, this was pitiful and it'd be wrong for him to take advantage; it would rob them both of their dignity.

He backed away from Eric as Devon got to his feet. Devon came at him and Luther raised his hands defensively, his fists just below his chin. Devon fired a series of fast punches at him; he went for the side of Luther's head and Luther blocked it, then Devon snuck one through, hit in the chest just below his collarbone. He repelled Devon's next two lightning fast punches at his head with powerful forearm blocks. Devon dropped low to strike up at Luther's gut but Luther moved faster, kicking him in the face. He knocked Devon on his ass, but in an instant Devon had rolled over, jumped back on his feet and sent a rapid string of four punches at Luther's stomach, which Luther blocked, keeping his arms low and leaving his face exposed. Devon capped off the barrage of punches with a powerful uppercut that caught Luther in the chin and rocked him back, sending the cage around him spinning.

Luther was dizzy and his vision was blurry, he instinctively brought his hands up to protect his head and started backing away, hoping he didn't trip himself up in his disorientated state. He saw a hazy Devon coming towards him, his view of the fighter tilting up and down, side to side. He didn't try to fight Devon, there was no way he could hit him in this state, all he'd do is leave himself exposed and even more off balance. Devon came right up to him and kicked him in the gut, knocking him against the cage. It really hurt.

The crowd had gone quiet, the tables had turned and the champ was in trouble. They went wild when Devon closed in on Luther and started hitting him so quickly that his arms were a blur and blood was running from Luther's mouth. Bane turned to Joe, he didn't look concerned.

Luther was taking hits all over. The more powerful strikes to the head and gut hurt so much more than the smaller strikes immediately before and after; so he hardly felt those at all. Devon had over the space of a few seconds created a world of pain for him, where only the most brutal blows were really noticed.

He kept protecting his head as best he could, waiting for the perfect moment. His vision was back to normal. The dizziness wasn't too bad but Devon's ceaseless attacks made it worse when one of them slipped past his defences and rocked his head. If he waited too long, Devon would beat him down; he'd get knocked out or he'd just collapse, his body too tired and sore to go on. He saw an opening and wrapped his arms around Devon. He pushed off the cage with his left foot and started charging forwards, forcing Devon back, moving with such force that it was impossible for him to get any leverage. Then in one fluid practised motion he planted his leg behind Devon's, released the hug and as the pair of them were separated and Devon starting to fall, he punched him in the throat.

Devon fell hard, clutching his throat and gagging. The crowd roared, telling him in their fervent shouts that they still loved him. Eric was back on his feet and pacing towards him. He didn't look great but he was still in the fight, with his slanting shoulders, head swaying around like he was drunk, broken nose and blood all over his face. He came right up to him and threw a wide right hook, yelling as he did so. Luther ducked clean below the punch and hit him in the gut with a mighty uppercut. Eric doubled over and Luther hit him in the face with a right hook of his own. Eric dropped.

The crowd cheered again. Luther glanced at Devon, still down. It was over, he'd won the fight, beat two men at once, two skilled fighters. He glanced down at Eric and was surprised to see him getting back onto his feet, a fresh river of blood pouring down from his broken jaw. He had a nasty underbite that hadn't been there a moment ago. Eric took a long deep breath, wobbled a little, had to right himself, never taking his eyes off Luther. He took in another long breath and then he charged, his shoulders bowed, going for Luther's chest. Luther readied himself and when Eric reached him he sidestepped, grabbed his right bicep and his ear and then turned and threw him at the hip. He slammed onto the floor.

He'd landed on his face and chest, it had looked ugly and painful but he was already trying to push himself back up. Luther stood over him and whispered, "It's over Eric, just stay down." Eric's pained eyes flashed open wider, he was more focused and determined than ever. He placed his palms flat on the floor; he paused for a moment and then started to push himself up. Luther sighed and backed up a bit to give him room. He glanced over at Devon just to be sure, nah he wasn't getting back up. Eric stood up, wobbled badly, nearly fell over and then steadied himself and began his advance. He was clearly having a lot of trouble breathing and he looked truly exhausted. Luther knew how he was feeling right now, he was completely out of energy, running on grit and his last dregs of adrenaline.

Luther decided to do something that he had never in his entire life done before. He was going to pull his punches. Eric was standing right in front of him. The crowd was completely silent. Luther waited.

Eric threw a left jab, Luther deflected it with ease and then tapped him in the head with his right fist. Eric dropped and this time he stayed down.

Bane turned to Joe and nodded, "I'll give him a shot."

Chapter 4

After the fight Luther was approached by Joe, "Great fight Luther." "Thanks." He said absentmindedly, "I've been talking with Bane and they're going to take you on." "Good. I'll talk to you tomorrow." He headed off before Joe had the chance to say anything, he had someone he'd rather spend his time with. He took care of the cuts on his face and knuckles. He was tired but he felt like celebrating after his win and there was something deeper to it, a primal urgency that hadn't been fully satisfied by the fight. He felt an animal hunger that enveloped his thoughts and focused him. He walked across Dantez, careful to avoid people who looked like they'd just seen him fight, right now he was in no mood to talk to drunk fans. He reached The Guardian's Palace without incident and went in through the secret entrance. He quietly made his way through the building, not wanting to be seen by anyone who didn't know that he was allowed to be there, or why he was allowed to be there. He slipped into the bedroom, it was empty. His skin felt hot and there was a bubbling excitement in his stomach. He undressed, washed and waited on the bed.

Shante sat attentively through another long boring meeting. As the Guardian of Dantez, she was in charge of the city and being in charge meant meetings, lots of meetings. Shante was a beautiful ebony skinned woman with flowing hair just below her strong shoulders. She had just turned twenty five and had been the Guardian of Dantez since her father died four years ago. She said something clever while she day dreamed about crawling under the covers of her big warm bed.

The meeting finally ended and she walked through the palace to her large private apartment. The moment she opened the door, she smelt him, the fresh sweat from a night in the cage and she felt fluttering in her stomach and a warm throbbing in her vagina, she no longer felt the least bit tired. He was here, waiting for her, her muscular powerful protector. She walked into the bedroom and saw Luther lying naked on the bed. He looked up at her and smiled. They stared at each other in silence for a long time, feeling the temperature in the room rise, understanding each other, practically able to read each other's thoughts. Then she spoke, "You just gonna sit there." He was up with her in an instant, moving with that speed that she found so sexy. He wrapped his big strong arms around her and she was kissing him and he was kissing her.

That night they joined their bodies together and they left their minds at the door. He was not a champion and she was not the Guardian of Dantez; they were just two lovers, experts on each other.

Chapter 5

Lakeitha had been treated for her wounds and had then gone home and slept for twelve hours. Sleeping a lot was common among Hell Hunters in their down time, especially after long periods of time spent outside the wall, when they would spend minimal time sleeping in order to limit the time they were vulnerable. Before she'd even opened her eyes, she noticed the horrible aching and stiffness throughout her body, and the shooting pain in her leg like she was getting bitten all over again. She grabbed her vial of potta juice and put two drops on her tongue and grimaced at the flavour, it tasted like dirt and oil; after a few minutes she started to feel the pain ease.

Potta juice was one of the most accessible painkillers around, but it wasn't a fun drug. The potta juice provided no high or feelings of euphoria, or even relaxation. It just tasted bad, dulled the pain and made you very sluggish for several hours. It could never be used outside the wall because of the effect it had on a person's alertness, but when Hell Hunters were at home they mainly used it as a cheap painkiller. The doctor had insisted someone with her injuries would be dependent on potta juice for eight days at the very least, so Lakeitha knew she'd have to keep using it for four before she could bear to go without.

Five days later she returned to training at the Hell Hunters compound. The compound was beside the wall, inside was the armoury, Bane's office, the weights room, swimming pool and the large outdoor training area that was split into three walled off sections. One for sparring without weapons, one for sparring with weapons and target practice and one for the obstacle course. They did sprint training on the stretch of ground beside the obstacle course. All long distance running was done outside of the wall, as well as trekking, tree and rock climbing and an assortment of other exercises.

She stretched, jogged and then got to work. She approached the pillars, they were both ten feet tall and cut from grey stone, placed roughly five feet apart. She gave herself a decent run up towards the left pillar, jumping before she reached it and throwing her arms above her head. She caught the edge with both hands and planted her foot against the pillar. She pulled herself up without much effort and stood on top. She leaned towards the other pillar, made sure her balance was good, and her hands were ready and then let herself fall forwards. She landed hands down on the pillar, and breathed a little sigh of relief, as she always did, that her feet didn't slip off the first pillar like they had the first time she tried to do this. She held herself horizontally over the two pillars, most of her body hovering over the gap, ten feet up.

She made fists, putting her weight on her knuckles and did the first press up, exhaling sharply on the way up. She did another one and another, getting into the rhythm. The pain in her arms was mild at first, but it mounted with each rep that she did. Her core started to burn. She tensed up her face, bared her teeth like a wolf. Down and up, down and up, her exhalations getting louder. She was really feeling it now, her arms hurting, a thick layer of sweat on her forehead. Her knees were shaking, they felt like they would give way at any moment. Down and up. She focused on steadying her legs and the shaking lessened. Down and up. Massive droplets of sweat were coming from her head, getting in her eyes and falling on the pillar like rain. Down and up, halfway through exhaling she broke into loud coughs, the press up halted halfway through and it was all she could do to stop herself from crumbling. The coughs were powerful, they made her shoulders shake and her knees were weak again. She was definitely going to fall. But the coughing passed, she couldn't stop her legs from shaking but they felt more secure. Her arms were tired and sore, she felt spent and ready to quit, but she still did another press up and another after that, and she asked herself. **Are you a fucking quieter?**

She did ten more press ups, then her knees gave in and her legs fell through the gap. She opened her hands and caught the edge of the pillar, her right shoulder jerked painfully and then she let herself drop. She rested against the pillar until her thirst forced her to get back up.

As she walked for water already wanting to go back to bed she saw Bane talking with some guy who wasn't a Hell Hunter. This area was for Hell Hunters only, so this must be one of the new recruits Bane was bringing in to make up the numbers. A lot of Hell Hunters had died this year. She was so tired and thirsty that she didn't recognise him at first. He was a cage fighter, meant to be one of the best, she couldn't remember his name.

As she poured herself a large cup of water Bane came over to her, leaving the fighter to talk with Malek. Bane told her that he wanted her and some of the other seasoned Hell Hunters to take Luther to The Stronghold that night, he told her that she didn't have a choice.

After that she did two runs on the obstacle course, sprints, weights, sword practice and knife practice, training for six hours in total. She passed on swimming and unarmed combat training, she was taking it easy today.

The Stronghold was a bar owned by a former soldier called Samuel and exclusively catered to soldiers, Hell Hunters and Grand Scrapers, who made up a class called The Strong, which was invented by Samuel and only officially existed inside the walls of The Stronghold. Everybody else was called The Weak and were never allowed in.

Lakeitha, Malek and Gideon took Luther into The Stronghold, as soon as Samuel saw Luther he beckoned them over. He was fairly old, about forty-five, most of his head was bald but there were a few thick, vaguely green, almost weed-like strands of hair. His nose was misshapen and bulbous, twice the size of anyone else's and his ears were hideously swollen. His skin had a little bit of a green tinge to it. And he was fat. "Who's this?" He asked, pointing at Luther impatiently. "He's a trainee." Replied Lakeitha, "We thought we should introduce him to the place." "Yeah?" He said looking Luther up and down, "Who the fuck do you think you are, coming in here? Just a trainee." He said, spitting the words. "You think I let just anyone in here. Trainee means you haven't done shit yet, you've got some balls on you thinking you're already one of The Strong." Surprise flashed across Luther's face, followed immediately by anger. He placed his fists onto the bar, showing off his marked red knuckles, as if they were weapons, which of course they were. Samuel's big meaty arms crossed defiantly, he sneered at Luther. No more words needed to be said, this was going to happen.

Before a punch was thrown, Samuel burst out laughing, "Eyy, I'm just busting your balls. Oh man, you should have seen your face, nah it's all good, a trainee Hell Hunter still gets his respect, don't worry about it. You, you've got balls, to be willing to go out there, on your own, with no back up. Scary shit man." He reached out a hand to Luther, Luther warily unclenched his fists and shook it, "I'm not scared of anything." Said Luther still a little on edge, "Hey man relax, relax. I'm just joking around. Somebody needs to keep things light, people around here are too serious,

I'm telling you. Probably because of all the constant danger." "Nah, it's because your ugly face puts us in a bad mood." Said Gideon, totally deadpan and Samuel laughed boisterously, slapping his arm, which was in a sling. "I love this guy. That's why I run this place, to give you guys a break. You can relax here, stop being so defensive and maybe even have a few laughs." Luther smiled, he decided that he liked this guy. "Can I get a beer." "What kind you want, good, bad or shit?" "Whichever's cheapest." Samuel laughed, and proclaimed another loud, "Eyy"

They all had a couple of drinks at the bar. After one sip of the shit beer Luther changed his order. They all got nice and loose, letting Samuel do most of the talking, then Luther said, "I've got a bone to pick with you Samuel." "Oh yeah?" Luther nodded, "I was on the Guardian's Force for all seven years of my mandatory duty. Why aren't we in The Strong. You got something against guards?" he chuckled, shaking his head, "No. My brother used to be a palace guard. When I opened the place I said you're not allowed in, this is a place for The Strong." They all laughed but Samuel fucking hollered at how hilarious he was.

Samuel got into telling an old story from his army days. "I was out there with a thirty man unit and we got attacked by this big pack of monsters, they were red but it wasn't like their skin was red, it was like you could see their bare muscles, like they'd been skinned, real freaky shit. They ran at us in this trail of green dust, there was a cloud of the stuff and when they hit us, we were covered in this dust cloud that came from their bodies. It burned our eyes and our skin, we could barely see and it hurt to breathe. And these fuckers were moving around in the cloud, tearing us to pieces. I got separated from my unit and I could hear my friends fighting and yelling all around me. I wandered around that cloud until eventually I found some fresh air, but I almost walked right over the edge of a cliff.

I stop myself from going over this massive drop, I don't even know how high, hundreds of meters and I turn around and I'm trapped by the cloud. I really have no room to move, it's just this one spot that's clear of the green cloud. A storm, that's what I'd call it, a dust storm and I'm trying to figure out what I should do and then all of a sudden three of these things come out of the dust and knock me over the edge." "Oh shit" said Luther, "I know right. We all go over together and then we're scrambling against the side of the cliff and the jagged rocks are tearing into my skin, but I managed to grab onto something. I look down and I see one of them falling right down to the bottom, but the other two had grabbed onto the cliff as well and they were climbing up towards me, really fast, way faster than I could ever climb, and believe me once upon a time I was in great shape, I could climb really fucking fast and I banged all the hottest girls, that's not part of the story but it's important that you all know that." Everybody laughed.

"Anyway, they catch up to me, so I get my sword out, find a really good hand hold and start swinging." He said, furiously waving around an invisible sword. "They started to spray more of their dusty weird gas at me and it hurts like nothing I've ever felt, I'm practically blind, fighting on the side of a cliff. I tell you the only time I've ever been more sure that I was going to die, was two minutes earlier when I fell off a fucking cliff." He said chuckling and taking a big drink to celebrate life. "They make their way a little closer and somehow I manage to catch one of them with my sword and it fell." "What about the other one?" asked Luther, totally sucked into the story, "Well this one came up underneath me and started grabbing and biting at my legs. So I kicked it in the face." He laughed, shaking his head at the memory, "I kicked it in the face and the fucking thing fell off the fucking cliff." Luther laughed with him and they bashed their beers together.

"So, so then I climb back up the cliff and when I get to the top, the green dust storm is still there and there's no way around it, unless I want to climb around it and fuck that, I'm never climbing another cliff ever again. So I lift up my sword and walk into the cloud and this time it hurts so fucking badly, my skin feels like it's being melted off, my eyes are getting worse, I'm terrified because I can still hear them moving around, fighting some other soldiers. I don't know how long I spent in there, but eventually I stumbled out of the cloud, I could hardly see but I knew I just had to get the fuck out of there, so I picked a direction and started running. I didn't get very far before I dropped onto the ground and started vomiting up blood. Luckily my unit eventually won the battle and some of my guys stumbled upon me and took me back home."

Luther gave Samuel a few small claps, "Now that's a story." "Oh I haven't finished yet. I woke up in the infirmary days later, my hairs falling out, my nose and ears are all fucked up. It turns out that the cloud that those things sprayed was extremely poisonous and now I look like this." "Shit, that's..." Luther trailed off, not knowing what to say, "But at least I have a cool war story to explain away why I'm so unattractive. Apart from being fat, nope, can't blame that on the poison cloud. I just drink beer and eat all day." He laughed, and poured Luther another beer, "I'm glad to have you round Luther, none of these guys appreciate my stories anymore." He said gesturing at the Hell Hunters. "That's because we've all got better stories Samuel." replied Lakeitha. Luther raised an eyebrow, "Really, care to share some stories guys." Lakeitha cringed and shook her head, "Nah, you haven't earned it yet." The other two nodded in agreement.

After a little more banter with Samuel the four of them split from the bar and sat at a table. Gideon asked him, "When do you finish training?" "In two weeks." Replied Luther, then he looked to Lakeitha and Malek, "Bane told me that my first mission is collecting samples of some crap that might be fuel, with the two of you." This visibly soured Lakeitha and Malek who had been reserved around Luther the whole evening. "What?" Said Lakeitha, "I'm gonna do a mission with you guys." Lakeitha shook her head, "There is no fucking way, that we're taking you on your first mission. That's babysitting, we don't do that." The smile on Luther's face fell and his alcohol inspired good mood died, "Babysitting?" Malek nodded, "We never take virgins on our missions." "Well, you're gonna be taking me and I don't care what the lingo is, don't you ever call me a fucking virgin again." Malek watched him with cold eyes, "We have been doing this for years, we know what we're doing, you don't and that makes you a fucking liability." Luther scowled at him, "Fuck you, I can handle it." Lakeitha shook her head, "We don't want to take that risk, get Bane to assign you some easier missions, with somebody else. This is a six day mission, nobody starts with a six day mission, what's Bane thinking?" "He thinks I can handle it." "No he doesn't, he knows you're not ready. Our numbers are down and he's getting desperate enough to throw a complete novice into the deep end. We don't want anybody on board that we can't trust not to fuck up." "I won't fuck up okay, and I'll be ready by the time I finish my training, I promise you that." "When did you start training?" "Five days ago." All three of the seasoned Hell Hunters laughed at him.

Lakeitha shook her head, "Three weeks of training, Bane really is desperate to fill spaces. You're meant to get four months before your first mission and even that isn't enough to prepare you for what it's like out there. There are thousands of things that you have to learn for yourself when you're actually in the wild. Things that no one can teach and things that no one else knows. The further from

Dantez you get the more uncharted, unknown and dangerous it gets. No one is ever ready on their first mission, a third of all recruits die on their first five missions, did Bane tell you that?" "Yeah he did and I don't plan on being one of them." "Then you better not come with us. You'll never make it. Go back and ask for some easy short missions and if you're still alive in a year then you can come with us, until then, go fuck yourself."

"That's not up to you." Lakeitha shook her head, "We'll talk Bane out of it. When we're out there we travel light, we take only what we need because anything more will slow us down and get us killed. You understand what I'm saying, there's no room for dead weight." "Oh fuck you. You gonna talk to me like that. I'm so much stronger than you, I know I could lift twice what you could." Lakeitha narrowed her eyes, nobody ever talked down to her about her muscle. She was one of the strongest Hell Hunters, man or woman, but this arrogant cage fighter prick clearly had bigger arms than her.

"A Hell Hunter needs to have luck running through their veins. No matter how much weight you can lift, you can still get bit by a anthtic and die within ten seconds, or one of a million other things could happen. You may be stronger than me but I've survived hundreds of days and nights out there." "Relying on luck doesn't sound like the safest plan." Snorted Luther and all three of the Hell Hunters laughed at him again. "Bitch if you wanna feel safe, then you should walk away right now. We can't have any pussies out there." Luther flinched, no one ever questioned his bravery. He felt hot, flushed and angry. He was the best fighter alive and he wasn't going to allow any insults. "Oh yeah, what about the one between your legs." Gideon laughed, but he wasn't laughing with Luther. Malek didn't have much of an obvious reaction, but Luther noticed a slight change in his demeanour. The man clearly wanted to do some violence, but he was holding himself back to let Lakeitha fight her own battle. Lakeitha was staring at him. Not angry, but focused, like she was studying him and he didn't like that, he wanted to get a rise out of her, so he poked her again. "There's a reason why no woman has ever gotten in the cage with me. You're weaker, slower, have less stamina and most of you can't even take a punch."

Lakeitha showed no obvious signs of emotion. But there was something in her eyes, before she had been dispassionately analysing him, now, she was feeling something. He'd managed to stir things up inside her head and that made him smile. Lakeitha leaned forward, "If you were stuck in a cage with me. I'd beat you." Luther shook his head, amused, "To death." added Lakeitha. Luther chuckled, "No chance." They stared each other in the eyes for several seconds, tensed up, both of them ready for the other to strike. Then they realised that neither one of them was going to cross that line, not just yet, and when Malek picked up on that he decided to change the topic of the conversation, "You ever kill anybody?"

Luther stiffened, withdrawing from his confrontation with Lakeitha. Lakeitha subtly licked her lips and nodded to herself, like she had won. "What?" They all waited. He saw the expectation in their eyes, they needed to hear an answer. He had to talk about things that he never, ever spoke about, with anyone. These people were killers, every one of them, and if he was going to do this, then he needed them to accept him as being just as ruthless as they were. "Yeah" He didn't look any of them in the eye. They kept waiting and he sighed, feeling uncomfortable, suddenly wishing that the bitch had hit him so that he could have gotten into a good old brawl, instead of this. "Four, all in the cage. Three with weapons; two with a sword, one with a knife. One just with my hands." The atmosphere at the table changed, becoming a little more respectful of him.

"Did you kill any of them by accident?" Asked Malek, Luther nodded, feeling an uneasy churning in his stomach. "The first time I killed anybody was in the unarmed fight, I hit him in the chest so hard that he drowned in his own blood right there in the cage. I tried to help him but there was nothing I could do." He felt his voice was starting to sound self pitying and weak, so he stopped. None of them said anything for a while, then Malek leaned over to Lakeitha and whispered something in her ear.

Lakeitha sighed, then said, "If you get through training and Bane vouches for you, then we'll take you on the mission."

Luther gave her a little look that told her he was going to ace his training.

Gideon asked him, "Have you walked The Passage yet?" "No I'm doing it tomorrow. I know I can walk that far in a day. You know I've made the journey a bunch of times before. When I was one of The Guardian's bodyguards." "On foot?" Asked Gideon, "No we were in vehicles. Tanks and armoured hover trucks." Luther allowed himself a small smile, thinking of the times they fucked in the Shante's hover truck, trying to keep quiet so that the driver wouldn't hear.

"I've always wanted to ride on a hover truck." Said Gideon, "Only the best for Shante." said Luther. Gideon switched gears, getting all sage and grizzled, "You really can't compare a vehicle to going alone on foot. You're walking and walking and walking, out in the open and the smarter creatures will follow you in the trees and wait for the right moment to strike. You never know when something could take a run at you and even if you stick to the centre of the road there are things out there that could cover that distance in no time and do it quietly enough that they'll still catch you by surprise. That's the real test of walking The Passage. They already know whether or not you have the stamina to walk that far in a day, what they want to know is whether or not you can do the whole thing, while remaining alert enough not to get killed. Do you honestly believe that you have that in you? Are you willing to bet your life on it?" asked Gideon, seriously, but not resentfully. Luther nodded, "I can do it." And he believed he could, there'd be no hover truck sex on this trip.

"What was it like being Shante's bodyguard?" "Pretty boring." lied Luther. "She's really hot." Said Gideon and Malek nodded. "Yeah you're right about that." grinned Luther. "Eh, she's not that hot." Said Lakeitha, "You reek of envy Lakeitha. You wish you had her beautiful, undeformed face." Jabbed Gideon, "Well duh." said Lakeitha and they all laughed. "And just for the record Gideon. My face is not deformed, it's mutilated." All three of them had pretty fucked up faces from spending years as hard living Hell Hunters. Luther had been lucky enough to avoid that fate as a bare knuckle cage fighter, maybe he'd managed to pull off the same magic trick with this new job.

"That's another thing you've got to be prepared for Luther. Hell Hunter's don't get to be handsome." said Gideon. "I don't know, Malek's still a bit of a looker." Malek raised an eyebrow, "Really?" "Yeah chick's dig scars man." It felt pretty good getting Malek to crack a smile.

Chapter 6

Lakeitha had a little house that she shared with her sick brother. Since his illness he'd become a hermit and the responsibility was solely on her to take care of him. The government had supplied him with medicine for the first year and then they forgot about him. After everything that he'd done for them, the years of innovation and invention that he had dedicated to protecting them, creating weapons and defences and all manner of other tools to keep the human race from being wiped out and at the end of it all they abandoned him after he got sick from one of the endless foreign diseases that plagued the earth.

Today Mikey was sitting in his chair, beside his bed, he wasn't doing anything, he didn't do much these days. He just sat in his chair, his big long beard stopping near his belly button. The scraggly black beard had many grey strands. Mikey was only thirty-one, too young to have a beard like that. When the portals started opening one hundred and thirty years ago the world had changed and become a lot harder for humans. The average life expectancy had dropped to forty-eight, but even so, no one Mikey's age looked as old as he did.

He smiled when he saw her, showing his teeth, many of which were black or missing. "Lakeitha how are you?

Actually I don't care, did you bring my stuff." Lakeitha patted his head and then dropped the medicine in his lap. Mikey picked up the little black bag and rolled it around in his fingers, feeling the marble sized balls of psychedelic medicine, "It's about time, I haven't had any in four days." "Oh well that's your fault. I told you how long that bag was meant to last you." "Yeah well, you try staying in this cupboard with nothing tah do and no one to talk to. While you're off on your adventures I have absolutely nothing going on. Hallucinating is the only fun I get to have." "I'm serious, you can't binge through all your medicine just because you're bored." "Yeah, well, maybe if you brought me more of it." Lakeitha sighed and sat down in the only chair. "Why don't you ever clean this place?" "Because I'm sick." "You think I like sweeping your floors." "Ughh, bitch bitch bitch, that's all I hear." She grinned and gave him the finger.

"How long are you back for?" "About a week provided that I mend in time." "You hurt?" "Oh the usual I fell out of the sky through a bunch of tries." "What? You fell out of a tree?" "Aghh, yeah, but I also fell out of the sky after this thing picked me up and then tried to drop me. But I tore it to pieces." "Good on you. I think." "Right well, I'll just be away for a day here, a couple days there, so I'll be around a lot over the next two weeks. After that I'm going to be collecting some fuel samples with Malek and this rookie, it'll be about three days each way." Mikey groaned, "Six days on my own, it's shit here, you realise that don't you, it is shit here, you're away half the time, but I have to live in this. The shitness of this room seeps into my soul and changes me on a physiological level. One day you will come to visit me and I will have turned into a shit, and then you'll realise that I was justified in my complaints." "Well at least then I won't have to listen to all your bitching." "You're the one who bitches, we established that moments ago." "Right of course."

They stopped speaking for a few minutes, just enjoying each other's company; savouring the peace and quiet, at least that was what Lakeitha was doing. Lakeitha spent so much time in constant danger, constant noise and tension, that peace and quiet were treasured things. Mikey on the other hand spent all his time on his own, doing nothing, in this very room. He hated peace and quiet.

"I got a visitor a couple of days ago, while you were away." "Really, but nobody likes you." Mikey smirked, "That's what I thought, but then Victor came around to talk. You remember Victor, we worked together years ago." "Yeah, he was…didn't he invent the World Saver." "Uh hu, he invented the World Saver Hand Cannon and the World Saver Turret single handedly." Mikey paused, looking at Lakeitha like he wanted some kind of reaction. "Get it? Because he blew his own hand off." Lakeitha frowned, remembering Victor and his stump. "You callous bastard." "Meh, it's not my joke, it's Victors, he's been telling it for years. Anyway he came around and we talked about stuff and I told him this idea I had. He brought me some materials and I got inventing." "Really, Mikey that's great.

When was the last time you worked on anything?" "Aghh, years. I just had this idea and I really wanted to make it. It could save your life one day." "Okay, let me see it." "Just bear in mind that the purpose of this project was for me to prove that I can still invent useful things, saving your life is just a potential biproduct. I don't want you getting the wrong idea or anything, I don't stay up at night trying to think of ways to make your life easier." "Okay, show it to me." Mikey sighed, "If anything, I actually quite resent that it could save your life, pisses me off really. But I have no one else to give it to so…"

Mikey took a box out from underneath his bed and lifted out two black metal discs. "It only took me five hours to figure it out. I bet no one else could have done it so fast." He handed one to her, "What does it do?" "You see the arrow on the disc." She looked at the blue arrow on the centre of the disc. The arrow was pointed straight ahead. "Turn around." Lakeitha turned her back on Mikey and as she moved the arrow started to rotate until she stopped and the arrow pointed backwards. "Wherever you are, the arrow will point directly to my disc, so you'll always be able to find your way back to Dantez." She looked up at Mikey, shocked.

Navigation hadn't been an exact science since the portals opened. As well as filling the earth with monsters, plants, magic, radiation and many other things, the portals had also corrupted the earth's magnetism. Compasses spun out of control, the needle never settling on any one point regardless of where it was facing. Mikey's invention would make a world of difference.

"This is incredible. This'll...Mikey thank you so much. The amount of times I've gotten lost out there, especially in unknown territory..." "Aghh quit you're babbling, I'm not finished talking. It's also a beacon. If you press the tip of your thumb against the arrow for more than five seconds, then the arrow on my disc, which always points towards you, will turn red and I'll know that you're in trouble and I can try to help you. Pretty cool huh." "Yeah that's great, Mikey every Hell Hunter should have one of these." "Maybe one day they will, but for now it's just for you. Consider yourself a test subject, but trust me it'll work, I know my craft. You'll need to hold onto this for a couple of hours so that it properly links to you, then after that it acts as a kind of death monitor. If you die then the arrow on my disc will turn black. I know this isn't a very nice thing to say, but if you were to die, that really would be very good for the test." "Yeah okay, I'll make sure to do that for the sake of your invention. What are sisters for? Oh and since I'm dead I guess you'll die here alone and with no medicine, because you're helpless without me." "Fuck you." "Fuck you." She made a fist and tapped him on the head as she walked out of the room, leaving him to enjoy his medicine.

Chapter 7

Mikey felt rejuvenated by Lakeitha's visit. It was great to have some company and he always enjoyed their banter. That disc that he had given her was the first thing he'd invented in a very long time and he was proud of it. He felt so happy after seeing Lakeitha that he didn't feel like taking his medicine just yet. The psychedelic episode brought on by the medicine was very intense and for the moment he just wanted to enjoy the good feeling that came from seeing his sister.

After about fifteen minutes he started feeling weak and knew it was time to take his medicine. He excitedly opened the bag, took out one of the little black chunks and popped it in his mouth, he swallowed it and waited. After thirty seconds he could feel time start to slow down, the air in the room feeling hot and dense, in a very comforting, slightly overwhelming way, like falling into a deep sleep. He was suddenly very aware of every individual hair on his arms and his beard felt ticklish. The tickling made him laugh like a toddler. He could hear a distant noise, not words just sounds, sounds that he could only detect, but not hear clearly.

His mouth tasted like chocolate, a food he had rarely ever had the joy of eating. He ran his tongue around his mouth savouring the taste. It oozed thickly off the inside of his cheeks, if he licked it hard enough it would break free and wrap around his tongue. His teeth felt funny, softer, not so hard and inflexible. As he chewed, the rows of teeth gently stuck together. One of them fell from his gums and started melting onto his tongue, he chewed his melted tooth and it released the most delightfully sweet flavours. The taste was so powerful and indulgent that he closed his eyes to fully immerse himself in the experience. Mikey's teeth all started coming loose as his gums melted, the thick texture and rich flavour of chocolate filling his mouth.

The noise was getting louder, he could really hear it now. It repeated itself on a loop, a loud, low blaring, drawn out for a whole second, flowed by a short clicking noise. It sounded as if the noises were being made by the mouth of a giant. He opened his eyes and saw that the dark grey walls had turned solid gold and the noise was sending vibrations through them. His beard started growing as the vibrations intensified. In seconds his beard was hanging below his waist.

He got to his feet, something which normally took a lot of effort, but now it was the easiest thing in the world. The walls were shaking furiously, like they were spasming out of reality, jittering so quickly that they became a golden blur. The noise got louder too, HUMMMMMM CLICK, HUMMMMMM CLICK. His beard passed his knees and then his feet and touched the floor. The vibrating got so intense that he could hear the room start to break apart, gold nuggets fell from the ceiling and popped off the walls. The noise got even louder until the gold wall in front of him was torn off and behind it was a great expanse, a vast open space with no ground, everywhere was the sky and that sky was bright red and pink with big veins of green running through it and five pointed yellow stars hovered among them.

His room was crumbling into a mess of gold nuggets, and this new space seemed to have sucked the noise into it, he could hear it in front of him, getting more distant by the second. His beard grew longer, running along the floor and out into the multi-coloured space in front of him. When the beard passed over the threshold it didn't fall over the edge, instead it continued to grow forwards, as if it was spreading over an invisible floor. He followed his beard out of the room, and stood on nothing, levitating with the sky above him and below him. It didn't feel like there was a floor below him, it felt like his feet were completely unsupported, and yet he didn't fall.

His beard stopped growing. There was ten meters of it, lying still on top of nothing. He reached into his beard with both hands. He parted it in the middle just below his chin with his thumbs and then he grabbed hold of both halves and drew his hands away from each other. He pulled his hands apart until the hairs on his face were pulling at his skin and stinging in their roots. Then he gave each side an extra yank and every single hair was pulled free without the slightest pain or resistance. He held a thick cord of beard hair in each hand which led down into the carpet before him. He felt that the hairs were all tightly bound together and knew that they would never break apart. The empty space below him started to shimmer, becoming creased and translucent. He looked around him, excited for the next development as he felt substance beneath his beard, something solid. A ground was forming underneath where he levitated. He felt a shift in the air behind him and he turned around to see a wave forming, a great translucent wave the texture of syrup. It was huge, a hundred meters tall.

The wave was going to crush him, he had to move and then he saw walls forming out of the shimmering ground around him and the ground in front of him, dense and solid, started to dip. A slope formed, a twisting, turning, rainbow, beneath a red sky. The slope got steeper and steeper transforming into a track that only the bravest of souls would ever attempt. He held on tightly to the strands of his beard and gravity did its job. He started sliding down the slope on his beard hair slay. He rocketed down it, flying at an impossible speed, the child inside him freaking out, while the inventor inside him marvelled at the tensile dexterity of his ridiculous vehicle. He heard the crashing as the wave hit the opening of the track and flooded down it, churning and buffeting against the edges of the wall. The thick waves raced after him.

He came up on a sharp bend to the right and steered through it with his hairy handles, hitting it at breakneck speed with the waves crashing against it a moment later, he felt the spray on the back of his neck, the water was so thick and sticky that it clung to his skin where it landed and he couldn't wipe it off, not without letting go of one of his hairy ropes.

He could see the waves now, on his left and his right, he could taste the water. He felt the slight drag from dense water sponging the hair on the rear of his slay. At any second the full bulk of the wave would swallow him. He laughed and yelled at the top of his voice. He looked up at the shimmering red sky for something that would save him. The bright stars and green veins were in constant motion but there was nothing up there that was going to intervene. He looked ahead of him at the track and realised that there was something wrong with this picture. There was no more than a hundred meters of track ahead of him. Not a dead end, but a drop.

His stomach was doing backflips as he approached it with no way to slow down. He sped over the edge. He clung onto his sledge in freefall, the water raining onto him, splattering his clothes. He was about to be crushed by the full weight of this new waterfall. Then he felt something beneath him, his soggy sledge had bounced off the sheer face of the track and then it happened again and again, each impact lasting longer, then he hit it again and he didn't bounce off. The track curved beneath him until he was rocketing forwards once more, somehow moving even faster than he had in freefall. He yelled as loud as he could, "Wooooooo!"

He looked at the rainbow slope ahead of him, saw it curve more and more until it abruptly levelled out, leading into a...oh no. OH SHIT! He hit the curve and was propelled up the fifty metre ramp and into the sky. Within seconds of taking flight he lost his grip on his beard and the billowing mass of hair fell away from him, leaving him soaring through the air on his own. He heard a boom, louder than anything he'd ever heard in his entire life and then silence. He'd broken the sound barrier, he was flying through the air and there was no sign that he was going to start falling soon. He spread his arms wide like a bird, he moved so quickly that the patterns in the sky turned to a streaky blur of warm colours passing by his head. He howled and screamed, loving every moment of this freedom, this exhilaration. He felt a burning in his fingertips, hot and getting hotter. He giggled in delight, let the heat build and build until he couldn't hold it in any longer and then he released a colossal bolt of lightning from each finger. He kept it going for as long as he could, he never wanted it to end.

The lightning faded, one finger at a time until there was only one continuous fork of lightning left and it got weaker and weaker until it was just a little shred of light dancing on his fingertip. Then it too disappeared.

He flew on with a massive grin on his face. In front of him way out in the distance, he saw a square, a little white square that stood out among the bright red and pink. The square grew as he got closer until it took up the whole sky in front of him, and then coming from within that perfect unblemished whiteness was a window, a couple of feet tall and a couple of feet wide, it didn't grow any larger as he got closer. He was heading straight for it at the speed of sound. He winced just before he hit it. He smashed through the glass and jolted back into his room, sitting in his chair, his heart racing. He blinked rapidly and looked around the room, at the walls that were suffocatingly close and drab compared to the vast beauty that he had left behind. He looked down at the bag of medicine in his lap and resisted the urge to take another one.

Chapter 8

That was without a doubt, the best blowjob Luther had ever had. He rested his back against the pile of cushions at the top of the bed and looked down at Shante, who was lying on his lap, with those big perfect boobs and hard nipples. He ran his hands through her luscious hair. Suddenly the idea of leaving her behind for any length of time seemed ridiculous. He wanted to stay with her forever, their minds and their bodies, intertwined in love and ecstasy. "I love you." He said to Shante, she smiled. They stared into each other's eyes for the longest time.

"Why would I ever leave this room?" her smile turned to a keen grin. "Because if you didn't, I'd leave first. I've got a city to run." "Oh yeah." "Yeah. I've got people to order around, as much as I'd love to live my life in this bed, drinking beer and brandy, with you as my fuck puppet." "Do you miss being able to order me around?" "Pff, Luther, I still order you around." "No you don't." "Yeah, I'll always have you wrapped around my fingers." "Nah, I've had you under my thumb since our first kiss." She giggled, Shante had a lovely giggle. "I wish you'd come back as my bodyguard. We'd be together every hour of the day." "Oh wow, that sounds incredible. We could fuck on the throne." Shante paused, "No. Don't joke about that. It's going too far." "Oh sorry." "I was thinking instead, we'd have sex on the steps outside the palace and make the whole city watch us." Luther looked down at Shante, "I love you so much." She giggled again.

He remembered what had happened the night before and he was riddled with such powerful guilt that he had to break his lover's gaze to stop it from showing.

Feeling the way he did about what happened last night, he realised for the first time that he had to change. He had to contain his animal side and only release it when he was in the cage, no not the cage, not anymore; from now on he would be fighting in a magical, monstrous, irradiated world, a blood orgy of unimaginable proportions that would dwarf his cage fights and truly challenge him. He was finally going to enter the real world that had always called to him from beyond the walls of Dantez.

He knew why he couldn't stay with Shante, he wasn't ready yet. He was a beast and beasts belonged outside the wall, not inside it.

"What are you thinking about?" asked Shante, snapping him out of his thoughts. "Going out into the wild." "Ah, it's a big thing." "Yeah, big…" He paused, thinking about how he felt. "You know, I haven't felt this way since the night before my first fight. I'm…" "Excited?" "Yes, but also, nervous. I won my first fight. I annihilated the guy and I've won every fight after that. I know I'm the best guy in the cage. Wherever I fight and whoever I fight, I always know that I'm the fastest, the strongest, the toughest. But the night before my first fight, I felt like I was... I felt like they were all going to be better than me."

Shante sat up and put her hands on his face. The novelty of romance with a fighter had long since worn off. At this point, she was rarely interested in what he had to say about his fighting. She was only intrigued at moments like this, when he was saying things that ran deeper than his celebrations and his declarations of invincibility.

But what was she going to say? Tell him that he was the best. She decided that would ring hollow, "Luther, you are the best fighter in the human race. But the cage that you are about to step into has giant monsters with teeth longer than your sword. You aren't going to be the best fighter there is." Luther pulled back a little and looked at her with a lot of different emotions moving across his face. "What?" Shante wondered if she'd made a mess of it.

"Luther we both know that this is infinitely more dangerous than any cage you've ever stepped into. Isn't that the point though?" Luther looked at her, thinking, breaking off eye contact and then glancing back up at her. He nodded.

"If you die out there, it'll tear me apart. But if you don't go, then it'll tear you apart. So you have to and I'll think about you all the time. You can't die, that's an order." He smiled.

She was really going to miss him when he was gone. Not just because of the love, the sex and the laughter that they shared. But most of all, because he was the only person in her life that she could be truly at ease with. Who she could talk to, without having to worry about her responsibilities, her reputation and her power. If he died, then she would be alone in the world, for the rest of her life.

"I think you need to cheer up Luther." "That sounds like a good idea, but how my fair and powerful leader, can I do that?" Shante straightened her back, raised her jaw and spoke in the elegant and forceful voice that she used to deliver her speeches. "Luther you must feel my tits." Luther sighed, "Yeah, that never gets old."

Chapter 9

Lakeitha met with Malek at the Hell Hunters armoury. She took her five blades, which she had sharpened the previous day, from her locker and grabbed her World Saver and secured it in its holster. Her armour was a lightweight and incredibly strong leather that held up fairly well to the heat and moisture of the jungle. Technically it wasn't real leather, but it looked and felt like it, so nobody bothered to learn the real name of the new material. The scientists really had done their best to design an armour that let the body breathe, but leather, fake or not, wasn't ideal for the jungle. Every single Hell Hunter had spent a ludicrous amount of time wishing that they wore some kind of fabric, rather than the sweaty leather, but they all agreed that the protection was worth the heat. Cloth couldn't stop a steel sword ninety percent of the time or the barbaric claws of a scorpion bear.

Sadly their armour wasn't as resistant to alien metals. Which were both of a similar strength, leading to endless debates over which was better among nerds and warriors alike.

One thing that should have happened a hundred and thirty years ago was for the alien metals to be given catchy names. Unfortunately they'd been named by long dead scientists who got carried away and used twenty syllable words that never had a hope of being adopted by normal people. Thanks to their lack of foresight, everybody nowadays just said, red alien metal and black alien metal.

Black alien metal was used for the forearm guards which they wore over the armour. It was too heavy and rare to be used to make an entire suit of armour. Steel would do just fine for the studs on the knuckles and the pads on the elbows and knees.

She did her final checks on her light pack with a few essentials like dry rations and a blanket and then joined Malek. Swords were standard, almost every Hell Hunter carried one, which might have been why Malek didn't. He had a red alien metal knife at his hip and a one handed mace with a cylindrical head and three inch, pointed flanges made from black alien metal. He also had a backup steel knife at his thigh that he rarely used. He chose not to carry a World Saver, because he thought they were too bulky, inaccurate and impractical for most situations. He was right on all accounts but Lakeitha still carried a World Saver. She'd used it to kill dozens of monsters that she didn't have a chance of hurting with her sword.

Malek was very good company on long treks outside the wall. He was good at talking but he was also good at not talking, which Lakeitha appreciated just as much. They waited for five minutes outside the armoury until Luther joined them. "You guys ready to go?" They both kept quiet and just gave him a look that said they'd been ready and waiting for a while. He definitely noticed but seemed not to care. Luther was quietly buzzing with excitement, it was obvious to both of them. Everyone was excited before their first mission, no one was excited before their second.

They walked across the city to the gates, waved to the Grand Scrapers and the gears started turning. The massive doors cracked open a few feet, a dozen soldiers raised their weapons and gathered around the opening, ready in case anything got through. The three of them walked through the gap and set off on their mission.

Chapter 10

They walked along The Passage for half an hour. As they walked Luther thought about his single day walk across The Passage two weeks. It had been tiring and draining on his focus. It's funny how you can be constantly expecting danger and be incredibly bored at the same time. The odd hover truck would pass him now and then. He had a few encounters with monsters along the way. He'd taken some scratches and got to use his World Saver on a monster for the first time, which was pretty awesome. He had arrived at Alcraze an hour before dark. It had just been a taste of what was to come.

That made him start thinking about Alcraze, about his trip there a couple of days ago. He thought about his last cage fight and what happened afterwards. Malek started to lead them over to the left, veering off The Passage, he took his mind off the troubling things when he reached the edge of The Passage. It was a clear line, on one side the ground was baron, the soil poisoned and flat, on the other side was grass and plants and trees. This was the edge of human territory. He stepped over the line. He looked down, noticed that he'd drawn his sword without even realising it. He looked at the others, their hands were empty.

Lakeitha glanced at him, "Everybody does it their first time. On my first day I never let go of my sword for a second." Malek didn't say anything. Luther made a point of sheathing his weapon, but as soon as he did he felt exposed. Lakeitha just shrugged and walked ahead. Luther felt slightly embarrassed, then he wondered how long it would take him to seduce Lakeitha, then he wondered whether or not he really wanted to have sex with her, her face was pretty fucked up. Then he felt ashamed, she was nothing compared to Shante and even if she was the most beautiful woman in the world, he still shouldn't even be considering it. His shoulders sagged, he was pathetic and a little bit glad that Lakeitha wasn't a looker.

They got through the first two hours without having to kill anything. Everything was going fine for Lakeitha and then Luther started talking and he wouldn't shut up.

Neither her nor Malek were in the mood to talk, not that Luther's offerings were particularly scintillating, but in spite of their almost aggressive silence, the guy just wouldn't shut up. He talked about his fighting career and his aspirations as a Hell Hunter, which were pretty naive and egotistical. He talked about the landscape and the handful of creatures he'd killed on his walk across The Passage and in his training sessions. His oneway conversation must have lasted for over an hour. She told him to shut up several times, so did Malek; but he kept running his mouth.

"Bane told me something about you Malek." Nothing from Malek. "He told me that you were magic. Or a mutant, I don't remember. He said that you've got a tentacle inside your arm and you can fight with it. I guess that's why you've got no palm on your right glove. I...ah, just have to see that shit." "Nah." "Come on, I don't get to meet many magic men. They're not allowed to fight in the cage. Unfair advantage I guess. I've always wanted to fight a mutant."

Malek didn't respond, leaving Luther to stare at the back of his head and keep pushing him for a demonstration.

Puppies get away with hassling people because they're cute, Luther wasn't, so he was in danger of getting punched in the face before the end of his first day. Lakeitha saw movement in the distance. She pointed and whispered, "Over there." The guys dropped low and looked to an opening in the trees. In that opening was a miniature pink-skinned bull. Just the sight of it made Lakeitha's mouth water. It was roughly two feet tall and pale pink with an underbite and horns that grew downwards from the head and jutted out below the mouth like an elephant's tusks. Luther leaned towards her and whispered, "Is that a-" "Yup" "Wow. I've never seen one alive before." Lakeitha swallowed to keep herself from drooling. The miniature pink-skinned bull was the most delicious creature that any human being had ever tasted. They were rare and fast, so Hell Hunters who brought them into the city were always given a substantial bonus.

"Malek you go right, I'll go left." Said Lakeitha drawing her sword. "What about me?" asked Luther, "Keep your distance and don't screw this up. If it runs your way then you take it down, and if you ruin the meat with your World Saver then I will personally cut off your head." Luther looked like he really believed she was serious. Good, she wanted him to be scared of her, even though she wouldn't really decapitate him if he tainted the meat. She'd probably just kick his head in.

Lakeitha and Malek split off into different directions. There was a thick spread of trees between them and their prey that provided cover. This thing was faster than even the fittest human, so they really had to take it by surprise.

Lakeitha became very aware of how much noise she was making just by walking. She kept her eyes on the miniature bull, taking quick glances down at the ground to make sure she wasn't about to break a twig or trip over something. She approached the clearing, with only one large tree concealing her from her prey. She stalked towards the tree, thinking about how close the bull was to her. The thrill of the hunt tickled her nerves. The excitement made her breathe faster and heavier through her mouth. That could give her away, she needed to keep quiet. Slowly take it in through the nose, gently release it out the mouth. Her heart was beating hard and her lungs felt stifled and demanded more air, but she kept her control, kept herself quiet.

She reached the big tree and pressed up against it. She looked to her right, it took her a few seconds to spot Malek. He was crouched behind a big spindly bush right at the edge of the clearing where the bull grazed. She peaked round the edge of the tree trunk, saw the bull standing side on to her with its back to Malek. It was maybe fifteen feet away from her and twenty feet away from him, just outside of his range.

She tightened her grip on her sword. Everything was very still, very quiet, she was alert to every little movement of her prey. She held up a hand to Malek and signalled that she was going to go first, pushing the bull towards him. He nodded and waited for her to make her move.

She sucked in one long, slow breath and held it for a second. Then she let it out.

She stepped around the tree and charged the little bull. It backed up instinctively, filling the air with a bellow. It raised its head, pointing its horns towards her gut. She'd expected it to run but this one was in a fighting mood. She sidestepped its charge and swiped down, slicing the skin on top of its head. It was a superficial strike but it brought a lot of red blood leaking onto the bull's pink skin and made the creature screech in pain.

It made a quick 180 turn and was on her before she was ready. Just before it reached her it slipped in the mud, its horns missed her but its head rammed into her leg and knocked her off her feet. She hit the ground and rolled away as Malek attacked.

Malek had his mace in his left hand, he kept his right hand empty. He was yelling and hollering, to distract it from Lakeitha. It turned towards him and then jumped away, ducking its head to avoid the mace. He turned to face it and they circled each other. He saw Lakeitha get up and start circling behind the bull. She raised her sword and was about to strike when the tiny bull charged at him. He dived out of the way, rolled when he hit the ground and came up in a crouch with his prey already coming at him for another attack. Staying low to the ground, he started his own crouched charge towards the bull. They ran straight at each other.

He raised his mace up above his head and then just before they met, he bent his knees, planted his left leg forward and used the tremendous amount of forwards momentum on his upper body to bolster the force of his downwards swing. The spiked head of the mace connected perfectly with the head of the bull. He bludgeoned its skull with a single blow and the creature's legs gave out beneath it and crumpled into him, one of its horns grazing his shin. It let out a low confused moan.

Malek stood to his full height and pulled the mace from the bull's head. He glanced at Lakeitha, she was fine. He heard Luther celebrating like an idiot back where they'd left him. He didn't indulge until he'd finished the job. He moved quickly and efficiently, showing the proper respect for his prey. He dropped his mace and pulled out his knife. He rolled the bull slightly as it continued to moan and he slit its throat. The bull's quiet moaning turned to a weak gargle that stopped after a few seconds. It was over. He exhaled deeply and smiled inwardly, allowing himself to enjoy the familiar rush of a victorious hunt.

This was not a cruel animal, nor had it hurt him, it was more important than most of the thing's he'd killed and deserved to be treated accordingly. Lakeitha was enjoying their little victory and being quiet about it. Malek appreciated that. She was one of his favourite people to hunt with, but Luther was coming towards him and with him came the inevitable death of the moment. He shouted as he got close; "Woo! That was incredible man, the way you bashed that thing's head in." Like a child he mimicked the swinging motion of Malek's mace. "You big white badass Malek." He came in for a high five, Malek just shook his head and walked away. This was one of the reasons why he hated working with rookies. They had no frame of reference for what was badass.

Luther glared at Malek, this prick wouldn't even give him a high five or accept his compliments. If his attitude didn't improve then they were going to have a problem. Then he turned his attention to the miniature pink-skinned bull. He'd eaten the meat of one of these things before, just a few times. Three or four steaks with Shante over the years and on one occasion he received a celebratory plate of sausages after a particularly big win. Those had been the best meals of his entire life. "How much is this thing worth?" He asked Lakeitha, who was tying the bull's legs together with rope. "About six hundred drogons." Drogons were the only currency anybody used anymore. "Great. Bane gets thirty percent right, so after that we'd each get…" "We're not selling this one." Said Lakeitha as she tied the last knot. Luther frowned, "Sorry, what. Why wouldn't we sell it?" Malek answered from behind him, "We can't sell it because we'd have to get it back to Dantez, today." "Okay, fine, let's go, Lakeitha's already got it tied up." Lakeitha shook her head. "We're moving it, but we're not taking it back home. If we'd found this thing on the return journey, then sure, we could take it back to Dantez, but we can't turn around and abandon the mission. Now if you don't mind this bull is leaking blood all over the place, every predator within two miles that has a halfway decent nose is already on its way here."

Luther's jaw clenched in frustration, "Then why did you kill it in the first place?" Malek grinned and so did Lakeitha as she hoisted the bull onto her back. Luther looked at the pair of them, confused. "We're going to eat it." Luther blinked, then a massive smile spread across his face. Maybe he'd misjudged the pair of them.

Chapter 11

Lakeitha carried the dead beast for twenty minutes. A lot of the blood had drained out of its slit throat right on the spot where it had been killed, but there was a near constant flow of blood droplets coming from the animal, leaving a trail. Lakeitha felt like she was carrying a live bomb on her back. There were creatures out here to whom the scent of its blood was a magnetic force that geared all instincts and senses towards tracking and eating it. Things could get very ugly defending their kill. More than a few Hell Hunters had died over one of these bulls, without ever getting to take a bite. This was one of the most dangerous things a person could do in an area crowded with all manner of carnivores; but just thinking about slow cooking the meat over a fire, letting the smell of it swarm her and tease her tongue for as long as she could bare before she finally sunk her teeth into it. If anything tried to take it from her, she'd tear it into a bloody mess of limbs and guts and her appetite would only grow.

As they moved Malek and Luther fanned out around her, with their weapons raised they watched the jungle, waiting for something to attack. If everything went without a hitch they should get through this patch of jungle in two hours, then they wouldn't be far away from a

Hell Hunter camp on top of a large rocky outcrop that would provide them with the high ground and about sixty feet between them and the nearest tree. It'd be a good spot to spend the night and cook their meat.

She stopped walking, the weight was murder on her back. "We'll break for a couple of minutes." Lakeitha took the bull off her back and sat down, keeping one hand on it and the other on her sword. She glanced over at Luther who was leaning against a tree trunk. After a moment of looking in his direction, she turned cold.

Malek was cleaning blood from the flanges of his mace when he noticed Lakeitha's shocked expression. He raised his weapon instinctively, turning on his heels ready for an attack. But nothing happened, so he looked to Lakeitha for an answer, and saw the way she was staring at Luther. He frowned, looked closer at Luther, he seemed fine, relaxed, hungry, bored but keeping watch and thankfully not running his mouth. Then he saw it too and his eyes widened and he looked back to Lakeitha but she wasn't doing anything either, she was just staring, looking worried. Malek tried to say something, his mouth was so dry, "Luther…" He whispered. Luther turned his head, "Hmm?" "That's not a tree." Luther looked confused, "What…"

A big wooden claw reached around him from either side and pulled him off his feet, forcing his upper body into the tree. He kicked out at thin air as the moist insides of the tree closed in around him. He realised that he was inside a giant mouth and he started screaming. There were rows upon rows of teeth all over the inside of the tree. Thousands of teeth snapped at him from all sides, scraping the skin on his face and digging into his armoured clothes. He kicked the screaming up a notch. He tried to pull himself free but those wooden claws were tightly closed around his body, keeping him trapped. His hands were pinned against the sides of the tree trunk mouth.

When Malek watched Luther get swallowed by a tree, he screamed. It had just opened up and pulled him inside its mouth. All those pointed branches that had pulled Luther in, were now tightly closed, fitting together and trapping Luther halfway inside the tree. His legs were kicking uselessly in the air and his hands were clawing at the tree bark. Malek could hear his muffled screams coming from inside. He was frozen to the spot. He was dwarfed by shock and horror and he couldn't move. This hadn't happened to him in years.

Lakeitha drew her sword and ran at the tree monster. She swung down at the lowest of the branches, just above Luther's flailing hands. Her blade bounced off the tree branch, and a small chunk of wood flew up into the air. She adjusted her position and struck the exact same spot again, making the cut bigger. She hit it again and again, as hard as she could, roaring with each strike, wood chips filled the air.

Luther felt the tree's reaction to every hit. He felt vibrations that the strikes sent through the wood and the pained quivering of the mouth. He couldn't stop screaming. He couldn't protect his face, there were bite marks all over his head.

She severed the lowest branch. Before it had dropped to the ground she had already switched her stance and taken the first swing at the next branch.

Luther felt the lowest branch that pinned his left hand get chopped off and he felt a surge of hope as his hand was freed.

The sight of Lakeitha taking out the first tree branch was enough to snap Malek out of his petrified state. Luther was still screaming and his legs were still kicking, so there was still something worth saving. He dropped his mace and pulled the knife from his belt as he started running towards the tree. Just before he reached the tree he saw one of the tree branches spring out from its tight formation and hit Lakeitha in the forehead before curling back into place. He passed her as she landed on her back, she was dazed but still conscious. He ran in front of the closed branches and started hacking at them, fast furious strokes across the ribbed wooden cage that ripped off the bark and left gashes in the wood.

The tree's mouth opened up and filled with light, Luther saw Malek standing in front of him, knife in hand.

The tree branches spread wide in front of Malek and he was fast enough to take a step back, but not fast enough to get away. The branches grabbed him, wrapping around him and digging into his back, it pulled him into its mouth with the strength of ten men. Luther and Malek kicked their legs against the closing branches. Luther screamed, Malek didn't. With four legs kicking they managed to keep the branches from trapping them inside. Malek felt a branch hit him in the back of the head and everything went black.

Malek slumped limply on top of Luther as the mouth continued to gnaw at the pair of them, but now he had his hands free, or at least free from the branches. Malek's body had pinned down Luther's left arm, but he could still move his right. Teeth bit into his forehead and more blood dribbled down his face.

As the little teeth bit into him he grabbed a hold of the knife at his thigh. He had a weapon, he'd done it, he'd won, he was going to cut it up from the inside. The teeth chomped on his right side and pinned his arm. **Shitting fuckedy fuck.** They couldn't pierce his armour but they trapped his arm, leaving him holding the hilt of the blade that was still in its scabbard. Then after a few seconds it moved back and Luther tore his knife out and started stabbing frantically into the mouth. He tore out meaty chunks and teeth, blood sprayed all over him.

Lakeitha got up from the ground, feeling slow and tired, her head pounding. She looked around for Malek, then she realised that he was in the tree as well, unconscious and stacked on top of Luther. The mouth of the tree was wide open and the branches mimicked the quiet flailing of a dying spider. She stared at the scene for a few seconds, then her brain caught up to speed and she grabbed her sword and ran in to help. She lobbed off one of the branches, then another and then she started stabbing into the tree trunk at head height. She cut through the bark, then the wood and then the blade sank into the soft inside of the tree's mouth.

Luther stabbed and screamed, until the tree was definitely dead, its mouth a tattered mess of meat and some combination of tree sap and blood.

Lakeitha pulled Malek out of the tree by his legs and then helped Luther out. Luther dropped to his knees in front of her and screamed at the tree. He brought his hands to his bloodsoaked face and started hyperventilating. Lakeitha winced and turned away from him, checking on Malek. He was unconscious and his face had bite marks, though not as bad as Luther's. He was going to have a concussion, but he'd be okay.

She looked back to Luther who was still freaking out on the ground. She took out her canteen and knelt down by his side. She held his shoulder firmly and poured water over his face, washing a lot of blood away and making him hiss at the fresh agony. His lips were quivering and he looked like he wanted to say something but he couldn't find the words. Then he started sobbing. She sat there with him, as he blubbered and cried. She didn't say a word.

Chapter 12

Luther composed himself after five minutes. Then he got up, took some medical supplies from his bag and tended to his cuts. He didn't say anything to Lakeitha, never looked her in the eye. When he'd done what he could with his face, he went over to Malek and treated his bite marks as he lay unconscious on the floor. Malek still hadn't woken up after half an hour, so they decided that they would have to carry him if they were going to make it to their camp before sundown. Lakeitha was already hauling the bull, so it fell on Luther to carry Malek through the dense jungle. Luther and Lakeitha never said a word to each other.

All the extra weight put them at a disadvantage defensively, fortunately the worst things they encountered were mosquitoes, hunger and back pains. Malek woke up after an hour and a half and Luther promptly dropped him on his feet and let him walk on his own.

They reached the campsite just after sundown. It was empty as expected. Luther prepared the fire, gathering tinder and wood and starting it with his lighter. Every Hell Hunter carried two lighters on them because they were light and saved a lot of time. Even purists like Malek used lighters. Malek went back to sleep and Lakeitha gutted, decapitated and skinned the bull, cut out some steaks and then put the rest of the meat into three sacks for them to carry later.

At first Luther was on edge about sleeping out here, in the open, but Lakeitha seemed pretty at ease about it. He didn't want to raise his concerns with her because… well he just really didn't want to talk to her.

He laid out his blanket by the roaring fire and held his sword at his side. He examined the blade. He liked this sword; he'd had a dozen swords to choose from, all made of red or black alien metal and this one had really stood out to him. It was black and had a hefty basket hilt, like a cutlass, with big sharp studs on it, even more dangerous than the studs on his gloves. It had a broad curved blade and was bigger than Lakeitha's sword. It had reminded him of the pirate swords that his mother had shown him pictures of, in those dusty old books that she used to read him. Only this weapon was much bigger, heavier and more menacing. It was bigger than any sword he'd ever fought with. He could handle the extra weight no problem, but it did force him to adapt his techniques. Luther had quickly taken to training with his new sword and now he wanted to kill some monsters. Next time, he'd be ready for the fight. It wouldn't be like with that damn tree. It'd be different, it'd all be different.

He was angry and he saw Lakeitha preparing the meat and then he felt embarrassed and shook his head. Would she tell Malek how he lost his shit. How he'd acted like a child. Of course she would, she was probably laughing it up inside. He had to prove himself to them; prove he was better and tougher than they thought. Otherwise they'd never respect him and then what. They'd probably tell Bane that he was a coward, spread doubt and gossip about him and he wouldn't get another chance to be a Hell Hunter.

Lakeitha was very aware of how hard Luther was trying to ignore her. He was clearly suffering from a nasty case of bruised ego. She had no problem with letting him sulk, she had better things to focus on, like the big juicy steaks that she was cooking in her mess tin. As the fat sizzled and the meat started to brown the aroma filled the air. Lakeitha breathed it in and licked her lips. The gorgeous smell woke Malek. He sat up impatiently checking the progress of the meat. The smell even seemed to cheer Luther up. Her stomach was growling at her. She'd barely eaten a bite since they left Dantez, because she'd wanted to indulge as fully as possible in the meal ahead. She'd eaten a few dry rations just to keep herself alert, but now it was time to feast.

She sat back, nestled into her blanket with her sword by her side and took one last moment to savour the smell, holding the meat in her hands, inches away from her mouth. Then she took the first bite.

Glorious.

After she finished her steak she dropped three more, smaller steaks into her mess tin and set it back in the fire.

After eating all the meat he could handle Luther felt much more at ease around Lakeitha and Malek. Now that he had finished obsessing, he could see that they didn't care about how he'd reacted after climbing out of that tree. They were both just happy to be alive and enjoying such delicious food. He nestled into his warm blankets; after all that walking and all that succulent meat, he was tired and ready to drift off into a deep sleep.

Lakeitha volunteered to take the first watch. She had a natural stamina that suited her well through all the walking and the lack of sleep that came with the job. She'd wake Luther in two hours, but now she was happy to sit back with her stacks of meat by her side and look up at the beautiful array of strange lights in the sky. Nobody knew much about the portals and the effects they had on the world. One of the many things they'd change was the night sky. She'd seen pictures of what the sky had looked like before the portals opened. Just endless blackness, with thousands of tiny little stars and one moon. So very different from what she saw now.

There were still countless small stars in the sky, little specks of light in the background; but few people could ever focus their attention on those far away burning lights, because of the clustered display of cosmic beauty that existed in all its spectacular chaos much closer to home.

The old moon was tinted strawberry red and hung in the sky surrounded for thousands of miles by pieces of its red rock that had broken off. Shards of moon bigger than any mountain glistened way up in the sky, looking no bigger than pebbles to Lakeitha's eye. She looked at the five new moons; they appeared tiny compared to the old moon. One was lime green, another purple, another brown and two were pale grey, like the old moon used to be.

Hundreds of massive comets blazed across the sky in every direction, cutting white lines through the black sky that took several seconds to fade. A fiery pinwheel coursed through the sky, it appeared to be three times the size of the old moon and obscured it as it passed, spirally sparks so large that they boggled Lakeitha's mind just thinking about them. How big they were, how hot they must be and how did the pinwheel never burn itself out. The pinwheel passed by once every night on its endless journey around the world; taking one hour to cross the sky and move on to grace another corner of the earth with its fire.

Lakeitha's favourite sight in the sky was the great streak. It was twice the width of the old moon and crossed the sky diagonally. It was the brightest thing up there, even brighter than the pinwheel. The great streak looked as if God had ripped a gaping tear in the sky and golden light bled through it.

Lakeitha spent half an hour staring in awe at the sky and savouring the meaty aftertaste. She would have gladly spent her entire shift right there, but she had responsibilities. She picked up her sword and stealthily wandered the perimeter looking for monsters. She did this, with occasional breaks, until the two hours were up, killing four small monsters with ease. Then she woke Luther and finally allowed herself to snuggle under her blanket and take one last look up at the sky. Her body softened and warmed and she sunk into a peaceful sleep.

Chapter 13

Shante personally performed four or five public executions each year. They were a show of strength to the people of Dantez. It solidified her position of power and the rule of law. There were many other executions carried out through the year in private by other people, but certain people had to be made an example of and she had to be the one to kill them. She stood at the top of the steps of The Guardian's Palace. There was a white sheet laid out beneath them. It was there to make removing the body easier and to make the blood more visible to the crowd at the bottom of the steps. On her right was a table with the bolt rifle resting on it. Much like a bolt pistol used for the slaughter of cattle, back when there were nice meaty docile cows everywhere, the bolt rifle fired out a metal rod with such force that it broke through the skull and into the brain, causing instant death. The extra size and length of the rifle was for show. This was a tool for public executions and it had to look impressive before it was even used.

At the time of public executions no civilians were allowed to stand on the forty steps leading up to The Guardian's Palace. There were fifty guards at the bottom of the steps keeping the crowd in check. The Guardian's Force guarded Shante and the palace; they were skilled and loyal fighters, entrusted with her safety. They were also there as part of the show. The Guardian of Dantez had to look powerful, and the intimidating number of warriors that she had gathered around her helped maintain this lofty image.

She stood beside the criminal, chained and on his knees and she looked over the square filled with spectators. The man beside her was called Sedrick and he had been a petty thief, sentenced to ten years of hard labour. Three years in, he'd killed a guard and escaped. Shante wasn't disgusted by him like she had been by some of the people she'd killed in the past. Hard labour was no joke, it was back breaking, dangerous work. The prisoners were sometimes sent to perform tasks on the outside of the wall that even the Grand Scrapers thought were too dangerous. If Shante had been in Sedrick's position she'd have done the same thing and it wouldn't have taken her three years to build up the nerve.

Before they were executed a lot of people begged and cried or they'd yell curses at her and everyone watching. Sedrick the rebel, seemed to be made from stronger stuff. He knelt there and he stared up at her. She could see his mind working. There was no chance of Sedrick living out the hour and he knew it. Nothing could change that, but right now with his fate sealed, he had a huge audience and was mere feet away from The Guardian of Dantez. She had a feeling that a speech was coming.

She glanced over at the square, it was full of people but the streets that lead towards it were still swelling with new arrivals, anxiously shuffling towards the centre of the city, not wanting to miss one of the biggest events of the year. She'd have to wait for about five minutes before the moment was right.

"Soon we'll all be free." Said Sedrick in an even voice that didn't portray any fear at all. "My fate and the fate of my friends are two very different things. You can't keep treating them this way, they'll push back with more fury than you could ever imagine and when they earn their freedom, you'll have to answer to them. Your slaves will not be forgiving." Shante didn't usually chit chat with the people she killed, but today she felt like making an exception. "You're not slaves, you're criminals. You did a bad thing and you're getting punished. If the work's too hard and the guards are mean to you, I don't care. You have it coming." Sedrick spat on the top step, earning himself boos and heckles from the crowd below, who couldn't hear their conversation.

"They beat us! They tortured us. Made us do the most dangerous jobs. They didn't care if we got sick, or the toilets didn't work or our clothes fell apart. I've seen over a hundred men die. I saw a friend of mine get torn in half setting up one of the traps outside the wall. I saw another man get his teeth pulled out by a guard. One woman got too sick to work so they blinded her for fun and then they threw her over the wall and watched her wander around until a monster ate her. They laughed the whole time. Not one of them died for anything they believed in and none of their deaths mean anything to you, do they?" Shante looked down at the man. He was bubbling with anger. She did think that those things were excessive, but she wasn't going to admit that to Sedrick. "No and neither will yours. It's not a nice world and we all ran out of mercy a long time ago." Sedrick shook his head and looked back at the crowd before him.

"You need to pay more attention to history. One thing that never changed, before or after the portals came. You can't keep slaves forever. The tables always get turned and when they do, you'll feel fear like you never felt before." "Uh huh" she picked up her bolt rifle. She held the hefty black bolt rifle in both hands and pressed it against the base of Sedrick's skull. The moment it pressed against him she noticed his entire body stiffen. He drew in a slow breath and then shouted loud enough for everyone to hear, "Fre…" Shante fired a metal bolt into his skull and out the other side, obliterating his face. The crowd went wild.

Chapter 14

Malek woke Lakeitha. She got up without any fuss, feeling refreshed and energised. She was used to only getting four hours sleep, or even less. Luther was not, he groaned and looked exhausted and miserable. Once again his spirits were lifted by a breakfast of the best meat in the world. The beautiful night sky was no longer visible now that the sun was up. Now it was blue and dotted with a few dull white clouds.

Malek told her that he'd had to fight off a few giant cockroaches in the night who'd been attracted by the smell of the meat. Then Luther mumbled something about killing a furry beast that walked on two legs and had six eyes. They packed up and started moving, with Malek out front having almost completely recovered from his concussion, Luther walking in the middle and Lakeitha bringing up the rear.

Not long after they left the camp, they came across much denser undergrowth. Bushes, saplings, giant blades of grass and leaves, were just some of the kinds of vegetation in their way. Lakeitha and Luther earned every step they took by hacking and slashing with their long blades.

It was tough work, but Lakeitha was strong and used to battling her way through the jungle. She was just relieved Luther had continued to keep his mouth shut since the tree attack.

Luther hacked through a bizarre rainbow coloured bush that was as tough as a mountain, he was too caught up in his moody thoughts to marvel at the migraine inducing colours. He couldn't take his mind off getting eaten by that tree; and how pathetically he'd reacted. He needed to earn their respect and he needed to find out whether these were the kind of people that he could trust. He had to prove himself as a warrior and a man, he had to show that after a moment of shock he was unshaken and could continue as normal. He realised that he'd barely said a word to either of them since the tree. They must think that his silence was a sign that he couldn't hack it, that his character had been destroyed by one short moment of terror. He had to start talking now or they'd never respect him.

Malek groaned inwardly the moment Luther opened his mouth.

"So what did the two of you do during your mandatory service? I already told you guys that I was in The Guardian's Force and I was Shante's bodyguard. Anyway, I was a low level guard for the first three years, then I got promoted to personal guard during the last year of Cust's reign. After he died, I was Shante's bodyguard for three more years. Oh I could tell you some stories." He smiled to himself. He found it almost impossible to think about those three years as Shante's bodyguard, without thinking about the constant out of this world fucking that went on from three weeks in, right up until now. Then he felt guilty again and that guilt killed his desire for conversation. A few moments passed in silence and then Lakeitha said, "I was in the army for the first two years."

Luther was quiet for a moment, then he asked, "How was it?" "There are eight thousand soldiers in the army and it wasn't until I became a Hell Hunter that I realised that seven thousand nine hundred of them are pussies. I did the usual stuff; manning turrets and guns on the wall, protecting Grand Scrapers. I rarely ever spent more than an hour outside the wall but I was good at it. They were even considering me to join the Blackmasks." "So why'd you become a Hell Hunter?" "When I was nineteen my older brother got sick. They call it chronic null. There's no cure and it kills you slowly, draining your strength, making you weaker every day, it ages him as well, he looks like he's fifty now, but he's only thirty-one." Luther winced, Lakeitha's conversation wasn't having the alleviating effect on his mood that he'd hoped for.

"They had a treatment that added years onto his life, but the medicine's rare and expensive. He was a really important guy, so the government got him the medicine at first, but they made it clear that wasn't going to be a permanent arrangement and he couldn't afford it forever on his own. Blackmasks do pretty well, but not as well as Hell Hunters and being a Hell Hunter I can find the medicine myself, rather than buying it from other people." Lakeitha seemed to be thinking aloud more than she was talking to Luther. "I served the five years left on my mandatory service last year, but Mikey still needs his medicine and he's not bringing in any money for himself, so I've stayed on to take care of him." "Huh." Said Luther, "What." She asked a little defensively. "That wasn't what I was expecting." "What were you expecting?" "I don't know. Just not that. How's your brother doing?" "He's dying a little every day. He never leaves his room, but his mind's still sharp. He spends most of his time taking medicine." "What does that mean?" "The stuff that keeps him alive is a really strong hallucinogen. He takes one, he trips for about fifteen minutes, and he never seems to stop at one." "Sounds like a fun guy." "He can be."

There was a lull in the conversation and then Lakeitha said, "Malek" "I guess we're talking then." "It seems like it." "Okay, I signed up to be a Hell Hunter when I was seventeen. I've been doing this for ten years." "Wow" Said Luther, "Ten years. Why'd you choose to be a Hell Hunter from the start?" "Same reason anyone does it at that age, I was too dumb to know better. Then it turned out that I had a knack for it." "Malek's the most natural hunter I've ever seen." "Exactly how good are you?" "I can go two days without water and still function normally, I can track animals for days on end. I can stay perfectly still for hours if there's a monster or enemy nearby. I can see in the dark.

I'm fairly good at telling whether or not an unfamiliar fruit or crop is poisonous to eat."

"You're leaving out the best one?" Said Lakeitha, "Which one?" Lakeitha looked to Luther, a grin on her face, "He can smell fresh water from a distance." "Bullshit." "He can, seriously. I swear it and it's not magic either, it's a skill he has." "There is no way." "I can." Said Malek, his voice portraying none of Lakeitha's desire to convince Luther. "Also, you don't seem impressed enough that I can see in the dark." "That's far-fetched but it's just impossible for a human being to smell water." "Show him." encouraged Lakeitha. Malek shrugged, "Okay."

He held up his hand for them to stop moving, then sniffed the air long and hard until he caught that subtle scent. He cocked his head like a dog and held onto the smell, connecting to it, focusing on it and where it must be. Without saying a word to the other two he started heading in the direction of water.

Luther was confused by everything that he saw, from the way that Malek was peculiarly sniffing at nothing in particular to how thrilled Lakeitha was acting and just the general strangeness of the idea that someone could smell water. The jungle vegetation grew sparser and they were able to walk without hacking their way through the undergrowth. They skirted around a blue hill and walked down a slope, then turned to face a narrow stream of clear water. He couldn't believe it. Malek had known exactly where it was. His first reaction was wonder and then that turned back to scepticism. He'd been a Hell Hunter for ten years, he must know this area like the back of his hand. He probably just remembered where the nearest water was and Lakeitha must be in on the joke. The pair of them were hazing the new guy with a far-fetched prank. He wasn't going to fall for it. "You expect me to fall for this?" The two of them frowned at him as they refilled their canteens, then Malek said, "Oh good, we've got a paranoid one."

The jungle thinned out more as they carried on. This made a big difference to the speed they moved at. There were fewer creatures in the canopies above them that they had to worry about and the humidity wasn't as bad.

They stopped to eat some beef and rest. It was a hot day and Luther was thirsty so he asked Malek to detect some more water. He said there wasn't any nearby. Luther still didn't believe he could smell water; he was even tempted to go looking around to see if there was actually water nearby, then he could prove Malek was full of shit, but that'd just be a waste of time and energy. He looked around and spotted a bush covered in plump dark blue berries, they looked delicious. "Are those poisonous?" He asked, pointing them out to the group. Lakeitha got up and walked over to them. Luther followed her. She looked at them for a few seconds but didn't touch them, then she said, "I have no idea. Hey Malek, come have a look at this."

Malek strolled over, looked at the bush for a moment and then sniffed it.

He felt like burning acid was being forced up his nose. He staggered away coughing and covering his nose. "Aghhh, no…" His stomach heaved, he bent over and dry wretched. He took a swig of water then spat it out. His running nose was raw with that noxious smell. "Those things'll kill you."

Luther shook his head. Shame, they looked tasty. Maybe Malek wasn't so full of it after all. Either that or he was even more of a fraud than he'd thought. Time reveals all. One thing's for sure, he wasn't going to test his theory on the berries.

While Malek took a few minutes to recover, Lakeitha talked to Luther, "Soon we're going to leave the jungle and reach some rocky ground and then a wall of cliffs. The best way through is a narrow gorge, we call it The Fucked Pass, because it's so fucked. Some of the smarter predators often hang around this pass waiting for idiots to come walking through. It's perfect for an ambush and a lot of people have died in there." Luther rubbed his lips together as he thought this over, "Is it really worth going through?" Lakeitha nodded, "It'll cut a day off our journey both ways. Before we go through, we'll split up and scout the area around the mouth of the gorge for an ambush." "What about on the other side of the pass, or on the cliffs above us?" "We go in blind." Said Malek, as he wiped his nose and then checked the sharpness of his knife for the hundredth time. Luther didn't like it, but it seemed like the only choice and he definitely wasn't going to be the one to pussy out. Anything the two of them could handle, he could handle.

Chapter 15

They walked on until they cleared the edge of the jungle. There were still a lot of trees and bushes spread around the area but there was also a lot of open ground and open sky above them now that they'd finally escaped the canopies of branches and leaves that stifled the sunlight. It felt good to be back in the open air and feel a breeze against his skin. The humidity was so malicious that it made him feel like he was marching around inside a skintight oven that weighed more than he did. They started walking uphill on rocky soil that gave way to hard unforgiving stone.

As he hiked he saw the tops of the cliffs sprout ahead of him and soon they took up the entire horizon. He realized as the slope started to level out that the cliffs were further away than he'd first judged.

"Split up?" He asked the group, Malek answered, "Soon." "Right, say if you've got a hound's nose, then why don't you just search the whole area with a few sniffs and a wag of the tail?" "That'd take too long. We have to do the leg work." "What you're saying is that you can't do it." Malek gave him a look that told him to back off, which was something that Luther rarely ever did. "Say, how come you didn't smell the tree monster? Maybe you're losing the knack." "Maybe. Or maybe I knew it was there the whole time and I was hoping that it'd swallow you up." "If that's true then how come you got swallowed as well." Malek glared at him and Luther glared back. Then Malek broke into a smile and after a moment of surprise Luther smiled back. "You were starting to scare me there." "Nah, when I want you scared…" "Hey sorry to interrupt your moment of bonding, but we've got shit to do." said Lakeitha.

They split up, Luther going right. There were all kinds of places where monsters could be hiding in the space between them and The Fucked Pass, which was a clear gap right down the middle of the cliff in front of him, maybe fifteen meters wide. There were boulders, bushes, clusters of trees, ridges, holes and piles of loose rock, some of which were more than forty feet tall. For the first time since he came into the wild, there was almost a full kilometre of relatively open ground laid out ahead of him and yet, he couldn't hear or see a single living thing. He didn't like that.

He walked in a wide arc, heading away from Malek who was heading straight towards the gorge. As he walked further away from the others, his view of them became obstructed by trees and rocks. He tried to keep himself in sight, but it was inevitable over this distance and in this place that sometimes Luther would be isolated.

The ground he walked on started to slope downwards towards the massive mouth of a cave standing in the middle of an even larger wall of rock. He could easily have skirted around the wall of rock, but he felt that this was exactly the sort of thing he should be checking out right now.

The inside of the cave was well lit by shards of sunlight that shone through holes in the stone. He approached trying to keep quiet but it was impossible to avoid kicking all the pebbles on the ground. He stepped cautiously inside, it was big with a ceiling even higher than the mouth of the cave, maybe thirty meters. The cave was empty, save for a large scattering of shattered and gnawed bones. Every surface was covered in a disgusting amount of dried blood.

He saw the mouth of a tunnel in the back of the cave, which was also very tall but much darker than the cave. He knew there was a risk in going deeper, but he went anyway.

He headed through the tunnel. At first there was just enough light to see by, but the further he walked the darker it got, until he could only just make out his hands in front of him. After walking for a couple of minutes he started hearing a crunching noise in the distance. It amplified and echoed as he walked further and he realised that something big was happening. He heard powerful impacts and the sounds of stone breaking and crumbling and getting tossed around. The echo changed and the tunnel ahead of him brightened, showing a wall ahead and a left turn.

He turned around the corner and there it was, the other side. The tunnel opened up at the bottom of a basin, with steep rock walls twenty meters high. In the middle of the basin, smashing boulders, was a monster. This was a freaky big monster. Luther didn't know what it was called, he didn't know the names of many monsters. Most monsters were only known to a handful of Hell Hunters, maybe only one. He'd never come across his own monster before. Just the tree monster, that wasn't an official name, but everyone called a tree monster a tree monster and everyone knew what they looked like, because they're trees. This was Luther's first, unknown, legitimate monster and it was horrific.

It had its back to him, a back that was twice as broad as Luther's and bulging with muscles. It looked vaguely human from behind, although its sandy coloured skin seemed almost leathery. It was hunched over a pile of rocks, a lot of which had been smashed into pebbles. It adjusted its position to smash another rock and Luther caught a good look at its front side. It didn't need any tools to smash those rocks. The thing had no hands, just massive round stumps of exposed bone, with skin and cartilage clutching around its base. Its big head was one massive eyeball with a skull around it with small ear holes. It had a huge gaping mouth on its whole torso, with razor sharp teeth that were almost a foot long. It was still hunched over but he reckoned that this thing was about eight feet tall.

This was what he'd been waiting for. A real fight, a real monster. He'd show those smug pricks what he was made of and he'd dominate this world of magic and monsters just like he'd dominated every fight of his career. He stepped out of the tunnel, it heard him and turned around, standing at its full height. Its massive eyeball looked at him for several seconds, its audible blinking made him shiver with revulsion. He stared back at it, sword steady in his hand, showing no fear. The monster threw its arms high over its head, opened its mouth wide and screamed the scream of ten men as it ran at him. He ran to meet it.

He came at it from the right side, slashing upwards into its muscular arm and then ducking underneath it. He stepped around the monster and slashed across its back. He back-peddled as it reared around on him. It made another run, he fainted with a lung to the right and then dodged left, running his blade along the creature's right side. It staggered and then came after him, getting up close and swinging its bludgeons at his head. Luther ducked under the first and backed away from the second. This thing's punches were easier to read than any cage fighter he'd come up against in a long time. He sidestepped a punch meant for his gut, then stepped in and punched upwards. The studs on his sword's hilt struck the monster just below the eyeball.

The monster howled and stumbled away from him. He started to follow it and then it screeched in fear and tripped over itself trying to get away from him. It reached the wall of the basin and then curled up into a ball and covered its head with its muscular arms. It was sobbing and he could see tears dripping from its massive eye. Luther stared at the monster, then he laughed, shaking his head in amazement. He'd beaten this big scary monster without breaking a sweat. The massive mouth of the creature was trembling and began to wail so loudly that it hurt Luther's ears. He couldn't wait for the others to see this.

He approached the crying monster, keeping his distance, wanting to examine the thing without pushing it to do something desperate. It seemed very distressed by the blood that was leaking out from the cuts Luther had made. Luther respected his weapon and he certainly hadn't been holding anything back, but still, this seemed like an overreaction to the damage he had done. This thing had come at him with such ferocity and power and now it was cowering in a ball. It was pathetic.

Malek appeared at the top of the basin wall and stared down at him and the screaming monster.

"Luther"

His voice sounded like a whisper yet it was loud enough that he could hear it at the bottom of the basin. There was a look on Malek's face that didn't make sense to him. "You idiot!" He shouted. "It's just a baby!" "What!" Luther called back.

"Run!"

"Why?"

But Malek had already turned around and disappeared from view. Luther could either run back the way he'd come or climb over the basin wall. He chose the latter, sprinting past the monster. **What had Malek said, a baby?** Luther ran up the side of the basin, scrambling on his hands as it got steeper. Just before he reached the top he heard a roar that turned his body to jelly and made him trip over in surprise. It was so much louder than the creature he'd beaten. It filled the air all around him with a potent, imminent dread. In that moment he was certain that every living thing in the area was hoping that they wouldn't come face to face with the source of that roar and suffer its wrath. Unfortunately, Luther knew that they had nothing to worry about.

Chapter 16

Ahead of Malek was Lakeitha, she was running too, heading towards the Fucked Pass, which now in spite of its name felt like a safe haven. He was uneasy about running this fast with his knife in his hand but he hadn't sheaved it before he started running and he sure as shit wasn't going to slow down. Up ahead of him was a ditch about six feet wide, if he fell in then he'd be a dead man. There were teeth chattering footsteps behind him; from the rate that they were hitting the ground he knew that it was moving a lot faster than he was. If it caught him the bracken would eat him alive, or maybe it would just pound him into a red paste in a vengeful frenzy. When he reached the edge of the ditch he leaped, lifting both legs up as high as he could. He cleared the ditch and rolled when he landed on the other side, trying not to stab himself.

Lakeitha stopped beside a few lonely trees and looked back at the others. She swore to herself when she saw the forty foot tall mountain of muscle and teeth with a single eyeball that was chasing Luther. It stepped effortlessly over the ditch a couple of seconds after Luther jumped it. Malek reached her and turned to look back at Luther and the monster. They both reckoned he was going to get stomped into the ground like a fence post. He paused for a moment and Lakeitha watched his mind whirling in search of a plan. "Shit" He cursed, he'd found one and he didn't seem to like it.

"Keep running and be ready with your World Saver. We're doing the bait and trip." "It's too big for the bait and trip." "Just do it." She turned and ran and Malek hid behind the thickest tree in the patch and watched Luther and the bracken approach.

Luther was twenty meters out and at this rate he might be crushed before he passed the trees. The plan would still work without Luther, it'd just be a shame if he was pulped before Malek got to save the day.

Malek was not a vain man, but he knew as a fact, based on life experience, references and the critical analysis of other human beings, that he was one of the toughest, most fearless people on earth. But when that bracken blocked out the sun, and made his bones shake with the vibrations of its footfall, he felt the unfamiliar sensation of fear, tugging at him, begging him to run away or dig a hole in the ground and crawl inside.

Its teeth were longer than his entire body, and it could topple a house with a single blow. This was a behemoth, an apex predator on a parental rampage, and his ridiculous plan was to trip the bastard up.

Luther sprinted past the trees, as he passed Malek caught a moment's glimpse of his face, up close. It was a split second but felt like so much longer. Even in his line of work it was rare to witness such pure helpless terror on the face of another man.

Malek hugged the tree with his left arm as tightly as he could and wrapped both legs around it. He reached out his right arm and splayed his palm. When the bracken passed by him its knee was above his eye level. He released the tentacle.

It flew out from the slit in his palm and wrapped itself tightly around the bracken's leg several times.

In the moment between the tentacle grabbing bracken's leg and the full force of the monster's momentum fighting back, Malek's mind was totally clear. Not one thought came to him. He was as relaxed and loose as he could possibly be. In his experience, that made it easier.

Malek's arm was pulled from its socket and he screamed.

Lakeitha watched the giant fall, it hit the ground and the entire valley shook.

Malek's dislocated arm hung limply by his side, with the tentacle still attached to the bracken's leg.

The bracken snarled, a sound so loud and deep and angry that she felt very foolish standing with her tiny gun in her hand, about to piss off the great beast.

The bracken was already starting to push itself up on its massive fists. She couldn't have that. She aimed and fired at its left arm. She hit it right in the centre of its elbow.

The bracken's elbow exploded and the bracken crumpled screaming in agony. She took aim at its massive eyeball head and the whole world started spinning. She didn't understand why, then she felt tremendous pain in her stomach and chest. She heard a short dull *thwack* and she blacked out.

Luther pulled out his World Saver. He needed to kill this thing right now. It had knocked Lakeitha through the air and into a rock. He didn't know if she was dead or not. He had to end it.

He was on its left side and since Lakeitha had almost shot the fucker's left arm clean off, he felt pretty safe standing there. He aimed at it and started to say a cool line that he'd been working on for weeks. But the moment he opened his mouth the giant's neck swivelled round and that big creepy eye was looking right at him. "Look's lik..." Moving with surprising speed and fluidity, the injured monster rolled onto its right side and kicked out its left leg.

He didn't enjoy the luxury of a clear shot into the air like Lakeitha had, instead he was sent tumbling head over heels at high speed along the ground. The bounces and flips turned to rolls which eventually stopped. He couldn't breathe, but there were more pressing matters than oxygen, like the World Saver that was five meters in front of him and the giant vengeful monster that was fifty meters away from him and closing the distance fast.

It crawled towards him and he crawled towards his gun.

Every movement stimulated new areas of pain. Spittle and curse words spluttered out of his mouth. He got a little closer to the gun and reached out to it. He touched it with the tip of his finger. He growled and then the monster came a little closer and the sound of it shaking the earth turned his growl to a whimper. He pushed himself a little further and got his hand around the grip of the World Saver. He rested it against the ground and tried to aim it but he couldn't raise his head to look through the sights. He hissed, he could feel something changing, he was getting weaker and...

Malek let go of the tree and started staggering after the bracken. It was still going after Luther the man who'd attacked its child, the man who just passed out. Doing the one armed commando growl this monster was still covering ground fast.

The bracken had stretched his tentacle taut. He wasn't sure which would snap off first, his tentacle or his arm, but he didn't want to find out. He released the bracken and his tentacle sped back into his limp right arm. He drew his long red knife and ran after the bracken. Now that its leg was free it was already starting to stand up.

He got beside its left leg and raised his knife in the air. As he prepared to strike this giant with his tiny little weapon he regretted not carrying a World Saver of his own.

He stabbed his knife a foot deep into the back of the bracken's knee. It hissed and tried to kick him with its injured leg. He rolled under the kick and ran past the bloody half arm towards the World Saver. As he passed the bracken's head it rolled over and swiped its right arm at him.

With all that movement, fear and adrenaline it almost felt as if time was passing by at a snail pace. The giant bone stump was arcing around, about to hit him in his side and shatter his ribcage.

He leaned back and jumped, raising his legs up over his head. Halfway through the backflip, at the peak height, the bracken's arm passed under him and he felt the woosh of air against his upside down face.

He'd overdone it and flipped 540 degrees, he didn't land on his head though, his dislocated arm broke his fall.

He rolled away from the bracken, got up and sprinted to Luther, agony riveting up and down his arm. He reached down and grabbed the World Saver from his hand, not having time to check if he was still alive.

He turned around and looked up to see the bracken standing at its full height. He stared into its gaping mouth. Its left arm was hanging limply by its side, much like

Malek's right arm. He rarely fought anything this big. It was truly awesome and terrifying.

The bracken took a step towards him and he blew out its knee. It fell and Malek felt like he was watching a building topple.

Its head landed ten meters in front of him. He was sure that he was outside of its reach, he didn't want to get sucker punched like Lakeitha.

It looked up at him with its big eyeball and moaned. For the first time, it sounded scared. The bracken knew it was beaten. He limped forward a few steps, he reckoned that was still safe. His arm had gone numb but he was still in a great deal of pain. His breathing was loud and raspy. It took a lot of concentration for him to stop swaying from side to side like a drunk. He raised his left hand and aimed the hand cannon at the bracken's eye. Its iris was green. It looked at him and he looked at it. It felt like they stayed there for several minutes, just watching each other. The only sounds were their pained heavy breaths.

He fired the World Saver. The bullet punched a hole through the bracken's eyeball and out the other side of its head.

His arm fell down by his side and he dropped the gun.

Chapter 17

He stumbled away from the bracken. He went over to Luther and kicked him gently in the chest; he didn't move. He checked his pulse and lifted his eyelids to check on his pupils. He'd be fine. He went over to Lakeitha, she was out cold as well, and there was a puddle of blood under her head.

He grimaced before he checked the pulse, he couldn't face losing her. She was one of the only friends he had and he didn't want to touch her. The moment he touched her, he'd know if she was dead and then he'd live the rest of his life with the memory of touching her lifeless body.

He checked her pulse, it was still going strong. He sighed in relief and lifted her head, checking on the cut. Her scalp had been scraped by the rocky ground she landed on. It was a surface cut, a lot of blood but no real damage. He checked on her arms and legs, they weren't broken.

He looked down at his own arm, "Fuck" He muttered. No one was awake to fix his arm for him, he looked over at the trees and knew what he had to do. "Fuck!" He yelled up at the sky.

He unclipped his empty scabbard and put it in his mouth. He bit down on it hard, it tasted of dirt, tree sap and leather. He pressed up against one of the trees, making sure that he got the angle of his shoulder right. He never carried painkillers. He was such a fucking idiot. **Big tough hunter, no World Saver, no pain killers, dumb fucking wanker, fucking,** "AHAHHGHG!" After the briefest muffled howl he lost his voice. He fell onto his back and rived around on the ground. He spat out the scabbard and tried screaming but his throat felt like it was clamped shut in a vice.

After he regained control he lay still looking up at the sky, savouring a moment of peace. He savoured it, but he didn't enjoy it, because of the agony in his arm and the knowledge that even though this giant was dead, there were many other predators in the area.

He got up, checked on Luther and Lakeitha again, neither of them had woken up. He patrolled a tight perimeter of his two unconscious companions for ten minutes. As he did this the pain and the exhaustion built up gradually, until he struggled to stand, sweat was thick on his face and he couldn't focus on his guard duty any longer. He rustled around in Luther's bag until he found some guaga. He wasn't going to pass out and let the three of them get eaten by the first thing to come along, just because he was too damn stupid to take a painkiller. It tasted horrible, he washed his mouth out with water and then ate some of the meat from the miniature pink-skinned bull. He felt like the meat worked better than the painkillers.

He sat on a rock, with his knife in one hand and his mace in the other, watching the valley around him. He didn't want to fight, not until he got some proper rest, but rest was never guaranteed and refusing to fight meant refusing to live.

Malek was no sweetheart, he was a survivor, but he wasn't a totally heartless pragmatic bastard. If he was, he would have left the pair of them. Retreated to somewhere safer for a couple of hours sleep and then attempted to walk through The Fucked Pass on his own. He wasn't going to do that though. He was going to sit on this rock and keep his eyes open, and if any monster was stupid enough to challenge him, he'd kill em, just like he'd killed all the others.

Luther woke up with a malignant headache. He was used to those. His body was stiff. He tried to get up and the stiffness turned to horrible pain. "Lakeitha" He groaned, "Malek. I..." It took a lot of effort to speak and all his words were drawn out and slurred, he sounded drunk. Somebody came over to him, he heard them coming from roughly twenty meters away, but by the time he managed to turn his head they'd reached him and their boots were inches away from his face. "You look terrible." "Malek. Is Lakeitha okay? "She hasn't woken up yet, but I think so." "Get me some guaga. I can't even move." "Yeah alright."

Malek grabbed some more painkillers from Luther's bag. He gave Luther a little bit of guaga, enough to get him on his feet for a few hours. The stuff worked fast, the pain in Malek's arm was tolerable now and Luther was moving around within minutes. Malek kept his guard up, as vigilant as ever. Luther might technically be awake but right now in a fight he'd be as useless as a slug.

It was another twenty minutes before Lakeitha woke up. She'd been hit even worse than Luther, but she wasted no time with complaints. She got up on her own, helped herself to a little guaga and within sixty seconds of regaining consciousness she was talking about heading for The Fucked Pass.

She clearly had a headache, one he reckoned was even worse than Luther's, but she didn't put up a fuss. Her nose started bleeding and bleeding hard, but again she didn't put up a fuss. Not even breaking her stride, she kept on moving while she wiped the blood away from her mouth.

They reached the mouth of The Fucked Pass without incident. They stood on the threshold, in the shadows of the two tall cliff faces. It was a very long pass and standing where they were, they couldn't see to the other side. Their view was blocked by the first of many tall piles of rocks that were ideal for ambushes. Everything about this fucking place was ideal for ambushes. Every time Malek walked through here he felt like a complete idiot.

Lakeitha looked over at Malek, she knew that every time they walked through this pass he felt like a complete idiot. It was a necessary step when travelling this direction but the risk they took was ridiculous. Knowing Malek, she reckoned part of him would like to grab a pickaxe and hack his own way through the cliffs. But that would be just a tad impractical.

As deadly as The Fucked Pass was, Lakeitha and Malek had successfully travelled through it together dozens of times. But they'd never done it with Luther. She still wasn't sure about him. He'd fucked up crossing the valley and almost got them pulverised by a giant bracken. Bringing a liability like that with you through The Fucked Pass, is no more intelligent than starting a fist fight with a swarm of acid hornets or jumping headfirst into a pile of human shit when you have a lethal allergy to large quantities of human shit. Still that's what they were doing, for no other reason than it would be too unprofessional for Lakeitha to cut off Luther's head then and there, just to spare herself the burden of his company.

Luther did not feel like going through The Fucked Pass right now. He was tired and in pain, he tried to stay focused but the pain, the tiredness and the painkillers all made that difficult. He was amazed by how Lakeitha and Malek were soldiering on, when both of them were easily as badly hurt as he was. He knew cage fighters and warriors who would have thrown in the towel after going through as much as they had, but the two of them were taking it in their stride and were ready to face something that could be even worse.

Chapter 18

Shante sat in her throne in the grand throne room that mainly served as an intimidating setting for her meetings with visitors from Alcraze. Today she wore a gorgeous bright gold dress. Her hair was impeccable, she looked gorgeous. The dress was tight showing off her figure and stopped at the knees for practicalities sake. Though she had never had to use it, Shante had been trained her whole life in weapons and hand to hand combat. She didn't just exercise to maintain her figure, but more importantly to be ready to run, fight and fuck. So far she hadn't needed to do much running or fighting.

Her throne sat atop three thick marble steps so that everyone had to look up at her. To her right side was Quentin, her trusty adviser and head of the army. She had twenty bodyguards in the room, all of them armed with an assortment of swords, knives and guns. Again the extra guards were only there as a show of strength. Everything had been orchestrated that day, after they received word that a representative of King Rodriguez was coming from Alcraze to see her.

The door to her throne room opened and the King's representative made his entrance, followed by two soldiers from Alcraze. His name was Vincent and when

Shante saw him she felt a terrible disappointment. Of all King Rodriguez's lackeys she hated him the most. He was the man that Rodriguez sent when he was in his most hostile moods. She had never once spoken to him without sweating with worry and wanting to hit somebody.

He was thin and grey with very pale skin and very blue eyes. Every time they met, he would bow his head slightly and she would see a little sarcastic smile on his face. But not today, he wasn't bothering with any sly jokes. This was a very bad sign.

His silver tongue started to slither, "Three nights ago, the King's son, Prince Angelo, was killed." The words sent a ripple through the room. It was not a noise, but a feeling of over twenty people tensing up at the same time. Shante knew that King Rodriguez loved his son. Rodriguez was a cruel man on the best of days, but right now he would be hungry for blood in a way that he had never been before. Vincent continued to deliver bad news, "His wife Princess Eleanora, betrayed him. She had sex with another man." Shante wondered if the bitch was already dead, or if Rodriguez had decided to keep his son's wife alive for a few weeks of torture. "Prince Angelo caught his wife with this man and he tried to take revenge." Vincent's lip curled in disgust at the next words he said, "This twisted bastard took Prince Angelo's sword from him and killed him with it."

Vincent paused and nervously, almost fearfully Shante asked, "Have you caught him yet?" Vincent shook his head, "He ran, he made it back home. To Dantez." Shante struggled not to curse out loud, in the corner of her eye she saw Quentin shaking his head.

"Vincent, I want you to tell King Rodriguez that I will do everything I can to help find and punish this killer." Vincent nodded, his face cold, eyes like a chess player. "What is his name?" "Luther Aprille."

Shante was relieved to realise that she was in a dream. This feeling of relief was scraped away as each long second passed. Her belief that it was all in her mind failed as she felt the stillness and expectation in the room. The depth of her senses and the brutal consistency of her surroundings told her that this was very real.

She let out a very slow breath. She could not be offended, she could not be angry, she could not be heartbroken. She could not cry or gasp or whimper or yell. She had to remain regal and powerful and presentable. She had to say, "Vincent, Luther Aprille used to be one of my bodyguards. He is a dangerous man." She had to turn her head to Quentin and say, "Quentin, where does Luther live?" Quentin told her what she already knew, "Luther joined the Hell Hunters and left yesterday morning for his first mission. He won't be back for four days." She had to nod and pretend that this was news to her. She had to turn her head back to Vincent and say in a most courteous manner, "I'm sorry that he isn't in Dantez right now. You are welcome to stay here and plan your next move. Is there anything that you need?"

Vincent nodded, "Things between you and the King haven't been good lately. He doesn't like you and you don't like him. When he found out that the killer was from Dantez and that he used to be your bodyguard, he was so angry that he knocked five of his daughter in law's teeth out. He suspects that you sent an assassin to humiliate and kill his son." Shante shot back with the appropriate, measured anger, "Tell him that…" Vincent held up a hand and she went quiet. She had never allowed Rodriquez or any of his men to silence her, but today she obeyed. "I don't think that you did send somebody to kill the prince. I think that if you attacked us, you'd go straight for the king. But I'm not certain and more importantly, the King is not certain. He wants you to prove your loyalty." Loyalty, she knew that was an insult. Vincent was acting as if Rodriquez was her king as well; but she let it slide. She waited for him to continue.

"The King has decided that you must have Luther Aprille killed and his body brought to Alcraze, to prove that you do not support this killer. You have until dawn four days from now." Shante's gut wrenched, but all she did was narrow her eyes, "He's demanding that I do his killing for him." Vincent nodded, "If you don't, then it will be taken as a declaration of war."

Now she felt that she was allowed to express her anger fully. She stood up and yelled, "What! That fucker would risk wiping out the entire human race, over one man?" Vincent held her gaze and said in a much quieter voice, "Over his son."

Glaring Shante sat back down in her throne and said, "Rodriquez has made up his mind?" "The King will not waver." "I want to speak to him. I won't go through a minion, I want to speak to him in person." "No." "No? You're telling me no." "Rodriquez has assured me that if he meets with you while Luther is still alive, then he will kill you with his bare hands."

Shante stared at Vincent. She could tell her twenty guards to restrain him while Quentin brought her bolt rifle. Nobody would stop her from punching a whole through his head. But she couldn't do that. She may have been sitting in the throne, but right now Vincent had the power.

"Come back here in three hours." Vincent nodded and allowed himself to be escorted out of the room.

After he had left, Shante got up, and walked firmly with a straight back and a composed face. Quentin came to her side and she said to him, "Give me twenty minutes alone." He nodded, didn't say a word. He was one of the few people who knew about her and Luther.

She walked through the halls and opened the door to her private apartment. There were a few servants working and she told them all to leave. She went into the bedroom, where she and Luther had shared so many hours of lust and love. She closed the door and screamed.

She screamed until her voice blew out. She cried and gagged and then screamed again. Her whole body was shaking. She crawled onto the bed, it must have been her imagination but it still smelt like him. She tore at her hair and wept.

The love of her life had sex with another woman. She hated him for that, but she didn't want him to die. She wanted him back, she still loved him far more than she hated him.

She loved his smile, his eyes, his laugh, his body, the way he touched her, the things he said to her.

But she was the Guardian of Dantez, she had a duty. She had to prevent war. Alcraze had a bigger army, but no matter who won, both cities would be doomed. One would be burnt to the ground and the other would be too badly hurt to keep the wild from getting in. Hundreds of different kinds of monsters would eat the children alive. Within a year or two both cities would be swallowed up by the forest.

Fuck him. Fuck him. Fuck him! Fuck him for forcing this decision on me.

As a leader she had an absolute responsibility to her people and as a lover she had an absolute responsibility to her man. It was tearing her apart, but she knew what she had to do. Even if she hated herself for the rest of her life, even if she would never be happy again.

Chapter 19

Nobody knew exactly how many Hell Hunters had died in The Fucked Pass. No bodies were ever recovered, even the drained husks of bone were devoured by the creatures who crawled through this death trap.

Luther and Lakeitha each had their swords out, while Malek carried a weapon in each hand. Malek wasn't ambidextrous, but he trained with his left hand so hard that it was almost equal to his right. Something he'd decided to undertake after training with Gideon, who was ambidextrous.

Though Malek and Lakeitha had travelled through The Fucked Pass many times before, neither of them took any complacency or made any assumptions about what they might come across. The ecosystem of predators between these long, tall walls of jagged black and purple stone was constantly changing. One day it was infested by giant furry abominations, with warped faces and claws longer than swords and thicker than tree trunks and then the next day those monsters were replaced by a swarm of razor raptors, little birds with metal claws and beaks, controlled by a deadly hive mind that would fit them together like a jigsaw puzzle, creating a giant flying blade and then the day after that a humongous malignant spore floats in and swallows up every single one of the razor raptors and digests the metallic birds alive. It was chaos and all experience got you was knowledge of the layout of the pass, which doesn't do all that much good considering that it's a straight line.

After five minutes, the purple and black gems started doing strange things. It was dark in there, but it was the middle of the day so they still had some light seeping in from high above them. That light caused the shiny black and purple rocks to sparkle and then the light reflected from those stones started moving and buzzing, forming patterns. The purple lights were brighter but there were far more black ones. As the purple lights twirled and danced, they touched the black lights and they seemed to bounce off each other. It was almost like the purple lights were fighting the black lights around them, striking out in all directions and every time they touched a black light it would retreat back before closing in again. Luther felt strange looking at all these lights, after twenty seconds or so the lights started giving him a headache.

There was nowhere he could look that wasn't covered in these bizarre lights. He felt dizzy. Then he saw a gap, an empty black hole on the wall to his right, with no light in it at all. He focused on it, trying to get his bearings back and stop his head from spinning. It was two meters above the ground and about as tall as he was. He looked into the emptiness and the calm and took a few deep breaths to still himself.

A giant screaming human head flew out of the hole. It was two meters tall and alive in spite of having no body. Its skin was grey, completely colourless. It had huge pulsing veins all over it, some of them seemed so clogged up that they might burst and leak out a torrent of grey blood. Its eyes were full of fury. It was coming right at him and Luther stabbed his sword upwards into the roof of its mouth and then it knocked him over and gnawed at his arm as strange fluids and giant lumps of pus were regurgitated up from some nonexistent throat. Luther was covered in this strange grey mass, it was gelatinous and hot and cold and he didn't know what it was but it was thick and it stuck to him and the giant head was dissolving as it leaked onto him. He screamed for help and the silver lava pus swarmed into his mouth.

"It's alive!" screamed Luther as he lay on the ground waving his sword around at the air. "His mind's been poisoned." "By what?" asked Malek, surveying the area for threats. "I don't know. If it doesn't wear off then what do you want to do with him?" Malek shook his head, "Now's not the time. Do we turn back or carry him the rest of the way?" Lakeitha looked down at the poor man, who was suffering some horror that was only real for him. "I'll carry him but I get to knock him out." "Fair's fair, Lakeitha." She kicked him twice, once in the wrist to get rid of that wild sword and then once in the head. He was unconscious in an instant. She picked him up and carried his weight, plus the weight of his equipment and the sack of miniature pink-skinned bull that he had been carrying. It all added up to a lot more than her own bodyweight, but she carried him without complaint.

Malek acted cool for Lakeitha's benefit but the frustration was getting to him like a big spider crawling under his skin. He kept his feet moving forward and his eyes on the potential threats around him. He hadn't gotten ten steps forward before something the size of his head jumped at him from the left. He didn't know what it was, but it was fast and black and he didn't want it on his face. He swung his mace and hit the little creature, it made a popping noise when it exploded. He waited for another one to attack, but they didn't. Either the thing had been going at it solo, or all its friends had decided that they didn't want to get splattered.

Each step Lakeitha took was arduous. She had a pounding headache and a great weight over her shoulders. Malek was leading the way, wading through small fry, but she had to remain vigilant, ready to dump Luther at any moment and fight for her life.

They reached roughly the halfway point when Malek stopped. "Lakeitha, we've got a problem." "What is it?" asked Lakeitha as she caught up to him. "Cunt" She said, as she looked down at the pool of twinkly grey quicksand. It covered the floor of the pass for about twenty meters. Malek didn't say anything more, he just stood there thinking. Then he knelt down, picked up a stone that probably weighed four kilograms and tossed it gently onto the top of the quicksand. It sank instantly, "Cunt" said Malek. He looked over at the jagged rock wall to his left and then to the one at his right. The right was better.

"We're going to have to climb along this side." "I can't do that while carrying him." "No, I'll carry him." Lakeitha raised an eyebrow, "Malek…" "You're stronger than me, but I have a tentacle. I'll wrap him up and then carry him on my back." She looked at the steep face of the cliff, there were some little holes and jutting bits of rock that would make good handholds and footholds. She'd do fine but she was concerned about how Malek would cope.

Lakeitha went first. She climbed ten feet up to get the best footholds and then made her way along. A few meters before she reached the other side she looked up and saw a figure standing at the very top of the cliff. She couldn't tell much from this distance, but the figure was black as night and bigger than she was.

She reached the other side and then pointed the figure out to Malek. He looked up at it for a few seconds, "You think it'll take a shot at us?" "Yup." he said with a shrug, then hoisted Luther onto his back and wrapped the tentacle around him. Immediately he felt the different pieces of bone within his damaged arm grinding against each other. It was excruciating. Still no point in complaining about it. The tentacle pulsed gently along with Malek's heartbeat and made subtle shifts around Luther's body, adjusting to changes in weight distribution caused by his movements.

He was going to put Luther's life on the line, relying on one arm to hold him, an arm that had just been dislocated and then forced back into its socket. He took a moment to be still and inhale a slow breath.

He grabbed a handhold, then changed his mind and grabbed a better one and pulled himself up. He moved very, very slowly. Letting go of his handhold to reach for the next one was nerve racking every time. With the weight of Luther on his back he felt like he was going to fall every time he made a move. He stepped blindly, feeling around for the next foothold. He stepped down on one and it broke as soon as he put weight on it. His left leg slipped and his right followed. He held on tight with his left hand and dangled over the quicksand, kicking against the wall, looking for footholds. "Oh fuck Malek!" Shouted Lakeitha. Their full weight was on one handhold. The black rock may have looked like diamond, but it wasn't no fucking diamond. The rock snapped and they fell into the grey quicksand and disappeared.

Lakeitha stared, shocked and scared. The quicksand had enveloped them instantly and the surface had settled a second later, there was no sign that there were people dying right below it.

She couldn't jump in after them. There was nothing she could do. She was torturously aware of how many seconds had passed.

Malek's tentacle broke through the quicksand and stretched into the air. It flopped over and landed on the surface of the quicksand before swinging back up and flopping in another direction. The tentacle kept reaching until it landed on the solid ground in front of her. Lakeitha grabbed the tentacle. It was a little moist and grippy despite a lack of suction cups. The second she grabbed the tentacle it wrapped itself all the way up her arm. She backed up, gradually pulling more and more tentacle out of the pit and then she saw the palm of Malek's hand emerge. It was hard work, fighting the quicksand and carrying so much weight, but she got Malek's head above the surface. He spat sloppy sand and breathed air, then she heard the muffled screaming. It wasn't coming from Malek. That was when she realised that Malek had to have let go of Luther in order to reach out with the tentacle. She kept pulling, dread rising in her as Malek got further and further out of the sand. Then Luther's head broke the surface of the sand and his piercing screaming echoed through The Fucked Pass.

Malek was pulling him up out of the quicksand by his hair. She got Malek up to the edge and kept pulling until he and Luther were both lying on the solid stone ground. They were both covered head to toe in damp grey sand.

Malek got to his feet, a big clump of Luther's hair in his hand. He was seething, his entire body trembled with rage. Luther jumped up beside him, still screaming. His mind still clearly poisoned, his eyes mad and afraid. Lakeitha tried to grab him and he hit her in the face. She dropped and Luther ran away screaming. He'd never seen anyone catch Lakeitha off guard like that.

Malek scratched his face and shook his head and slapped himself and swore. He shook his arms and looked around for something to kill.

Luther screamed, he'd fallen and there were giant orange centipedes crawling out of the cliffs and climbing on top of him. They bit him and pinned him down as he hallucinated. Malek started running and yelling a war cry like he had a thousand men behind him. He drew his blade and jumped into the pile of centipedes. One wrapped around his stomach and he cut it in half, then another one crawled up his leg and another latched onto his knife arm. He roared and struggled and cleaved the centipedes until his other arm was pinned to his side by five centipedes that were trying to bite through his armour. He staggered back and the centipedes tripped him up. He fell and they climbed onto his body.

One of them came up in front of his face, it had sharp black teeth right the way around its mouth. The mouth widened and the teeth stretched out, preparing to bite into his face but he bit it first. He sunk his teeth into the centipede below its mouth and shook his head, green blood spraying into his mouth. It tasted like unbearably bitter lemon juice and tar. He tore out a chunk of it, spat it out and then bit into it again. He kept biting and tearing until it stopped struggling. A second one came for him and he bit that one too. He bit them until his arm was free and he started stabbing them, laughing and cheering until all of them were split up into a pile of torn red flesh and green blood.

The other centipedes retreated away from Luther, into their holes in the stone. But Malek wanted blood. He threw the knife up into the air, freeing his right hand so that he could fire his tentacle at one of them, he caught it just below the teeth and he pulled it away from a hole in the wall, catching the falling knife in his left hand. He reeled the centipede in and as it passed by, he stabbed down on it again and again, puncturing its body eight times in the space of a second. He dropped it dead on the ground.

He looked around for something else to fight, then he looked up at the top of the cliff and pointed at the big black figure. "You! I fucking want a piece of you!" The figure stayed still for a moment and then turned around and disappeared from view. "Ye fucking coward." Muttered Malek. He shook his head and wiped the green blood off his face.

He checked on Luther, he was still rolling around on the ground, he didn't look great. He'd heard of people who'd had their minds poisoned and had hallucinated for the rest of their lives. Luther could do that on his own time, if he was going to be a part of the team then he had to get his head together. He turned to Lakeitha, she was on her feet and walking over, blood pouring from her left cheek. "He sure can hit."

Lakeitha looked Malek over, he'd gone calm again, the anger was gone. He was an alchemist, he turned feelings into piles of gore.

In the state that he was in Luther couldn't be carried. In spite of Malek's terrifying actions, the creatures who were watching them at that very moment wouldn't be held at bay by fear for very long. They had to move or they'd get attacked again by the centipedes and if they killed all the centipedes then the dark figure on top of the cliff would drop down and try his luck. Nobody holds The Fucked Pass for long.

"Do you want to kick him again?" asked Malek. Lakeitha shook her head, "I don't think I'd enjoy it as much the second time." "Fair enough." he kicked Luther in the head, putting him to sleep. "What a headache he's going to have." Said Lakeitha, Malek nodded, turned around and started walking towards the tall pile of shiny black rocks ahead of them. Leaving Lakeitha to pick Luther up again.

They climbed over the rocks. The pile was more than twice their size. They could hear quiet breathing and slight movements beneath them. There were things in the pile and they didn't have the guts to attack. When they got over the pile they could see the other side of the pass a hundred meters ahead of them.

Chapter 20

She left her bedroom and sat down on one of her sofas in her living room. It was full of rare luxuries from the previous century. She had shelfs stacked with books and a carefully maintained TV. She had a big stack of old DVDs and Blu-rays. She liked the TV but she never had any time to watch it. The movies were a window to the past, to the crazy world that had existed before the portals started opening. She also had music, music that she liked to sink into, leaving her body behind and letting herself be moved by rhythms and energy from another era. Suddenly she wanted to put on a song and escape. She stood up and went over to her stereo system.

There was a knock on the door and she heard Quentin say, "Shante can I come in?" Shante sighed, disappointed. "Yes Quentin, come in." She had, subconsciously, been expecting him to enter the room like he was at a funeral, instead he came in like Luther at one of his cage fights. He was buzzing with anger, like he was going to pounce on somebody and tear their ears off. "I'm sorry Shante." She knew that he was holding his tongue. That he wanted to rant and rave about Luther's betrayal.

She gestured for him to sit down. "We don't have any choice here Quentin." He nodded and she saw a little relief in his face. As much as he knew that she was wholly committed to her duty as The Guardian of Dantez, a little part of him had clearly been worried that she would try to protect Luther. "Get Bane, I want him in the room when we speak to Vincent again."

A horrible thought crossed Shante's mind and she shivered with revulsion. She tried to stifle the emotion and focus on being ruthlessly pragmatic. "Quentin, if Rodriguez ever finds out about me and Luther, then he will be certain that I was behind the killing. He'll go to war immediately. We can't let that happen." He was looking at her with eyes just as focused and heartless as her own. "Agreed. Who knows?" "Two servants who I trust and two that I don't. At least a dozen of my guards past and present. I'll give you the names." Quentin scratched his chin, "I think that every guard that worked your personal guard at the same time as Luther, needs to be on that list as well." "No, most of them didn't know. They couldn't have." "They all knew Luther. It's possible he bragged about fucking the most powerful woman in the world, to his friends." Shante narrowed her eyes at him, "No it isn't." Quentin held her gaze, "Would you have thought it was possible that he would cheat on you with the Alcraze Princess and then kill the Prince?" Shante felt like she'd just been slapped in the face. "You're right, kill them all and get me new guards."

"I'll have Bane take care of it." "No, we might not be able to spare enough Hell Hunters to discreetly kill fifty trained guards and soldiers. We have to do it in a way that's instant and arouses no suspicion." Quentin looked uneasy. He'd clearly been hoping that he could pass it off on Bane, so that he wouldn't have to personally orchestrate the deaths of his own men. "We could frame them. Accuse them of treason and have them all executed. Takes away the need for secrecy." "No, that won't work either, it draws too much attention. Vincent will want to know the details and if he starts sniffing around then one of them might say something. No…" She paused, thinking about the best way to kill dozens of guards who had protected her for years. Loyal men and women. Many of them had been close friends to Luther. They didn't deserve what they were getting. "Have Bane send them on a suicide mission. No, five different suicide missions. Break them up into groups, send them far away and let the monsters do the killing for us." Quentin seemed to both approve of and be disgusted by the strategy. "That'll work."

"I want you and Bane to volunteer your very best men. I want mean bastards, with magic if possible. They'll have the best weapons available. And a sensitive to keep us informed. Make sure they know this is important and necessary, but don't tell them any details for the time being. The fewer people who know about the threat of war the better. I want them to leave at dawn."

Chapter 21

They walked out the other side and started heading through a field full of long grass that reached above their knees and was green like a granny smith apple.

As rough as it was, this was a pretty typical trip outside the wall, with two big differences; the heavy slab of muscle and liability that she carried on her back and the knowledge that soon her taste buds would be blessed again with the meat of a miniature pink-skinned bull.

Malek held up his hand and she froze, he sniffed the air and then crouched in the long grass, Lakeitha did the same. She didn't see anything, hear anything and she definitely didn't smell anything. But this was why Malek was special, more so than his tentacle mutation; he was the most natural hunter in the human race. If the cities fell and people had to survive in the wild, then she reckoned that Malek would live to be the last of the species.

"Drop Luther." he whispered, "You need to be ready." Lakeitha laid Luther down on the ground softly. "What is it?" She asked, "Oh this thing is good. It's quiet."

He started to rise up and she followed suit, sword at the ready. As her head rose above the grass, she saw a figure fifteen meters in front of her. It too was rising up from the grass, just as slowly as they were. She stood to her full height and this thing kept on rising. It was pitch black in the middle of an aggressively green field. It stood taller and taller, reaching over nine feet tall. Its whole body was shrouded in black.

It stood unnaturally still, the only part of it that moved at all was the black cloak that covered its entire body and gently waved in the wind. In its right hand it held a six foot long black sword. The array of sharp points and shapes along the edge of the sword was an almost mesmerising symmetrical pattern. Darker than an ink blot and more perfect than one could ever be. That sword looked sharp enough to cut through a mountain without dulling.

This was who Lakeitha had seen standing on top of the cliff. Up close, it looked to her like a picture of death.

She wondered how it had made it down the steep cliff face so quickly. Had it flown, glided, levitated, teleported or just jumped?

It remained still and quiet. Lakeitha broke the silence, "What do you want?" It continued to stare at them and at first Lakeitha thought that it was challenging them. She thought that it had drawn its blade to stand off against them.

But as the seconds evaporated, she started to feel something. Not a thought, a feeling, a strange understanding that grew until it was undeniable in her mind. The more time she spent around this eerie figure, the more she understood what it wanted. "It wants a trade." She whispered to Malek. "I know" said Malek, sounding just as mystified as she did. "It wants the meat." Said Malek, "It wants a bag of meat, in exchange for the crystal." She finished.

As they watched it, the stranger reached its black hand into its cloak and took out something small and turquoise.

Lakeitha realised with a shiver that this tall stranger didn't cast a shadow.

She knew what the crystal was for. It was going to cure Luther's poisoned mind. She was deeply creeped out by the things that she was becoming convinced were true. She felt violated and she also felt that she had no choice but to accept the trade. Going deeper than an opportunity to save Luther, she was compelled, like this was a moment of cosmic importance, that all time had led up to this deal of meat for medicine and she had no ability to deny it, just like she'd had no power to stop herself from being born.

It began walking towards them. As it got closer they started to hear its breathing. The sound seemed not just to come from its head but also from the rest of its body. It was loud and rattled against itself, like the wind on a stormy night.

It stopped a few feet away from them. They stared up at it. Even this close, when they looked under the hood they didn't see a face. All they saw was a shadow as dark as the cloak itself.

She didn't know what material the cloak was made of. It looked brand new, but she felt that it was very old.

It reached out its arm, which was disproportionately long, even for its nine foot tall body. It clutched the crystal in its hand. A hand that didn't look like it was made of skin and bone but shaped from the dark gaps between stars.

As she listened to its loud breathing, she felt her throat catch and she struggled to draw in air. She held out her own hand and it dropped the turquoise crystal into her palm. Then it reached out to Malek and he lifted up one of the bags of meat and dropped the bag in its open hand. The bag must have weighed over fifteen kilograms but the hand didn't dip under the weight at all. Like it wasn't even there.

It left them. Both Malek and Lakeitha felt the uncontrollable urge to turn around, averting their gaze as it moved away. After twenty seconds or so the urge left them and when they turned back they saw nothing but an empty field of tall green grass.

Chapter 22

She went to the throne room fifteen minutes before Vincent was meant to arrive. She wanted a moment with Bane and Quentin. Bane came through the doors first with Quentin trailing behind him. He stormed into the room outraged. "You want to kill my hunters!" he yelled at her. "Bane, it has to be done. Luther…" "Quentin told me about Luther, but he…" "Don't you fucking interrupt me Bane. I am in charge, you little shit. You show me the proper respect or I'll fucking kill you!" She got up and marched down from her throne to stand toe to toe with Bane. He shut his mouth but there was still defiance in his eyes, "There's a pile of bodies being made right now. It could be a very big pile…Do as your fuckin told."

Bane didn't look scared, but he showed her some respect. "I don't like betraying my own people. But Luther has to go. The idiot made his own bed. He's new anyway, so not many of my hunters will give a shit." It made Shante very angry to hear somebody talk about Luther in such a callous, insulting way. How dare he. How dare she. She struggled not to let the mounting guilt show.

"But Malek and Lakeitha are innocent in all this. They're two of the very best Hell Hunters that I have. I can't let them down. They're not to blame." "Bane, are you to blame?" Bane blinked, "No" "Am I to blame?" "No" "Is a single person currently in Dantez to blame for this?" Bane shook his head, "No" "And yet, it's still happening to us. I understand that you want to protect your people. But I have the same responsibility, you are trying to protect two people and I am trying to protect seventy thousand people."

"It isn't necessary to kill all three of them. Just kill Luther." Shante shook her head, "Bane, do you really believe that after spending four days together in the wild, constantly watching each other's backs and building trust, that Lakeitha and Malek would step aside and let Luther get killed?" Bane thought about it for a moment, "I think they might." "That's not good enough. I need a guarantee, because if we give them the opportunity to hand Luther over, then we sacrifice the element of surprise. Luther is a great fighter and you just told me what great Hell Hunters Lakeitha and Malek are. I don't want them to have a fighting chance. This is the best way to do it. This is exactly what you would demand be done, if these weren't your people." Bane winced, "I don't like this." "Me neither."

"Quentin talk to me." "The equipment is ready and I have selected my very best soldiers." "Good. Who leads the missions?" "Akira" suggested Bane. After a couple of seconds Quentin nodded in agreement. "Your men won't have any objections to taking orders from a Hell Hunter?" "They won't if I tell them not to." "That's what I like to hear. Bane, how many Hell Hunters can you have ready to leave at dawn?"

Bane thought it over, "Our numbers have been down for a while. We have thirty two healthy hunters in Dantez right now, most of them rookies. The problem here is that all my best hunters know Lakeitha and Malek. Akira, I can guarantee that he'll follow through and his pal Roth is reliable but some of the others might refuse. Mason, yeah, he hates Lakeitha and he's pretty cold on Malek so I can count him in. Let me work on it. Small groups are faster and stealthier but we will need a formidable force to kill all three of them. Plus a couple of medics. I say sixteen in total." Quentin nodded, "Agreed."

The big doors on the other side of the throne room opened and Vincent walked in. Shante returned to her throne. He didn't waste time with pleasantries, he just asked, "Are you going to kill him?" "Yes"

Chapter 23

It wasn't smart to make camp near The Fucked Pass. After fifteen minutes they stopped in another forest.

Malek made a fire and then he filled a mess tin with water from his canteen and held it over the fire until it boiled. Lakeitha placed the crystal on a large flat rock and crushed it into a fine powder with a smaller rock. She palmed the shiny turquoise dust and dropped it into the boiling water. Malek stirred it until the water had turned deep turquoise. They did all this without talking. Somehow they just knew how to prepare it. If someone had asked Lakeitha how to use the crystal to help Luther, she wouldn't have been able to tell them, yet she still performed the task through an impossible muscle memory.

The world never ceased to bewilder her.

They leaned Luther's back against a tree and Malek gradually poured all of it down his throat.

Lakeitha and Malek sat on either side of the fire, watching Luther.

The pair of them had spent so many days and nights together. They were totally comfortable around each other. Malek was her favourite person to go on missions with. Gideon was good too, but there was nobody like Malek. Spending this much time together outside the wall, they got to know each other very well, they trusted that they would protect each other and they had an understanding that went beyond words. They had both seen the other person at their fiercest, their angriest, their weakest and their most afraid.

It had been a hard, strange day and neither of them felt like talking. They dug into one of the remaining bags of meat.

After about an hour Luther woke up. His head snapped up and he looked around the fire in tense confusion. His eyes glistened with fear. His mind had been bombarded by horrific hallucinations, things that only he would ever see and believe to be real. In that moment when he woke up and hadn't yet realised that it was over, Lakeitha and Malek saw him so clearly they could practically read his mind. Like a dog, he was showing all his emotions, feeling something raw and making no effort to hide it.

He let out a deep relieved breath and covered his face for a moment. He looked back up at them, composed and guarded. "What happened?" "A few minutes into The Fucked Pass you lost your mind. You were poisoned...and then you hit me." she added, "I don't remember hitting you." He blinked, "I did hit something though." "It was me. Then I knocked you out and we took turns carrying you." Luther seemed surprised, "I hit you really hard." Lakeitha shrugged, "Then you carried me through The Fucked Pass?" "Yeah." Luther took a moment to think this over and then he gave her a look that was almost respectful and said, "You're pretty tough for a girl." Lakeitha gave a little shrug, "You're pretty weak for a cage fighter." Luther grinned, "Ah fuck…"

He leaned over and slapped Malek on the shoulder, "Thanks man." Malek nodded and handed him a cup of water, "You feeling alright?" "Yeah, I feel great actually." "Then we should cover some more ground. It's only the afternoon." "Let's go."

They walked until an hour after sunset. Luther seemed to be taking the horrifying hallucinations and almost dying very well. They made another campsite and Malek went to sleep before Lakeitha had even started the fire. Luther looked over to Lakeitha, "I'll take first watch if you want some sleep. Lakeitha considered it for a moment. "I wanna look at the stars for a little bit." "Okay"

She leaned back and looked up at the night sky, beautiful as ever. "Luther" "Yeah?" "How often do you look up at the sky?" "Occasionally." "Yeah, we never do pay attention to the stars when we're in Dantez. We're always focused on the people around us, the activity, the noise. We sleep inside, under a roof. We forget what's above us." Luther didn't say anything back, he was looking at the stars too. The only thing that she could hear now was the crackling fire and the chatter of life beyond their campsite.

"When I was a kid, I loved to look at the pinwheel." Said Luther wistfully. "It was my favourite." "How about now, what's your favourite?" "I haven't had a favourite in a long time." "Well, pick one." Luther smiled. "Maybe the great streak." "No, that's my favourite." "Oh, would you mind sharing?" "Yes, I mind." he chuckled. "Fair enough, I choose the purple moon." a few seconds went by. "Loser" Malek piped up, "Sorry to interrupt your moment of bonding but I'm trying to sleep." They all laughed.

Chapter 24

They were up before the crack of dawn to wash in a pond. The water was unusually warm, it must have been a bit of a hot spring. Lakeitha loved it when she found those. None of them had had a proper wash in two days and they were all eager to clean themselves. They went in one at a time, while the other two guarded them by the edge. They went in completely naked, leaving everything behind except their weapons. Malek went first, a mace in one hand and a knife in the other. He stopped when he was in four feet of water. You never know what's lurking in deep water.

Luther went in second. He took off his clothes and waded into the water. Some first timers were uncomfortable about being naked in front of the other hunters. Most of them were too eager to wash off the grime to care.

Lakeitha was most definitely not attracted to Luther, but she had to admit to herself that she was impressed by his body. His muscles were really something; big and toned and powerful. Living as a pro fighter he'd gotten a fair few cuts and still had some bruises that hadn't faded yet, but his skin was pristinely smooth compared to the circus of scars that covered her and Malek's bodies. She indulged in a little peaking, while still staying alert for monsters.

Then it was her turn. It felt glorious to wash herself. Get all the dust and dirt and blood off her.

She towelled herself off and then reluctantly put her dirty clothes back on. A second set of clothes was too much extra weight and it wasn't wise for them to clean their clothes in the water and then stand around naked for a couple of hours while they let them dry off under the sun. It was tempting to walk into the stream wearing the dirty clothes and then let themselves dry off as they walked but wearing soaking wet clothes in this environment was stupid for a number of reasons. It was very uncomfortable, it caused rashes and it attracted swarms of insects, all of which were irritating by themselves, but together became dangerously distracting. It was one thing to ignore pain but trying to remain focused on your surroundings for twenty hours straight while ignoring pain and soggy discomfort was a challenge that even Malek, hardcore as he was, would shy away from.

With her clothes back on she no longer felt wholly clean, but it was an improvement. They continued on their journey. They'd reach their destination by dusk and would do the collecting in the morning. She'd been to this area before and had occasionally found some of Mikey's medicine. She was always on the lookout for the stuff.

After half an hour of walking they found themselves at the top of a steep ridge. There was a six foot drop that led onto a slope. At the bottom of the slope was a clearing with a few trees and a three foot tall green stalk with a single orange fruit hanging from the top. Luther had never seen a fruit like it. It was shaped like an apple and looked juicy, with no leathery skin like an orange had. "Do we climb down or go around?" He asked Lakeitha and Malek. "We can just walk around." Said Malek.

A bird flew down into the clearing and landed beside the fruit plant. It stood at over two feet tall, had big black wings and grey feathers on the rest of its body. The bird bit the fruit, tore it free and ate it whole. Malek and Lakeitha had already started to walk away, Luther was just about to follow them when he heard a stark, skin-crawling choke. He turned his head back and looked at the bird. It teetered from side to side and then started frantically flapping its wings. It got a few feet off the ground and couldn't get any higher. It swung from side to side desperately. "Hey guys, what's up with this bird?"

They came back over to him and Lakeitha started to say, "Come on Luther it's just a bir…" The bird exploded. Its body parts and blood scattering through the air. A piece of orange fruit fell to the ground. It was completely intact and three times the size that it had been before the bird ate it. "What the fuck." Said Luther.

"Hey Malek, I'll give you five drogon if you eat that fruit." joked Lakeitha. Malek grinned and slapped the shocked rookie on the shoulder. "Let's get out of here." "Yeah alright." As Luther watched it, the fruit grew a green stem, plunged it into the ground and started to grow until the stalk was over six feet tall. Within seconds it looked like it had been growing there for months. It made him shiver.

They moved on. The jungle got thicker, forcing them to cut through giant leaves. After nearly being eaten by a tree and then witnessing that fruit, he was becoming very aware of the fact that literally anything in this jungle could potentially kill him, in ways that he couldn't even imagine.

They spent four hours getting battered by the drudgery and heat of the jungle. He was drenched in sweat, he was thirsty no matter how much water he drank and his headache was back. He felt the jungle draining him of his energy. It was a sticky prison that stole a man's determination and wore him down until he could barely put one foot in front of the other. The jungle was full of predators who were watching them and waiting until they were utterly exhausted and downtrodden so that they could pounce and get an easy meal. But Luther wasn't going to let them win, he'd burn this whole jungle to the ground before he let them win.

They broke through the other side. The trees thinned out enough that he could actually feel a cooling breeze. Malek sniffed out a pond where they could fill up their canteens. Luther decided that he believed that Malek could smell water, and that it was nothing to do with his mutation or magic. He trusted in Malek's ability as a hunter. "Say Malek, if you can see in the dark, how come you don't travel at night." "I do when I'm on my own." "Oh, yeah that checks out." "Paranoia never dies." Luther smirked, "I guess not."

They drank their fill and then ate lunch. Luther dunked his head under the pond. He felt refreshed when he came up for air, but the rest of his body was still covered in jungle sap and grime. He was really missing the cleanliness of Dantez. Lakeitha and Malek joined him in dunking their faces in the pond and then they moved on.

Now that the trees and plants weren't so densely packed they were able to move much faster. A thought occurred to Lakeitha that Luther was probably having a lot more trouble than her and Malek with the pain. He didn't really have any experience tolerating this kind of pain. He was a fighter, he fought for maybe ten minutes while his body was so full of adrenaline that he barely noticed his injuries. Then he got to properly recover, putting his feet up in a cool, dry, soft city. He'd never spent day after day on the move, coping with this kind of pain. It was a very long time since she had been a rookie, she supposed that she had forgotten how hard it was to be new at this crazy job. "Hey Luther, how are you holding up?" "I'm fine." he said casually, "Good." "Aren't you going to ask how Malek's holding up?" said Luther, being a little cheeky. That was a good sign. "Malek, how are you coping?" "Fabulously."

They stopped so that she could take a crap and then moved on. Another thing occurred to her about Luther. A mistake that only a rookie could make. "Hey Luther. You haven't been masturbating out here have you?" "What?" "Because that attracts predators." "No I haven't been masturbating. Bane told me that's a no go." "Okay good." "You haven't been getting your period have you? Cause that's a bit of a magnet as well isn't it." "No Luther, I haven't, I never go on missions when I have my period." "So you get a guaranteed holiday for a few days every month." "In a way." "What do you do when you're back in Dantez?" "Oh I train, I drink, I spend time with my brother, I sleep." "Uh wild. How about you Malek. Do you tear things up?" "I train, I sleep, I eat." "Oh yeah eating, I do that too." Chimed in Lakeitha. Luther looked between the pair of them, "Do neither of you do anything besides this?" "Not really I just like to rest, hang out with Mikey and Malek and Gideon. I get ten to fifteen days at home every month but that time flies by pretty quickly." "Malek?" "I'm out hunting twenty five days a month unless I'm injured." "What? Twenty five days a month, that's ridiculous." "Nobody hunts as much as Malek." "Why do you do it so much?" Malek took a moment to answer, "I like it out here."

"Okay...What about sex?" Lakeitha shrugged, "With a job like this and a face like this, sex is pretty hard to come by." Luther nodded a little awkwardly, feeling sorry for her. "Okay, how about you Malek. You must be a hit with the ladies. Classic strong and silent type. Not ugly either, for a Hell Hunter." Malek made a noise that might have been a little laugh. "Keeping a girlfriend is hard, working like I do.

But every now and then. If I'm not too tired." "Yeah, yeah." said Luther, hungry for some sordid details, "I have sex." "Cool."

"Isn't anybody going to ask me how much sex I have?" "Is it a lot?" Asked Lakeitha sarcastically, "Yes it is. It is a lot." "Congratulations. Hey Malek, remember Nicholas." "Yeah" "Remember how he spelt all his free time having sex with women who were impressed that he was a Hell Hunter. Then one day he came back from a mission and couldn't have sex anymore." "Yeah poor guy." Luther was horrified, "What happened to him. Did he lose his penis? Was he crippled?" "No, he just smelled the wrong flower." "What?" "He sat down near a flower for a few minutes, smelling it and resting. After that, he lost all of his sex drive and he never had another erection. Just because he sniffed a flower." Luther nervously looked around for any flowers. "What kind of flower was it?" "A red one, maybe." "I've seen hundreds of red flowers in the last couple of days." "That is true." "Oh no, no no. I can't go without sex. I can't." "Take it easy, it only happened to one guy. Or only one guy has ever admitted to it." "Oh fuck me." said Luther desperately.

It occurred to him that this was a mean joke, "Wait a minute. You two are fucking with me aren't you." Lakeitha shook her head, "No we're not. You can ask Nicholas yourself." "Where is he?" "He killed himself." "What!" Malek started laughing. He laughed so hard that he had to lean against a tree to stop himself from falling over. "Oh you bastards. It was a joke." Lakeitha was laughing as well, "Of course it was a joke." "So Nicholas was made up or what?" "Mmm? Oh no, Nicholas is real and he really did lose his libido because of a flower. I just joked about the suicide." Luther glared, "Fuck the pair of you."

Malek stopped laughing and held up his hand. Lakeitha went deadly serious, watching Malek and her surroundings. In a whispered voice, Malek said, "We're being hunted." "Where?" Malek sniffed the air and cocked his head, "Nine o'clock." Lakeitha turned to her left, there was a slope that started a few meters from where they were standing and went up at a thirty degree angle. The slope was covered in trees and bushes and big leaves, she couldn't see any monsters in there. "How many?" whispered Luther, "Just one."

"I think I know what he is. I've come across one of them before. He's maybe seven feet long and four feet tall. Moves on four legs, heavy but fast. He's got metal claws, like knives, metal teeth too and he's smart. He's hiding in those blue leaves." "He hasn't attacked yet. He's waiting for an opportunity." said Lakeitha, "We should set up a trap. How about the flank and trip?" Malek shook his head, "After what happened to my arm yesterday I don't think my tentacle could take it." "Could try a wire trap." Malek hesitated. "This thing's pretty clever, he'd see us setting up the trap and know better." "We can do it subtly." Insisted Lakeitha. "We turn our backs to it, we tie out lengths of wire together and then we both walk in different directions. We tie the wire up to some trees and then we wait." Lakeitha and Malek looked at each other for a moment, communicating in that near telepathic way of theirs. They both knew that the wire trap required bait. They turned their heads to Luther.

"Luther, we need you to be the bait." Unenthusiastically Luther said, "What do I have to do?" "You need to sit down with no weapon in your hands and wait for the monster to try to eat you." Luther sighed, made an angry face and then said, "I'll do it." She was impressed, she'd expected some pushback. "And we need to leave the meat with you." said Malek. "Wait no. No way. I'll take the meat to keep it safe." Malek looked at her sternly, "We have to leave it with him for the bait to work, if you have it on you then it might follow you instead." "But no Malek. We can't risk losing that meat. It's the best food I've had all year." "You seem to care more about whether or not the meat gets eaten than if I do." Said Luther, glaring at her. "Oh Luther you can run and you can fight, but this is literally dead meat that we are talking about. It can't defend itself." "It's the only way Lakeitha." Insisted Malek. Lakeitha shook her head, "Fine."

Lakeitha and Malek took out their razor wire and carefully tied the lengths together. It was so sharp that they had to be careful not to cut their gloves on it. Malek told Luther where to sit with the bags of meat behind him. His hands were empty, he focused on where the monster was meant to be. It really was time to test his faith in Malek's senses.

As they started walking away from him Lakeitha said, "Try to look tasty." He smirked and waited.

He couldn't see Lakeitha or Malek. He couldn't hear them either. All four of them were lying in wait. Listening to the chattering of insects and the singing of birds. Luther had his hands splayed in front of him. They were sweaty inside his gloves. This thing was supposed to be fast so he had to be faster. He had to draw his sword and jump to his feet before it reached him. He didn't know if that would scare it off, which would mean that it wouldn't reach the razor wire. He didn't want to ruin the trap but he also didn't want to entrust his life to a bit of wire.

This was the problem with sitting still and waiting to get attacked. You start to overthink things. He had to focus, clear his mind and trust that his friends would protect him.

The monster leaped from the blue leaves on the slope and hurtled down the hill. With each bound it seemed to cover five meters. From where Luther was he could see the big metal teeth and claws that stood out against the monster's deep blue skin. It reached the bottom of the slope and jumped at him. He stared up at it, looking into its open mouth, its row of metal teeth and its tonsils. He held off for as long as he could, then his hand flashed behind his head, he grabbed the handle of his sword and pulled it free. He started to lunge out of the monster's path as it hit the razor wire. There was a look of shock and pain on its face. Blood leaked out of its front left leg and its head tipped downward. Luther got one foot under him and started to push off the ground as the monster's leg dragged over the razor wire and its back raised up over its head. Luther got clear just as the monster finished its mid-air somersault and landed heavily on its back.

Luther stood to his full height and swung his sword at the monster as it scrambled up to its feet. He cut into its shoulder, it hissed and swiped at him with its right claw. He blocked it with his sword, his weapon clanging against the blades on its hand. He pushed the claw back and then slashed the monster across its face. It howled and raised up, standing on its back legs, with blood pouring down its face. Its front left leg, which hadn't been too badly hurt by the razor wire, lashed out at Luther. He ducked under it and drove his sword into its side. The blade didn't go right through, it pierced the skin and got a few inches into the tough muscle before it was stuck. He stepped back and pulled the blade free.

The monster made a terrible rumbling noise, twisted unmistakably by pain. He saw Malek running up behind the monster. He started swinging wide at the creature's chest, not hitting it, just keeping its attention and repelling its strikes for a few seconds as Malek ran in and slammed his mace into the monster's back left leg. It lurched and fell, then rolled over and came back up into a four legged stance. It was bloody and the leg that Malek had hit looked weak, but this was still a formidable animal. It snarled at them, blood glistening on its metal fangs.

Lakeitha appeared at his side, sword in her right hand and a long knife in her left. She didn't wait for it to charge at them, she ran up to it and he followed her. It lunged at him, its front legs rising up in the air, its big jaw open wide, ready to tear him down and bite his head off. As it passed her Lakeitha stuck both her blades into its side and the monster's momentum carried it along as the weapons sliced across the length of its body. Luther ducked out of the monster's path and it stumbled on the ground, bleeding from the two six foot long cuts on its left side.

Before it could get its bearings Malek smashed his mace down on its head. It scrambled back, roaring and bleeding all over the ground. It stood up once more on its back legs and tried to cut Lakeitha's head off. She blocked it by slashing both her blades across its leg. She followed through with the motion, stepping under its leg and then turning around and slashing her sword down the other side of the same leg. With that slash she cut its leg clean off.

Blood spouting from the wound, it gargled and screeched until Luther drove his sword up through its neck. It went stiff and quiet, blood rolling down the edge of his sword. He pressed his foot against its body for leverage and pulled his sword free, letting it fall dead on the ground.

He looked at Malek and Lakeitha panting and grinning.

Chapter 25

"Yeah! Oh man, that was great!" Celebrated Luther jumping around and waving his sword over his head. He giddily recounted the entire fight to them, acting parts of it out. "And then you came in and hit its leg with your mace and the big blue cunt started hobbling like an old man." He said, pointing at Malek. They laughed along with him. It felt good to win. Lakeitha was proud of the kill.

Luther mimed his upward stabbing motion that had finished off the monster and then roared triumphantly like one of his fans when he won a fight. He felt like a champion. He was a champion. His blood was fire.

He ran over to the dead monster, "Not so tough are you now, yuh rusty prick!" He gloated and kicked its blood soaked chin, closing its mouth of shiny, unrusted teeth.

Lakeitha had beaten up plenty of corpses in her time, but in this case it was bad form. None of them had been hurt fighting this monster and they had no reason to want revenge. A celebratory kicking was uncalled for. But this was Luther's first big kill of the mission, so he could be allowed some indulgence. She remembered her first big kill, she'd felt ten feet tall and higher than the moon.

Luther was kicking the dead beast in its chest and yelling, "I'm the champ! I'm the champ! I am the champ! Yeah!" She winced and looked over at Malek, he wasn't smiling anymore, he was shaking his head distastefully. "Hey Luther." She said, trying to catch his attention. He jumped on top of the dead body and struck a pose. "We're invincible!" "Luther, we need to move on." Said Lakeitha. Luther looked down at her and grinned.

He jumped down from the corpse and started leading the way, his whole body vibrating. He kept talking about how great they were, how great he was. He was in a volatile state and Lakeitha didn't like it. Getting pumped up was common under the circumstances but this was too much, she started thinking of him as a prick again.

She shared a look with Malek that told her he was thinking the same thing.

Luther was charged up like a lightning bolt. He wanted to go again; his face was hot, his sword was sharp and he wanted to kill something. There was a rustling in a bush to his right, he lunged at the bush, swinging his sword. He sliced the bush apart and then he saw something run away. He stepped over the tattered remains of the bush and ran after it. He closed in on the little thing that ran on four legs. It tried to jump away from him. He punched it out of the air and it bounced off a tree and dropped onto the ground. It wriggled and then he stabbed down on it, splitting it in half. A big smile spread across his face as he breathed heavily.

Lakeitha rolled her eyes. **Idiot**. She came closer to Luther and then she saw the lifeless little body. "Aww, you killed a grimba." "Hmmm, what?" replied Luther, "A grimba, we don't kill grimbas. They're cute and soft and harmless. Look at that little guy." Luther scoffed, "Can you believe this Malek." Malek shook his head, his face hard as stone. "Luther, we don't kill grimbas." Lakeitha looked down at the poor thing, with its short green fur, soft little nose and big dark eyes. It had been cut in two and there was a lot of blood on the ground. "What a shame. Gideon has one of these as a pet." "Alright, nobody told me about these things." "Fucking rookies." Said Malek. It was the kind of thing that most people would say under their breath, but Malek said it loud enough for both of them to hear. Luther grimaced and then scowled, "I didn't know what was in that bush. It could have been a threat. Maybe next time I won't do anything and then one of us will get killed." "You were hyper and you jumped into that bush like a maniac." Spat Malek, "You've got no restraint and no experience and now a grimba is dead." "Fuck the grimba." Malek punched Luther in the face. It was a light jab that knocked him back a step and burst his lip.

Luther instinctively swung his sword at Malek's head. Malek's hand blurred to his thigh, he drew his knife and blocked Luther's sword creating a small burst of golden sparks. They both took a step back and eyed each other.

Luther instantly realised he'd made a mistake, he'd overreacted by bringing the sword into it and now this might end in one of them killing the other. If Malek made a move, he was going to block the knife, trap his wrist, disarm him and then get him in a sleeper hold before he could draw his mace.

If Luther made a move, he was going to parry the strike and then slit his throat from side to side.

Lakeitha watched the pair of them and waited. She didn't want them to fight, but she wasn't sure how to diffuse the situation. If she told them to stop and got their attention then one of them, probably Malek, might use that distraction to cut the other one's head off. These guys were fast and deadly, she didn't want to create an opportunity for either of them.

"Luther" Said Malek, "You wanna put that sword down?" "Yeah, how about you?" "I don't wanna kill you." "I don't want to kill you either." "Well there's not much chance of that." Luther smirked, "We cool?" Malek nodded and lowered his weapon. "Sorry about the grimba. I won't do it again."

Lakeitha was relieved and then something very strange happened. From every direction, from the ground and the trees above, grimbas leaped out from hiding. They all jumped at the same time and landed on the three of them. One second they were standing around, glad that they'd avoided a fight to the death and the next they were all staggering around with cute soft green animals climbing all over them. Biting and clawing at them.

Their teeth and claws weren't very sharp so they barely felt anything beneath their clothing, but their heads and necks were exposed to the onslaught. One of them scratched her cheek. She grabbed it, tore it off her face and then threw it away from her. She threw it so hard that when it hit a tree, it exploded.

She felt a horrible punch of guilt and then one of them jumped onto her head and started clawing at her scalp. She started punching and slapping them off her and then she drew her sword and sliced them apart as they jumped at her. Blood sprayed all over her as her sword whirled its way through the cute little creatures. Luther and Malek were killing them as well, but as they fought back the storm of grimbas seemed to intensify. One of them jumped up and hit her forehead. She stumbled and whirled as another one collided with her arm, knocking her sword from her hand.

She batted them away with her empty hands until she had her bearings and then she drew her twin knives and started slashing through them. She glanced over at Malek and Luther as she always had to do during any fight to check if they needed her help. Malek had his knife and mace out, he appeared to be swinging wildly in every direction, but she knew from his level of skill and the number of grimbas that he was hitting, that he was using a method of precise bedlam.

Luther was also going wild but with less success, still he had good reflexes and a big sword that did plenty of severing.

A cute, green, cuddly grimba jumped at her from the side, its little teeth bared. It hit her in the shoulder and she stumbled, her feet tripping over something soft and grimbay. She fell and they crawled over her. She had dozens of grimbas on her, something that would have sounded lovely mere moments ago. She punched and stabbed and rolled, getting up into a crouch and butchering as many as she could. She killed seven in the space of a second and then two of them jumped onto her face at the same time and sank their teeth into her skin. They knocked her on her back and she skewered the pair of them and then pushed herself back up.

She killed a few more and the rest retreated. The three of them stood surrounded by over a hundred dead grimbas. They were covered head to toe in red grimba blood. Luther wasn't amped anymore and Malek looked sad. She didn't often see Malek sad. She'd seen him cry dozens of times. Cry because of pain and even once because of fear, when he was injured and bleeding everywhere and thought that he was going to die. But she couldn't think of a single time that she'd seen sadness in him.

Luther saw this as well and he looked concerned, although it was a little difficult to tell facial expressions because of how much gore was stuck on his face. "Malek, I'm really sorry." He said sincerely with a hint of trepidation. Not trepidatious of getting attacked by Malek, but trepidatious of Malek's hurt feelings. She'd definitely never seen anybody show that kind of trepidation around Malek. Malek shook his head and then walked away from Luther.

Chapter 26

Being covered in blood was a dangerous business. It attracted all kinds of predators. They spent almost an hour killing various monsters and animals that had smelled the grimba remains on them. None of them gave them too much trouble. After a while the small monsters gave up on attacking them and instead ate the even smaller monsters.

Malek wanted to sniff out a body of water for them to clean in, but all he could smell was blood. The stink attacked his sensitive nostrils. He had to go by memory, which was why it took them so long.

They waded into the muggy swamp fully clothed. They knew that they'd suffer for it later, but they had to get the blood off their clothes as quickly as possible. There was nothing refreshing about crouching in this hot bubbling green water. Like they'd been dropped in a pot of gross soup. The ground was six inches of thick slime that climbed up their boots. A dead purple lizard floated past Malek's head. Sick looking trees grew out from the swamp. Their trunks were twisted and warped.

He remembered one time he'd run out of water and found a swamp much like this one. He'd resorted to drinking from it. He'd vomited for two days, Gideon had to carry him back to Dantez.

Being surrounded by this swamp, it was impossible for Malek not to think about the days he'd spent throwing up his guts, weak as a kitten or a grimba.

They reached their destination. An area ripe with a new source of fuel. It was green and thick, glowing softly as it oozed out of various rock clusters and then joined a thin and slow moving stream that only ran for about fifteen meters before going underground. They were standing twenty meters away from the nearest drop of the stuff, yet the temperature had still jumped fifteen degrees. Lakeitha could feel her clothes drying as she stood there. They were all drenched in sweat.

This was Luther's first mission and normally when someone reached the goal on their first mission there would be a fair amount of back patting and congratulations. But neither of them felt like patting Luther's back. Without saying a word they took out the sturdy glass jars from their packs, removed the lids and collected some samples of the fuel. They were careful not to get any on their hands, they didn't know anything about this stuff, it might burn their hands down to stumps if they touched it.

They stuffed the jars into their bags, turned around and started walking back the way they had come. They were all exhausted and it would take them another three days to get back to Dantez. "We'll set up camp as soon as we're clear of that shit." Said Lakeitha, pointing her thumb over her shoulder back at the raw oozing fuel that they'd left behind them.

Energy was always a concern. The cities had figured out sustainable sources of food and water, but they could never have enough fuel. If the scientists liked the samples that they brought them, then there would be poor bastards continuously making the same journey that they had just done in order to collect more. A lot of people would die for this stuff, if it worked.

The sun was still out when they reached a good spot to camp. Luther started collecting tinder and firewood. She stood opposite Malek, each of them leaning against trees. "Some fucking day, huh." Malek nodded. "We should sharpen our weapons." Lakeitha took in a deep breath, "I'll do mine later. I just need some time doing absolutely nothing." A few seconds passed, "I don't know how I'm going to look Gideon in the eye when we get back to Dantez." Some people might have mistaken the way that Malek said it as a joke, but Lakeitha knew better. He was being serious. She didn't say anything back. "Some fucking day." Said Malek and then he walked off to help Luther with the firewood.

Malek had just taken out his lighter and was about to light the tinder when he smelled something. He snapped his head up and went totally still. He started hearing things that matched the smell. He grimaced and spat on the pile of wood. He had hoped that the day was over, that he wouldn't have to deal with anything else. He was tired and hungry, he wanted to eat some meat and doze, not fight.

"That blue monster we killed earlier, his friends are here." Luther and Lakeitha drew their swords and stared at the jungle around them, "Where?" asked Luther. Malek pulled out his own weapons and pointed with his mace, "Six of them." "Six, fucking six." Stammered Luther. "They must only have found the body about ten minutes ago." "We can't fight that many." Said Luther, sounding scared. "Yes we can." Replied Malek. "How?" "I have no idea." "I do." Said Lakeitha. She slung her bag off her back and took out the fuel sample, "We tear up our blankets, dip them into the jars and then set the blankets on fire." Malek and Luther stared at her for a moment and then they hurriedly opened their bags and started tearing their blankets.

Lakeitha crept towards where Malek said the monsters were. At first there was no sign of them, then she saw the rustling in the trees and two of the big blue creatures prowled out, their metal teeth shining in the light of the setting sun. They could see her and they started roaring. The noise spread, coming from creatures that she couldn't even see. Not until the other four leaped out from the bushes and the trees. Her skin crawled looking at the pack of giant vengeful monsters.

The three of them were standing on top of a slight slope, with the creatures four feet lower than them and thirty feet away. "Wait for it." She whispered. The jar was in her right hand and her left hand held the lighting an inch below the rag. The growling got louder as the monsters crawled closer.

She swallowed stale saliva and mumbled, "Wait" The blue beasts charged and without even bothering to give the order, she lit her rag and hurled it overhand at the approaching tidal wave. It exploded in mid-air, before it had even hit anything. The explosion was painfully loud and so bright that it forced her eyes shut, imprinting the image of a hot white blur and six black figures around it.

There were two more loud noises and flashes of light that she saw behind her eyelids. After a few seconds she opened up her eyes. Everything was a little blurry, but she could see a bunch of monsters scrambling around and shrieking, with white and orange flames thriving on their bodies. The earth around them was scorched black and the air smelled of smoke, burning flesh and a uniquely toxic stink.

One of the monsters staggered towards them, its entire body engulfed in two different colours of flame. It stared at her with half its face burnt off, its metal teeth still in place. Staring into its eyes she could see that through all the pain it was focused on one thing. It wanted to kill her, it knew it was already dead and it wanted to take her down with it. It wanted to spill her blood and feel it sizzle on its superheated claws.

It prowled forward a few meters and then fell heavily and suddenly on its left side. It grumbled and kicked its legs at the air, then died. The fire continued to burn up its body.

Lakeitha thought it was all over and then she turned to her left and saw a monster charging up the slope towards Luther. Its whole body was burned and disfigured, but the fire had burnt out and it was moving very fast. She saw Luther raising his sword and getting into a bold defensive stance. That was the wrong thing to do, he was being charged by a big, heavy, angry juggernaut and he didn't have a hope of repelling its attack, he had to dive out of the way. It was going to hit him at over twenty miles an hour and it was going to kill him.

Moved by pure instinct, Lakeitha ducked down, reached her hand into her boot and pulled out the concealed throwing knife. She stood up, drew back her arm, turned her hips and then threw the knife at the point she expected the monster would reach in the almost imperceptibly short time between her throwing the weapon and when it would reach its target. The blade whistled gently as it travelled through the air, a noise that nobody heard because of all the screaming and burning and growling.

The knife shot through the monster's eye and into its brain as it leaped through the air. When its front legs landed on the ground they crumpled and the corpse's momentum carried it onward into an ugly roll. It landed on its back, at Luther's feet.

A badly burnt monster ran at Malek and he ran to meet it. He was going to try and give it the slip at the last second and then fight it toe to toe. The monster did a mighty leap three feet up in the air, its mouth open and its fangs ready to sink into him. Malek dropped from his run to a slide and the monster passed by over his head.

Before he'd finished his skid he had already rolled over to face the monster and placed his hands down on the ground so that he could push himself up as soon as he stopped moving. The monster turned and came for him as he got his feet under him. It didn't have anywhere near as long a run up, so when he struck its head with his mace, instead of barrelling him over, the monster stumbled, its head lulling to the side as it grunted in dizzy pain.

It swiped its claw in his general direction, he dodged to his right and then stabbed it in the shoulder. He'd stabbed with a lot of force but his blade only cut two inches deep into its tough flesh. It snapped at him but he jumped back before it could take a bite out of him. He swung his knife into its open mouth, the blade clanged against its metal teeth. It groaned in pain and then clawed his arm. Sparks flew when it hit his metal forearm guard and his knife was knocked from his hand.

He only got one step into a tactical retreat when it jumped on him, knocking him to the ground. It was on top of him and its mouth was wide open and close to his face. He shot a desperate uppercut into its chin, snapping its mouth shut. It stepped on his right shoulder and pressed down on him. It hurt but more importantly it pinned his arm. He'd lost his knife and his mace was in his right hand. He propped up the mace onto his belly and then grabbed it with his free hand and started smacking the mace against the monster's ribs and head. All he was doing was holding it off and buying time.

Lakeitha could see that Malek needed help, he was pinned and about to get his head bitten off but at that moment she was unable to help him because she was flying backwards through the air, with her legs and arms splayed open. Her stomach felt pretty nasty having just been kicked by one of the burnt up monster's back legs with the force of a cannon.

Luther stood in front of the monster that had just kicked Lakeitha, casual as a fish in water. It rose up onto its back legs, planning to flatten him just like Malek had been flattened. He used his sword like a true artist, slicing all four of its limbs in a flashy blur and then ducking to one side as it tried to knock him down. He plunged his sword into the back of its front left leg, piercing through the other side. He pulled the blade free and in a single elegant motion, he raised the sword to his shoulder, switched from a one handed grip to a two handed grip and then stabbed the blade down into a section of its neck that had been badly burned by the bombs. His sword cut deep into its throat. It thrashed around at him, but it was slow and off balance after his last strike at its leg. He was able to easily remove his sword and get clear of the creature. It growled and stumbled as blood squirted out from the back of its neck.

Luther looked over at Lakeitha, she was shuffling across the ground very slowly, wanting to get up and fight but barely able to sustain a crawl. She wasn't an emergency, but Malek was. Luther hurried to him and the monster that was crushing him. He went to stab upwards into its torso below the ribs, where it would be softer and there would be a lot of organs to cut into. He didn't even scratch it, because it saw him coming, shifted its body and kicked him with its back leg, sending him flying through the air. As he soared, he was less concerned with the pain or Malek's life, than he was with the embarrassment of making exactly the same mistake as Lakeitha.

Nobody was going to help him, he had to get himself out of this or he was going to die. Malek knew that he only had one chance left, he had to use his tentacle. He had hoped that he wouldn't have to use it again for the rest of the mission, but he didn't have a choice. His tentacle emerged from his palm, wrapping around the leg that pinned his shoulder and then running up to the monster's neck. It wrapped around the neck three times. He had its leg and head pinned in place, but he wasn't in a strong position and holding the powerful creature in place as it struggled was agony.

It growled and snarled, spitting all over his face, then it placed its other claw down on his other shoulder just above the chest. It tried to claw into his skin but his protective clothing held it off, then its sharp metal claws pierced his clothing and dug into his skin. He hissed and then he screamed into its face as it started dragging its claws down his chest, carving four bloody furrows in his skin. He hollered madly, banging his mace against its ribs but all that seemed to do was make it madder. It snapped its giant teeth over his face. Their angry roars blended together.

It cut below his chest and kept going lower. He hit its leg with his mace. This just seemed to make it clench and dig its claws deeper into him, but he didn't let up. He hit it again and again, as hard as he could. It tried harder than ever to break free but he held onto it with his tentacle as he bashed the leg. It withdrew its claws but he didn't stop hitting until the leg snapped; the skin torn and the broken bone exposed with the foot clinging onto the rest of the leg with nothing but bloody muscle sinews.

The monster screeched and struggled. He held onto it, "Fuck you!" He shouted at it as it tried to pull away from him. He wasn't going to let it get away, not if it cost him his whole arm, he was going to kill this bastard. Its efforts didn't free it but it did manage to shift the trapped leg to the left and gave it room to move. He tensed his tentacle as hard as he could trying to stop the leg, but it kept on moving closer and closer until it placed the tips of its claws down on his forehead. His eyes widened and he was wracked by the terror of knowing what was about to happen.

The monster slashed its claw down his face, from his forehead to his chin. His vision went red, his nose opened up and his lips split. Blood leaked all over his face and filled his mouth as he flailed on the ground in silent agony.

His tentacle's grip weakened and the monster was able to pull back and limp away, dragging him with it. He rolled around on the ground, his cut-up face getting smeared into the dirt. It stepped down on his back and all of the air was forced from his lungs. He released his grip and pulled his tentacle back into his arm. He wasn't giving up though, he still had his mace in his hand. It took its foot off his back and he rolled over, smacking his mace across its jaw, interrupting its killer bite. He rolled away and pushed himself up onto one knee, turned his head and saw the monster's face a foot away from his own.

For three seconds they stared into each other's eyes. They could feel each other's breath on their faces. They hated each other and they were both in so much pain, they were messy and angry. They had their mouths open, their cut, bleeding lips spread in wide toothy grins. Only one of them was going to live and that was exactly the way they wanted it.

Malek swung his mace up into the monster's chin, snapping its head up. He jumped to his feet and hit it again across the face. He raised it up high and started swinging downwards on the head, one of its eyes flew out of its socket. Black spots started appearing in his red blurry vision. He hit it over and over, knocking its metal fangs out of its mouth. He wasn't sure if it died standing or lying down but he kept on hitting it after it fell.

He walked away from his dead enemy, his mace was covered in gore so he dropped it. He went up to Luther who had just gotten to his feet. He spat out a mouthful of thick blood and then he mumbled wetly, "How's my face?" Luther blinked; this guy had fucked up many faces in his life, but he looked queasy at the sight of Malek's. "My eyes?" Luther swallowed and then reached out at his face and started gently wiping blood out of his eyes. Malek twitched and hissed as he touched his face but he didn't stop him. Luther nodded, "The eyes are okay." Malek was satisfied with that. He took out his canteen, opened it and tipped it upside down over his face, washing the blood away.

The water stung. In situations like this, the mind clings to whatever comfort it can find. Malek's comfort was that when he healed and had four deep ugly scars running down the length of his face, he was going to look like even more of a badass. It wasn't much, but it was something.

Chapter 27

Malek lay down on his back and bled while Lakeitha and Luther treated his wounds. They gave him some guaga for the pain. Eating the stuff hurt like a bitch because of his badly cut lips. It wasn't going to spare him any pain for a couple of minutes. "Close your eyes Malek." she said as she took out her blood clotting powder. He closed his eyes and she started dropping the powder in the cuts on his face. It burned, making him scrunch up his face, which aggravated his cuts and made the pain even worse. The powder moved down over his eyes and his nose and then onto his mouth. A muffled scream rattled behind his tightly closed lips. The clotting powder would take a little time to fully stop the bleeding.

Luther was crouched beside her, watching her work.

She moved on from the face to the chest. Between each cut there was still a ribbon of his strong clothing. She had to saw through these ribbons in order to fully expose his injury. There was a lot of blood, but it didn't seem to have cut through his ribcage so his heart and lungs were okay.

She winced at all the blood, there was too much of it, she needed to clear most of it away from the wounds before she could clot them. "Luther give me some water and your towel." He gave her the towel first so she had to wait for the water. She poured the water on his chest, washing away the blood and making the cuts clearer. She pressed the towel on top of the cuts as fresh blood leaked over the fleshy ridges. Malek gurgled. She held the towel down for three seconds, then she lifted it up and poured some clotting powder onto the wounds. She stopped halfway through the first cut, she was running low and odds were she'd need some for later. "Luther give me your clotting powder." "I don't have enough." Replied Luther and then he said, "We can use those leaves." He said pointing at some large green dower leaves. "Good thinking." Luther ran off to pluck some leaves, "I hate the leaves." Mumbled Malek. She patted his shoulder, "Keep your fucking mouth shut."

Luther came back with an armful of leaves. They tore the stocks off, ripped the leaves in half and then stuffed one half into their mouths and started chewing. It had the texture of a salad leaf but the taste of coal and rotten oranges. He leaned over Malek's wound and spat the mouthful of chewed leaves onto his chest. He worked the gunk into the cuts with his fingers and then stuffed another half leaf into his mouth. He finished his first leaf and then took a swig of water for the taste. He swirled the water around and then spat it out.

Lakeitha was during the same thing as he was, only faster. As he was spitting up his second half onto Malek's chest she was already smearing her fourth into the cuts. All that speed came at a cost though, she turned her head away from Malek and threw up. He stuffed in a third half and chewed it up, his mouth was going numb. Lakeitha was vomiting uncontrollably, it was all on him. He chewed five entire leaves on his own.

When he was done Malek's chest was a green and red mess, soggy from blood, saliva and the moisture in the dower leaves. It wasn't pretty, but they'd stopped him from bleeding to death. Luther forced Malek to sit up and wrapped some bandages around his chest, over his clothing. He reached the end of his bundle of bandages and tied it off, but there was still an unsightly smear underneath the white fabric, so he took some bandages from Malek's bag and wrapped him up some more.

He wiped some congealed blood out of Malek's eyes and asked him, "How you feeling?" Malek didn't respond, he was keeping his mouth tightly shut. His eyes were closed and twitching. He wrapped Malek's arm around his shoulder and led him away from the scorched earth and dead monsters, as Lakeitha followed them, looking nauseous.

Her nausea was not helped when she dug her throwing knife out of a monster's brain.

They walked towards Dantez. Malek was weak and tired after all the fighting and blood loss; he fell asleep as Luther carried him. They stopped to make camp after just a few hundred meters. Lakeitha sat with a blanket over her knees and a sword in her hand, drinking water and cooking meat. Luther left the two of them there, walking in the dark past the site of their fight, to collect three more jars of fuel.

Chapter 28

Lakeitha and Luther took turns sleeping for three hours each. They let Malek sleep through the night. It was rare that any of them got six hours sleep while out in the wild. They both kept an eye on Malek's face and bandaged chest. The bleeding had stopped for the most part, but his skin had gotten paler as the night went by. When it was time to wake him he looked weak and ugly. The cuts on his face had turned scabby and stood out against the drained skin.

"How are you feeling Malek?" She asked, feeling a tad concerned. "Hungry" He replied. She remembered that he hadn't eaten anything the previous night, he'd gone straight to sleep. She reached in her bag for some food and when she looked back at him he was already sitting up and eating his own rations, not wanting to waste the flavour and time it would take to cook up the miniature pink skinned bull meat. He looked like he'd been dead for a couple of days, but he wasn't letting that hold him back. He quickly ate some nuts, dried fruit and dried meat, grimacing at the discomfort of eating with such badly damaged lips. Then he pulled himself up onto his feet. "You good?" She asked him. He nodded gently and said, "I can't smell anything." "Oh" That was not good. "How's your hearing?" He stood still for a moment, looking intensely focused. "Ughhh" He exhaled, "It's bad." "Alright, it'll all get better. We'll get you back to Dantez and it'll be fine." "It better. Let's get moving." And then he started walking towards Dantez. Luther gave her a look, "Don't worry, I've seen him walk away from a lot worse." They followed him.

A lot of colour came back into his face as they walked. He hadn't taken any more guaga, so he was feeling every little thing. If he was in pain he didn't show it. Much.

"Malek, you'd make a great cage fighter." "No shit" said Lakeitha. "You too." He said to her and she grinned, "We'd embarrass the lot of you." "I wouldn't go that far." "I would." said Malek. "I've seen a couple of those fights. One time a guy gave up just because of a few broken fingers." Lakeitha scoffed, "What a wimp." Luther shrugged, "You might be right. Some of those fighters could learn a lot from a couple of days out here. Still skinny guy like Malek might get smeared all over the floor if he refused to give up." "No one has ever called me skinny." "Well that's because you're not associating with the right people. Look at me, look at my muscles and then look at you. You're tiny compared to a lot of the guys I fight." Malek seemed in high spirits as he argued with Luther. "Maybe they're bigger but I'd walk up to them, knock all of their teeth out and they'd start crying and I'd kick them until I got bored. No contest." "I don't doubt you would Malek. Lakeitha on the other hand, you've got some bulk to you. More muscles than some of the guys I've battered. And you're tall for a girl, you're the same height as me. You'd have a shot at being the champ, if I weren't already the champ." "Oh you think you could beat me?" said Lakeitha, having fun with all the competitive banter. "I know moves that no other human knows. Stuff I've learned from monsters." "I don't buy it, there's a limit to the moves a human being can pull and I've seen them all. There's nothing that you could do in the cage that would surprise me." "Oh you just wait and see. You'd try to hit me and the next thing you knew, all the bones are missing in your arm and the skin is hanging by your side like an empty shirt sleeve." "Nah" "Nah?" "Nah." "Malek, are you hearing this. "I am." "You'd back me in a fight right?" "Well…" "Seriously Malek." "Out in the open, with weapons, sure you've got it, but locked in a pit or a cage, I don't know. You don't have nearly as much experience fighting in enclosed spaces and he is stronger than you." "Yeah" Said Luther and caught up to Malek just to give him a fist bump.

"Oh come on, that's ridiculous. I'd take him to pieces." "You might, or you might not. Luther would have to win quickly though." "Ohhhhh" Said Lakeitha, drawing out the word and hamming up the intrigue for the sake of fun. Luther frowned, "What are you talking about Malek?" "I'd have to give it to Lakeitha for endurance. I know that you're tough Luther but this bitch is hard as nails. If you didn't end her in the first few minutes, I think she'd turn the tables on you, little by little. You might turn her face into mashed potatoes but she'd give you a death by a thousand cuts and a broken neck." "Uh Malek, you're not making sense, she already has a face like mashed potatoes." Lakeitha laughed, "Alright pretty boy, a few more missions with us and you'll realise that I've held myself together with a level of grace that Shante could only dream off."

The mere mention of Shante flicked a switch in his head. He zoned out of the conversation and started thinking about her again. He missed her laugh, he missed dancing with her in her room where nobody else was around. She was a great dancer and she had great music that he'd never heard anywhere else. And he missed the sex. This was his fourth day out in the wild. He couldn't remember the last time he'd gone four days without a good fucking.

Lakeitha noticed Luther drop out of the chatter. She kept on talking with Malek for a while about hypothetical fights. They brought Gideon into it. Gideon was stronger than both of them and fast too, but did he have the skill hand to hand. He was great with a sword, knife, mace, axe, bow, club, anything, but unarmed he wasn't at their level. Good, very good, but when they'd spared together she'd found it pretty simple to trap his arms and from there she had a hundred different ways to press the advantage. He could hit like a bull, but years ago she'd worked out his defensive weaknesses. She'd tried to help him out with it like a good friend, show him where he was in trouble, but still he was something of a predictable fighter. They agreed that they could both probably take him. A conclusion that was easy to reach without him around to defend his honour, which also made it a bit unsatisfying. Maybe he was easier to take apart, but he was also very good at taking people apart. It would take him fewer hits to win because he was so strong.

The conversation died down and they walked in silence. Lakeitha was looking forward to seeing Mikey again. It had been a grizzly mission, as always and she wanted to be safe back in Dantez, hanging out with her brother, able to relax, able to fall asleep without worrying that she wouldn't wake up again, able to drink water without being suspicious that it might dissolve her tongue. Still in spite of how much she hated being out in the wild, she also sort of loved it. This was her life. She'd be bored without it. This was the absolute edge, a place where no human should be able to survive and yet she'd managed to survive out here for five years. She wasn't thrilled about retirement. It was unheard of for a Hell Hunter to keep going after they turned thirty. She reckoned Malek would probably manage it, he was already twenty seven and he hated the idea of giving it up even more than she did. Even if she went that far, her years in the job were numbered. A life where she never got to fight to the death, sounded unbearably boring.

They stopped for a short break. Lakeitha leaned against a soft green tree trunk. It was a very hot day and she was glad for the shade. At the start of the mission Lakeitha had told Luther that he didn't need to carry his sword the whole time, that it was a rookie move but now all three of them had their weapons out at all times. There had been a lot of violence during this mission and they weren't taking any chances.

She yawned and looked up, then yelped and jumped away. High above her was a massive orange ball. It was the little fruit that they'd seen yesterday, only now it was bigger than a house and it was hanging from the top of the stalk she had been leaning on. The guys stared up at it, looking very creeped out. They all backed away. "What ate it, for it to get that size?" asked Luther in disturbed awe. "Maybe a bracken. Maybe something bigger." Said Lakeitha.

It was a very unsettling feeling, to stand near this thing. It was almost like it was watching them. "I feel like it's watching me." Said Luther. Lakeitha shivered at hearing Luther say the same thing that she had been thinking. "Let's get out of here."

Chapter 29

Luther got excited. Very excited. He was so excited that he would've done a backflip if he wasn't so tired, hurt and weighed down. "Look" He pointed, "Miniature pink skinned bulls, six of them. No seven, we're gonna be rich. Rich." "Pfft" Said Lakeitha as she walked on. Luther frowned, confused as a man in a field. "Guys, what the fuck?" "Those aren't miniature pink skinned bulls Luther." Said Lakeitha, "Yeah, they are." "Nah" said Malek "Those are girls." "Girls? So what?" "Don't you know what a bull is?" Luther paused for two seconds, "Oh. Cows." "Yup those are miniature pink skinned cows, they taste like dirt and they give people diarrhoea." "That's the most disappointing thing that's happened on this mission." Lakeitha raised an eyebrow, "Really, what about when Malek had his face torn off?" "I wasn't planning on seducing Malek so what do I care about his face." Malek laughed hard and then broke down into a coughing fit, he capped it off by spitting blood and making a loud *uugghh*. He took a swig of water, swirled it around his mouth and spat out a twisting streak of pink water surrounded by a fine mist. He took another swig that he swallowed. The whole ugly ordeal took more than ten seconds to play out, then he looked over his shoulder at Luther and grinned, "Good one"

It was a hot day, as the jungle thinned out around them the sun beared down harder. They all had growing beads of sweat on their faces, in Malek's case the sweat was gently liquifying loose bits of the brand new scabs. It was gross.

His ears and his nose weren't working nearly as well as they normally did. He didn't like that. His finely tuned senses were an edge that he relied on for every waking moment he spent in the wild. He would rather be out here totally naked than have to make do with this. Once he was in Dantez the doctors would sort him out, but it might take weeks and that thought was hard to bear. He needed to be out here. He was different than the other Hell Hunters. Their home was inside the wall, his was outside. He spent more time on missions than any other person. He often went out without a mission, just to live. He'd hunt or he'd gather, just enough to keep Bane happy. He was a feral and he loved it.

In spite of his disdain for a long dull stay back in Dantez he also felt proud. These cuts on his face were proof of his toughness. He already knew that he was going to regularly check on his reflection in the mirror, watching the scabs break off and the scars come out. He'd do it with a grin on his face. It was worth the pain to know that he had won the secret competition. The one that every Hell Hunter competed in but only he knew about. The never ending contest to determine who was the most hardcore hunter. These four vertical scars on his face were his certificate that he could shove into the face of all the losers without ever having to say a single boastful word.

Lakeitha felt something, something that confused her. It wasn't a big feeling, but it was there and it felt out of place. It was fear, she felt afraid, but afraid of what. This wasn't normal, she didn't get scared for no reason. She took a drink of water and then poured some over her head. It was still there. It was slight but difficult to ignore, it added a hesitance to her. She waited for something to happen, but nothing did.

Am I losing it? Hell Hunters go crazy all the time, like Storror and Jessie. But I'm not crazy, I can't crack. I won't.

A few more minutes went past and the fear faded.

She licked her dry lips. The heat was getting to her. It was easier to focus in a fight. Fights are fast and urgent and short, but the heat was something totally different. It slowly drained her energy and softened her up. A lot of people got caught off guard because they sweated out their vigilance.

They were walking on level ground, there was a slope to their left with a lot of trees and bushes on it. On their right there were more trees, as always they were surrounded by life, but nothing big. Just insects and rodents and birds. They were more than five klicks away from The Fucked Pass. The plant life around them was going to gradually get sparser, leaving them with less shade to protect them from the sun.

A breeze picked up, but it didn't do much to cool her down. To her left, on the slope, the breeze lifted two dozen or so leaves off the ground and carried them through the air. They tumbled over each other randomly. The breeze carried them behind a thick tree trunk but only five of them passed by the other side and carried on their journey, while a few offers fell into view, dropping onto the ground. Lakeitha froze, the wind hadn't slowed down. The leaves had been blocked by something behind the tree.

"MalekLuther" she said in a quick hushed voice, the names blended together into a single sound that was sharp and clear. They both snapped out of their humid thoughts and turned to her, their knees bending slightly, their shoulder's leaning forward, their heads cocked and hands twitching. "There's something hiding." She whispered.

Instinctively she looked to Malek, expecting him to sense what was going on. She just saw him curl his upper lip with clear disdain for the fact that he couldn't hear or smell what was behind that tree.

She didn't bother with strategy or options. In those first few seconds there were no options. They were in a purely reactive moment, waiting. Her and Luther's heads turned in unison when they heard the same noise. Metal gently hitting tree bark. The sound came from behind a different tree.

First she started turning her right shoulder, then her head, followed by her right leg. She was halfway through turning around when saw people stepping out from behind trees and bushes all over the slope. She made a quick count of ten, but she couldn't be sure of the full number as the more she turned her head away, the less she saw of the slope. Her left heel raised off the ground and her hip started to turn as she saw that the closest man on the slope had his arms outstretched and was raising them up with the hands splayed. She made out the man's face. His name was Kalep and he had magic. She completed her turn and started running.

When Malek saw her start to turn, he copied her.

Luther didn't understand why they were running, not after he recognised some of the faces as Hell Hunters and soldiers. He didn't really know any of them, but he knew they were on their side.

The ground that Lakeitha sprinted over was full of animal holes and small ditches. She stepped over and around them until she saw one that was deep enough and wide enough for her to fit in. She jumped and while she was in mid-air she heard the first tree splinter and Luther's shout of surprise.

She landed in the ditch, crouched down and put her hands over her head.

Luther yelled and then spluttered a short gasp as the wind got knocked out of his lungs. As brief as the gasp was, it still hadn't finished before he was lifted weightlessly off his feet and started to fly backwards. He saw plants getting ripped out of the ground and then a bush whacked him in the leg and he started spinning as he hurtled through the air. Tree trunks twisted, snapped and burst into storms of splinters. He saw Malek underneath him. He was lying behind a fallen tree trunk bracing himself and looking up. He didn't have time to see the look on Malek's face because he'd made another flip and was now looking up at the sky. He didn't seem to be slowing down at all.

The booming noise of breaking colliding trees made her flinch in the hole. If anybody up there was screaming she couldn't hear it. She didn't dare look up even though a forest flying and falling to pieces a few meters above her head would be a rare sight.

Malek's feet had lifted off the ground, his grip on the tree branch was the only thing that anchored him. He couldn't hear it but he felt the tree branch crack. He winced and then ducked his head down to avoid a flying stone. It would've killed him for sure, but now all it did was tickle a few stray hairs at the back of his head and then bounce off his back and move on. He felt the tree branch crack again, he was sure it was going to break but then it had the pressure taken off it when the entire tree trunk started to roll towards him. He had to let go of the tree branch otherwise his hands would be crushed under the tree trunk.

He expected to go flying but he hadn't been moved six inches before the powerful wave of air cut out. He dropped onto the ground and immediately got up into a crouch and started running. He ran diagonally away from the death squad. He looked back at them, everything beyond the tree trunk that he'd hid behind was now gone. The forest had been levelled by the force of Kalep's shockwave and it had become eerily quiet. One moment the sound of destruction was so loud it hurt his ears and the next all he could hear was his feet hitting the dirt. It didn't last long though. A mere second after Kalep's magic ran out, he collapsed and as he fell half a dozen machine guns started firing.

The gunfire was thunderous and he was an open target. There was nothing tall enough to protect him as he ran. He was conscious that he hadn't been hit yet. For as long as he hadn't been hit he knew he could survive. He always survived, he always won, but if he got shot in the leg or the arm or the torso, he'd be weak and bleeding everywhere. A bullet that didn't kill him, would soften him up for the blades that would finish him. He couldn't keep running. Lakeitha had found herself a hole to hide in, Luther dead or alive, was out of sight, he was the only target and he had to stop running. He dived over a cracked lump of tree and hugged against it.

Bullets crackled against the otherside of the tree trunk. He stayed put, lying down on the floor, careful not to let any part of him peek over the top of the tree trunk. He could wait out the shooting here. Ammo was hard to come by and easy to lose, soon they'd run out and then they'd walk in with their swords and Malek would open up their arteries.

A bullet tore through the tree trunk a few inches above his head. He squirmed, rolled over and started commando crawling further along the tree trunk. He muttered swears to himself as he moved away from the pathetically thin tree.

Luther lifted a log off his chest and started clambering over the pile of woodland debris. He could hear guns firing but was too far away to see them. He'd been carried a long way and he was in a lot of pain that he ignored. Back here there was still cover. There were still trees and bushes with their roots in the ground.

He got himself clear of the wreckage and stood with his big sword in his hand, fuming. They'd been betrayed. Soldiers and Hell Hunters from Dantez were trying to kill them. He wanted to run back and fight but he made himself stay put. Here he had cover but if he ran to his friends then he'd get shot to pieces before he got within ten meters of another person. Waiting was the only move.

They were still shooting and that meant that at least one of her friends was still alive. Lakeitha felt scared. She was trapped, if she got out of the hole then she'd be standing right in front of those guns.

It was a tight fit. She was sweating and breathing hard.

She had her knife in her hand in front of her, she wondered if she'd get a chance to use it or if they would kill her first.

Malek crawled further away, lumping uprooted bushes and clumps of dirt onto his back to hide him. He was staying close to the ground but he felt exposed. One positive of all the trees getting blown over was that they couldn't ricochet bullets into him from all angles, all he had to worry about was the shots being fired from one direction. He covered a lot of ground but he still hadn't reached the cover that he needed. When it came time to fight back, that cover would be the difference between life and death.

Lakeitha gasped when she heard the shooting cut out. Had they stopped because Malek and Luther were dead or had they stopped because they'd run out of ammo. She wiped dirt and sweat off her forehead, or at least tried to, all she really did was smear it around.

A minute passed in the sweltering heat of the cramped hole. She started hearing them, they were coming closer. She didn't hear them speak a word, they would be using hand signals. How many had she seen, more than ten. She couldn't fight that many of them. And magic, if they brought Kalep then who else did they bring.

She heard an especially close set of footsteps and then a man stepped into view. He was standing by the edge of the hole, he looked down and his eyes widened. Lakeitha dropped her knife and jumped up, grabbing both his legs and pulling him into the hole. They were crammed in together, almost nose to nose, their arms jammed against the walls of the hole and each other.

Lakeitha knew him, his name was Mason and he was a Hell Hunter and a dickhead. They went on a mission together once, two days they'd lived together trusting each other with their lives.

Her knife was stuck at an awkward angle at the bottom of the hole, prodding their legs but not cutting into them. He shifted trying to get his hands free, pushing against her. She did the same, closing her left hand around one of her twin knives, she pulled it from the scabbard and then he moved, jamming her arm in place. She tried to yank her arm free but it wouldn't budge, then suddenly Mason had a knife in his hand, the blade a few inches away from her chin. She grabbed his wrist with her free hand. He pushed against her and she pushed back. She was stronger than the bald bastard, but he had two hands and she only had one. The knife got a little closer and she knew that she couldn't win like this.

She switched up her grip, instead of pushing the knife towards Mason, she pulled it down towards her. Mason wasn't expecting this and he let the blade dip a few inches, scraping lightly over her armoured chest. With the knife out of the way she headbutted him, then switched her grip again and pushed the knife up as hard as she could. The knife stabbed briefly into the curve of his jaw and neck. He wrenched the knife back out, but the blood was already draining from the narrow cut. He struggled madly and tried to stab her back but she held him at bay. He was dead and he knew it. He was going to get weaker until he couldn't fight her for the knife anymore and then he was going to die. There was no way out.

In his eyes there was a panic sharper than the blade between them. She looked into those eyes, at the child within him who was regretting everything. "That's what you get." She whispered to the traitor.

He died.

She clambered over him, moved him around until she could get her knife from under him and then climbed out of the hole. "Hey!" someone yelled. She started running and they chased her. After a few seconds of running Malek burst out from under some bushes twenty meters to her right.

Some of them were fast, faster than her and she could feel them gaining. An arrow flew over her shoulder. She waited for the next one to dig into her liver. Malek reached the tree line first and then she joined him.

They had trees and bushes and tall plants, massive leaves and shadows.

Somebody tackled Lakeitha from behind. They hit the ground, she twisted and saw the face of her attacker. Sort of. It was a Blackmask, sleek pitch black metal with an excellent killer inside of it. She wriggled out of his grip, kicked him in the chest and got to her feet. Blackmasks wore a gauntlet on each hand with a two foot long retractable blade on either side of the fist. All four of these blades snapped out. Lakeitha wasn't afraid to fight a Blackmask, but she had just gotten to the tree line and in seconds there'd be more people here. She was definitely afraid of fighting five Blackmasks.

She turned tail and ran deeper into the forest. After about ten seconds Luther appeared out of nowhere and collided with the Blackmask. She would've liked to help Luther fight the Blackmask, but two against one was a luxury she didn't have time for.

She went looking for a fight and left Luther to it.

Lakeitha left him to deal with the Blackmask, he was fine with that, for about two seconds. The Blackmask's black blades, like giant claws, moved in a blur, he could barely keep them at bay. His sword got batted around, he was on the defensive and he was doing a crap job of it. He was no match with the sword but he was good at the foot work. He didn't let the Blackmask get close, every time the Blackmask lunged he stepped out of the way. He could keep himself a few feet away from his enemy at all times but that was all he could do.

He swiped at the Blackmask's neck and the Blackmask ducked to one side, slashed across Luther's chest and disarmed him. Luther backed away from the black whirlwind, empty handed with his chest stinging. The slash hadn't pierced his armour but it had left two shallow cuts. He could've drawn his two knives but he decided to try something different.

With the blades out he was no match for this Blackmask, he'd lose the knives just like the sword but if there was one thing that Luther knew for certain, it was that he was the greatest hand to hand fighting in the world.

He stopped backing up and dancing around the elite killer with the intimidating mask and the even more intimidating blades. He went at him head on and empty handed. The Blackmask swiped at his head and Luther ducked under his arm, rose up and punched him in the face. The black metal studs on his knuckles collided with the black metal of the mask. The Blackmask tried to turn and slice at him with the back of his claws but he grabbed ahold of his arm behind the elbow and snaked his foot inside his leg. He had him trapped. As the Blackmask struggled and tried not to trip over Luther's foot, Luther hit him in the head again and again. Punch, punch, punch, elbow, elbow, punch.

The Blackmask struggled to pull his arm back but Luther was stronger and held on tight. The Blackmask tried to stab him with his free hand and got close a couple of times, those long double blades made it very different from trying this move on an unarmed opponent. Luther had to duck his head out of the way a few times to avoid getting stabbed but he held on tight until the Blackmask took the only way out. He leaned back and allowed himself to get tripped up. As he fell, he swung wildly, knowing that Luther wouldn't dare follow him to the ground and risk getting impaled.

Luther backed up and waited as the Blackmask jumped to his feet. Not wasting any time he ran at Luther.

Luther snaked a wicked fast jab around the outside of the Blackmask's raised arm, then sidestepped the other way, leaving him to slash at thin air. He kicked the Blackmask in the stomach, batted his arms down and then got up real close to him. They were standing toe to toe, the Blackmask could afford to take a lot of hits but Luther would be dead if he let a single strike through. Jabs. Head. Right, left, right, left, right. His forearms caught the Blackmask's before the blades could get anywhere close, then he raised up his knee and fired off three quick kicks from the same leg. One to the stomach, one to block his other arm before it could swing and then the last kick to his chin.

The Blackmask staggered back but Luther never let him get more than three feet away from him. When he was within three feet he could control him, keep those arms down and leave the Blackmasks head and torso exposed but between three feet and six feet away from him, that was the danger zone. The Blackmask was light on his feet, he was backtracking fast but Luther stayed on him like glue. He hit him with three mighty uppercuts to the body and then cracked an elbow into his face.

If it wasn't for that mask, his face would've been halfway to hamburgers. He swung those big blades at his head and this time Luther was too slow to block it so he ducked down underneath the swing, rose up and grabbed the Blackmask's head with both hands and pulled it to his right so that he could knee him in the side of the head, twice. Then he took his right hand away and cracked his elbow into his head. The big round studs over his knuckles make a loud clinking noise as they hit the metal mask over and over. He felt like he was in the cage again, totally and utterly dominating his opponent, controlling the rhythm of the fight, hurting him exactly the way he wanted to at exactly the right time.

The Blackmask's backtracking took him close to a tree. Luther stepped back and kicked the Blackmask in the chest, knocking him into the tree. With his enemies back pinned against the tree Luther could really let loose. He launched into a wicked pitter patter of devastating punches and elbows. His arms moved as a blur but the sound of the impacts was clear. He sent out more hits per second than any other man could. He ran smoothly up from the chest to the head and then back down to the torso. His relentless barrage only paused to deflect the Blackmask's increasingly futile attempts to fight back.

He hit the Blackmask five times in the head, each blow forcing the back of his head to knock against the tree trunk and then rebound into the next punch. He kept hitting him until one of his punches broke through the mask, leaving a spider web of cracks and the indent of three knuckle studs.

Luther stepped back and the Blackmask toppled, like a plank of wood.

Lakeitha had gone deeper into the trees and had stopped when she reached the top of a slope. It was good and steep. She started to backtrack and hadn't walked ten meters before she saw three of them running at her. One Blackmask, one soldier and Roth, another treacherous Hell Hunter. The Blackmask hurled a spear at her. It flew towards her, fast, perfectly aimed. She stepped to the right and held her sword with both hands as she deflected the spear to her left, sending it spinning over the edge of the slope behind her. They were sprinting towards her, the Blackmask was especially fast. Even if she had wanted to run, she knew that he would have caught her. She headed towards them at a fast walk, shoulders leaning a little forward, knees a little bent. She drew her largest knife, going akimbo to take on multiple opponents.

The Blackmask reached her first and they duelled. It was like fighting a small tornado that had picked up a set of knives. They moved around each other, her weapons licking at his, keeping him at bay and trying to create openings. He was an intelligent fighter, he seemed to know all her moves before she tried them and wherever she was standing there was always a pair of blades stabbing at her.

She batted his right hand down but it came back up in a powerful uppercut aiming for the underside of her chin. She blocked it with both weapons parrying the blades, forcing the Blackmask's arm down to the ground. She left the knife in place and swung the sword up at the Blackmask's head but he blocked the sword with his other set of blades. For a split second they stood locked together, blocking each other's weapons and then the Blackmask's hip turned and his leg flashed up into her gut.

The kick separated them, freeing up the Blackmask's weapons, he came for her and she backed up, blocking him as best she could, getting panicked as black metal tore towards her, sparks flying everywhere, fast and jarring and hard to follow…she felt one of the Blackmask's blades whisper past her chin. She'd been lucky that it hadn't decapitated her. She'd slipped up with her defences and now he was very close to her and throwing a backhanded swing at her head. She blocked it with her forearm, the metal guard shuddering and letting a healthy dose of pain reach her arm.

He was already starting to pull away from her but there was a fleeting moment when his left blades were still jammed against her forearm, leaving the space in front of her open. She took a step forward and turned her hips as she slashed her sword against the side of his head. The sword made a beautiful clattering noise when it bounced off his helmet, leaving behind the slightest of dents and making him stagger away. Blackmasks often liked to stay quiet because it added to the intimidation factor of their outfits but when she hit him she heard a loud muffled, "Ahh!"

She felt the air shift behind her and heard a little something. She ducked under a sword swing, turned and struck her elbow into some cunts belly. She shifted her position and stabbed both her blades up at his belly. As he stepped out of the way he knocked both her weapons aside with his short sword and then with his free hand he punched her in the face. She fell from her crouch landing on her back. Her nose felt numb as she rolled away, the short sword stabbing into the dirt.

She hopped up onto her feet, noticed that Roth was the one who had punched her and started deflecting his attacks, realising that she was in a lot of pain and her chin was covered in blood. The Blackmask *had* cut her.

Ideally she would have liked to stab Roth in the throat and then move on, but she didn't get the chance to whittle down the numbers because the soldier was on her already. She was using her sword to fight Roth and she was using her knife to hold the new guy at bay. It was hard, she had to give one hundred percent of her attention to two places at once. On top of that she saw the Blackmask out of the corner of her eye as he approached, she couldn't see his face but his walk was angry.

She had to try something. With her knife she parried the new guy's sword off to the left and then swung her sword round at his head. His sword was being held back and his head was totally exposed, that sword should have killed him, but it didn't, because it never reached him. When the sword was about three feet away from the guy's head, six inch glowing green and red circles appeared around his body, encasing him in a sphere of laser rings. The sword hit three diagonal rings of solid light and pushed them back about a foot before they bounced back, repelling her sword.

The rings remained around him, protecting him. She was shocked, her eyes wide but not so shocked that she forgot to keep herself alive. She blocked Roth's attacks and then the rings disappeared and the man inside them disarmed her left hand, the knife flying away. His sword went for her head and she ducked. It barely missed her. She scampered back, getting some distance between them. All three of them followed her, the guy with the forcefield had a face covered in sweat, while Roth seemed to be enjoying himself immensely.

She stopped retreating when she reached the top of the steep slope. This slope behind her could be her saviour or her doom. They tried to rush her, all three of them coming at her at the same time. She couldn't let them overwhelm her, she had to split them up, so she picked the weakest one and tried to mow him over. Roth was formidable but had no magic and was also shorter and a little thinner than her. She used her superior size and strength to push him back, swinging her sword at his head and forcing him to constantly be on the defence. The other two were right by her side so every other move she made she was blocking and countering their attacks. This left a lot of windows of opportunity for Roth, so she had to be fast in order to keep him from slipping a cheeky decapitation past her. She didn't just have to be fast, she had to be the fastest person in the fight.

Holding her red bladed sword with two hands she let her weapon flow between them, never faltering, always where it should be, clanging against another blade and keeping everybody away from her. She was in the zone, but the forcefield threw her off. He hadn't been using his forcefield, he'd been letting their swords meet in the middle until she disarmed him and went for his belly, fully committing to an upwards stab that had enough force behind it to cut through his armour and out the other side. Then the rings materialised and her sword pushed a single ring almost two feet back. It was a strange sensation, because it seemed like there was nothing but empty space in the middle of the rings, but that empty space was holding her back. She couldn't see anything but she could feel something solid. Then the ring popped back into place and the force knocked her back. She stumbled and tripped over herself.

She had started the roll before she even hit the ground and was back up on her feet within a blink of an eye, but still, she'd fucked up. In a one on one fight she could take her time to get a feel for her opponent, how his power worked and how she could exploit it, but this was a three on one fight and the rules were completely different.

The Blackmask's blades screeched along the edge of her sword. He tried stabbing at her with his free hand and she kicked his wrist down then cracked her knee into his head. He staggered back and she stepped in, getting her leg behind his. He fell and she stepped over him, planting her boot on his head and lunging at Roth. He blocked her first two slashes and then she disarmed him, grabbed his right wrist, kicked him in the stomach and then slashed her sword down his leg, from his thigh to just above his knee. He roared startlingly loud, it sounded more like anger than pain. She backed up dragging him with her and kicking him every time he tried to straighten up or resist. She held off the magic soldier every step of the way and then reached the top of the slope and threw Roth head over heels down it.

She turned to face the last man standing, although the Blackmask already seemed to be recovering. She just couldn't catch a break. The magic soldier turned on his shield and started whirling his sword around to show off. At first he went with the simple wrist roll that was super cool and almost every fighter indulged in it from time to time but then he made a dick of himself by executing a more complex series of moves that he had clearly spent a pathetically long amount of time practising.

She went for him, tapping her sword all over his shield, testing not only the strength of the rings but also the temperament of the fighter. Rings all over him absorbed the attacks and then recoiled until the entire forcefield disappeared and his sword went for her throat. She blocked and countered with a stab at his left eye which he batted aside and tried to faint at her knee before going for her chest but she saw it coming and deflected it, then she whipped the tip of her blade up at his neck. His sword was down and that would have been a lethal move against any other opponent but his rings saved him again.

As they fought she worked her way towards the Blackmask, who had gotten up on all fours and was about to rise. Without breaking the rhythm of her sword she kicked the Blackmask in the head. Her steel capped boot clanged against the mask.

Every time he attacked he had to let his shield go down, so if she knew exactly when he was going to attack she could catch him. She swung at one of the lowest and furthest rings and when the ring bounced her strike back, she let her sword linger for just an instant. She was wide open and it was irresistible. The shield disappeared and he stabbed at her. She sidestepped the strike and slammed her forearm into the side of his head as hard as she could. Her forearm guard dropped him into unconsciousness.

No time to celebrate, the Blackmask was back up on his feet. But it was a one on one fight now. He looked around, at his allies, one unconscious, the other missing. He gave her a nod of respect. Possibly sarcastic. She raised her sword and said, "Alright pretty boy."

In a thicker part of the forest, where the jungle was creeping in, the trees were large and the canopy blotted out most of the light, Malek was on the hunt. He'd reeled one of them in, led him away from his team and now they were alone together. Malek knew him a little bit, his name was Darrius and he had a knife in one hand and a revolver in the other. He didn't know where Malek was but he knew he was close.

Malek darted out from his hiding spot, hit his enemy in the knee with his mace and then disappeared back into the jungle. Limping and muffling his cries of agony, Darrius fired two random shots into the jungle before remembering to conserve his ammo.

Adrenaline carried Malek's injured body towards precise moments of luscious violence. He crept out, grabbed him by the hair, kicked out his weakened knee, took his knife from him and then vanished before Darrius could turn his gun on him.

He whimpered, Malek could taste his fear. He hopped and stumbled, his left leg barely able to support any weight. "Please don't kill me Malek. I'm sorry, please I'm so sorry. I was just doing what I was told, you get that right. The mission. I didn't want to hurt you. Please." He was crying with his eyes and his voice; heaving like a child. "I don't wanna die." Malek hit the knee for a third time, he heard the leg break. Darrius dropped and howled. Malek snapped the gun from his hand and pressed it against his forehead.

The sniffling wretch closed his eyes, his face scrunched up in an ugly mask of pain and misery. "Did you really think you could hunt me?" "Please…" he sobbed, "I'm no threat to you man. Please. My leg's all fucked up. I'm just a dumb fuck, I do what I'm told, I never wanted to hurt you, please have mercy. I'm not worth it, I'm…" "Whatever happened to dying with dignity." He moaned and cried even harder. Malek sighed, "I'm not going to kill you Darrius." Pure relief filled his face, lighting up his eyes. A relief so pure that it seemed to smooth over all the pain he was in. He smiled, showing his top row of teeth and Malek shot him in the head.

Malek spotted Luther, he was getting his ass handed to him by a soldier and a Hell Hunter. He had fresh cuts in his armour that were welling up with blood. The soldier was a big man with a black double edged broadsword that he wielded with obvious skill. The Hell Hunter was a woman, he knew her. Her name was Clara and he'd been on half a dozen missions with her. She was shorter than Lakeitha, about five eight and not as strong either. Really she was average in all things, except for swordsmanship. Luther's main focus seemed to be on keeping the soldier's big sword from killing him, meanwhile he was leaving gaps for Clara's light blade to sting him. Malek ran in to help, knowing that at any second Clara might cut Luther's throat.

He ran towards them and Clara peeled away from Luther to face him. Luther was still in trouble though, blocking the juddering strikes from the big sword, his every counterattack failing.

Malek chose to fight Clara with the mace in his right hand. He knew he would probably have to use his tentacle at some point and he wasn't looking forward to it. But he knew he could take Clara without it.

"I was hoping I wouldn't have to face you." She said, as she approached with noticeably less confidence than she'd had while fighting Luther. Malek didn't waste words, he just attacked. She blocked and countered with a stab at his face, he ducked his head out of the way and tried to break off and get some space to manoeuvre. She stuck to him, keeping his mace trapped and whipping her thin blade at his neck and face. He forced her back with a shin kick that hit her just below the ribs. He danced around her trying to create an opening to bludgeon her. She kept him back, her blade colliding with the shaft of his mace, learning her lesson from the kick. Up close and personal she could control his weapon but she couldn't keep him from beating her up. They both knew how much stronger and tougher Malek was.

Clara took a swing at the left side of Malek's head and Malek purposefully let her get close before blocking it with his forearm. As her blade retreated he swung his mace into the tips of her fingers. Before the gasp of pain had started to leave her lips, Clara had already tossed the sword up into the air and reached for it with her other hand. Malek was faster, he snatched the sword out of the air and Clara froze. Her eyes were wide, full of shock.

Empty handed, she said in a voice dripping with fear, "Malek" He smashed his mace into her jaw as hard as he could, breaking it and knocking teeth out.

He dropped the sword and stepped over Clara, passing the mace from his right hand to his left as he approached Luther and the soldier. He raised his right arm with the palm open. He took a moment to aim and the tentacle shot out of his hand. It wrapped tightly around the wrist of the sword arm and Malek yanked back. The soldier's arm was forced wipe open and Luther took a swing at him. The soldier blocked the strike with his forearm guard and then Luther kicked him in the groin. His arm dropped down instinctively to his groin and Luther cut his head clean off.

Luther froze. He'd just done that. He'd just cut a man's head off. Blood was spurting out of the raw wound halfway up his neck. The present moment became fuzzy as he replayed the decapitation over and over in his head. The brief sound that it made when his sword had passed weightlessly through skin, spine and throat.

Malek shook him. "You with me?" There was something in his eyes, but Luther was too dizzy to understand what it was. Some kind of emotion, it didn't matter, they were all the same anyway. "Ehhhhhhhhh" He droned. Malek kept on talking but Luther stopped hearing him as his eyes drifted over to the head on the ground. It was facing him. It vaguely resembled the grim expression of pain and surprise that had been on his face during the last moments of the fight, except that without any life in his eyes the rest of the features on his face didn't really fit together.

Malek's hand was on his chin, forcing him to look at him. "Luther, we don't have time for this, Lakeitha needs us." "Uh yeah." he said in a faraway voice. "You ready to fight?" Luther looked down at the black blade of his sword that had blood rolling down it. He looked back up at Malek and nodded.

There may have been a battle raging, but that didn't mean that life had stopped for the inmates of this jungle. Birds fluttered their wings and a hundred thousand insects nibbled on the fresh corpses that they'd just left behind them.

They stepped around a few small clusters of white fungus. Like slimy cauliflower. Luther cut his way through a row of massive purple leaves and then something big, scaly and six legged jumped at his head and he impaled it against a tree with his sword, then yanked his sword free without even looking at what he had killed.

He could hear Lakeitha fighting somewhere in front of them. He saw one of their enemies off to his right, running through the trees towards Lakeitha. He peeled off from Malek to follow him while Malek went ahead to back up Lakeitha.

Lakeitha had beaten the Blackmask, the fight had sent both of them rolling down the slope and when they'd reached the bottom she'd found the other guy she'd already thrown down it. He was out cold after knocking his head on a rock. Lakeitha had taken the rock from under his head and used it to hit the Blackmask until he stopped moving.

She stood up and turned around, not knowing which way to go and then a man walked into her line of sight. They locked eyes. She knew him, his name was Akira and he was one of the most dangerous men on the planet. He started sauntering towards her. He was a few inches shorter than her, lean and muscular with a closely shaved head of black hair. In each hand he held a long metal club, the same length and shape of a baseball bat, except that they weren't hollow and they had two rows of metal studs near the top which had bashed in many a head. He had two black alien metal knives at his belt. He was a Hell Hunter, he was smart, he was tough, he was ruthless and on top of all that he was also magic.

As they approached each other she felt her nerves tingle and adrenaline rush her system. "So you're the one they put in charge." She said, "I thought we were almost friends." "Almost" replied Akira, not showing a morsel of regret. They stopped walking with six paces between them. "Before we do this, I want to know. Why?" Akira shrugged, "They must have their reasons." "You didn't ask Bane?" "Doesn't matter to me." "Well, I'll have to ask him myself." Akira nodded, "Is the talking part over now?" "I guess so." She lunged swinging at his head, he ducked out of the way and then batted her sword down on the return swing. He fainted at her head with his right club and then took a sneaky swipe at her knee with his left club. She jumped over the club and backed up, deflecting his attacks, holding her sword with both hands so that she could repel the power of those heavy clubs that he wielded with graceful speed.

He took a swing at her right knee and then a fraction of a second later he swung the other club at her head. She blocked the knee swing with her sword, one handed and then used her left arm to block the head shot. Blocking both strikes sent a judder through her body. She shoved the club away and shot a left jab into his face.

Akira backed off, blood running from both nostrils but she kept on him, hitting him with a whirlwind of light slashes all over his body. He was good but his clubs couldn't stop every viper strike from the blurring red blade. She hit his shoulder, not breaking through the armour and then cut his thigh, this time drawing blood. The inside of his left elbow. Just above his right nipple. His right bicep. His cheek, with a slash that carried on and nicked the outside of his ear.

Then his elbow hit her temple and one of his clubs punched into her gut. She took a swing at his head to force him back but he blocked it with his left club and trapped her arm on the other side with his right club. He kicked her in the chest, knocking her on her back and disarming her.

She rolled away before he could crush her head. She got back to her feet and pulled out her largest knife. He kicked her sword away and grinned, "You know..." He lunged trying to take her off guard but she sidestepped him and brought her knee up into his ribs. He stumbled a single step and then he was back on. She ducked and dodged most of his attacks, trying to avoid having to block with her knife. Every block against those clubs would take a toll on her.

She ducked under one of his swings, leaving his head and his side wide open. She stabbed at his neck but he was faster. He let his club fly from his fingers, turning his hand around and catching her wrist just after it had passed over his shoulder. He turned into her, kicking at her knee but she stepped out of the way. They each had a hand wrestling for the knife while Akira's other hand still had a club in it. He swung down at her head and she blocked it with her forearm guard. She took a second hit and felt like a nail getting hammered. He pulled back the club, readying himself for a third strike and in that short gap her free hand drew one of her twin blades and she saw his eyes widen as she stabbed at his belly.

He pulled back, dodging the stab and managing to yank the big knife from her hand. She drew the matching knife and went for him. He fought her with one club and her own knife. It was a deadly combo; with a knife he was even faster and he still had a big blunt club to break her bones and squash her brain.

She tried to slash his face but he caught the inside of her arm with his forearm and held her arm in place while he swung his club up into her chin. Her bottom row of teeth smacked painfully into the top row and her vision became a shapeless black and white void. She staggered around like she'd just been spinning on the spot for a full minute.

His club hit her in the back, returning her vision as it toppled her. She rolled onto her aching back and lifted up her legs, kicking the bat away from her. He leaned forward and slashed her shin with her own knife. It hurt but then she kicked him in the face and that made it worthwhile.

She jumped to her feet and realised that her hands were empty. She saw her twin knives on the ground and then Akira walked in front of them, dirt from the sole of her boot on his face, getting washed away by blood. His eyes seemed to radiate a strength even greater than he possessed. Like he had the soul of a giant inside him.

With as much speed as her battered body could muster, Lakeitha bent down, grabbed the throwing knife from her boot and hurled it at his neck. Akira casually blocked it with his club, the little knife clinking loudly as it failed.

Lakeitha gave a disappointed sigh. "How many fucking weapons do you have?" he asked with a smirk on his face. She pulled the World Saver from its holster. Akira darted forward and swung his club. It hit the barrel of her gun, knocking it from her hand before she could fire. Akira stabbed at her with her own knife and she grabbed his wrist with both hands, disarmed him and danced back, taking an organ mashing hit from the club.

Panting, bleeding and not quite able to stand up straight, Lakeitha faced off against Akira, her knife raised. He took a step forward and then Malek's tentacle wrapped tightly around his neck. His eyes widened and then his upper body leaned back and he was struggling to breathe and stay standing. Lakeitha took a hold of the opportunity and charged up to Akira, kicking him in the stomach as hard as she could.

He grunted, doubling over and then Malek wrenched the tentacle and he practically flipped onto his back. Malek started dragging him across the ground, pulling the tentacle towards him like a rope, the slack flowing back into his hand. Akira was choking and his face was turning red. Akira dropped his club so that he could claw at the tentacle with both hands. He rolled over, his face mashed against the ground. He managed to prop himself up on his knees and then Malek pulled him along and he fell flat again.

Lakeitha walked close behind him to keep him from breaking free. He let go of the tentacle with one hand and grabbed one of his knives from his belt. Lakeitha jumped on him, grabbing his arm and digging both her knees into his stomach. She disarmed him and then took the other knife from his belt before he could. He was almost gone, she could see it, they were so close. Nearly there.

Fire spat out from Akira, singeing her armoured clothing. She rolled away cursing and Malek howled, retracting his tentacle. Spluttering and rubbing his throat, Akira propped himself up on one hand and then got to his feet. There were small orange fires burning all over his body, one by one they burnt out.

She looked to her left and saw Luther running with four people chasing him. Akira was up again but he was hurt and tired, Malek looked solid, better than she felt. Luther on the other hand, needed the help. She exchanged the briefest of glances with Malek and then she hurriedly picked up her weapons and ran after Luther.

Lakeitha picking up her weapons seemed to remind Akira that he was empty handed. Malek had him at a disadvantage. He charged Akira as fast as he could, reaching him before he could get a weapon. He swung his mace at Akira's head and Akira ducked under it, came up and kneed Malek in the ribs. He blocked Malek's mace on the back swing and then shot two lightning fast jabs into Malek's chest and one into his face. Malek blocked his next punch with his forearm and then punched Akira in the face with a right hook.

He swung his mace down at Akira's head but he sidestepped it and then kicked him in the right leg. He backed up, Akira followed him and he elbowed Akira in the face until he gave him room to manoeuvre. He fainted a lunge to the right and then went left, aiming a backhanded strike at the right side of Akira's temple. Akira barely ducked under it and then caught Malek's forearm and held it there while he stomped down on his knee.

Malek's face briefly contorted in pain but he powered through it, drawing his knife with his free hand and slashing it across Akira's face. The blade whipped into

Akira's open mouth, cutting through his left cheek. He backed off, bleeding and gargling. Malek's mace hit Akira's stomach and he fell on his back.

Akira splayed the palms of his hands up at Malek and he dived out of the way of two jets of fire. It burned his face a little bit, but his face was still doing better than Akira's. Akira started running, still hunched over, towards his weapons. Malek dropped his mace, splayed his own hand and his tentacle shot out, wrapping around Akira's leg and tripping him up. He fell hard and Malek retracted his tentacle quickly, learning his lesson from last time.

He picked up his mace and ran after Akira. Akira rolled over and raised his hand, but nothing happened. He swore, frustration on his face, then got to his feet and started running for his clubs. Malek caught up with him just before he reached his first club. Hot on his tail, Malek took a swing for the back of his head and Akira dropped and rolled under the swing. He came out of his roll behind Malek and kicked him in the back of his knee, sending him to the ground. Akira stepped on Malek's back as he ran on to collect his clubs. By the time Malek was back on his feet Akira had a club in his hand and was about to pick up his second.

Akira's clubs were almost twice the length of Malek's mace, but his skull wasn't any thicker and that was all Malek needed to know. Akira charged Malek with a club in each hand and Malek charged Akira. There was no frustration on Akira's face anymore, just ruthless focus. As he ran, fire started spitting out of the air around him and his bounds got longer and longer and then he took a bound and stayed in the air, flying towards Malek. He was flying a lot faster than he'd been sprinting, moving through the air with his head forward and clubs out, his entire body covered in roaring flames. Malek kept running at him, mace up and just before they would have hit each other Malek threw his mace at Akira's head. Akira blocked the mace with his clubs, throwing off his balance. Malek dropped into a slide. As Malek slid under Akira, he reached out his empty hand and his tentacle grabbed Akira's fiery leg. He grabbed his wrist to strengthen his grip as he wrenched downwards, slamming Akira onto the ground and extinguishing his fire.

Malek retracted his burning tentacle, pulled out his knife and pounced on top of Akira. Akira caught him by the wrists and held the knife back. They rolled around wrestling for the knife. Malek kneed Akira in the chest, knocking him on his back, but he didn't let go. He planted both his feet on the ground for leverage and started lifting the knife up, trying to wrench it from Akira's hands. Akira pulled even harder, forcing Malek to lean down, weakening his position. Akira kicked out Malek's left leg and he fell. Akira took Malek's knife from him and then Malek elbowed him in the face, right in his cut cheek.

As Akira grunted and hissed at the fresh pain, Malek knocked the knife from his hand. It landed a few meters away from them as they wrestled on the ground. Akira had an arm around Malek's neck and was trying to pull him into a headlock as Malek punched him in the ribs and pressed his full weight on top of him, keeping him from wriggling free. With each punch Akira's grip around his neck got weaker. Akira let go prematurely, leaning forward, drawing Malek's backup knife from his thigh and stabbing at his neck. It was a lightning fast attack but Malek was faster, he caught his wrist, the tip of the blade grazing the stubble under his chin. He held Akira's arm in place as he punched down on his face. Akira struggled and bucked like a wild animal as Malek hit him and hit him.

Malek had one of Akira's legs pinned but the other had some room to move. As Malek knocked out one of Akira's canines, Akira snuck his leg up over Malek's right hip, wrapped it around his body, wrenched his knife hand down to the left and started the roll. He flipped Malek onto his side and then Malek killed the roll by grabbing his head, pressing it down to the ground and kicking him in the groin. The kick connected well and hurt Akira, but he still lost the grip on the knife arm.

Akira slashed and stabbed frantically at him, nicking him a few times. Malek raised up both his legs and kicked Akira's body as many times as he could, creating some distance between them. He rolled away and got up into a crouch as Akira did the same. Akira's knife darted at him and Malek kicked the blade out of his hand. He moved in with a quick combo of three punches. Right uppercut to the chin, left jab to the chest, left uppercut to the chin. The first punch landed but Akira blocked the other two and then kneed Malek in the ribs. He tried to pull back after kneeing him, but Malek wouldn't let him, he hugged him in close, one arm wrapped around his back and the other clasping his head and keeping it jammed into his shoulder.

Akira pushed back against him but Malek held on. He tried to get his legs behind Malek's to trip him, but Malek blocked him off and kicked his shins. Then Malek grabbed Akira's ear and pulled his head away from him, headbutted his bloodied face and then pulled his head back into his shoulder. He did it again. Akira was still strong in spite of all the damage he'd taken, but he couldn't break free from Malek. Malek didn't want to have to headbutt him to death so he decided to try another move. After his next headbutt he was going to push Akira's body back and sweep his legs, then stomp on his face a couple of times before grabbing a knife off the ground to finish the job with. But it didn't work. He pushed Akira's head back and in the brief moment between the push and the headbutt, Akira's arm snaked up and blocked Malek's forehead.

He pushed Malek's head back, weakening his grip and his stance. He gave an extra hard shove on his head and then broke Malek's grip and gave him a headbutt of his own. Immediately after the headbutt, Akira punched him four times in the face. Malek backed up and Akira kicked him in the stomach. The kick made Malek stumble and Akira took that opportunity to dart in and smash his palm into Malek's face.

Malek answered it by punching Akira in the face, and again and again and then he tried a fourth time and Akira caught Malek's arm. Malek threw a punch with his other arm and Akira caught that too. Akira pushed Malek and Malek pushed back, both of them leaning forward, creating a clumsy arch. Akira had good leverage which he abandoned for a fraction of a second to kick Malek in the side. Malek wheezed and gritted his teeth. Their heads were locked a few inches away from each other. They could hear each other panting and grunting. Akira tried the same kick a second time but Malek saw that shit coming. When Akira lifted one foot off the ground, Malek pulled him back, taking him off balance. He sidestepped him, stuck his foot out in front of him and threw him as hard as he could.

Akira landed on his back, rolled, got his right foot and his left knee under him and then Malek kicked at his head. Akira blocked his kick with both arms, shoved the leg down, lunged forward and punched Malek in the stomach. He rose up and punched Malek across his face and then Malek hit him back. Akira jabbed at Malek's head, Malek blocked it and then elbowed Akira. Both their faces had become cracked and mushy. Akira hit him in the mouth, knocking out a few of Malek's teeth and then Malek punched him twice in the face, taking a few of Akira's teeth. Akira hit Malek with two powerful body shots and then Malek kicked him in the chest, knocking him back a few steps.

Akira paused and so did Malek. He backed up a couple of steps, getting his breath back. They watched each other. Malek was in so much pain. Akira's face was slashed and battered, one of his eyes was totally bloodshot. Malek had zoned out of the battle going on around them, all he could hear was his breathing and Akira's.

Akira was not a man, not a Hell Hunter, not a traitor, not an enemy. He was a lump of meat that didn't know he was dead yet.

Malek roared, "UUURRRAAAGGGHHHRRAAAAA" Akira roared back, "AAAAAGRUUUUAAAAAHH" They ran at each other.

He swung with all his might at Akira's head, he was going to knock it clean off. Akira ducked under the punch and snapped his fist into Malek's eye. Malek fought through the blurriness and the pain. Akira hit him in the ribs and then Malek elbowed him in the face. He jabbed at Akira and Akira sidestepped his arm, stepping in and kneeing Malek in the ribs again. Malek felt one of them break but that didn't stop him from grabbing ahold of Akira's ear, wrenching his head to one side and then punching Akira in the face. Punch, punch, punch, punch. He hit Malek back but he didn't even feel it. Hitting Akira got him high. Akira broke free from the hold and took a wide punch at Malek's head, Malek ducked under the swing, turned and kicked Akira in the back.

Akira stumbled and when he turned around Malek's fist met his face. He hit Akira with a barrage of fists, palms and elbows, every blow landing and fucking with Akira's balance. Akira swayed and staggered, throwing a punch at Malek that he easily batted aside. Malek stomped down on Akira's knee. Akira fell on his back and Malek mounted him and rained down punches on Akira's face. Then he wrapped both hands tightly around Akira's throat and started squeezing.

Akira choked, spitting up blood. He struggled, hitting Malek's arms but he couldn't break his hold. Malek had a big grin on his face as he strangled Akira. He gave up on breaking the hold and reached out his open palm at Malek's face. A few sparks fluttered and died in Akira's palm, then nothing. Akira's eyes were full of panic. His magic wasn't going to save him.

In his panic Akira desperately patted the ground around him. It wasn't going to do him any good, he was going to black out at any second. Malek felt the pain first. He half coughed, half whimpered and withdrew his arms. Then he noticed that there was a large splinter sticking out of his cheek. He looked back down at Akira, who had once again splayed his hand up at him. A jet of flame blasted Malek in the face.

Malek covered his face and dived clear of Akira. He smushed his face into the dirt until the flame went out. He was in so much pain, but he could still move and he could still see, so he wasn't done yet. He rolled away from Akira's next fireball, got up to his feet and pounced at Akira. He batted down Akira's arms and threw a punch at his face. Akira ducked under the punch and then wrapped his arms tightly around Malek. Malek struggled but he couldn't break free as sparks and little flames started dancing around Akira. One of those little flames burned Malek's neck, it made a sizzling noise.

Akira was seething loudly into Malek's ear, he sounded pained. Malek tried to trip Akira up, but he couldn't. Akira had both his arms pinned under his hug, so Malek couldn't hit him. The heat got a lot worse, it singed his armoured clothes. Malek grunted and hissed, Akira was making a lot of noise as well, the seething sound getting louder and louder. He was grumbling curses to himself as the pair of them lifted a few inches off the ground. "ARRrraaAcca NO!" Yelled Malek, in a strangled moment of hot fear. Akira let out a single relieved breath.

The pair of them flew up into the air, engulfed in a big ball of fire that roasted Malek but didn't hurt Akira. They shot upwards at a ridiculous speed, leaving the trees behind them. The fire that burnt up his bandages and raged around his head was the most painful thing he had ever felt.

He struggled against Akira's tight hug, until Akira let him go.

He fell, looking up at the clear blue sky, the blazing sun and the ball of fire who dropped him. The wind rushed around him, extinguishing some of the fire. The fear overpowered the pain, as he watched the blazing Akira get smaller and smaller. He was existing in a brief moment of heat and speed, where his life was over, but he hadn't died yet.

His first thought when he hit the ground and his bones snapped, was that he missed falling. He looked up at the blurry sky, his vision turning red in patches. There was nothing that he would've done differently and there was nothing that he still felt the need to accomplish, but still this felt like the wrong time to die.

Chapter 30

Lakeitha saw a big mess of fire soar up into the air and she saw her friend break off from Akira and fall a terrible height as he burned alive. She'd seen a lot of friends die before, but she'd never lost someone like Malek. There was no one like Malek. This was a lifechanging moment and it was interrupted by a dirty cheap shot. A heavy fist slammed into the side of her face. A spiderweb of excruciating pain spread across her cheekbone. She watched the end of Malek's fall at a jaunty angle as she toppled sideways.

Malek was dead. She got up, half her face was numb and it felt like there were loose shards of bone moving around under her skin. Malek was dead. He was tall and broad, had a lot of muscle. He came at her with his hands raised, moving like a boxer. She stood and waited, her hands down by her side. Malek was dead. He sent a powerful swing at her head and she ducked under it, came up and hit him with an uppercut to the throat. She batted down his blocks and counterattacks, held onto his right arm to keep him close. She broke his nose, elbowed him a couple of times, broke his jaw. He hit her in the face, hard but she barely felt it. She hit him in the mouth again and again. Malek was dead. She knocked out his bottom row of front teeth, then turned into him and threw him at the hip. He went head over heels and landed on his back. She stomped on his face and then dropped down, grabbed ahold of his left arm and got him in an armbar. He struggled, gargled, gasped and yelled. Malek was dead. She snapped his arm.

She got up and looked around her. She saw Luther running towards her. He had a look on his face. A lost look, in need of guidance. Fight or run? Was the question on his face. She wanted revenge, but she'd already lost once against Akira. She was okay with dying in an effort to avenge Malek, but she didn't want to get Luther killed with her and more importantly she had a responsibility to her brother. Mikey needed her alive. "Run!" She shouted at Luther and then she started sprinting.

They headed away from Akira's men, out to where the trees got thinner. Luther was by her side in no time at all. Then he overtook her. They were both beaten and bloody but tough, fit and fuelled by the adrenaline that came from the certain knowledge that running fast was the only way to survive.

She felt someone running behind her, gaining. As they ran the trees around them thinned out until they were running in an empty field of brown dirt. They ran deeper into the field, Lakeitha pushing herself as hard as she could. In spite of her efforts the guy behind her was still gaining, he was about to tackle her. Then he made a strange yelping sound and suddenly he wasn't behind her anymore. She couldn't look over her shoulder without slowing down but he definitely wasn't close.

Two things happened at once. Lakeitha heard the man let out a scream of terror and a creature leaped out from under the dirt and slammed into Luther.

It was about six feet tall, black and grey with spindly limbs and a broad head that seemed to be covered in moss and roots too black to be alive. It had Luther pinned to the ground and was clawing at him with its oddly shaped limbs. Not slowing down at all Lakeitha ran up to it and jumped, lifting her leg in the air. Her boot smacked into the creature's head, knocking it off Luther. She landed on her feet, drew her sword and stabbed it down into the creature's head before it could get back up.

She helped Luther up and they started running again, each of them holding a sword at the ready. Once again Luther ran out ahead of her, but he didn't go as far ahead, leaving a gap of about three meters between them. Another monster jumped from under the earth, going for Luther. Luther slowed his run, turning around and slashing his sword across the creature's body, as Lakeitha did the same from the other side. The monster lurched in the air, Luther ducked out of the way and it landed on the ground. It tried to stand and raised its strange bristly limbs up at Lakeitha and Lakeitha cut the top halves off them. It writhed in pain, bleeding everywhere and making a strange screaming sound. Lakeitha raised her sword to finish it off, but before she could strike down another creature leaped out from the dirt behind the wounded monster, leapfrogging over it.

Lakeitha already had her sword up, so all she had to do was change the angle a little. She shifted her left foot back a few inches to sure up her stance and then she stabbed down as hard as she could just before the creature would have hit her. The tip of her sword cut through the airborne creature's head and then went down to the ground, skewering both monsters. Another one jumped out at Luther, who barely managed to dive out of the way. It landed and immediately started worming its way back underground. Within the space of a second the top half of its body was already underground, then Luther ran up and cut off its two hind legs. That stopped it from digging any deeper, it was stuck in place, blood squirting into the air like a double fountain.

Lakeitha pulled her sword free and saw that there was another guy chasing after them, he'd just entered the field. A couple of creatures jumped at him and instead of fighting he just dodged them and kept running towards her and Luther. If that strategy didn't get him killed, then he'd be on them in seconds. "We need to move." She called to Luther over her shoulder, already running away.

There were trees ahead, there weren't any trees in this field and there hadn't been any of these monsters back in the forest so she assumed that the treeline was the safe zone, where she could stop and quickly kill the prick that was chasing her.

She was expecting a grand charge, with monsters jumping around her, every moment brimming with near misses, but instead the monsters left them alone. Maybe they'd lost confidence in themselves after all the maiming and killing. She had the breathing room to risk a few quick looks over her shoulder at the guy chasing them. He was gaining on her. She didn't recognise him.

He closed the gap to about ten meters. They were very close to hitting the trees. This guy was the only other person in the field, if they could deal with him quickly, then they would be able to disappear into the forest.

She saw Luther reach the treeline and turn to wait for her. Lakeitha was a whisper away from the trees herself, when her foot fell into a deep hole in the ground that hadn't been there a moment ago. She toppled, almost tearing her quadriceps as her body fell forward but her leg didn't budge, stuck in the hole that had closed tightly around it.

She frantically tried to lift herself up but she couldn't, she was trapped. She looked behind her at the man who'd been chasing her as he lowered his outstretched arm, a predatory glimmer in his eyes. He drew his sword as Luther ran at him.

Luther didn't use his sword, he didn't know what would happen if he killed him before he released Lakeitha, he couldn't risk it. He dodged the first swing, then grabbed his sword arm and dragged him backwards, kicking up at his groin. But the guy turned and took the kick to the leg, then caught Luther's raised leg, stepped in and swept his other leg out from under him. Luther fell, but didn't let go of the sword arm, forcing his enemy to hunch down with him. Their faces were inches apart, Luther tried getting his feet back under him and then the ground swallowed them all the way up to his hips.

A grin spread across the bastard's face. Luther held on tightly to his sword arm, he had to keep him off balance and tucked in close. If he managed to break free then the fight would be over. He could easily kill Luther now that he was two and a half feet tall and stuck to the spot. With one hand he let go of the arm and grabbed the back of the guy's head, threading his fingers through his hair. He tried to break his hold but Luther was stronger.

Luther pulled his head in and headbutted his face. He did it again and then the guy kicked at his stomach. Luther let go with both hands and caught the leg just above the ankle before it hit him. He twisted the leg, making him hop around a few times before falling flat on his face and dropping his sword. He pulled him in closer, dragging him by the leg as he kicked and struggled, trying and failing to reach his sword. He pulled him in up to his hips, then the guy drew a knife and stabbed at him from an awkward angle. Luther caught his forearm with one hand. He held onto the arm as he slowly pulled him in closer with one hand. The guy put up a fight but there was nothing he could do to stop Luther from reeling him in and then letting go of his belt, reaching up and grabbing ahold of the hair on the back of his head. He pulled back as hard as he could, making him gasp in pain. Luther took the knife from his hand, threw it away and then grabbed him by the armpit and pulled him in close. He wrapped his arm around the man's throat, putting him in a chokehold.

He put on a little pressure, cutting off his air for a few seconds to show his power. The guy struggled uselessly. Luther loosened the choke a little and then said into his ear. "Let us go, or I won't stop squeezing until your head pops off." The ground around Luther's legs widened giving him space to awkwardly clamber out of the hole, without surrendering the chokehold. He watched Lakeitha get up to her feet and then he started squeezing again. He was unconscious in seconds.

Luther got up to his feet and looked over Lakeitha's shoulder, for the moment the field was empty, but there'd be more of them here in no time at all. "Take his World Saver. Yours is empty." Luther nodded and took it from the unconscious man. He checked the ammo, one had already been fired. He tossed away his own empty gun and holstered his new one. "Come on, we have to go." He said, turning away.

"Wait" said Lakeitha. He looked back at her, "What is it?" "You gotta kill him." "What no, he's out cold and we need to get out of here." "He's too powerful. If we don't kill him then he'll come after us, sink our legs into the ground and then we're dead." Luther grimaced, she was right there was no arguing with her on that, but still, he couldn't do it. Killing an unconscious man, that went against his code. The code of the fighter, he'd do all kinds of damage to his opponent when the fight was on but as soon as he was knocked out the fight was over. "I'm not going to kill him. I won't do it." She shook her head, looking disappointed, then she stepped forward and stabbed her sword down into his throat. He didn't react at all, he was just as limp as he had been before, only now he was leaking blood all over his neck.

Luther stared at her, not even sure how he was feeling. Not shocked. Not particularly surprised. He just felt disgust at being a part of something wrong. Rational and necessary, but wrong. She walked past him and said, "You fucking coward." Then she started running. Luther twitched and then turned away from the body and ran after her.

Chapter 31

They sprinted through the forest, weaving their way through the trees, jumping over holes in the ground, low bushes and foot and a half tall creatures that looked like giant green porcupines with needles made of gleaming steel. Lakeitha was running ahead, she was used to dealing with these little pricks. If she stepped on one of them then she wouldn't be able to run or even walk and her enemies would come and kill her, if Luther tried to carry her then he'd die as well. She had to be careful but to be slow was death as well.

She was paying so much attention to the porcupines on the ground that she almost didn't realise that there was a cliff right in front of her. She looked up, saw that she was a couple of meters away from the edge and knew that she was moving too quickly to stop in time. Thankfully there was a tree in front of her, she collided with it, wrapping her arms around the trunk to stop the juddering impact from knocking her on her ass. She peered over the edge as Luther arrived beside her. "Oh fuck!" She ignored him as she judged the height of the cliff, the choppiness of the river below and the direction that it led. It was doable, about forty feet, the water was fast moving but deep enough to stop them from breaking their legs on the riverbed.

"We're jumping." She told Luther. "Have you lost your fucking…" She had already jumped.

Luther stood at the top of the cliff, watching her fall. It was a long drop. She hit the rushing water and disappeared, a moment passed and then her head popped up. "Lakeitha you crazy fuck." He said to himself and then he stepped over the edge. He rocketed straight down. At first all he really felt was his stomach churning. Then he found his scream. It was a scream that tickled his throat with a thousand feathers and kinda shaped his thoughts into a weird synchronicity of body and brain. His mouth screamed like fuck and his mind screamed like fuck. The world around him was a blur. He looked down and saw the fast approaching water, it was the only thing that he could see clearly, as it magnified at a terrifying speed, making his stomach feel even worse.

He hit the water. He sank deep down into the river, water swarming up his nostrils and into his mouth. He stopped sinking and started swimming up through all the bubbles he had created on the way down. His head broke the surface of the water, he spat and breathed as the river carried him along at speed.

He had to kick and struggle to keep his head above the water. He looked for Lakeitha but he couldn't see her. He started worrying that she had drowned, then he felt the current change and the water started rushing downwards. He felt it before he saw it. His first thought was that he was going over a waterfall and was about to die, but thankfully it was just a small drop of about three meters. When the river levelled off he saw Lakeitha ahead of him. She was alive.

He got to enjoy a brief moment of relief and then he saw something up ahead that made him utter a string of the worst swear words he knew. One of them was cunt.

Lakeitha had thought that it was over. She thought that she had escaped from the people who were trying to kill her and that this river was going to carry her along until she decided to clamber up onto the riverbank. But no, there had to be a head rising up from under the water, no more than thirty meters ahead of her. It was scaly, jet black and big, the size of ten human heads, it had a long almost rectangular nose like a dog's. It had huge sharp teeth that were chalk walk. Behind the teeth was a big red tongue. Its eyes were pupilless and whiter than its teeth. The head rose up higher, revealing a long neck. It was terrifying watching it rise up higher and higher as the river carried her closer to it. It stopped rising when the head was fifteen feet above the water, even at this height its entire neck wasn't visible. Running down this neck were many four foot long spikes that looked as sharp as her sword.

It looked right at her and opened its mouth wide.

The river was too strong for her to turn back, if she was going to live then she had to go through it. Something wrapped itself around her waist and before she had even realised what was happening the monster's tentacle pulled her under the surface.

Luther saw Lakeitha go under the water and she didn't come back up. The monster was huge and it was fighting in its element; they didn't have a chance but still Luther had no other option but to take a deep breath and start swimming downwards. He saw her kicking and struggled against the massive tentacle wrapped around her. Her hands were empty and she was trying to get ahold of one of his weapons as she was thrown around the water with such ferocity that he saw a cloud of vomit swell up from her mouth and start to spread around in the water. A second tentacle wrapped around her, pinning her arms to her side. She couldn't do anything to fight it, the tentacles held her in place.

Luther swam faster. Right now it was drowning her, but at any moment that massive head was going to come down and eat her whole. As he swam towards it he realised the full size of the beast they were fighting. Its body was huge, twenty meters tall not including its neck and it was broader than three houses side by side. One of its tentacles came at him. He drew his knife just before it wrapped itself around his hips. He stabbed down on it, the blade piercing the scales and going deep into its flesh. He pulled the knife back out and then stabbed again, again, again, again; until it couldn't stand the pain anymore and released him.

Each time Luther stabbed the creature Lakeitha felt the tentacles around her twitch and spasm, then the tentacle pinning her arms loosened enough that she was able to draw her largest knife and start stabbing it. Green blood filled the water around her.

It let her go and she swam up to the surface. Her head broke through the water and she gasped for air, a moment of relief that was ruined when she saw the giant head of the monster leering down at her, its mouth wide open. It sped down towards her, coming to eat her whole. Lakeitha ducked back under the water and started kicking as hard she could. There was a brief moment of stillness as she swam downwards, then the monster's head crashed into the water behind her, creating thousands of bubbles and sending Lakeitha spinning head over heels. She swallowed a big mouthful of water, it went up her nose burning her sinuses. When she stopped spinning and the water settled she realised that she was just under the monster's head. She was within a metre of it. She could see the gentle flapping of its gills. Its head was upside down and she was practically level with its big white eyes. She reached out and stabbed her knife into one of those eyes.

She didn't let go of the knife. It swung its head back up out of the water, lifting Lakeitha high into the air. She was on top of it, looking down at its body. It swung its head this way and that, flinging Lakeitha around. Then the monster's eye came loose from the socket and Lakeitha was hurled weightlessly through the air, the knife still in her hand and the eye still on the knife. She was flipping through the air, looking at the empty sky, the cliffs, the river, the flailing monster and then back up at the sky. The water got closer and closer with each cycle until she was just above it. She took a deep breath, covered her head, pointed the knife away from her head and tried her best to go limp.

She hit the water. It hurt. She sank deeper into the water, not doing anything to swim back to the top, just feeling the pain. It was fuzzy and covered her whole body. Then she felt a need to breathe and started kicking. Thankfully neither of her legs were broken. She reached the surface and watched the big scaly black creature wrench its head around in the air as the current carried her away from it. She guessed that its species couldn't scream but it looked like it wanted to. One of these wild agonised swings of its neck caused its head to crack against the cliff face. After that it dropped beneath the surface. She waited for something to happen, but it didn't.

After a few minutes the cliffs along the riverbank gave way to even ground and she was able to swim over to it easily enough. She sat on the dry ground, panting and waiting. After about a minute Luther came along.

They sat next to each other for a little while, enjoying dry land and then Lakeitha said, "Why the fuck were they trying to kill us?" "I have don't know, I thought you might have some theories." Lakeitha shook her head, then said, "That was an authorised assassination." "What?" "Those were some of the best fighters in Dantez. Soldiers and Hell Hunters, I knew some of them, so did Malek. I was not their enemy and neither was he. Those guys did not assemble on their own and decide that it would be fun to kill the three of us. Somebody told them to do it." "Who?" She sighed, "There are very few people who could give that group an order to kill three active Hell Hunters. There is no way that Quentin didn't sign off on the soldiers and there is no way that Bane didn't sign off on the hunters." "You do anything to piss them off?" "No, never. So it must have been you." Luther's eyebrows shot up, "What? I didn't do anything." "Luther, my best friend just got killed. Tell me why, right now or I beat an answer out of you." Lakeitha's voice hadn't changed, she said those words in exactly the same deflated way that she had said everything else, but the words made Luther's skin go hot and a new nervousness forced him to speak. "We're going to be okay. Shante is going to fix this for us."

Lakeitha slowly turned her head to look at him. She said her next words very slowly, "Why would she do that?" Luther swallowed and then said, "Because we're in love." Lakeitha got so angry that her hands started shaking. "She's behind this." "No" "You made her angry, so she told Bane and Quentin to have you killed and me and Malek are collateral damage." "Fuck you. She would never do that to me." "Did you fuck somebody you shouldn't have fucked? Did you break up with her? Did you hit her?" Luther froze, realisation dawning on his idiot brain. "I made a mistake." She leaned closer to him, almost snarled, "What did you do?"

"It was two nights before the start of the mission and I was in Alcraze. I was drunk and hyped up. I just won my last fight, against the best fighter in Alcraze. I wanted to celebrate and sometimes after such a big fight, I get really horny." "ughhh." He shot her a look and she wanted to punch him for it. "Shante was back in Dantez and after winning a fight like that there are a lot of beautiful women who wanna night with the champ. And this girl's nipples were." "You vulgar cunt. I don't wanna hear about this bitch's nipples." He grimaced, looked ashamed, as well he should. "She was the hottest girl there, so I let her take me somewhere and after we'd been together for a while, this guy busts in the door and attacks the pair of us. I'm almost blackout drunk so a lot of it was a blur by this point, but I remember blood on my knuckles and the sound of his neck breaking. Then this slut starts telling me who she is and who I just killed. After that, I got out of Alcraze as fast as I could." "Who were they?" Luther pursed his lips and then reluctantly admitted, "The princess and prince of Alcraze." Lakeitha closed her eyes, cringed and let out a long groan.

"Lakeitha…" She punched him in the face, hard and fast. He jumped to his feet, his nose bleeding, fists raised ready for a fight. She didn't bother getting up. "You stupid bastard! Malek's blood is on your hands and soon we'll both be dead." Luther shook his head, "Shante'll call them off. She got angry when she found out what I did, but after a few days, she'll calm down and she'll remember that we're in love and she'll want me back. She's a very forgiving person." "She personally carries out several public executions a year." "That's different. Believe me, she's going to have a change of heart."

Lakeitha put her head in her hands and contemplated how fucked this situation was. "I didn't want to take you on. You were a rookie, I said you'd cause problems and you did. You've killed us." To Lakeitha he sounded like a child, "Please, we can count on Shante. Our love is real and she's going to come through for us." "You don't get it. It isn't her decision." "What?" "Because you killed King Rodriguez's son. You humiliated him and then you killed him. Those people trying to kill us are from Dantez not Alcraze. So Rodriguez is making Shante take care of the killing to prove that she doesn't condone it. If Shante doesn't get it done then Alcraze will go to war with Dantez. Even if Shante forgives you, she can't let you live."

Luther slumped, sitting back down and staring at the cliff face on the other side of the water. It was steep, very steep, with lots of little bits of stone jutting out at odd angles. The stone was grey with hints of beige. Luther noticed that the stone that was lower and closer to the running water was darker. There was a clear watermark from the rise and fall of the river. Luther looked further up, at the way that the cliff curved inwards and outwards. He wondered what kind of stone the cliff was made of. He wondered if this cliff had existed before the portals had opened.

Lakeitha watched Luther sit quietly, staring at nothing, a few tears running down his face. She wasn't a fan of Luther at the moment but she still empathised with what he was going through. Regardless they were being hunted, so they couldn't sit around moping. "Luther we need to go." She waited. He didn't move, didn't speak. "Luther" Nothing. She sighed, "Luther. We can't go back to Dantez because they'll kill us. We can't go to Alcraze, because they'll kill us and we can't stay here because they'll kill us. Our only option is to turn around and start moving until we come up with something better." Luther still didn't respond. She had really hoped that would work. She had to come up with something in the next few seconds. Something that could cut through Luther's catatonic fog.

She bent down so that she could talk into his ear. She opened her mouth, then hesitated, turned her head away and then turned back and started talking. "Luther you have ruined your own life and failed everybody. I'm the only one that's left, the only person that you have a responsibility to, that you can still help. I'm your last chance not to be a fuck up. The odds of me surviving are better with you by my side. So how about it?" Luther turned his head and looked her in the eye. "I'm sorry." "Fuck sorry. Are you ready?" Luther sniffled and wiped the tears off his face. "I'm ready."

They started walking and then Lakeitha remembered Mikey's present. She reached into her bag and pulled out the device. She pressed her thumb down on the blue arrow and held it there until it turned red. Mikey now knew she was in trouble. She didn't know what he could do, but he was a genius and he was relentless. She had faith in him like no one else.

Chapter 32

"Fan out and find everybody we're missing! If they're wounded do what you can for them or call for somebody who knows what they're doing. If they're dead then leave them until we've found all the wounded!" Akira shouted as he strode through the cooling battlefield. He saw one of his medics Vikas hunched over Roth's leg. "Hey Vikas. Get away from him. You're wasting time on this bullshit. Get out there and see if you can find somebody who's bleeding to death, I'll take care of Roth." Vikas left them and Akira started stitching up the wound. "You alright?" "Just a scratch." said Roth, through gritted teeth. "You look terrible. Try not to drop any of your face in my cut." Akira laughed painfully. Roth and Akira had been best friends for years. As he worked on Roth he shouted to the rest of his team, "Who was the last person to see Lakeitha and Luther?" "I saw Terry chasing them." shouted Kalep. "Anybody seen Terry?" "Akira!" "Yeah!" He looked around, saw Maximillian approaching.

"What have you got?" "Malek's still alive." Akira frowned, "Is that a fucking joke?" "No" "Tough bastard." He looked back down at Roth's bleeding leg, shaking his head, "Malek's still alive can you believe that shit mate? Is this his handywork?" "Lakeitha" hissed Roth. "She's a tough bitch isn't she." Roth nodded, "She get the best of you, too?" "That still remains to be seen. I might've killed her if Malek hadn't come along."

Akira finished up the stitching and then he felt something that killed his momentum, made him pause and shiver. The fear, that low, inexplicable fear that he'd felt already felt twice today. He looked into Roth's eyes, "Do you feel it?" he asked, "Yes, I'm...scared." "I think it's something about this place." Said Akira. Neither of them spoke for a few seconds as they focused on the emotion. "I feel like a rookie." whispered Akira. "I'm not afraid of anything." said Roth and Akira knew that he wasn't bullshitting. "What is this?" "I don't know, but we've got more important things to worry about. You good?" "I'm good."

He left Roth, following Maximillian towards Malek. Maximillian was covered in mud for some reason, he didn't bother asking what happened.

As he walked he shouted, "Who's still missing?" He heard a disappointing number of names. Some of them were probably still alive. "Has anybody seen Terry!?" he shouted again. "I found him." "Good, where is he?" "He's dead." "Fuck." That was a big loss, Terry was one of his best, there was nothing like having a man on your side who could sink people into the ground. He looked around, saw Kalep carrying Renn, the soldier with force field powers. He winced, he didn't want to lose two fighters with magic in the same day. "Is he dead?" Kalep shook his head, "He'll be alright." "Good"

They stopped walking and looked down at Malek. Large parts of his body were badly burnt, turned red or black. He was bleeding, he'd clearly broken a few bones and his face was bashed in. His eyes were closed but there was still a rise and fall to his chest and his breathing was surprisingly strong. He had landed in a bed of gross white fungus or some kind of plant. The stuff was slowly latching onto him in places, sticking to his cuts and burnt flesh.

"Alright kill him and move on." said Maximillian. Akira took out his knife. He stayed standing, weapon out, looking at Malek. He sheathed the knife, "We're not killing him." "You fucking what?" growled Maximillian, "We'll send him back with the wounded and the doctors in Dantez will save him." "He probably killed some of the guys we're still missing. He doesn't get away with that." Akira glanced down at Malek, "You call that getting away with it?" "He dies." "I've given my order. Get him a medic." Maximillian didn't move, he stared down at him, looking angry. Maximilian was a good few inches taller than Akira and he was a soldier, a captain in the Dantez army who wasn't used to taking orders while on a mission. Especially from a Hell Hunter. More than half of the team was made up of soldiers and even though he hadn't said anything it was obvious that Maximillian thought he should be in charge. Akira didn't have time for this.

"Maximillian, did you do this to him?" asked Akira in a calm voice, "Did you fight him one on one, did you take the hits, did you burn him and fly him up into the air? Did you drop him?" Maximillian didn't say anything, he just kept up his stare. A stare that suited his stature, his scars and his reputation; a stare that undoubtedly worked most of the time. "No, I did. I beat him. But even if you had, it wouldn't matter, because I'm in charge." Akira saw something out of the corner of his eye but waited until Maximillian started speaking before addressing it. "You..." "Hey, is he dead?" He called to the Blackmask who was approaching, carrying another Blackmask. "No but he's hurt real badly." replied the Blackmask, who he could tell was Efron, because he was the one who carried a spear. That meant that Theo was the injured one.

"Mason's dead." yelled Kalep. "That's two dead so far." Said Akira as he started walking away from Maximillian. Maximilian grabbed his shoulder and Akira whirled round and broke Maximillian's hold without hurting him. Hurting him would be a bad idea, it would humiliate him, in turn forcing him to retaliate to retain his standing among the other soldiers. Before Maximillian could do anything like hit him or start another staring contest, Akira started talking, "I was happy when I heard that you were going to be on this team. I know a lot of people who'd talked about what a great fighter you are, how good you are at this and that. I was on board with you as a soldier, not a rival. I've got people dead, people wounded and people missing. I don't need a fucking rival. I'm in charge, you do what you're told or I'll send you back with the wounded and I'll finish this mission with the professionals. This is your one and only warning. I'm going to walk away now and take care of my team and if you grab me again, I'll murder you."

He left Maximillian and checked on the wounded who had all been gathered together. Dominic was gingerly removing the damaged helmet from Theo's head. He had clearly been punched a lot, judging by the dents the metal studs had created. The mask came off. Theo was missing teeth, his cheekbones had been pulverised, his eyes were swollen, there was blood everywhere. With the mask off he could hear his raspy breathing. "He's going back to Dantez." said Akira and then moved on to Renn, who was still unconscious but would be alright to continue the mission. He knew Roth's cut hadn't been too deep and he'd be fit to carry on.

Next to Roth was James, he was a soldier. He was a really funny guy. During the two day journey they'd taken to get here James had made them all laugh many times. Somebody had broken his jaw and one of his arms. It looked like they weren't going to have his hilarious company for the rest of the mission. "James is going back to Dantez as well." He turned around and saw Efron the Blackmask carrying Clara over. It hurt him, seeing Clara like that. She'd been his girlfriend for a few months a few years ago. He still had a soft spot for her. They'd even shared a charged moment yesterday and he had wanted to kiss her. Her jaw had been broken as well. It had clearly been done by a mace, Malek's mace. He pushed that thought aside before it could lead to something dangerous.

"I found her next to Angus." Said Efron, "Angus is dead?" "They cut his head off." Akira sighed, "This fucking clusterfuck. Well nobody said it would be easy. She's going back to Dantez." He went over the damage in his head. Three dead, Three going back to Dantez, not including Malek. Who was still missing? Darrius and Regus were missing, who else? He couldn't think of anybody else. "Who's still missing?!" He shouted. "Regus!" Somebody called, "Angus!" called somebody else. "No Angus is dead!" replied Akira. There was a heavy silence from the person who had called Angus's name. "Darrius!" Maximillian shouted. Alright, just two left. He looked around and was glad to see that nobody was standing around doing nothing. Everybody who was able was either taking care of the wounded or out searching for the missing.

Maximillian called from a distance, "Regus is dead." "I found part of his leg. At least, I think it's his."

He looked to Roth, "How you feeling?" "I'm alright, I got some pain relief in me." "Can you walk?" Resting his weight against a tree Roth slowly got up to his feet and then walked over to Akira. He was sweating a lot and limping a little, but he'd be alright and his stitches would hold, Akira knew he had done a good job on them. "I need you to go and track Luther and Lakeitha, figure out which way they're going." Roth winced, "I don't know, I'm not feeling great about that." "I'm sorry but you're our best tracker by far right now." "What about Darrius?" "Darrius is missing." Roth paused, "Theo's pretty good." Akira pointed over at Theo's swollen red face. "Ah, okay I'll do it, but I'm going to need somebody to come with me, make up for this leg if I get in any trouble." Akira nodded, "Maximillian you're going with Roth to track Luther and Lakeitha. If you find them, don't attack, just watch where they go and then come back here." Maximilian went along without complaint, he was a good soldier in spite of his ego.

Akira turned around to the rest of his men. His two medics, Dominic and Vikas were working on the wounded, Renn was still unconscious and both Kalep and Efron were out looking for Darrius. Everyone was doing what they were supposed to be doing. He had a moment to think, but he also knew that he couldn't be seen to stand around doing nothing at a time like this, so he went over to Dominic who was working on Clara. "Dominic I'll take it from here, Malek needs some help. Do what you can to keep him alive." "Malek?" Asked Dominic, clear disapproval in his voice. "Yes, Malek. Get the fuck out of my face and help him." He did what he could to help Clara out, which wasn't much. She already had a bandage wrapped around her head, holding her broken jaw in place. Akira had never wired a broken jaw before and he wasn't about to try it now. He wiped the blood from her mouth and gave her some more painkillers.

As he helped his ex-girlfriend out, he thought about who he was going to send back with the wounded. He had four wounded at the moment, Clara, James, Theo and Malek. He knew Darrius was probably dead at this point, so he worked with that assumption. There were eight healthy people left. Himself, Maximillian, Renn, Roth, Kalep, Efron and the two medics Dominic and Vikas. He was definitely going to send Vikas back to take care of the wounded, but Dominic had the magical power of telepathy. He could only communicate with a handful of other telepaths but it was very useful on a mission like this as a means of communicating back to Dantez from any place in the wild. He had to keep Dominic with him. He also wanted Roth by his side. Efron was invaluable as a warrior and his special training and Blackmask suit made him extremely skilled at stealthy attacks in the middle of the night. He needed Maximillian. Renn's forcefield magic and Kalep's shockwave magic were very effective as well, he didn't want to give them up.

Shit, this was a problem. He didn't want to give any of them up. The truth was, his most expendable people were dead or injured. Maybe he'd get lucky and Darrius would still be alive and then he could send him back with the wounded. But if Darrius was dead, then he needed to come up with a new plan. All of his wounded looked bad, they'd all been hit a lot in the head, which would hurt their balance and ability to stay awake and focused. Maybe Clara had gotten off most lightly and her jaw was fucked to pieces. He didn't feel great about any of them having to walk all the way back to Dantez. But they only had two stretchers, only one man to carry those stretchers and Malek, who needed the stretcher more than any of them.

He had an idea. He could leave Vikas and the wounded here and call for more medics and fighters to come from Dantez and then take them all back. All Vikas would have to do is protect them and keep them alive for two days. Two days. Plus two days travel back to Dantez. They'd have to survive out in the wild for four days. Malek would never make it. And it was a real risk for the others. Then he had another idea.

"Dominic" he called over to the medic who was working on Malek. "I need you to see if you can get in touch with any other telepaths who are currently on missions and are closer to us than Dantez. Tell them that they have to drop everything and come here to take our wounded back to Dantez. It's a top priority, they can ask Bane or Quintin for approval, they will back us up."

"Should I do that now or should I finish helping our enemy first?" asked Dominic sarcastically, "A bit less of the smart mouth dickhead. Get it done."

Dominic sat down, closed his eyes and didn't move or make a sound for five minutes. As he did his thing Kalep came back. "Darrius is dead." Akira sighed. "Alright then, you and Efron and Renn, if you can wake him up, should go bring in all the dead, pile them over there. If Roth finds the targets then we go after them now; otherwise we'll set up camp and then burn the dead first thing in the morning." "What about the wounded?" asked Kalep, "Dominic's working on it."

Dominic found a group of three Hell Hunters who could get to them just after dawn the next day. Then Dominic got in touch with a telepath in Dantez who told Bane and Quentin that their first attempt had been a failure. They had four machine guns with a little ammo left. He decided to give half of them to this other group of Hell Hunters to protect the wounded. With all that sorted, he ran through another mental inventory of supplies and problems before finally allowing himself to sit down and have his own face treated by Vikas.

Chapter 33

Lakeitha and Luther had been moving for half an hour before they finally stopped to tend to their injuries. The sun was about to set so this was their last chance to do it in daylight. They applied some blood clotting powder and bandages and sewed up a few of their worst cuts. Lakeitha had been hit in the mouth quite a lot, she lost teeth but her jaw thankfully wasn't broken. They both had some broken ribs that were painful and would slow them down, but they hadn't punctured any organs and would heal on their own in time. They took as many painkillers as they could without making them sleepy or hurting their coordination.

Lakeitha started moving again and Luther followed her asking, "What's the plan for tonight." "No fires." "Yeah, I'd guessed that wouldn't be safe but what about sleep." Lakeitha sounded exhausted as she spoke, "We walk till we drop. They've got Blackmasks with them, they're likely to come after us in the night. We can't afford to sleep." "They'd have to find us first, they can't track us past the river." Lakeitha scowled, "Of course they can. Just because we didn't leave any tracks doesn't mean that they can't find us." "How come?" "Tracking is about more than just footprints. When they figure out that we jumped into the river, they're going to check on all of the riverbanks that we could have climbed ashore on. When they do that, they'll find the one we used in no time, they'll see the little drops of blood we left behind and follow them to the footprints in the mud and follow them to us and kill us in our sleep. That's if they're feeling merciful, which they won't be after we killed so many of them." Luther groaned, "Okay, I get it. But we need a plan, what are we gonna do, walk all night and all day and never sleep?" "I once went fifty-five hours without sleep." "Were you this badly injured?" Lakeitha didn't answer. "I'll take that as a no. Great, just great." "Luther, sleeping means dying. So we avoid sleeping until that changes." "I know. I know."

Luther's thoughts had gotten slow and numb, the tiredness was seeping away at his brain. He wondered if Lakeitha thought he was being whiny, he didn't want to be whiny. He wanted to sleep. He felt himself start to fall asleep. He pinched an uninjured part of his face, harder and harder until the pain woke him up.

Chapter 32

It had failed. She had tried to kill the man she loved and she had failed. She thought about him, walking through the trees, bleeding and hurt. Was he confused? Had he realised that she must be behind the attack. Until now she hadn't considered that he would ever know it was her. It had felt like he had died the moment she gave the order, instant and painless. But he was still alive and this was going to be drawn out torturously. He was going to suffer so much.

Quentin was still talking but she hadn't heard anything he'd said. She made an effort to focus on the discussion. "They're staying put with the wounded until morning, then another group of Hell Hunters is going to come and take the wounded back here, while they go after the targets." Shante grimaced impatiently, "Can't they finish this tonight?" Bane shook his head, "They've lost them, the sun's already gone down. They're very unlikely to find them tonight. Akira made the right call, taking care of his men." "Malek" said Shante. Neither of them said anything, "Do you approve of Akira's decision?"

Quentin refrained from answering the question, just as Shante had expected him to. Akira and Malek were both Bane's men. After a moment where Shante could see Bane carefully choosing his words; he nodded his head. "Malek wasn't the main target and he's a good man. If it's possible to bring him back alive, then I support it." "Will he try to take revenge on us when he gets back here?" "Not in his condition. They burned him and broke him, it's a miracle he's still alive." "But he is and he'll heal and it will take a long, long time. He'll spend months in a hospital bed thinking about nothing but revenge. He will not forget this. Am I wrong Quentin?" Quentin shook his head, "He'll kill us all if he ever gets the chance." "Then why are we giving him that chance?" She said, her eyes flicking to Bane, "Because he deserves it. Because he's a good man and a great hunter. If I can spare him, then I owe him that." "I respect your dedication to your hunters, but he's a threat that I can't let inside of Dantez." "He won't be a threat for a long time." "He'll be a threat the day he speaks and tells people what happened to him. Is he friends with any other Hell Hunters or soldiers or anybody who might get angry at the idea that we tried to kill our own people?"

"I have a suggestion." Said Quentin, "Yes?" "We could keep him separated from everybody else. Guarded twenty four seven by reliable people. We tell his friends he died on a mission." "You want him to be a prisoner?" asked Bane. "No, not a prisoner. Just a secret, until he's recovered. Then we give him a choice. He can choose to be killed or he can choose to be sent out into the wild, for the rest of his life. I know a little about Malek. I know he spends more time in the wild than anyone else. He's born for it. He could survive for months, even years on his own.

But he'll never be allowed back into Dantez. He'll live but he can't possibly threaten us by roaming free in the city."

Shante considered it. To her being banished in the wild for the rest of her life was a fate worse than death, but Malek was built different. For him, it was the best future he could be allowed to live, but she wasn't sure if she wanted to give it to him, rather than just ordering Akira to kill him now. She didn't care all that much about Malek's life, but Bane did and so did Akira. This mercy meant something to them and she needed them. She had ordered them to betray their own people, something they'd never done before.

"Okay. We'll do it. But, If Malek comes back after his exile, for any reason, you kill him." Bane nodded.

"Now that's sorted, we need to discuss Vincent. What are we going to tell him?" asked Shante. "I don't think that we should tell him that our team failed. We keep Vincent and King Rodriguez thinking that they haven't found the targets yet. Until they kill them and then we tell Vincent that the mission was a success. They don't need to know anything else." Shante made a face, "Is that all you got? Lie to them indefinitely. Are we meant to tell Vincent that there's been no progress, every day? He'll get suspicious and then he'll tell Rodriguez his suspicions and right now there is nothing that Rodriguez won't do if he feels like we're fucking him."

"You want to tell him the truth?" asked Bane. "Well, I wouldn't go that far. He doesn't need to know just yet, but I don't know, Vincent's ultimatum runs out at dawn two days from now. We really don't have much time to work with. If we don't make the deadline, then we tell Vincent that there has been some trouble, some of our men are dead and the rest are still on the job. Then we just hope that they take the news well and decide to give us more time." "You think he won't let us finish the job?" asked Quentin. Shante shook her head, "Eventually he'll get sick of waiting and he'll send an army to walk the earth killing everything that they come across until they cut Luther to pieces. And after that, they'll come here." She glanced at Bane, "Make sure Akira understands that."

Chapter 33

They'd been walking for a while, Lakeitha wasn't sure how long. Moving through the trees, in the dark, faintly illuminated by the kaleidoscope of distant lights in the sky. She was very tired. Even her breathing sounded tired. Listening to her own tired breathing made her even more tired. As she breathed she walked and as she walked, she started to talk. At first she talked just to keep herself awake, then after a while she started talking about important things. "I killed Mason and that magic guy who sunk us into the ground. How many did you get?" "I killed one guy." Said Luther, his voice sounded even more exhausted when he admitted that. "Do you know how many Malek got?" "No. I didn't see him kill anybody. I did see him mace this one girl. She didn't die but he really messed her up." "You think she won't be able to keep coming after us?" "I dunno, she might be able to if she holds her face together with one hand the entire time." "You hurt anybody that badly?" "Maybe. I beat up this one Blackmask." "You beat up a Blackmask?" "I punched him a lot." "Cool. I injured one guy." "Just one?" "Well I fucked up Akira as well, badly and then Malek hurt him even more. But he'll keep coming after us. Akira's different. There's only two ways that we could stop him hunting us. We kill him or we take out his legs." "So that's three dead and three injured. Oh and there was that guy who got taken down by those monsters that jumped out of the ground. You think he's still alive." "No I don't." "It's safe to assume that Malek got at least one kill right?" Lakeitha shook her head, "He probably did, but we can't afford to make assumptions. All we know is that we've got four dead and three wounded. So their number is down by seven."

"And what is their number? I have no idea how many of them there were when they first attacked." "More than a dozen." Said Lakeitha. "Fourteen, fifteen, sixteen, maybe seventeen. No more than seventeen." "So there could be as many as ten people after us?" "No, even if there were seventeen, a few of them will have to take care of the wounded." "Meaning if they had fourteen to start, there might only be four of them still coming after us. Maybe even less, if Malek killed or injured more of them, which we both know he must have." "Maybe, if we're very lucky. But I think it's more likely that we have five to eight people on our tail." "Oh" Sighed Luther.

Lakeitha's mood suddenly improved when she saw a gaffa bush. She practically skipped over to it and started tearing off the leaves. "This stuff is like cocaine." She said to Luther. "What's cocaine?" "You should read more." She said with a grin on her face. "It'll keep us awake. Give us energy for hours." "Really." She shook her head happily, "We're not getting murdered tonight." She handed a bunch of them to Luther. "They taste pretty good if you crush them up and make tea. But we can't risk the time or the exposure of making a fire, so we have to eat them." "How do they taste as leaves?" "Bad" "How…" "Very" Luther sighed.

Lakeitha shoved two handfuls of leaves into her mouth and started chewing. With each bite she released a foul acidic liquid from the leaves. It stung like she was eating live bees. She forced it down with some water.

She watched Luther, whose neck was clenched, face was red and eyes were watering. He gagged, swallowed, gagged again, took a swig of water, chewed, gagged and then let out a gag that propelled itself into a gruesome burp. As she watched him struggle to keep the leaves down, the world around her became heightened, it became realer and bigger and she felt like climbing a tree. All the aches and pains that bullied her body disappeared.

A second later a big grin hopped onto Luther's face. Those leaves kept them going strong and ecstatic for another hour and a half. Then they started slowing down again. The stiffness and soreness returned and the headaches were worse than ever. They still had a little energy left but they once again felt like they were about to topple over, asleep before they hit the ground.

Luther had bumped into dozens of trees in the dark. Lakeitha had by some magic managed to avoid hitting a single one, even though she was walking right in front of him. The trees around them thinned out again, giving way to stony ground and wide open space. Finally he had conquered the odyssey of the rude trees.

They kept walking for fifteen minutes or so before their path was blocked by a deep gorge, like the one they had jumped down the previous day only narrower and deeper. They couldn't tell how deep. In the dead of night it was just a black void at their feet. The other side of the gorge was about ten meters away; at the top of a jagged cliff. Lakeitha looked to the left, and then to the right. The gorge went on and on. It was going to take them a while to walk around it.

Lakeitha took out her binoculars and looked off to the right for a few seconds and then started walking. "Hey, what are we going to do?" asked Luther as he trudged after her. "We're walking on stone." said Lakeitha. Luther frowned, "And...?" "We're not leaving any footprints." Luther's drained brain realised that this was important but he was too tired to figure out what Lakeitha's point was, so he just waited for her to tell him. This passive approach briefly made him feel a little stupid, but he was too tired to worry about whether or not he was a big old dummy. "They've got trackers in their group, who will easily be able to follow us up until the point that the ground turns from dirt to stone. Then it'll get a lot harder for them. They'll have to scour the ground for any sign of us. And that's why we're walking this way, where there are patches of dirt here and there, rather than the other way, which is all stone."

"Wait, what. But we're going to leave footprints. We should go the other way so that we'll be untrackable." Lakeitha shook her head, "No, we're leaving footprints on purpose. When the hunters get here they'll see the footprints and they'll follow them." She pointed ahead. "See there, the patches of dirt stop and it's just stone for mmm... a long way. How far do you reckon until the dirt crops up again?"

She handed him her binoculars. The pinwheel, the great streak and the many moons and stars gave off a bit of light but it was still dark. The stone was grey and the dirt was brown with a yellow tinge. The stone ran on, pure and grey until it met the treeline far ahead. "There's no more dirt." he said, not understanding why it mattered. "It's all stone. There might be a few tiny little patches, but it's basically all stone. So they won't notice that our footprints disappear suddenly." Luther nodded, "Alright I like it. So we turn back after we reach the end of the dirt and hopscotch in the other direction?" Lakeitha winced, "Not exactly." "What do you mean? How else are we going to give them the slip?" Lakeitha raised her arm and pointed at the massive gorge to the left.

Luther glared at her. She shrugged, "That's the price of being a badass." "I can't make that jump." "No, not that jump. But a little further ahead, it gets thinner." Luther's gaze traced along the crack in the ground. "It doesn't get much thinner." "Ah true. But it's doable." "Who are you Jackie Chan?" "Who's that?" Luther looked at the gaping crevice and sighed, "Some guy from history. He was good at jumping." "huh"

They carried on walking until they reached the narrowest point. He peered over the edge. A death drop. He turned back to her and asked, not even trying to keep the fear out of his voice, "Lakeitha are you sure we have to do this? We're both really badly hurt. We need sleep. We can barely walk. We could both die and if you go first and you die, then it's going to be really hard for me to attempt it after that." Lakeitha patted him on the shoulder, "We'll jump at the same time." "Aren't you going to address the other stuff." "I don't see any point. Now, I reckon that those trees are four miles away. It will take them roughly an hour twenty to walk that far. Then they realise what we did, which will take a while because tracking footprints in the dark is harder than in the day. Then they take another hour twenty just to get back to this spot. Then they have to figure out that we jumped rather than backtracking like you wanted to. Fifteen minutes if they're smart, which they are. Then they jump over and try to figure out which way we went, which will be hard for them, because it's all stone on the other side as well. After we jump we walk for a few more miles to be safe and then we sleep for four glorious hours."

Desire is a funny thing. For years he'd had two things on his mind, two things he craved every day. Winning fights and fucking Shante. Every day he'd had sex with a bodacious woman who he loved more than oxygen and every few weeks he'd won a fight. He'd had everything he ever wanted on a regular basis. And yet, at this moment he wanted sleep more than he'd ever wanted love or sex or victory. This jump was the price he had to pay to sleep. "Same time" Lakeitha nodded, "Same time"

They took off their bags and hurled them over the gorge to lighten the load. Then they did the same with all their weapons.

As they walked away from the crevice, preparing their run up; Lakeitha felt like every step made her calmer and readier. She didn't think about death or injury or her making it but Luther falling and leaving her with the guilt of talking Luther into his own death, all she thought about was her many hours of training back in Dantez. But she didn't focus on the agony, the struggle, the failure and frustration; all those details were glazed over and she just felt the triumph, the rush of endorphins and the proof that she could do it. Her body could be counted on to meet any occasion. She had earned her invulnerability.

She turned around and shared a look with Luther. "Before we jump, do you want a hug?" Luther hesitated for a moment and then raised his arms. She laughed and shoved him, "I can't believe you wanted to hug me." Luther looked scorned for a moment and then he burst out laughing. "Wuss." "Evil bitch." He shook his head, still laughing. "Let's do this shit." They started running.

They ate up the ground, their minds consumed by acceleration until they were within five meters of the edge and then all they cared about was how close they were to jumping. No fears or instincts, just step after step of mounting anticipation.

They launched themselves over the gorge, soaring through the air, raising their legs up in front of them. Not looking down, but still feeling the oblivion beneath them.

She was going to make it. She was going to make it. She saw Luther start to dip down and realised that he wasn't going to make it. Her eyes widened and then her feet hit the ground and she skidded forward, her butt hitting the stone and then her back following it.

Luther's feet didn't make it over the edge. They hit the cliff just below the edge and he thought he was dead, then his knees bent over the top and his body kept moving forwards. He landed hard on the other side, dragged his feet away from the chasm and jumped up, "WOOOOOH!" He wrapped Lakeitha in a hug and they jumped up and down. She laughed even when she lost her footing and fell backwards, Luther's arms still wrapped around her. The weight of him knocked the wind out of Lakeitha.

He rolled off her, punching and kicking at the air. It felt good to be alive.

Chapter 34

Mikey woke up from a long warm sleep after spending a good while wavering, half awake but in no hurry to get up. He sat up on his bed, glanced over at the table and noticed that the arrow on the beacon had turned red. "Fuuuck"

He struggled into his clothes as fast as he could and limped out the front door with his staff. It looked to be just after dawn and there were a lot of people walking around the street. He spent a full minute scurrying his way through the hustle and bustle before he questioned where he was going. Instinctively he had been following the arrow on the beacon but there was no way he could walk out into the wild and find Lakeitha himself. He had to tell somebody. Gideon, it had to be Gideon. He was his friend as well as Lakeitha's, he was a Hell Hunter and he lived nearby. He knew Gideon was in Dantez, he hadn't been on a mission since he broke his arm a couple of weeks ago.

He hurried to Gideon's as fast as he could, leaning heavily on his wooden staff. Somebody bumped into him by accident and knocked him over. He landed on his side, it hurt and getting back up was infuriatingly difficult. The guy who'd knocked him over helped him up and put the staff back in his hand. He kicked off again. Gideon only lived five minutes away but it had been a long time since he'd walked for that long.

He reached the house, sweating hard and banging on the door with the head of his staff. He heard Gideon grumble from the otherside, "I'm coming, I'm coming." He opened the door, looking pissy about being woken up, then his eyes widened. "Mikey what are you doing here?" "Lakeitha's in trouble." Gideon instantly switched from a leisurely off duty Hell Hunter into a sharp survivalist. "What happened? Is she back from the mission already?" "No, she sent me a distress signal." "What?" "I invented a device that lets her alert me if she's in trouble." "Do you know what kind of trouble? Can you communicate with her?" Mikey shook his head, "It can't do that, it's just a prototype, this is the first time she's ever used it."

"All you know is that she's in trouble. Is that it?" "No, it also points me in her direction." He pulled the device out of his pocket and showed it to Gideon. They both looked down at the wavering red arrow. "This arrow is always pointing at her?" "Right." Gideon paused and then did something very out of character. He wrapped Mikey in a tight hug, "This thing is going to save so many lives." Veneration was for people whose sisters were safe, Mikey didn't have time for it. "You have to go tell Bane, right now and get some people out looking for her." "I'm on it. Is there anything else that thing can do to help us?" "Yeah if she dies the light will go out." Gideon instinctively looked back down at the metal disc, just to check that the arrow was still glowing red.

Gideon knew that Bane started his days early and spent most of his time at the Hell Hunter compound. Mikey couldn't walk that far and Gideon only had one bike, not that Mikey was fit enough to ride one. Mikey gave the beacon to Gideon and Gideon raced across Dantez on his bike, reaching the training camp in record time. He ran towards Bane's office, asking everyone he passed if they knew where he was. One of the rookies he'd been training since he got injured turned him around and sent him over to the sword training area. He found Bane beating the shit out of a rookie with a wooden practice sword. "Bane! Hey Bane, I need to talk to you." Bane immediately abandoned the sword fight, recognising Gideon's urgency.

"What's going on?" "Bane. It's Lakeitha. She's in trouble, we need to send her help." Bane paused and then sighed, shaking his head. "It's too late, Gideon. I just found out this morning. She's dead, so are Malek and Luther, the rookie." "What?" Gideon said, confused. "Their bodies were found by some other Hell Hunters. They had a telepath with them. It's horrible, but we've lost them. There'll never be another pair like Malek and Lakeitha." Gideon looked at Bane. Utterly puzzled, trying to make sense of what Bane was saying and then he understood. Part of it at least. He understood that Bane was lying about Lakeitha being dead, so he had to be up to something. He had to be the reason that Lakeitha was in danger. Gideon looked shocked and sad, doing his best to hide his rage at the traitor in front of him. "I better go tell her brother." Bane nodded.

He went back to his house, where Mikey was waiting. "Is it sorted?" asked Mikey hopefully. "No." Mikey's whole body seemed to clench, "Why not?" "I talked to Bane. He told me that all three of them are dead." "What?" "He's lying. He has to be, he says that some other hunters found the bodies. But if Lakeitha's definitely still alive then there's no way that's true. You're one hundred percent sure that your machines haven't malfunctioned." Mikey scowled, "There's no fuckin way I'd give my sister a tool that didn't work. She's alive." "Then Bane's trying to cover something up." "He's trying to kill her isn't he. That bastard is trying to kill my sister." Gideon hesitated. "Yeah I think so."

Mikey sat down in one of Gideon's chairs. His eyes filled with an angry focus that made him look to Gideon like a predator with a hundred teeth, lying in the jungle, itching to sink his teeth into something. "If Bane's trying to have them killed, then he must have sent other Hell Hunters to do it." Something dawned on Gideon, "Two days ago a lot of Hell Hunters disappeared. They were around the day before, then in the morning they were gone, no word of warning." "That's not normal is it." "No, we always get at least a day's notice before a mission. This was a last minute thing and secret. They left two days ago, then they attacked Lakeitha, Malek and Luther early this morning." "Or maybe last night. I go to bed around seven." "Okay. I can't remember everybody who was on that team but I know that Akira and Roth were two of them." "I don't really know those guys. Do you think they'd betray other Hell Hunters?" "There isn't a creature on this earth that the pair of them wouldn't kill if Bane told them to."

"We need to find out who else Bane sent." "I'll go round The Stronghold, the guys there will remember and there'll be no chance of running into Bane. He's an alcoholic, never sets foot in the place." Gideon paused, "I just can't think why Bane would do this. He's got no reason to turn on Lakeitha and Malek." "Why don't we ask him." said Mikey, a hard edge to his words. "Ask him?" "We grab him, tie him up and hurt him until he explains himself and then we make him call off the attack." "And then what, we kill him?" Mikey shrugged, then nodded.

Gideon had hated Bane for the last fifteen minutes, but this idea made him squirm. Bane was his friend, his mentor and there were a lot of professional killers who would protect or avenge him. "I don't want to do that." "What's the alternative?" Asked Mikey, "Never mind, I'll tell you the alternative. You, all on your own, with only one arm, go out into the wild with the beacon in your hand and follow the arrow for days, until you either get killed by a monster or by Bane's hunters. You can't save Lakeitha alone and there isn't a single Hell Hunter who we can trust to take our side over Bane's. Going after him is our only chance."

Gideon wondered if Malek and Lakeitha would do the same for him; then he scolded himself for even questioning that. Of course they would. That was the deal; every time they left the walls of the city they knew that they would put their life on the line for their partner. That meant really putting their life on the line, not just fighting a creature that was dangerous. It meant that, given the choice between walking away and facing near certain death, they always took the latter.

It was a pact that he sometimes lived up to with reluctance. But he always did it and he was always proud to do it. Especially when it came to friends like Lakeitha and Malek.

Bane and Akira and Roth and the rest of them, had broken that deal. Fuck em all.

Chapter 35

After four hours Lakeitha and Luther woke up in a dry hard cave, pulled off their blankets, pissed and started walking. It was just after dawn. They chewed dry rations and drank water. They'd lost what was left of the miniature pink skinned bull. There had been so much going on that neither of them could remember at what point they'd dropped the precious meat. The sleep had helped but they both had terrible headaches and weren't the least bit refreshed.

Luther would have stayed asleep for a full day, but Lakeitha had a disciplined internal clock that allowed her to wake herself up, with reasonable accuracy, when she needed to move on.

They hadn't walked a mile before Lakeitha realised that they couldn't keep this up. "We need more sleep." "What was that?" "I said we need more sleep. Like this we won't be able to run or fight. We need at least a couple more hours if we're going to make it through the day." "You think it's safe to stop here?" "Maybe. We're still on stone so we'll be hard to track. We just need to find another cave or a hovel or somewhere we can hide away."

They stopped at the first spot they found. A curving pothole almost two meters wide. They climbed in, going five meters deep before the tunnel became level. They lay side by side in the dark and fell asleep.

Luther was woken up by a horrible pain all over his head and neck. He hollered and scrambled around in the dark. His knee slammed into Lakeitha's back and then he crawled over her. She was making a fuss as well. They felt around in the dark trying to get out of the tunnel. The pain was so fierce. There were things on him, stinging him unbearably. He grabbed a hold of one of them, on his cheek and tried to pull it off. It held on, the pain getting worse for two or three seconds before he was finally able to tear it off. It was almost as big as his hand, squishy but strong. It barely moved inside of his hand. He dropped it and carried on crawling up the pitch black tunnel. It was a lot harder going up than down. After a while it got light enough that he could see again. He couldn't get a good look at what was hanging from his neck and face, but he could see that they were big and red. "Aghghh!" He gargled as he tore one from his neck. It looked like a big red slug, with row after row of tiny little teeth. He dropped it and pulled out another one and another one, panting and hissing. They had turned him into a frantic mess. Lakeitha crawled up past him and over the edge of the tunnel. Tears running down his face he followed her.

Lakeitha was hopping around as she tried to rip them off her. After she pulled two off and said cuntfuck five hundred times, she had an idea. "Hey Luther, you do mine and I'll do yours." Luther stumbled over to her and they stood face to face, ripping the little monsters from the other person's skin. The ones that were dug into hair were the easiest to pull free. When they were finished they had big red circles all over their heads and necks. Blood trickled from them.

They looked grimly at each other. Lakeitha reckoned that they had gotten about an hour and a half of sleep. It would have to do.

They got in a solid twenty seconds of walking before the hard stone ground in front of them cracked open and a giant purple monster climbed out. It had a huge head on top of its oily eight storey tall body. Its hungry eyes focused on them, as it panted with anticipation. There were dozens of smaller mouths up and down its body and all of them were doing the same thing.

Luther licked his lips. It was twenty meters away from them and if either of them made a move it would cover that distance in no time. "I'll do it." he whispered. The towering monster inched forwards and Luther snatched his World Saver Hand Cannon from its holster and fired dead centre at its torso. The hefty bullet tore its way deep into the monster's body until the barbed wire stopped it in place and the poison got to work.

The monster fell forwards, shaking the earth. It started screaming from its dozens of mouths. It was down but not dead, it would take more than a minute for it to die from poison and blood loss. Lakeitha wanted to put it out of its misery, but she couldn't afford to waste their last bullet and there was no way she was going to risk getting close enough to kill it with her sword.

Luther started walking, giving the monster a wide berth. Lakeitha followed him. "It never fucking stops." Said Luther, in a defeated voice. "Course it does. Today's the day it stops for big boy over there." "We're going to die out here aren't we." "You know Luther. When we first met you were an egotistical, aggressive, dickhead." "And?" "Since then you've revealed a tender, sensitive, weak side to yourself. You remind me of an old woman, with no redeeming features." Luther couldn't help it, he laughed.

Chapter 36

After jumping off the cliff and crossing the river Akira and his team had made good time tracking Luther and Lakeitha. They had a whole new attitude towards their quarry. Before the battle there'd been a tinge of unspoken shame at what they were doing and a desire to finish it quickly and painlessly. Then five of their men died and they were told for the first time that the purpose of their mission was to prevent a war. Now they all wanted blood.

They didn't have any serious monster attacks, they never lost the trial, it all went fine. And then the fear returned. This time they all acknowledged it to each other, these men were rock solid but they were all affected and he could tell that it was getting to some of them, especially Renn and Kalep. They swapped theories of what it could be, the most popular one being that it was some kind of magical atmosphere that had recently surrounded patches of this area. But they'd covered a lot of ground, so if that was the answer, then it had to be massive.

They broke through the vegetation and then wasted almost three hours trying to track their targets across stone, before Roth realised that they'd been duped.

"You sure?" asked Akira, "Yes. It's the only thing that makes sense and it's a smart move. Kinda thing Lakeitha would think of. This stretch here is the only part that's narrow enough to jump." They both knew that there was no way Roth could make the jump after getting stabbed in the leg yesterday. "Okay, we need to figure something out here. Roth definitely can't jump this far." "Could you fly him over?" asked Dominic, "Oh there's a thought. Hey Roth, what are your feelings about third degree burns?" "On myself or other people?" "Yourself." "Not a fan." "Yeah, not a fan. Fuck's sake Dominic, you're the medic. You're not supposed to suggest that I set members of the team on fire." Dominic looked like he wanted to swear at him or punch him or put an arrow through him, but he held himself back. Not a man used to being put down.

"Do the rest of you think you could make it?" He asked his team. They all nodded, some of them more hesitantly than others. Nobody wanted to be the first to back down. This was a death drop, it was no time for egos. "Renn and Efron, you just got your asses kicked. I'm not sure I want you taking the chance." Efron's face was blank as always but his posture smacked of protest and Renn had a look on his face like he was about to talk back. Akira raised his hand for silence. "I've got an idea. Maximillian you and me are going over, then I'll chuck a length of rope back and Roth will climb along it. Does everybody think they could handle that? Good. Who's got rope?" "I do." said Roth.

Akira went over to Roth as he opened up his bag. "Good plan." "Thanks. It was either that or me and the captain pick you up and swing you over by your arms and legs." "That sounds fun. I liked it when you silenced Renn and Efron. Not many people get to make a Blackmask their bitch." Akira chuckled, "He's not so scary during the day. But when you bump into him in the dead of night on your way to take a piss." "You piss yourself." "Maybe you do, but I held it in." "Here's your rope dickhead."

He stepped away from Roth and turned his order giving voice back on, "Alright, everybody throw your bags and weapons over when it's your turn to cross. Efron and Kalep will hold the rope from this side, while Roth and Renn cross, then I'll fly back over and take the rope while Efron crosses. That leaves Dominic and Kalep. Do you guys want to take the rope or jump?" "Fuck you." said Dominic, "Okay, Dominic's jumping. Kalep?" Kalep took a moment of pause and then said, "I'll take the rope." "Pussy" said Roth loudly between coughs. Everybody laughed, even the ones who didn't think it was funny. There hadn't been enough laughter since Lakeitha beat James half to death.

The plan worked.

"Which way did they go?" Renn asked Roth after they'd all spent five minutes watching him wander around the valley looking for signs of their targets. "I don't know, it's stone in all directions and they didn't leave any tracks." Akira gave Roth a reassuring look, knowing how frustrated he could get when his tracking skills let him down. "Let's split up into three groups. Group one will be Maximillian, Renn and Dominic. You'll go that way. Group two will be me and Roth, we'll go this way. And then group three will be Efron and Kalep. You'll go that way. If you don't find anything then meet back here in an hour. If any group hasn't made it back here in an hour, that either means that group is in trouble or on the trail of the targets. Either way we go looking for them. And if you are the lucky team that finds their trail, remember to put down some fucking markers so the rest of us can have an easy time following you."

Akira and Roth found a giant purple monster lying dead between a huge hole in the ground and a little pile of red parasites roughly five inches in length, also dead. Roth had a grin on his face, "Don't you just fucking love dead giants." Akira nodded, he had a point, there was nothing like it. "This was probably them." Said Akira, "World Saver I reckon. How fresh is it?" "Judging by how much of it's already been eaten away by scavengers I'd say they came through here bout three hours ago."

Akira took out his roll of markers and dropped one on the ground beside the dead giant. The markers were little adhesive discs that could stick to stone, wood and soil. They came in yellow, red and blue, so that they would stand out against any surface.

The pair of them carried on after Luther and Lakeitha.

Chapter 37

Shante didn't want to see the head of the Grand Scrapers, the head of the police or the people in charge of water, food and plumbing and street maintenance and building maintenance and on and on and on. Shante had given up on all of her duties as The Guardian of Dantez that weren't centred around killing Luther and Lakeitha. She'd completely ignored the people that she used to speak to for hours every day, hoping that they would hold the city together on their own. She only wanted to speak to Bane and Quentin.

She had experienced a brief and conflicted moment of delight when she heard a knocking on the door to her private living room and opened it to see Bane. They didn't have a meeting scheduled, so she had briefly assumed that he had run in to tell her that the mission was over. But it wasn't and that disappointment deflated her. She slumped into an armchair as he spoke.

"Gideon came to me this morning to ask about Luther and the others. He was worried about them, which is odd. I said that they were all dead and I'd been on my way to tell him." "Why?" Bane winced, "He put me on the spot and I thought that would get him to spot asking questions. I know it was risky but it should work as long as our team does actually manage to complete the mission." "Fair enough" Said Shante with a shrug, "Is that all?" "No, I just found out that Gideon was asking around The Stronghold." "The Stronghold is open in the morning?" "A lot of the retired guys are alcoholics." "Right…can you get the point please Bane." "He was asking which Hell Hunters and soldiers left for the mission two days ago." Shante frowned, "Really." "I think he might suspect that we're trying to have his friends killed." "How the fuck could he know that?" "I don't know. There's no reason why he should think that there's anything going on."

Shante thought for a moment, "It's only Gideon who suspects?" "For now." "Then kill him. Kill him today." Bane looked pained but he nodded and then turned to the door. "Bane." He stopped and turned to face her. "How do you know he's working alone?" "Everyone he questioned said he did it alone." "But why was he suspicious in the first place? He had no reason to think that his friends were in trouble." Bane frowned, "You think he's been communicating with them?" "It's the only explanation." "But that's not possible, the only way to communicate with somebody out there is with telepathy and none of them are sensitives." "Then they must know somebody who could invent a new way to communicate." She saw the realisation behind Bane's eyes. "Lakeitha's brother, Mikey." "Yes. He has to be with Gideon, so he has to die as well. I know it's unpleasant, because of his sickness and everything that he did for Dantez, for all that's left of the human race. But it has to be done."

Chapter 38

Lakeitha was really feeling her injuries now. All the little cuts and bruises, all the damage she'd taken in the battle. No adrenaline, no guaga, just drudgery and pain.

They had finally left the stone behind, it may have been protecting them from trackers, but it was also tough on the knees. Now they were walking on grey soil and leaving footprints with every step. At first they had brushed over their footprints, using their hands, tree branches would have been better but there weren't any trees around. That tactic had slowed them down so they abandoned it after a hundred meters.

She did a mental inventory of their supplies. Their water wouldn't run out for a few hours and they had two days of dry rations. At this rate they'd be lucky to live long enough to run out of food. They hadn't lost any of their weapons, though they only had one World Saver bullet left. They still had a fair amount of medical supplies as well, although they were running low on clotting powder, so they'd do well to avoid any more gaping wounds.

They continued trudging in silence, the incline picking up. They walked up a long but slight slope for almost an hour. They saw a river about four hundred meters away that ran parallel to them. Lakeitha liked the change in landscape, they never would have been able to spot a river so far away in the jungle. It was also a relief to get away from all the noise and the constant threat that at any moment, something might jump out at them from behind a bush or a tree. This wide open space didn't guarantee that monsters wouldn't attack, there were still creatures running around but they could see them from a mile away and so far none of them had attacked. The only way they could be taken by surprise out here was if another monster came out of the ground. Or from the sky. "Keep a look out for anything with wings." She told Luther.

They got some more water and then walked alongside the river as they talked. "Did Malek have any family?" asked Luther, "No not for a long time. Parents died when he was a kid." "Then who raised him?" "After they died, nobody. He lived on the street from twelve until seventeen, then he signed up to be a Hell Hunter." That made Luther feel sad. He didn't ask any more questions about Malek.

"Who do you think would win in a fight, an adult Bracken against that thing I just shot?" Lakeitha smiled and gave him a sideways look, "Okay. Uh, I'd back the Bracken." "Really, that thing was so much bulkier. Must have been stronger." "Maybe but a Bracken can fight. I've seen them take on other big monsters and they do have some skill. Those massive bone boulders will pulverise anything and I'd take its one massive mouth over that thing's hundred small ones." "Ah but you never saw the purple monster fight. Maybe it's even more skilled than the Bracken." "Or maybe it's worse. You don't know." "Yeah okay, you win. Your turn." "Who do you...oh no." They both stopped in their tracks. They'd crested the top of the hill, on the otherside was a vast empty valley. It was flat and open and grey for miles upon miles. In the far distance they could see a green mountain, to their right and their left the valley went all the way out to the horizon. There was nowhere to hide out there, they'd be the tallest things for miles.

"We have to turn back right?" asked Luther. Lakeitha looked back the way they'd come, the only landmark for miles was the river they'd been walking beside. "Fuck. How did I let this happen? We're totally exposed." "Come on, we don't have time to waste." "No we don't. We can't turn back." "No Lakeitha, we can't walk through that valley." "Luther, we're already in the middle of the valley, we only just realised it. There isn't a single thing over two feet tall in any direction. It'll take us two hours to get back to the stone and there are almost no landmarks on the stone either. It might take us five hours just to find something to hide behind. They'll find us before then, spot us from a distance and then they'll come and kill us." She saw the brutal reality dawn on Luther's face. "We have to cross the valley. That mountain is our only chance."

At that moment Luther noticed just how hot it was out there. The river didn't make it very far into the valley. There was a horrible churning in his stomach. He walked in a slow circle scanning his surroundings, it was a brutally clear day, the mountain really was the closet piece of cover. He felt a feverish certainty that he was going to die in that valley.

Chapter 39

Agony.

Chapter 40

They were six miles into the valley. Twenty minutes in the river had disappeared underground. It was hot, hot, so hot; the sun hated him and he hated the sun. They'd drunk almost all their water. Luther was so thirsty, he promised himself a good swig in a mile. The mountain ahead of them was such a luscious green that it was certainly drenched in water. That was something to look forward to. "Can I have a drink of your water?" "No" "Mmmphh" he grumbled.

How far had he walked in the last five days, a hundred miles? No, it just felt like it. They hadn't covered that much ground on the first couple of days because they'd spent so much time fighting through the thick jungle. Fifty miles? Seventy miles? It didn't matter. He hadn't had eight hours sleep in ages. He'd been hurt a lot. His body was somehow still functioning but for how long. He wondered which of his knees would give out first. "How far have we walked in the last five days?" He was surprised at himself for asking the question, he thought he'd given up on that train of thought. "It doesn't matter." Said Lakeitha. "Uh huh."

Luther was hungry as well but he couldn't eat any of his rations because their saltiness would be a cruel joke on his thirsty mouth.

They walked another couple of miles. It took them a whole hour. Luther spent a lot of time looking back at the edge of the hill that their enemies would inevitably walk over. "How...ah long have we been in this valley?" He asked Lakeitha. "Almost four hours." He groaned. The mountain was a little over a mile in front of them; somehow it looked further away now than it did four hours ago. Maybe he was losing his mind, "Lakeitha am I losing my mind?" "If you have to ask." It took Luther way too long to get the joke. "You're funny." "Shit." "What." "It's taken desert delirium for you to finally admit that I'm funny." "Is this a desert? I've never been in a desert before." "It's not really a desert. Deserts have sand, this is soil. But it's pretty much the same." "Have you ever been in a desert?" "Yeah, if you turned around, walked back the way we came and then carried on past The Passage for fifty miles you'd reach a desert. It's smaller than this valley and has orange sand but otherwise."

"Can we just stop for a minute?" He asked, having already stopped. "No we have to keep moving." He looked at her, begging with his eyes but she was unmoved, "You can rest when we get to the mountain." With a huff he started walking again. Why had he joined up. He'd loved his old life, plenty of sleep and glory. There was no glory out here, no cheering crowds when he won a fight. It was all about survival. There was nothing about being in the wild that he preferred to his old life. What an idiot he'd been to try and play at being a Hell Hunter. Sure if he hadn't signed up he still would have fucked the princess, killed the prince and been assassinated by the king, but he would have been spared five days of torment and counting.

He knew why he'd signed up of course, he'd never forget. He wanted to prove that he was the champion, the toughest, strongest, most resilient bastard in the world. He did it for his ego. Now in this vast empty space, under the gruelling sun he felt so small and pathetic. There was nothing here for him to conquer, there is no champion in the desert. What was he even doing in this place? Running away from a fight. Struggling to run away from a fight. He had to admit to himself that he wasn't even the toughest bastard in this desert. Lakeitha was better than him. Look at him, his life depended on it and he couldn't even keep walking.

"Luther get up, we're almost there." "I...just, I need a moment. You go ahead, I'll be right behind you." "Luther, if I leave you, you'll fall asleep." "No, I wo..." He was surprised by how sluggish his voice was. "Luther, we're too close." It felt right, sitting on the ground. "I'm not giving up, I just need a few minutes." "Luther, they could appear at the other side of the valley at any moment." "So, it took us more than four hours to get this far, it doesn't matter." "It matters, If we're already gone when they get here then they're not going to race as fast as they can to catch us. What if Akira can fly that far. What if they have somebody else with them who can. What if they have some kind of super rifle that one of Mikey's friends invented that can hit a target from this range."

Luther looked up at Lakeitha's gnarled black face with the sun blazing behind her. Maybe she could have been beautiful if she hadn't chosen this life. He'd never met a woman like her.

He was surprised to feel a mischievous little tingle, a part of him that he thought was dead. The delight of competition. "I wonder which one of us will live longer." She grinned and he let her pull him to his feet. They started walking, "Me obviously. I'm more experienced, I clearly have better stamina, better with weapons." "Come on, I'm stronger, so much stronger." "Not that much stronger." "I could beat up two of you." "Alright, now you're just being ridiculous."

Chapter 41

Akira and Roth reached the top of the slope and looked out at the valley and the two sets of footprints walking into it. "Beautiful" said Roth as he took out his binoculars. After a few seconds he grinned and handed them over to Akira. "Silver linings." Said Roth, "What was that?" "If that bitch hadn't stabbed me in the leg yesterday then I would have had to run through this valley to try and catch her. Instead I get to have a nice little rest." Akira smirked, "If I take the two of them out on my own then imagine how sulky Maximillian is going to be on the way home." "On the other hand…" "Go on." "If you go at it lone wolf style and the pair of them kill you, then I'm going to have to listen to Maximillian gloating for days." Akira had under 1.3 seconds to come up with a quip, or the friendly banter would lose its momentum, after 0.4 seconds a giant snake broke his concentration. It jumped up from under the ground wrapping itself around his torso and over his shoulder.

"Fuck" He yelled. It started to tighten around him, he could feel its strength. It pinned his legs together and his arms to his sides. He focused in on the magic within him and started sparking. He didn't even bother trying to struggle free, he just ignited himself. His entire body was roaring but the snake kept tightening. Akira started to panic for the first time. He turned to tell Roth that it wasn't burning but his friend was way ahead of him. The snake's head was circling his throat when Roth's sword chopped down on its neck. He barely even made a dent, a tiny bit of blood eked out and hissed briefly in the inferno. It tightened around his throat, cutting off the air. Now Roth was panicking too as he started hacking at the snake.

Akira started falling backwards, there was nothing he could do to stop it. When his back hit the ground the air was knocked out of his lungs and then the snake squeezed his neck tighter, robbing him of a chance to get it back.

Roth stood over him hacking down uselessly at the snake. Akira's flames burned out. He looked at his friend's desperate face and tensed up as death glided towards him.

The snake went limp and he saw a magnificent relief on Roth's face, another hack and the head split from the body. They'd both lost count of how many strikes it had taken Roth to kill it. Roth helped Akira get untangled. He took a moment to breathe. "You alright?" "Yeah. I just need a minute."

"It's not burnt at all." Said Roth. He looked down at it for a moment and then he looked back to Akira, "I have an idea." "Yeah?" "It's fucking crazy." Akira raised his head to look Roth in the eye, "I'm listening." "I think we could attach ourselves together, using the snake as a rope and you could fly us across the valley." Akira blinked, "You're crazy." "It's like your suit, it won't burn, it's probably sturdy enough to take my weight and it's long enough that your flames won't touch me." "I'm never having that fucking snake wrapped around me again." "Come on, it's already dead." Akira felt the marks around his neck. What can a man say at a time like this, except, "Fuck it."

A giant grin popped onto Roth's face, he clapped his hands, excitement swirling in his eyes. "I've always wanted to fly."

Chapter 42

Lakeitha saw it first, an ever-growing flame in the distance. It was miles away but clearly moving at speed, close to the ground. "Akira!" She yelled and started running for the mountain. They were so close, within half a mile. Lakeitha sprinted as fast as her knackered body would allow but she already knew that Akira was going to catch her. She looked over her shoulder, the fireball had gotten a lot bigger and now she could see something dangling underneath it. It was still too far away for her to make out what it was. Luther was managing to keep pace with her, running on adrenaline alone.

She looked back again and this time she could clearly see that there was a man with some kind of rope wrapped around his waist that Akira was carrying through the air. **What the fuck**, she thought. Akira was within a hundred metres of them and Lakeitha saw him start to slow down and raise his arms to point at the two of them. As he thundered towards them, she could hear Roth shout, "Time to die, bitch!" "Dive" She yelled to Luther and then leaped as far to her left as she could as a stream of fire blazed past her. She jumped back up and ran past the scorched earth, drawing her sword. She looked round for Luther, he was unburned and lagging behind her.

Akira had passed over their heads, turned around and now with a swipe of his arm he created a wall of fire twenty metres wide and three metres tall that stopped them in their tracks.

They stood tensed and ready with their weapons in their hands, unable to see their attackers through the roaring flames. They expected to get roasted at any moment, but oddly enough nothing happened for twenty seconds. They stood in fighting stances and waited, feeling the heat on their faces.

Then suddenly the wall of fire dropped and there was Akira and Roth. Roth had a sword drawn and Akira already had his hands splayed and sparking. Lakeitha and Luther sprinting towards them. Twin streams of fire burst out from Akira's hands, Lakeitha ducked under hers, rolled to her left, got up and continued her charge. The streams of fire cut out and Akira started shooting individual balls of fire at them. Lakeitha dodged one, Luther dodged one, Lakeitha dodged one. They were closing in and then Luther got hit in the torso. He dropped and rolled and then she reached Akira.

He raised his hand to ignite her face and Lakeitha jumped, lifting her legs, pointing her boot at Akira's head. She kicked him in the face. They both hit the ground, she rolled, came up into a crouch and punched Akira in the head, then blocked Roth's sword swing and rolled again to get away from him. She jumped up and stabbed at Roth's stomach but he deflected her sword and then hit her in the face with his forearm guard. She stumbled and he kicked her in the chest, knocking her on her back.

Luther was already up and running when Akira got to his feet, he tackled the magical cunt, tried to pin him but he wormed his way free and they started wrestling. The whole time Luther was punching Akira wherever he could, the ribs, the gut, the face, the groin, hoping that if he kept him in pain then he wouldn't be able to burn him. Luther's knees were pressed down on Akira's legs. He had his bicep pinned with his left hand as he punched down at his face with his right. With his free hand Akira pulled out a knife and slashed across Luther's ribs. It sliced right through the armour but only gave him a superficial cut. He made for a second, stronger strike but Luther knocked the knife from his hand, sending it bouncing well out of reach.

He hit Akira four times before he managed to wriggle his way out from under Luther's left arm. Then he grabbed ahold of it and pulled it to the right, forcing Luther to turn his body side on to Akira's face, his right arm now unable to reach him. Luther tried to pull back, but the awkward position he was in didn't leave him with much leverage and Akira was bucking furiously. He was forced to shift his weight to pull his arm back, in doing so he got off of Akira's legs and the second he did that Akira kicked him in the belly. The first kick knocked the wind out of him and made him double over. He let Akira kick him a couple more times while he drew his knife, then he wrenched his arm free and jumped down at him, the knife in a two handed grip aimed for his face.

Akira rolled out of the way and the knife dug deep into the ground where his head had just been. Luther turned his head to face Akira's fist a moment before the knuckle studs hit him in the forehead. Everything went white, then black. He was still conscious but he couldn't see and everything was fuzzy and painful. He was aware of more punches, he didn't feel any more pain he just recognised the impact.

Akira got to his feet, wiping his bloodied face and briefly considered the danger of a stranger's blood being smeared over his open cuts. Even a stranger who went for the classiest ladies. For all he knew Shante and the princess were as diseased as a couple of plague rats.

The job was done, he'd tracked Luther, beaten him and now he just had to kill him. He reached behind his back and pulled out one of his clubs. He looked over his shoulder, checking in on his partner. Roth had Lakeitha on the retreat, her red blade barely able to hold off Roth's spinning black one, there was fresh blood spilling from her cheek. She stumbled almost losing her footing and as she struggled she made a desperate two handed swing. Powerful but obvious and easy to block for someone as skilled as...

Roth's head hit the ground. Akira's heart stopped. He hadn't blocked it, he was dead. Akira numbly raised his empty hand and pointed it at Lakeitha. He told his magic to burn her alive but nothing happened. He concentrated. Nothing. He gasped, his breathing suddenly heaving and unsubstantial, tears streaming down his face. He grabbed his other bat and started walking towards her. He was going to bash her head into a brainy pulp. No, too quick, he was going to turn her entire body to pulp starting with her legs so that she'd stay alive for longer.

An arm wrapped around his neck, it wrenched him back and started squeezing. The air was instantly cut off, he kicked and struggled but Luther kept dragging him backwards, his feet skidding uselessly across the ground. He tried swinging his clubs behind him but he missed the first few times and then he started getting weak. Luther was so strong, the hold so effective. It was all going black. He had nothing else to look at but the woman who killed his best friend.

Luther dropped him and then kicked him in the head to knock him out for longer. It was against his ethics but the sleeper hold just wouldn't last long enough for them to get away. He went over to Lakeitha, he was dizzy, couldn't even walk in a straight line but at least he was alive. "You good?" She nodded. "You didn't kill him?" "Ah no." "You choked him out and now you have a moral objection to doing what you should have done in the first place." Luther winced, "Sorry, I should have finished him, I was just going by instinct." Lakeitha's gaze was drawn to Akira, her skin got hot, her wounds hurt worse, everything that wasn't Akira became a blur as the unconscious body grew more vivid. He was right there in front of her, defenceless. "I know it needs to be done but…" said Luther, snapping her out of it. She took a breath, tried to find the right words. As she spoke she zoned back in on Akira, "Next time, I'm not going to do your killing for you. But I'm glad you didn't do it. This mercenary parasite killed Malek. He's one of us you know, Akira is a Hell Hunter. He burnt Malek alive…" She took a breath, glanced back at Luther. His eyes had gone a little red, she could see that she'd roused some anger in him and he looked nervous of her, his shoulders inching back as they made eye contact. "I'm going to fucking kill him."

Lakeitha walked past him, sword in her hand. She never got to Akira. There was a brown blur and then Akira was gone, carried off by a giant bird. "Shit!" She shouted, a second bird landed in front of her and Luther, spreading out its wings and shrieking at them. Standing at its full height it was taller than she was and had a wingspan of about fourteen feet. Luther slowly backed away but Lakeitha stood her ground looking the monster in the eye. "He was mine!" She shouted and it squawked back, ten times louder than her. Her ears hurt, it took a couple of steps towards her. "Lakeitha" said Luther nervously. She swung at the air a few times, "You stole him from me! I'll cut your fucking wings off for this!" "Lakeitha! Leave it alone!"

A third bird swooped down and stood next to its friend, they stared down at Lakeitha squawking over and over, flexing their giant claws. Lakeitha returned to her senses and backed off. The third bird turned, picked up Roth's body and flew away with it. Lakeitha scanned the sky for any more, without needing to be told Luther kept his eyes fixed on the bird so that it didn't think for a moment that it could take them by surprise.

The bird gave one last warning squawk, "Yeah fuck you too." said Lakeitha bitterly. It grabbed Roth's head and took to the sky.

They watched them fly away. "I'm sorry La..." "Just don't...talk about it." She cut him off and started moving.

They reached the mountain. Grass beneath their feet, bushes and a few trees but not so many that they didn't have room to breathe. They collected a few swigs worth of semi clean puddle water and started walking up the mountain. It wasn't particularly steep or tall, they'd easily get to the top in an hour.

Chapter 43

Gideon was a little drunk. He'd spent all day in a bar, he knew every person he had questioned and half of them had asked him to have a drink with them. He'd stopped before he got too inebriated. He'd just been to Mikey's to tell him the names of everybody on the hit squad and now he was walking home alone. He'd come to realise that Shante had to be behind it all. That weighed heavily on him. Mikey hadn't taken the news well either.

The sun hadn't set yet but the street was quiet. Walking along the paved roads always felt like a bit of a novelty after all the time he'd spent in the wild, even though he'd lived in Dantez his whole life. The tarmac was layered on top of five feet of stone to prevent monsters from burrowing under the wall.

He walked past a dark alley and two guys jumped out of the shadows and grabbed him. He switched into survival mode before he even had time to flinch. He pulled back, tried to shout for help and then a hand clamped over his mouth. He kicked one of them in the knee and tried to break their grips. There was no way they were getting him into that alley. As he struggled one of his attacker's fingers slipped into his mouth and Gideon bit down. He yelled and the hand was pulled away from his mouth. "Help..." A fist smacked into the side of his head and then there was a third pair of hands grabbing him from behind. The three men dragged him into the alley.

They shoved him against a wall and one of them stepped back, drawing a knife. He started to lunge in at Gideon but he was faster, drawing his own knife and stabbing it up into the man's throat. He kicked the dead man away from him, pulling the knife out of his neck. He cracked his elbow into the head of the guy to his right and then stabbed the one on the left in the gut. His knife cut through his coat but didn't go any further. This guy was wearing armour underneath loose clothes.

He barged into Gideon, pinning him to the wall and stabbing at his ribs. Gideon wasn't wearing his armour, he had to be a lot more careful. Gideon dodged one stab, deflected another, wrist to wrist, then blocked a third, blade to blade, half by accident. He tried to push him off but this guy was even bigger and stronger than he was. The attacker to his right had gotten back up and tried to stab him in the head. Gideon ducked his head away, but the blade still sliced his cheek. He kept doing what he could to block the knives but he knew that at any moment he was going to fuck up and a knife would dig into his liver. The guy to his left grabbed his one good arm and pinned it against the wall.

He kicked and struggled; a knife went at his face and he pushed the big guy back enough that he could slip off to the left and knee him in the head. As he broke free the knife that had been coming for his head cut deep into his right arm, just below the shoulder.

He backed up and the big man came after him with a slash. Gideon dodged it and then hit him in the face with a roundhouse kick. He dropped and Gideon stepped over him to meet the other guy. Their knife's clashed and then he kicked Gideon in the knee and whisked the knife out of his hand. Gideon ducked one slash, dodged a second and then a third sliced across his chest.

His old white shirt was soaked with blood. He caught the knife arm on the fourth attack, held the forearm in place, stepped in and headbutted him. He wrenched his arm to the side, opening him up and kicked him twice in the chest. Then he turned, charged forward and swung him into a wall.

The big guy came running up behind him. Gideon waited until the last second to slide out of the way, making the big guy ram his knife into his friend's back with enough force that he pierced his armour. Gideon disarmed the big man, grabbed his arm and slammed him face first into the wall. Holding the arm, he stood behind the big guy, planted his foot on his back and then pulled the arm back until it loudly dislocated.

The big guy roared. He let go of the arm, turned him around and shut him up with a punch across the jaw. Knocking out a few teeth without knocking him unconscious. He shoved the big guy to the ground and stomped on his belly, then he went over to the guy that he'd accidentally stabbed.

He was still breathing so Gideon stuck his own knife through his head and left it there. Gideon picked up his knife and grabbed a hold of the big man's jacket. He dug the tip of his knife into the fabric at his collar and sliced it from top to bottom. Underneath it was a set of armoured clothing, standard for all soldiers and Hell Hunters. He didn't recognise any of them so they had to be soldiers.

He put his knee on the big guy's chest and applied pressure until he sounded suitably uncomfortable. He sneered down at him, "You should have brought the whole fucking army." He'd been planning on asking him questions and hurting him until his answers sounded honest but he realised that they'd already given him the answers. All except one, "Do you know why they're trying to kill my friends?" The big man looked scared. "No, no I swear I..." Gideon stabbed him in the throat. "Didn't think so."

Mikey was sitting on his bed, worrying about his sister, thinking about the very long list of names that Gideon had just told him. There were sixteen people after her, the best of the army and the Hell Hunters. They had Blackmasks and several of them had magic. Powerful, brutal, combat magic. He'd checked the beacon every few minutes since he found out. The light on that disc was his only way of knowing if she was still alive.

He heard the front door of the house open and a moment later a man walked into his room and sat down in his chair without saying a word. Mikey's heart started beating painfully hard. He'd never seen the man before, he was black, broad shouldered, had short hair, a stubbly face and hard eyes. He held a broad bladed knife in one of his big scarred hands. Mikey reckoned that the man was a few years older than him, although most people wouldn't realise this, since Mikey's disease had brought a lot of grey into his long beard.

Mikey looked away from him, looked down at the floor, the walls. He could feel his invasive stare on him and it took him a while before he could bring himself to look the man in the eye. "I didn't think that today would be the day. You guys are quick. So you're the piece of shit that they send to kill a sick man." The man across from him didn't say a word. "You planning on using that knife, or are you going to smother me with my own pillow?" Nothing. "Five years ago, they would've been scared to cross me. I was a respected, dangerous man. Now, this is what they think of me." A tear welled in Mikey's eye, this was going to be very difficult for him. "I'm going to take my medicine. It'll make it easier for me." The killer shook his head. "I wasn't asking permission." He reached over to his table, picked up his pouch of medicine, took one out and ate it.

There was a frown on the man's face. "I bet you wanted to stop me from doing that." Mikey shook his head. "Why would you come to my home. Do you have any idea who I am. The things I've invented, the lives I've saved. I made traps, you idiot. Traps good enough to protect Shante and her dad before her. I made weapons, I made all kinds of things." The realisation on his face was quickly followed by absolute terror. He couldn't move. What panic he must be feeling, "You were dead the moment you sat down. In fact you were dead the moment you walked in, it was just a matter of you choosing which trap finished you off."

Pain was bubbling on his face. "When you came in, you were being strong and silent, huh. But right now, asshole, you'd beg if you could."

The only measure of his agony was how his face contorted and his eyes shifted. Mikey didn't like watching him suffer. He lay down on his bed, closed his eyes and let the medicine build something new around him. It would take the chair a couple of minutes to end him.

Chapter 44

They'd been at the top of the mountain for two hours. Luther had been asleep the whole time and Lakeitha had stayed up on watch duty. It was quiet up there, plenty of green grass and moss but very little real life. The little mountain wasn't quite the infinite mound of fresh water they'd been hoping for. Sunset was in a couple of hours, the evening was clear and with her binoculars she could watch the death squad approach. There were five of them and they were already more than halfway through the valley. She couldn't make out their faces yet, but she could tell that one of them was a Blackmask. They seemed to be in better shape than Lakeitha and Luther were. She guessed that they'd reach the top of the mountain in under three hours, if they didn't take any breaks.

It was time to move on, she wished that she could have gotten some sleep but they couldn't afford to lose any more of their lead. **We could stay here, make a stand. Two against five. We might win, our odds were a lot worse yesterday. But we did lose Malek and we got injured. Too risky.**

She nudged Luther and he bolted up into a sitting position, knife in his hand. **Good Man**. She handed him the binoculars, "They're getting close, time to go."

Chapter 45

While Gideon had been asking questions at The Stronghold, Mikey had set up six lethal and two nonlethal traps in his room. He hadn't, however, devised a method for removing the body. He definitely couldn't move it himself. He decided that his best course of action was to wait for Gideon. If Gideon had also been attacked, then his first move after would be to come back. After his medicine wore off and he had to spend ten sober minutes sitting in a room with a dead body, it occurred to him that Gideon might not have survived his assassination attempt. Being alone would make taking care of the body a lot harder, not to mention rescuing/avenging his sister. Mikey started to wonder if he was already fucked.

Back in the day he might have taken them on single handedly, but now he was a shell of that man.

The door opened. He breathed a sigh of relief. He was covered in blood, a lot of it his own but he was alive. "Stay there for a second." He told Gideon, then reached under his pillowcase and pulled out the little wooden box with the controller in it. As Gideon stood in the doorway, Mikey flicked all eight switches off. "You're good now." Gideon nodded, stepped over the dead body, without addressing it and sat down in the chair. "You got any medical supplies." "Sure" Mikey opened a drawer and pulled out his med kit. "You want me to fix you up?" "Yeah"

Mikey took out a pair of scissors and started cutting Gideon's shirt off. He'd been cut three times, two nasty looking but fairly shallow slashes, across the face and chest and one much deeper just below the shoulder. "There were three of them. They had knives, dragged me into an alley." "Who were they?" "Soldiers. I didn't recognise any of them. They were all wearing armour." Gideon looked down at the dead assassin. "I recognise this guy though. Another soldier, got banned from The Stronghold for starting too many fights, mean fucking piece of shhhhaa..." hissed Gideon as Mikey wiped down his arm wound with disinfectant. "You got any painkillers?" Mikey chuckled, "Yeah, but I think they're a bit heavy for you." "Just give them to me." "They're a hardcore hallucinogen, once you take it you won't be able to speak or walk for fifteen minutes. Actually, it's fifteen minutes for me, but for you it'd probably last close to an hour."

Gideon winced, "Maybe later." "We need to get out of here as soon as I've fixed you up. More of them will be coming." "I know. My place isn't safe either. But I have to go back and pick up Lilly? I know it might not sound important but..." "No, I get it. You need to take care of your grimba." "The quicker I go to pick her up, the better."

"After you do that, I say we need to hit them back tonight." "You want to go after Bane?" "Exactly." "You know this thing is a lot bigger than Bane." Mikey reached for a bandage, busying himself with the task, trying not to panic. "Yeah, but he's a good place to start. I guess. I mean how the fuck can we fight them? It's two of us against the whole army, all the Hell Hunters and all of The Guardian's Force." "Even if we had an army, are you really ready to start a war that could destroy the whole city?" asked Gideon. Mikey looked up from the bandages, "Of course I am. Are you with me?" "As far as you want to take it." "Then we grab Bane tonight."

Chapter 46

Shante was in the strategy room with Quentin and her main bodyguard. His name was Bogatar, he had a stubbly face covered in scars and he wore a black iron kasa on his head, a large disc-shaped hat. He was probably the only person left on the planet who could wear a kasa in a room full of people not wearing kasas and look like a badass, rather than an idiot. He had been her main bodyguard ever since Luther had quit to become a full time fighter. All three of them were watching the telepath, waiting for Dominic to make contact. If she didn't hear that Luther was dead, then she was going to stay in this room all night. If the job wasn't done by morning then she would have to tell Vincent that they'd failed.

The telepath's name was Steven and he was the only source of amusement she was going to have tonight. As she understood it there were two kinds of telepaths. Those who went outside the wall and those who stayed and communicated with them. This division was not down to their magic. She was told that Dominic was an intense tough guy with a bow and arrow. Steven was the complete opposite. He was a nervous skinny man, he had nice hair but an awful beard. He seemed unable to stop tapping the table, even though Quentin had ordered him to stop several times. He was eager to please her but afraid to speak to her, unless she spoke first, which she had seldom done in the three hours they'd been sitting there. He couldn't seem to look her in the eye. He was clearly afraid of her but also couldn't stop staring at her tits.

It would be hilarious to call him out on this, but she had to be restrained, because she needed this man and couldn't humiliate him. But she could mess with him a tiny bit, just a smidgen. With the odd impatient look and disapproving raised eyebrow. Just to tickle herself.

Steven was a welcome distraction from her panic, her regret, her self-loathing, and her doubts. Her mind had been an unwelcome place for days. **What if I had sex with Steven?** The thought made her laugh out loud, drawing surprised looks from the room full of subordinates.

She drew her smile back and started thinking about telling Vincent that she'd failed. The very idea made her muscles contract and squeeze her, reminding her that shitty leaders should never be comfortable in their own skin. What about shitty girlfriends. She'd done everything she could. She'd sent a kill team sixteen strong after three people and if they couldn't deliver then she'd done her best. I did my best, was that really what she was going to admit to Vincent tomorrow. We're just not good enough, please don't kill us. Pathetic.

"Dominic" said Steven and all heads turned to him as he closed his eyes. They watched him as he sat perfectly still, his breathing very light, his eyes moving beneath their lids and gently twitching from time to time. After a minute he opened his eyes again and looked reluctantly at Shante. He was clearly wishing he was somewhere else. "Akira and Roth are dead." With great effort Shante stopped herself from yelling swear words. "What happened?" asked Quentin. "They split up. Akira and Roth went together, they were following Luther and Lakeitha for most of the day and the others were behind them. Their tracks ended in the middle of an empty valley, their bodies were missing but there was blood on the ground. Luther and Lakeitha killed them but they think their bodies were taken by scavengers."

She didn't need to hear the details, they were dead that was all that mattered. She'd sent sixteen and now there were only five left and time had nearly run out.

"How close are the rest of them to catching the targets?" She asked. "They said they were a few hours behind?" "A few hours. What does that mean, two, three, five?" Steven shrivelled in his chair, "They didn't specify." "Then find out." She said through gritted teeth. He closed his eyes again and as he tried to make contact Quentin came to her side and whispered to avoid disturbing Steven. "Maximillian will take over. He's a good man, he could finish this." "Akira was the best. You and Bane agreed. You picked him over any of your own men. His magic is so powerful, he's so smart and fast and strong and he'll kill whoever we tell him to. But he couldn't deliver." "There's still a chance." Steven had reopened his eyes, "Three to five hours, they couldn't be more specific." Shante grimaced. "You tell them that they can't rest until morning. They have to keep going no matter what it costs them, Luther must die tonight." "There's no need." Said Quentin, "They already know." Shante sighed, "I'll be back in a minute."

She got up and her bodyguard followed her. She went to her apartment and sat down in her favourite chair. Her mind was empty, her eyes wandered aimlessly. Then after a while her arms started trembling and she hunched over, her face contorting like she was screaming but a dry gasp was the only noise she made. She cried for a full minute. Her face bunched up and overheated, fat tears spilling from her half open eyes. Then she got up, washed her face, did a pee and walked back to the windowless room.

Chapter 47

Akira opened his eyes. His vision was a little blurry but he could see a giant moving mound of brown feathers. As he looked more closely he saw blood and bone scattered on the floor of the bird's nest. **That was Roth**, he thought to himself. He started crying, crying loudly. The birds turned around and started sculking towards him.

He sat up and set himself on fire. He slammed both his hands down as hard as he could and the entire bird's nest exploded into flames. He jumped to his feet, pointed his hands at two birds and hit them with everything he had. They screeched and blackened. One of them flew away, up into the sky, its wings on fire. Akira launched himself after it.

It was moving fast, the wind putting out the flames, its scorched wings still strong. Akira soared upwards faster than he'd ever done in his life. He flew past it, his momentum carrying him higher and higher as he tried to slow down. He looked down at it and it looked up at him. He sent an inferno straight down onto the filthy monster.

The sun had already set, he reckoned he'd been out for about six hours. He flew for five minutes in one direction, over rock and forest and when he still couldn't see the grey valley, he turned around and flew the other way. It took him fifteen minutes to find it. He landed beside the same footprints Roth and him had followed for hours, saw their own footprints and the footprints of his team. They'd already passed through, they had to be at the top of the mountain by now. He was drained, he'd just flown for longer than he ever had in his life but he made himself take off again and sore to the top of the mountain. He saw his team. They were staring at him in shock. He cut off his magic before he'd even landed. The flames extinguished and he fell hard to the ground, taking the impact in a crouch. He was dripping with sweat. He took a few seconds to breathe and then stood and faced them. "Lakeitha is mine."

Chapter 48

After the mountain's peak there was a descent of about a hundred metres before it plateaued. The sun set as they walked along the rocky ground. "We need to find somewhere to hide for the night." said Lakeitha. "They have a Blackmask with them and they're at their most dangerous in the dark." "Do you think any of them know this area? asked Luther. "What?" "Well you've never been out here, but some of them might have." "Maybe, nothing we can do about that." "We haven't seen a single good hiding place since morning." "I know, I was just thinking the same thing." They'd seen another ridge in the distance before the sun had set, it would take them another hour and a half to reach. Anything could be on the otherside, or nothing could be on the otherside, it could just be another open, flat space. After spending a whole day exposed like this, Lakeitha longed for the rough jungle that made every step a struggle.

Fifty minutes passed. Lakeitha felt a sharp pain and she fell, her body tilting sideways, hitting the hard ground. "Ackhhh." She groaned at her twisted ankle, and then something passed over her head and stuck into the ground in front of her. A spear. "Shit." She turned and drew her sword, looking for the thrower. Luther crouched down beside her, sword ready, "Can you see anything?" asked

Lakeitha. "No." It was dark, but they should still have been able to make people out, unless... "Fuck, it's the Blackmask." "Oh" "Yeah, yesterday there was a Blackmask with a spear." "How did he catch up with us so quickly?" "Fucker must have run. On your right!" She yelled, Luther dodged barely avoiding the Blackmask's claws. It took two more swings at him that Luther blocked then it kicked out his knee and slashed him across his waist. He howled in pain and then Lakeitha hurled her ankle knife at his head. It hit him, bounced off his helmet. She raised her sword but he had already retreated back into the shadows.

"You okay?" She asked Luther, "Uhh...It's not too deep." "Stay alert." They watched the darkness, couldn't see a fucking thing.

She scrambled up, her bad ankle giving her a weak stance. "Back to back." Luther got into position. They watched the darkness until a rock flew into Luther's head. He fell sideways and the Blackmask jumped out and slashed at Lakeitha's head. There wasn't an ounce of grace in her blocks, sloppy, panicked amateurish but somehow her red sword kept the long claws away from her. The onslaught forced her to back up and her ankle gave way. She fell on her back but managed to keep her sword between them. Luther charged at the Blackmask, but a kick to the chest knocked him down. He got back up though, so the Blackmask decided to leave Lakeitha to take Luther on.

Their weapons clashed and Luther, of course, was losing. In the dark it was almost like watching Luther fight a shadow. Lakeitha pushed herself back up and limped towards them. The Blackmask had his back to her but she knew he was aware of her. She got closer and closer, she had to time this just right. Luther came in, attacking the Blackmask's left side and Lakeitha attacked the right side. The Blackmask, blocked both swords and the instant metal hit metal Lakeitha let go of her sword, wrapped her right arm up under his shoulder and grabbed him behind the head. She tightened the half nelson, trapping his right arm in place. She stuck her foot out in front of him and took him down to the ground. She put her knees on his back and Luther grabbed ahold of his left arm.

With her free hand she reached under his mask and undid the clips that held it on. He bucked and struggled but she still pulled it off, exposing the back of his bald head. She drew one of her twin stiletto's and pushed it deep into his skull.

She took the knife back and then crawled away from the dead body. "Good move." said Luther, "Thanks. You know this twisted ankle saved my life." "Can you walk?" "Barely."

Luther helped her limp along. Their three hour lead was going to shrink and shrink until they were caught and killed. Lakeitha looked up at the crowded night sky, feeling compelled to enjoy it for as long as she could. The pinwheel looked particularly magnificent tonight.

If there was nothing on the otherside of the ridge then she was going to tell Luther to leave her. He would object at first, offer to go out in a grand stand but she knew he would leave in the end. They went on without Malek and now he was going to move on without her.

Luther stopped, "No." He said in quiet awe. Lakeitha looked over her shoulder and saw a streak of fire land on top of the mountain. "He's still alive."

She tried her best to speed up, but it didn't really make any difference. She kept up the effort for as long as she could. As the minutes trickled away she imagined getting burned alive by Akira. Her senses dulled and her feet got heavy.

Luther grabbed Lakeitha as she passed out.

Keep moving, keep moving, don't look back, don't trip up. Keep moving.

He took a step and his foot sank into the ground. He tripped over and the pair of them hit the ground as it started swallowing them up. He struggled, but it just made him sink faster. He couldn't find any purchase. Quicksand, fucking quicksand.

He craned his neck to keep his head above the sand. He reached over to Lakeitha and lifted up her head, then his arm went under the sand and then his head.

He took one last breath of air. They sank and sank, the deeper they got the heavier the sand became. He wasn't touching Lakeitha anymore, he tried to find her but he couldn't move an inch. Going without air was torturous. He passed out.

Chapter 49

Bane may have been well into his forties but he was still strong and fast. He had spent seven years as a Hell Hunter, then spent the next twenty years or so training and commanding them. Gideon kept this in mind as he watched the house. Even if he had both his arms, there would be a good chance that Bane would beat him. He'd watched Bane come home twenty minutes ago, he wasn't sure if he planned on staying the night or leaving again. Lights were on behind drawn curtains.

Bane lived two blocks away from the Hell Hunter compound, he probably had some kind of alarm in his house that would alert every Hell Hunter on the premises that he needed help. There were hunters training there at all hours of the day and night. He would definitely have weapons hidden throughout the house and maybe some traps as well, taking him on at his home turf wouldn't be smart. So Gideon waited and waited, crouched in the darkness.

Occasionally drunk people stumbled past, some of them were even bold enough to sing, some of those singers got the shit knocked out of them by the people they woke up.

He'd been there for two hours, the lights were still on.

Bane stepped out and headed down the street. Gideon followed him at a distance. He didn't have much experience with this, stalking in the city was very different from stalking in the wild. It was closer, you could never lose sight of the person you were following because they weren't going to leave any tracks on the paved roads and they could be lost around corners in seconds.

Bane seemed to be heading towards The Guardians Palace, Gideon had two minutes to grab him before they'd reach streets swarming with guards. He sped up, got a lot closer to him and looked around to make sure the coast was clear. He took his sap from his coat pocket, stepped up behind him and hit him over the head with his little club. Bane fell forward, face planted and didn't get back up. Gideon hid his sap, knelt down and picked Bane up, loudly saying. "Easy buddy. I told you not to drink that much."

He'd really been expecting more. That Bane would realise he was being followed and put up a fight. He carried him across the city, keeping up the act for the benefit of passers-by. Occasionally he spotted people who might recognise him or Bane and had to skulk into the shadows to avoid being seen.

They had him tied to a chair in an abandoned house that Gideon had picked. Gideon had told him that he could handle this himself but Mikey wanted to be there. He wanted answers and he wanted Bane to see his face as he suffered.

Gideon had hidden his adorable pet grimba Lilly in another room. He didn't want her to be distressed by what he was about to do.

Bane stirred, then his head snapped up, eyes going from foggy to alert in an instant. "Gideon?" Then he looked at him, "Mikey. Why are you doing this?" "You know why." said Mikey, "What? I really don't." "He's a good liar." commented Mikey, "Not good enough." said Gideon, "You were my friend Bane and you tried to have me killed." "No Gideon I would never." "You tried to have me and Mikey killed, because we were asking questions about Lakeitha, Malek and Luther. Don't bother denying it. There are no fools in this room and there isn't any mercy either. You're going to answer every question we have or we'll torture you."

The blubbering and the scorn fell away from Bane's face, replaced by a stony defiance. "I am truly sorry about what has happened, but it had to be done. I'm not going to tell you anything. Unless you have a very low opinion of me, you know I'll never break, no matter what you do to me."

Mikey was seething, he wanted to hurt Bane, just to punish him, just to make himself feel better. But he held back, this was Gideon's job, Gideon wasn't going to get carried away. There'd be plenty that Mikey would get to do later.

"I know that you would never give in, under conventional torture. You're a very tough man aren't you Bane. If I didn't know you, then I'd never be able to break you, but I do know you. I know the one thing that you are truly afraid of." Gideon reached into his bag and pulled out two full bottles of very crude vodka.

Bane went pale, all the defiance melted and he was a baby afraid of the world. "No, no Gideon please." He blubbered, "I...I...I" He was shaking, his voice caught over and over. "Seven years since your last drink." He opened the first bottle and held it under Bane's nose. "You remember that smell." Bane's face was a mess of flinches. "If you don't tell us what we need to know, I'm going to make you drink this whole bottle and then I'm going to ask you again." "No! Gideon you can't do this to me!" "Why are you trying to kill my friends?" "I can't tell you, I can't." "Bottom's up." "Gideon my wife. She'll leave me if I ever drink again." "That's none of my business, after tonight no one is going to force you." "My marriage..." "I don't give a fuck about your marriage." The bottle came closer and Bane clamped his mouth shut.

"Mikey, please hold Bane's nose shut." Mikey walked over to Bane, looking deep into his eyes, drinking in his dread. He squeezed his nose and felt Bane squirm. Gideon waited until the inevitable gasp for air and then he forced the bottle into his mouth, pungent booze spilling down his chin. He gargled, tried to spit it up but there was always more and now he was swallowing great gulps of hard alcohol. He stopped fighting it and started suckling greedily at the bottle.

Gideon gave him the nod and Mikey released his nostrils. Gideon didn't have to force Bane anymore, all he did was hold the bottle for him.

He pulled it away and Bane tried to hold on with his lips wrapped around it, trying to get another sip. Less than half of the booze was left.

They left him alone for five minutes, watching the blur of emotions on his wet face. Mikey had never seen a man break before, but he was certain that this was what it looked like. No matter how devastated he was, Mikey didn't feel the faintest flicker of remorse.

Gideon went back over to Bane, "You can have more if you answer our questions." Bane looked up at him, his eyes glassy and his head bobby around. "I'm going to kill you Gideon." Gideon stared coldly down at him. Bane's angry gaze eventually turned back to the bottle. "Why are you trying to kill my friends?" "It's not about Lakeitha or Malek. It's Luther. He was in Alcraze last week, he had sex with the princess and got caught in the act by the prince. There was a fight and Luther killed him. Lakeitha and Malek never did anything to deserve this, they were two of my best." "Shut up."

Gideon turned around and shared a look with Mikey. Mikey didn't find the explanation satisfying but he believed it was the truth. "Are they still alive?" asked Mikey. "Yes. Malek's half dead, they're taking him back to Dantez, I fought for him, she didn't want to but I got Shante to spare him. The others are still on the run."

"Are you doing this because King Rodriguez told you to." Bane nodded, "It might be the only way to prevent a war. A war that would kill everybody in Dantez. We had to do it." "Uh huh. You couldn't wait to see if Luther made it back from his very first mission, so that you could kill him on his own?" "They wanted an immediate response, Shante was not in a position to bargain." Bane swallowed and then asked, "Can I have some more?" "Not yet. "How many of that sixteen are left?" "Five" admitted Bane. Gideon laughed, "You fucked with the wrong people."

He let Bane drain the rest of the bottle. "Can you call off the attack?" "No! Only Shante can and she'll never fookin do…" Bane threw up on himself. "You spend a lot of time in the palace, it may not be your job to know about the security systems but you always taught me the importance of being observant. You're going to tell Mikey about any changes that have been made to those security systems since he stopped working on them." "Sure." mumbled Bane, he wasn't afraid of anything anymore.

Bane told Mikey everything he knew and apologised to him about his sister several times. When he was done, Mikey stepped back and watched Gideon execute him.

Chapter 50

Agony with no end, that rushed his nerves and twisted his mind.

Something else. Something that was teeming inside him, making him feel like an ant hill.

Chapter 51

They found Efron face down, with his mask off and a knife wound in the back of his head. They stood around him, gave a moment of silence. Akira looked over at Maximillian. He knew what he was going through. In his brief time as leader of the group the one decision he'd made had been to send Efron to his death. At the time he'd probably hoped that the mythical nocturnal ruthlessness of the Blackmasks would wipe out the pair of them. But it hadn't.

It didn't need to be said that Efron not having any backup made it worse. "I liked him." said Maximillian. "He was a good dancer." The rest of them laughed, "Really?" Maximillian nodded, "He loved to dance, at parties everyone would watch him." "I can only picture him dancing in his suit." Said Renn. Akira grinned, shaking his head at the image. "Come on, let's get them for Efron." said Maximillian.

They carried on, it didn't take long for the tracks to stop at a pit of quicksand. "It's over right?" asked Renn. Akira spat, "No. We don't know that they're dead." Renn snorted, "Of course they're dead, the quicksand got them." Akira walked up to Renn, standing almost nose to nose with him, "It's not over until I see her body." All amusement was gone from Renn's face, he kept his eyes down. Akira turned to the rest of the group. "It's not fucking over!" They watched him nervously and he stared defiantly back at them. Then he looked back at the quicksand. "Fuck" he started pacing.

Maximillian stepped forward, "Akira, there's no way to test the quicksand." Akira stopped, "There's one... I'll go in, see how deep it is, see if I find their bodies. Then I'll fly out." Maximillian made an almost disgusted face. "That's insane." "It could work." Maximilian stepped closer, "It's not worth it." "She killed him in front of me!" Akira roared right into his face, spit flying from his mouth. "She cut his fucking head off! I'm not turning back! And when I find her she better hope she's already dead!"

Chapter 52

Gideon approached the Hell Hunters compound under the cover of night. He had to get some weapons from the armoury, right now all he had were a couple of steel knives. He didn't want to leave this till morning, he had to get in and out before anybody realised that he'd taken Bane. For all he knew everybody was already looking for him. By now Quentin and Shante must know he'd survived their assassination attempt. Every soldier and Hell Hunter could have been given a kill on sight order.

The compound was never empty. After living on so little sleep out in the wild it was hard for some hunters to sleep through the night and so they came down here and trained in the wee hours of the morning. He slipped in through a side entrance and prowled along a corridor that led past the weights room and outside into the unarmed combat zone. Four men were training in the dark. Big Don was beating the shit out of Riz, while Felix and Clint grappled. Gideon kept his distance, sneaking around the outskirts and through the gate that separated the obstacle course from the unarmed combat zone.

There was only one person here, it was Marie. She was gracefully climbing, vaulting and jumping through the obstacle course. Few people were as good at this as Marie. Gideon liked her, he thought that they might have had sex once while drunk but he wasn't sure. It would've been nice to ask her for help, but he couldn't trust her.

He passed by the obstacle course and reached the weapons area with the massive armoury in the corner. Inside there were over a thousand swords, knives, bows, guns, maces, axes, clubs, shields, spears and so on. Weapons made of black alien metal, red alien metal and more pedestrian metals. Hell Hunters were only allowed to carry non alien metal knives within the walls, all other weapons had to be deposited inside this building, made of a foot of concrete and metal with a complicated magical security system designed by one of Mikey's friends. Gideon was betting everything on Bane not removing him from the system yet. He doubted he would have thought to do it immediately after ordering the assassination.

He wished that he could have brought Mikey with him to deactivate the security system, but if the shit went down there was no way that Mikey could outrun a Hell Hunter. He stood in front of the door and took a deep breath. He really needed this to work. He put in his code, 4636256. Green. The thick metal door slid open and he stepped inside. The weapons were split up into five long lanes. He kept his locker on the furthest lane to the right. He walked quietly down the centre lane, full of communal weapons that were displayed openly. There wasn't even a shred of alien metal in this lane. He turned right at the end and passed a private lane full of lockers. He reached the top of his lane and was suddenly standing five feet away from Hamish. He was a big man, like a bear with a blond beard. Hamish was looking right at him, in his hand he had a spiked cylindrical mace similar to Malek's but bigger. One step forward and he'd be close enough to smash Gideon's head in.

He stood, waited for him to make a move, but Hamish just nodded and said, "Hey Gideon how you been?" "Alright, couldn't sleep so I thought I'd stop by for some training." Hamish nodded approvingly, "Good to keep in shape when you're injured. You remember when I was in a wheelchair for six months. I practically lived in this place. You wanna get a few drinks at The Stronghold some time?" "Yeah, let's do that." Gideon stepped aside and let Hamish past, then he walked down the lane and opened his locker.

He had a black alien metal katana, a big broad sword also made of black alien metal, seven knives of varying metals and lengths, a World Saver with four bullets in a special case and two old revolvers with twenty two bullets. He took everything, putting on all his holsters, sheaths and an X-shaped double scabbard that he wore on his back. Now he was ready.

Chapter 53

Lakeitha woke up. Before she had even opened her eyes she knew that she wasn't outside anymore. There was no wind, she was aware of a roof above her and walls on all sides. There was something sloppy covering her from head to toe. She opened her eyes. It was dark, almost pitch black. "Luther" she whispered, not knowing if they were alone. No reply. She still had her bag, she rooted around inside it and found her lighter.

She flicked it on and the small flame revealed a dirt roof that gently dripped quicksand. She saw Luther, lying on his back, she could see the rise and fall of his chest. She stayed quiet, looking for signs that anything was living here. She crawled over to Luther and shook him, but he didn't wake up. She gave up and slumped onto the dirt floor beside him. Her mouth tasted like sand. She drank some water. Then she slapped Luther across the face. He snapped up, fists at the ready. She patted him on the back and then handed him her canteen. They were both running dangerously low on water.

He looked around them, "Luther, what happened? Where are we?" "We must be under the quicksand." "Fucking quicksand."

They got up, crouching under the five foot roof. They found a tunnel, it was pitch black, there was no way of telling how long it was or what was in there. "I don't like the look of that." said Luther, "It's the only way out. Can you take point?" "Yeah, how's your ankle?" "About the same." They started walking slowly through the tunnel.

The lighters only let them see three feet in front of them. They both walked with their swords outstretched, ready to impale anything that was stupid enough to jump out at them. "How long do you think we were out for?" asked Luther. "I don't know. An hour, two, maybe more. How long was I out for before you fell into the quicksand." "Not long."

They walked for five minutes in silence. Luther found the feeling of Lakeitha at his shoulder very reassuring. The tunnel split off into two directions. They couldn't see any light in either of them and they were both about the same height. Luther went right and Lakeitha didn't protest.

She looked closer at the walls of the tunnel. "This was formed by a creature. A giant worm, ant, maybe a phlain, burrowed its way inside the mountain." "You think it's still here." "No, these tunnels haven't been used in a long time." "They have to lead out of here right?" "I would assume so. The question is, are we heading further out or further in?"

Forty minutes later, the ground started shaking. They crouched down as small clumps of dirt fell from above them. "Let's just ride it out." said Lakeitha. Luther looked up, "What if there's a cave in." Lakeitha grimaced "Shit, alright. We need to move fast." They rushed through the darkness with her arm around Luther's shoulder. The further they moved the more intense the shaking got.

Luther tripped and took Lakeitha down with him. More dirt was falling from the roof, they got back up and hurried on. It got a little brighter, a little more and then they turned a corner and they could see the light at the end of the tunnel fifty meters ahead of them. Dawn must already have come. A big clump of dirt fell on Luther, it felt like a punch to the face. He wiped it out of his eyes.

They reached the end of the tunnel and both of them stopped in their tracks. They stared, stunned by the realisation that it wasn't an earthquake. There was a bowl shaped valley in front of them and in that valley was a rushing mass of six legged monsters. They were black with orange stripes and looked to be about ten foot tall. There were tens of thousands of them. An unstoppable wave rampaging at high speed, devouring every living creature that was unfortunate enough to be in the valley that morning.

They were standing halfway up the mountain, there wasn't a lot of cover for them so they lay down on their stomachs and watched. Thankfully the horde seemed to be moving from the right side of the valley to the left. They were in the clear for now. They were around five hundred metres away from the creatures but still they didn't dare move. All it would take was one of the frontrunners to spot them and turn the entire horde in their direction. Lakeitha and Luther could do nothing but stay still and hope that the creatures didn't have the eyesight of eagles.

Near the centre of the valley there was a giant statue. It was probably a hundred metres tall standing up, but it was lying on its side on top of a pile of rubble. It was a monument to a strange creature with two heads and six muscular arms, dressed for battle, it was made of gold and it shimmered in the sun. A portal must have dropped the statue into the valley; recently considering how shiny the gold was. Lakeitha wondered if it was built to scale by a race of giants.

The horde reached the statue and was forced to split into two streams that ran around it, tens of thousands of them on either side.

After ten more minutes the horde reached the end of the valley and ran over the top of the bowl, taking their rampage somewhere else.

It took five more minutes for the ground to stop shaking. "Okay, let's get moving." said Lakeitha, "Keep an eye out for Akira." "Is there a chance that they think we're dead and have already turned back." "Don't get your hopes up just yet." Staying hunched over they started treading down the hill towards the statue.

They reached it without seeing Akira or any of the others. As they approached the massive statue Luther saw something in the distance. "Look" He said, pointing out the creature that flew above them. "Under the statue." They hurried to the statue, climbing up a pile of rubble to get underneath it. They hid behind one of the arms and watched the flying monster get closer. It was gliding slow enough that they got a good look at it as it passed by. It was nine or ten metres long, orange and scaly with a fish like head and two long sabretooth tiger teeth. Its wings looked very short and their buffeting motion looked different from any other winged creature that Lakeitha had ever seen.

They watched it fly on by.

Luther took out his binoculars. "If they're still out there then maybe we can spot them." "Good idea." Luther fiddled with the focus and then scanned the walls of the basin. After a couple of minutes he spotted them. "I see them." He handed the binoculars over to Lakeitha. "We've got almost a mile between us and them." "But we can't move. As soon as we break cover we'll stand out and there's no way I can outrun those guys on my ankle."

"We'll have to move eventually, which way are we going to go." "Straight down the middle." said Lakeitha pointing to the very end of the valley, where the two sides closed in, leaving a small gap. "That's the furthest distance." said Luther, "Yeah, but it's the flattest, we won't have to walk up the sides of the basin. We can't go back obviously and left isn't an option, because of the horde." "What makes you think that straight on is better than going right? We don't know what's on either side." Lakeitha shrugged, "It's just a feeling." Luther's cheek twitched, "Fuck. Straight ahead." "We just have to pick our moment." "I hope our moment comes before we run out of water." said Luther. She didn't say anything in reply to that, just ran her tongue around her sandy mouth.

Chapter 54

Morning had come. It was morning right now, she wished it wasn't but it was. The sun was up and the mission had failed. Dominic had reached out one more time, to tell them that Akira was alive, Efron wasn't and the targets were missing.

Now she had to meet with Vincent and tell him. Admit to her enemy that she had failed her city. She couldn't remember the last time she enjoyed having power. For her, being the Guardian of Dantez wasn't about power, it was about the burden of seventy thousand lives. Her father had been a wise, fair minded, disciplined man, but she knew he'd also revelled in being in charge. He made sure to get his kicks in. He'd wrestled control away from Regus Solomon the previous Guardian. It was his great victory that he celebrated every day for the rest of his life. Shante never had a reason to celebrate. She'd had a colossal burden dropped on her the day her father died. The two best things she ever got out of being the Guardian of Dantez, were her love for Luther and the satisfaction that she got from keeping all those people safe. It was tearing her up inside.

There was a knock on her door, "Come in." Quentin entered her living room, he saluted her. She raised an eyebrow, he only did that during public events. "Sit down." He took his seat. "I've prepared some early strategies for the first few days of war. Top priority is seizing The Keep so that we can control The Passage and post a brigade of men there ready..." "They have seventeen thousand soldiers and we only have ten thousand." She interrupted him, sounding defeated, feeling defeated. "Yes." Said Quentin. "They have more Hell Hunters as well, over two hundred. If there's one thing we've learned it's that they can't be underestimated." She grimaced, "Or overestimated. I have every faith in your abilities as a general, but if we go to war, we'll fucking lose." Quentin didn't say anything to contradict her.

A moment passed, Shante's shoulders sagged lower, she looked away from Quentin. "Bane's missing." Shante's head snapped up, her eyes wide, "Is this Rodriguez? A pre-emptive attack." "Maybe. Very possible." This was terrible, this was wrong, this wasn't how war was supposed to start. "Although, it is worth mentioning that yesterday's attempts to deal with Mikey Gleeson and Gideon Murdoch failed." "Well, you better get after them. Find out if they took Bane. If it was them, then there's a better chance that he's still alive and we can get him back, wouldn't you say." "Maybe." "No more fucking maybes. Not today." She looked away, shaking her head, this was the last thing she needed. Bane was very useful and she was weaker without him.

She sat for a moment, her mind speeding from one catastrophe to another, everything seemed to be getting worse by the minute. To her surprise Quentin broke the silence with words of encouragement. "You are the Guardian of Dantez and you are very good at it. You care about this city more than anyone and you make all the smart moves. You sacrificed the man you loved to protect your people…" Quentin seemed to run out of words, he tried to think of more to say and then chose to end it with, "I'm proud to have served under you." Shante thought about saluting him, but she'd never really been one for salutes. This was a rare moment of empathy with Quentin, the stoniest, bluntest man she knew. **Shake his hand.** She stuck out her hand and he took it. It felt insubstantial.

They left her private rooms and met with the excessive number of bodyguards out in the hallway.

They entered her ridiculously grand throne room, she sat in her shiny throne with the admittedly glorious black marble back, though it was fucking uncomfortable to sit against. Five guards stood on either side of the door at the other end of the room, two rows of five guards stood on either side of her throne and ten lined each wall in between. They were all dressed in identical uniforms. Quinten was standing to the left of the throne and on her right, standing closest to her was her most trusted bodyguard Bogatar.

The doors opened and Vincent walked in alone. Even with her forty-one guards in the room, she felt impotent. He stopped just shy of the throne and the twenty guards and looked impatiently at her. **He's making me speak first. What a dickhead**. "I'm sorry to tell you that we haven't accomplished the mission yet. We sent our best after them and they're still hunting as we speak. They might finish this within an hour." She stopped, leaving a gap for him to speak, a gap that grew and grew. "I'm not promising that, but it's possible." "How many did you send?" asked Vincent and Shante found herself relieved to hear him speak. **Shit, he's good.** "Sixteen." "Sixteen and yet you have forty soldiers standing in this room and thousands more inside of the city. Seems to me like instead of doing everything you can to kill Luther Aprille, you have been saving your resources, almost like you're preparing for war." There it was, that smug little smile. She wanted to tell him to go fuck himself like she always used to. He'd never had this kind of power over her.

"I don't want a war and if we sent a thousand soldiers instead, they would have been less effective. An army that size is slow moving, attracts monsters and easily falls through shallow ground over caverns, or quicksand or traps and good luck squeezing them through The Fucked Pass…" Vincent raised an eyebrow and she shut up. "I don't need to hear any excuses. You had a deadline and you missed it. My job is done, I'm going back to Alcraze and the King is going to decide what happens next." "And what will that be?" "I can't speak for him." "You're a message boy fuckwit, it's your job to speak for him." **Fuck, Fuck, Fuck, Fuck, Fuck. You dumb cunt!** Vincent shook his head, looking displeased. "Old habits die hard, huh." He said and then turned around and started to leave.

"Vincent!" She called after him, "Before you go, you've got to think about what a war will do to all of us. You like your life, you like your city? It all ends if we go to war. It'll weaken your city and the jungle will eat Alcraze in under two years." He kept on walking without giving her an answer. He passed through the giant doors and they closed behind him. "FUCK!" She screamed and all forty-two heads in the room whipped around to her, before hastily looking away.

Chapter 55

Akira was picking up a general reluctance from his team. They all thought Lakeitha and Luther were dead, or at least, they were willing to accept it so that they could go home. Nobody had said much since they found the quicksand. They were all resenting him and thinking about Efron. He didn't much care what they thought but he wasn't immune to the atmosphere that had fallen on them. They were all very aware that they had left Dantez with a team of sixteen and there were only five of them left. He reckoned that every one of them wished they'd been wounded in the ambush two days ago. They'd almost be back in Dantez by now, free from the dread that mounted higher and higher the further they got from home. If one of them got injured now, Akira wasn't going to be sending them home and they knew that.

"Hey look, something's coming our way." Pointed out Renn. Akira looked up and saw something orange flying towards them. It was far away but moving fast. "Duck and cover!" shouted Akira. They all dropped down onto their bellies, crawling towards the cover of small bushes and clumps of wildflowers. He waited and watched as it got bigger and bigger, quickly realising that it was heading straight towards them. He could see its giant teeth and fish like head and the strange way it flew, its short wings buffeting it through the air with fast snapping motions. It dived down towards them and Akira shouted, "Shoot it." Maximillian and Kalep came up into crouches, raising their machine guns and Dominic notched an arrow.

They hit it with forty bullets and two arrows, small puffs of blood jumped from it as it came down on them. But it wasn't dead, not even close. Just before it reached them Akira yelled, "Scatter!" They all jumped up and started sprinting in different directions. The monster hit the ground and bounded towards Renn like a giant rodent, using its wings because it had no front legs. Its giant mouth closed around Renn as his forcefield appeared, the rings of red and green light took the impact and pushed back, causing the monster to scamper back in confusion.

Kalep marched towards the monster, unloading his machine gun into its head. Annoying it and scraping its face without going deeper. The gun clicked empty, Kalep dropped it and the monster lunged towards him as he splayed his palms and sent it spinning through the air with a powerful shockwave. It also picked up Renn, causing his forcefield to bounce high across the ground as the monster rolled painfully. Kalep sagged to his knees, drained by the use of magic.

The creature recovered quickly, within seconds it was back in the middle of them. Akira hit it with a jet of fire and the monster turned away, taking the flames to the back until it jumped out of the way, heading towards Dominic.

Maximilian ran in and tackled Dominic clear before it could eat him. "Rally on Maximilian!" ordered Akira as Maximillian and the creature got up at the same time.

Akira ran with a club in his right hand and his left hand empty to use his magic.

Maximilian stabbed the monster, cutting into it, making it roar and then it snapped its back up and wrenched the sword from his grip. One of its wings clattered into Maximillian, knocking him on his back and then it stepped on him, pinning him and leaving his head exposed between its giant talons.

Still running, Akira blasted it in the side, it turned away from Maximillian and screeched at him. Dominic shot an arrow into its neck, making the screech intensify. It stepped off of Maximillian and lunged onto Dominic. Its mouth engulfed his head, shoulders and torso. It bit into him and raised its head, lifting Dominic's dangling legs as his blood gushed down its neck. **Not Dominic**, thought Akira, he was so shocked that his fire failed. Its scales just seemed to have surface burns.

The monster swallowed most of Dominic and then dropped the legs. Blood spurted out from the red raw stumps.

Maximilian got back up, drew a knife and charged it. The monster tried to knock him aside with its wing but Maximillian jumped up, grabbed the wing, stabbed his knife deep into its back and climbed on top of it. He took out a second knife and stabbed it again.

Akira ran in with a club in either hand as the monster span around trying to throw Maximillian off. He was just about to reach them when the monster launched itself up into the air. It flapped its wings going straight up, higher and higher. Akira watched from the ground, watched the dark line on its back that was Maximillian holding on for dear life. Akira didn't know what to do, part of him wanted to fly up there and fight it, but that would certainly end in Maximillian falling to his death, possibly while on fire. All he could do was stay on the ground and hope it came back.

Renn finally returned after Kalep had thrown him like a ball. He was looking up at the sky. "Fuck me? Is that Maximillian?" "Yeah" "Oh shit, we can't lose him too, we just lost Efron. No, no this is fucked." He looked around, "Where's Dominic?" Akira was about to answer when Renn spotted Dominic's bloody legs barely connected by what little remained of his hips. "Oh no. Not Dominic. He's dead, uhh hea uck mnooo..." Renn started crying. Akira kept his eyes up, waiting for them to return to the ground. He was still in combat mode and he couldn't deal with Renn's crisis.

"And he was our only telepath and our only medic. What are we..." "Look out!" yelled Akira as the monster rocketed to earth. It hit the ground and rolled, knocking

Maximillian off. Akira didn't have time to check if he'd survived the impact because the monster was coming right at them.

He ran out of the way and Renn activated his forcefield. The monster jumped up and landed on top of the forcefield with so much force that it dug six inches into the ground. It bit and clawed at the laser rings, pushing them as far back as they would go. They started to bounce back but the monster was pushing so hard that it held them in place. Akira could see the strain in Renn's body language, he was about to give in.

With a club in each hand he started running at the monster, small flames spitting out around him and then he jumped into the air and caught fire. He flew full pelt into the monster, it turned its head as he approached and Akira raised up his clubs and slammed them across the monster's face. He knocked it off Renn's forcefield and then span out, losing all control he hit the ground and rolled. He stopped and jumped back up as the monster lunged at him, its bloodied jaw hanging low on one side.

Its massive red mouth was open wide, it was going to chomp down on him and tear him in half just like Dominic. Akira raised his empty hands and blasted everything he had up into its mouth. He immolated its throat and burnt its organs. The monster landed short of him, flapped about a few times and then lay still.

Akira sagged, "Renn!" He called, too drained to raise his head. "Go check on Kalep and Maximillian."

Chapter 56

They made the move the second the monster attacked. Lakeitha had her arm around Luther's shoulder. It was going to take them almost an hour to reach the end of the valley; every few minutes they rested and Luther checked to see if the hunters were following them. Even after they killed the monster the hunters still didn't move, they seemed to have lucked into a head start.

Akira sat alone, unused binoculars in his hand. He couldn't stop thinking about everyone who had died on this mission. Mason, Darrius, Angus, Regus, Terry, Efron, Dominic and Roth.

Maximilian was sitting on the ground while Kalep treated his cuts. The damage hadn't been serious but hanging onto that monster by two knife handles as it flew up into the air had been the most terrifying experience of his life. His whole body was shaking from an adrenaline rush unlike anything he'd ever experienced. Kalep kept looking over at Akira. Renn had been blubbering ever since the fight ended. "What a fucking mess." said Kalep. "Yup." "Captain, he's never going to stop. He wants Lakeitha more than Luther, it's personal and it's costing us too many men." Maximilian didn't say anything, but he'd been thinking the same thing ever since Efron died. "He's not fit to be leading us. You're a captain, you should be in charge." "I know."

"We need to do something." Maximillian narrowed his eyes, "Like what?" "Renn's lost his nerve and Akira's obsessed. We're the only ones who can do what has to be done. He'll never let us quit so we need to take over." "You want to kill him?" "I don't want to, but we have to. We do this captain and we go home, me, you and Renn. We get to live." Maximilian looked Kalep over, "You want to kill our commanding officer?" Kalep nodded, "Right now. He's got his back to us, we take him by surprise. It'll be easy." "Let's do it."

Kalep helped him up and they approached Akira. "Do you want to do it Captain?" asked Kalep, "Your plan, your privilege." Kalep had his knife in his hand, hidden behind his leg. Akira heard them approaching, he put down his binoculars but didn't turn around. "I can see them, you guys ready to move?" Kalep didn't say anything. Maximilian could taste the tension coming off him. Kalep got within two paces of Akira and raised the blade. Akira turned around, saw Kalep's face, saw the knife and the beginnings of a lunge.

Maximillian wrapped his arm around Kalep's head, wrenched back and stabbed him in the throat. He held him as he bled and struggled. He was dying, not yet dead; as those crucial seconds ticked by, the longest seconds of Kalep's life, he started to feel something. Up until this moment Maximillian had been thinking practically; he'd been removing an enemy, a traitor, but now he was killing a friend. He dropped the body. He looked down at Akira's surprised face. "I always thought he was better than that. Disappointing." "Thank you." "It's my job sir." Renn had seen the whole thing from out of earshot. If they thought he was freaking out before. Akira stood up and handed him the binoculars. "Ready to go?" Maximilian nodded, wiping his knife clean against Kalep's leg. "Let's finish this."

Chapter 57

Agony. His world had been nothing but pain for so long, but now his eyesight seemed to be improving. It was still hazy, with blurred patches and black spots but he could see faces, see trees moving above him and people carrying his stretcher.

The teeming had grown, now it felt like there were snakes crawling under his skin. The moving and eating of this other presence had become more painful than his burns and cuts and broken bones.

Hours passed, they carried him, stopped and carried him again. Watching them was his only distraction from the pain. Six of them were healthy, three were injured, there was another guy on a stretcher. His hearing came in and out, at one point he heard them laying bets on whether or not he would survive the journey.

Why are they helping me? They tried to kill me. He thought to himself. He remembered seeing some of the injured people, running around fighting. The injured girl, he couldn't remember her name but he could remember breaking her jaw with his mace. His mind wasn't very sharp.

They stopped again, set his stretcher down on the ground and then the shouting started. Then the screaming. Things flew over his head and he distinctly heard a man being gored. Some monsters roared and others made scary high pitched noises. There were a couple of different sizes and colours of monster. A cross species team up.

One of the monsters stepped into his field of vision. It drooled over him, a massive ball of spiky orange fur with four strong legs. It didn't really seem to have a face, no visible bone structure, just four black eyes, a snout and a gigantic smiling mouth peeking out of the hair. He was looking up into the roof of its mouth, it had four rows of teeth.

It was about to eat him when his skin split in spots all over his body. It felt like he was being stabbed by more than ten knives at once, except the cuts were coming from under his skin. They were all confined by his clothing, so they slithered up his legs and arms and torso and neck, over his collar. They pressed down on his neck, making it hard to breathe. As soon as they reached open air they shot into the ball of fur. They pierced its skin and started sucking blood from it.

The tendrils undulated as they pumped the blood into him, making him stronger, making his vision clearer and his mind sharper. He watched the tendrils grow and felt them bulge inside of him. The monster strained back, stretching the tendrils, the bigger they got the more they sucked from this creature. He realised that they weren't just sucking blood, they were stealing its energy, taking its strength. He could feel it.

The monster lurched back so hard that the tendrils broke, spilling blood up into the air. The monster scampered away as the tendrils retracted back under his skin. They were a lot bigger now; it hurt a lot more having them inside him.

Malek felt better, stronger, the injuries didn't feel as bad, but he also felt the strength of this thing inside of him; it was very separate and far greater than his own.

The feeding had changed it, he was starting to sense a mind. Its thoughts were in his head. Only, they weren't really thoughts and they weren't really plural. There was just a single instinct to grow and devour.

Chapter 58

The ceiling was snowing, every snowflake that landed on his skin turned into toffee. It landed in his mouth and he chewed it; delicious. The more it snowed the higher the toffee grew. It started wrapping around his arms and over his clothes, encasing him. He was serene. It tasted too good, it smelled too good. It covered his eyes, everything looked golden. How could he fight this, his mouth was full of toffee. He hadn't had toffee since he was a little boy. It had closed over his nostrils and corked his mouth, he didn't have any air but it was so sweet that he didn't mind.

He didn't suffocate, he was in his tasty chrysalis for a few minutes and then it cracked and opened up. He stepped outside and saw a thousand faces, free from their bodies and bunched up in concentric circles. They were the faces of the thousand most beautiful women he had ever seen in his life, they were perfect, just how he remembered them, except that they were all bright green. He giggled and they giggled with him, he giggled harder. They mimicked him as he laughed and laughed. "Weird" and they all agreed with him, which made him laugh even harder. What a beautiful sound to hear those thousand different laughs joining in with him.

The laughter lessened and the green started to fade as the faces disintegrated. At first they went one row at a time, then it became a random and rapid shrinking until every one of them was gone and he was back on the floor in the dingy room with Gideon who was preparing his weapons.

He was back in this dreary hole. It was mid-day but the only thing keeping the dark out was the little light that could shine through the old brown rag in the window. There was dust visibly floating through the air. "How you feeling?" asked Gideon. Mikey waved him off, "I'm fine, I'm just saving my energy." He got the feeling that Gideon thought he was too sick to do this, but there was no way he was going to stay behind. He was perfectly happy to die tomorrow, as long as the plan worked. Not really, that was just something he said to himself to feel strong and motivated. He really didn't want to die.

Mikey looked back at the pile of tools and devices he'd been working on before he took his medicine. These were the things he needed to deactivate the booby traps and alarms. There were also his own weapons, the sonic gun and the gravity bomb, he'd opted not to build the bone liquefier because it was just a bit too horrible to use on guards and soldiers. "I think I can get this done by three in the morning, if I work nonstop. We could do this before dawn tomorrow, if you'd prefer to do it at night." Gideon mulled it over, "I don't see much advantage to doing this at night. There are going to be just as many guards inside at night, there's no cover of darkness because we'll be inside the whole time. But if we do it during the day then you'll have had more rest, which is a plus. There's no specific time of day when Shante is easiest to get at, she's always got her bodyguards."

Gideon stroked his grimba. He had a sad smile as he looked down at her little green face. Then she climbed up his arm and around his shoulder, licking his face. He laughed, picked her up, cuddled her and then put her back in his lap. "I love you Lilly." He looked up at Mikey, "I need to step out for an hour or so. I have a friend I can leave Lilly with. She's an old girlfriend and she absolutely loves her. She'd take good care of her if I don't come back."

A moment passed and then Mikey said, "Gideon I can handle this." "Yeah, you better. I'll never get close without you." "You're okay with taking somebody as slow and weak as me into combat?" "I haven't got a choice, there's no way I can disable the security system." "Alright, tomorrow." "Light still glowing?" Mikey looked around for the beacon, every time he was about to look at it his body was numbed by fear for just a moment. The beacon was glowing red. "She's still alive."

Chapter 59

Lakeitha and Luther reached the otherside of the valley. They rested at the mouth of a ten metre wide stone corridor, it went straight for about a hundred metres then veered off to the left. Lakeitha let out a long groan as she lowered herself to the ground resting her back against the stone. Luther peered through the binoculars, "We've got about twenty minutes before they catch up with us." "Let's eat." said Lakeitha. They chomped on some dry rations, wetting their tongues with the last few drops of water that they had left. "A lot of my stitches are broken." said Lakeitha, "Yeah mine too. We don't have time to fix them." "What does death by a thousand cuts mean?" Luther frowned, "Uh...I'm not sure. Is it like the straw that broke the camel's back?" "Maybe. If we go for long enough without fixing these stitches we might bleed to death from all of our cuts added up. But I don't think that's what it means." "Don't be ridiculous. We'll never live long enough to die that way."

"There better be some water through this pass. I'm telling you I'm not going to die thirsty." "What are our odds that it's a dead end after ten minutes and just when we get back here they arrive to block us off and kill us." Lakeitha stretched her legs, "About a hundred percent." Luther laughed, hoarsely and briefly. "Oh Lakeitha I'm gonna miss you." "Miss me? Do you expect to outlive me?" "Well yeah." "Yeah?" "Yeah" "Is your ego creeping back, champ?" "No, I just plan to run away next time we're in danger and you can't run so you'll get killed as I make my escape." "Well, now that I know you're planning on deserting me, I'm going to stab you through the thigh at the first sign of trouble. Then we'll see who's faster." "Ah, that's cheating, ungentlemanly conduct." "I have a vagina." "Bloody loopholes."

They chuckled and Lakeitha looked back to the dots in the distance. "Two against three. Not such bad odds." "That monster really did us a favour." "If it wasn't for my ankle, I might suggest that we head towards them, get it over with." "Maybe the horde will come back and wipe them out." "No, they're too good at killing to bother coming back to the same area twice in one day."

"You ready?" "I'm ready." He helped her to her feet and she started limping through the pass with Luther at her side.

The walls were only steep for about fifteen feet before they started to curve outwards, making it much more open than The Fucked Pass and there weren't any traps or monsters, or blind spots, it was nice and flat and empty. Boring and safe. They reached a left turn and followed it. The stone was about twenty five feet tall and smooth, there was no way over so they had no choice but to follow it. There was a right turn after, then a left, right, left, right and then a crossroads. "Shit" said Lakeitha, "Are we...?" asked Luther, "Yup, we're in a maze."

Lakeitha looked to Luther for a preference, he just shrugged and went right.

Two hours later. "Fuck" whispered Lakeitha "I told you. I told you this was a dead end. We've been here five times before?" she quietly scolded Luther, "How the fuck can you tell, it all looks exactly the same." "I just remembered this part, okay." They'd been whispering for over an hour. They knew that the others had to be in the maze even though they hadn't seen or heard them yet.

Something popped into Luther's head, "Hey, why hasn't Akira flown over the maze to spot us?" "I don't know, maybe he's dumb." "Maybe you're dumb." "He must be conserving his energy, or he just can't do it. How much water do you think they have left?" "None." "Yeah, none. Maybe he can't use his magic when he's dehydrated." "I guess we still have a little luck on our side."

Left, right, left, right, they wandered through the maze until they heard a voice, "Akira, let's just take a break for a few minutes." They froze, the words had carried over the top of the wall beside them. Their enemies were only a few feet away from them.

Lakeitha and Luther stared at each other, standing so still that they felt every little vibration that their bodies made. "Okay, just a few minutes." said Akira, "They must have found their way out…" said a third voice, "We've been in here for almost two hours, we would have bumped into them by now." "Fucking stone, if there was soft ground here we would have caught them in minutes." The harder Luther tried to keep his breathing quiet, the louder it got. His heart was thumping and lurching, his skin felt a little strange and his breathing was so loud it was impossible that they wouldn't have heard it yet. Fuck his breathing was loud. Lakeitha had hers under control, he was standing three feet away from her and he couldn't hear a thing.

They were both trying to calm each other with their eyes, while visibly freaking out. After a minute or so they started watching the fat drops of sweat trickling down each other's faces.

"Alright Renn get up we're going." ordered Akira and a moment later they heard them move off. They hastily tiptoed in the opposite direction. They communicated with hand signals. Once or twice they heard them, but the voices were distant. Then they got more space between them. They stayed quiet just in case the others were actually nearby and being stealthy.

Lakeitha was cool and focused. Then she wasn't. She was scared. Her pulse quickened, her face flushed, her breathing got faster and shallower. She exchanged a look with Luther and knew that he was feeling it too.

She was shuffling on the spot, feeling the powerful urge to start running but she didn't know which way to run. "I think we should keep moving." said Luther in a voice that sounded solid, but she could see the naked fear in his face. She nodded five or six times, she'd only meant to do it once. They crept on. Tensing up at every corner, expecting something on the otherside. Something that their puny weapons and injured bodies would be no match for. In the blink of an eye, the fear doubled to a new level of mind grating intensity. **Why, why am I so scared?** asked the quivering voice in her head.

Roaming through the maze he had felt like a predator, zoning in on his prey. He had turned every corner with confidence, feeling a buzz of anticipation that he would get to use his clubs. That changed for Akira the instant the fear returned. Now he moved like he was the one being hunted.

Lakeitha reached a crossroads, there was a right turn and a left turn. She went left and saw Akira and what remained of his team. They were about thirty metres away. They made eye contact. Lakeitha turned and ran as fast as her ankle would allow, as Luther sprinted ahead of her. Something about running made the fear swell in them, like they were giving in to it. The maze took a right turn that led them out to the exit they'd been looking for. It was a clearing with a cracked and eroded wall, roughly eleven foot tall.

No words needed to be exchanged between them. They both ran to the lowest section of the wall, Luther hunched onto one knee and put his hands together. Lakeitha put her foot on his hands and he started to boost her into the air. The three hunters reached the clearing and one of them threw a small black knife into Luther's thigh. He dropped her before her hands reached the top. She landed on top of him.

Luther was gritting his teeth and stifling a yell. Without asking him for permission she grabbed the knife handle and yanked the alien metal blade out of his leg. "AGGGHHH BITCH!" He hollered.

They looked up at the three killers who had finally trapped them. They didn't attack. All five of them could feel it and then Lakeitha saw it. Akira, Maximilian and Renn turned around and they all looked in terror at the source of their fear.

He was at least six foot eight with broad strong shoulders and in his hand he held a massive axe. It was made from black alien metal, with a five foot long staff and a curved axe head with sharp tips jutting out at the top and bottom, and a narrow blade coming out the back. He had two machetes on his belt and eyes with more confidence than any human being should have. Looking up at him, she felt the way that little insects must feel when a human takes notice of them.

With blood gently pumping from his wound and through his fingers, Luther stared breathlessly, his mouth hanging open, at this man who had haunted him from a distance. He took a single step closer and the fear wrenched higher, making him scream.

Maximilian dropped his sword and tried to run around him. In one fast motion he changed his stance, swung his axe and split Maximillian's head like a piece of fruit. Even Lakeitha gasped at that.

He swung at Renn just as he activated his shield. The axe head bounced off a couple of the laser rings and then Akira's instincts kicked in and he lunged past the shield and sent his club at the beast's head. He blocked the club with his staff and that was enough to crack Akira's little drive of adrenaline, heroism, whatever you want to call it. Standing three feet away from this man was unlike anything Akira had ever experienced in his life. The fear overcame him, it didn't make him run or scream or cry, but it made him flinch and close his eyes like an amateur. He side stepped Akira and snapped the axe staff into the side of his head. Akira dropped and the man turned back to Renn, who was curled up into a snivelling ball inside his forcefield.

He stood looking down at the forcefield, intensifying the fear to the point that Lakeitha swore the air started to shimmer. The forcefield disappeared and Renn was exposed. He had his back turned to the axe wielder, facing Lakeitha, so she could see the blood running from his nose and ears. His eyes were glassy and already faraway, before the narrow end of the axe dug into his skull.

Chapter 60

Five days earlier

"What does this job pay?" King Rodriguez nodded eagerly, "Anything, I'll give you anything." The right side of Alejandro's mouth twitched upwards, "And if I refuse." King Rodriguez narrowed his eyes. He felt the presence of all ten of his bodyguards leaning forwards, closing in around him. This made Alejandro smile. He let the fear grow and expand and play. He kept it slow, a subtle change in the atmosphere just strong enough to put some unease in the squad of guards and make the king twitch, his steady stare faltering. "If I refuse, then you'll use your royal authority to punish me, one way or another. Is that it? Are you trying to intimidate me?" He laughed, "I don't get scared, the same cannot be said for the ten bedwetters you brought here to make yourself look tough." The almighty king looked as if he was going to start squirming in his chair.

King Rodriguez felt the tightness in his throat and coldness of his face start to fade and he exhaled in relief. He glared at the man in front of him, no one ever disrespected him like that. No one ever made him scared. He calmed himself, rained in his ego, this man's magic was why he was so good at what he did. This man was not one of his soldiers, and he could not be treated the same way. "You kill people. It's what you do. I'll give you anything you want, anything. In return for you doing what you do better than anyone else. I need to see this animal dead and you can kill him." "Naturally." "So we have an agreement?" "Wow, not so fast. First I have to be wooed." The king's lip curled in disdain.

"I've already offered you anything that is in my power to grant." Alejandro nodded, a wicked smile on his face, "I think, I'd prefer it if you started with some specifics. What do you think I would find enticing?" "I'll give you ten thousand drogon." Alejandro sat in silence for a moment, his eyes focused on his axe, that he'd laid on the table between them. "Go on." "A bigger, nicer house with more land to train and luxuriate on." "High quality real estate huh. Now that is a rare thing these days." "I'll give you the pick of any whore from any whorehouse in the city and I'll pay for her to live full time in your new mansion and fulfil your every desire." Alejandro chuckled and then looked over his shoulder and shouted, "Girls, come meet the king." Two beautiful longhaired women, one with brown skin, the other much lighter, came strolling excitedly out from Alejandro's house. One wore a tight corset while the other wore a black shirt. Neither of them had sleeves and both of them had fantastic bodies. "Hello your majesty." They crooned.

As his girls approached Alejandro loosened his hold over the magic inside him and let it have more of a taste. Last time he'd just been playing, but now he was really encouraging his power to wreak some havoc. King Rodriguez froze in his chair, momentarily paralyzed by terror. Most of the soldiers ran away from the table, many of them screaming like they'd seen the face of pain winking at them and tapping its watch. A couple stayed frozen to the spot, until one of them fainted. Both Roxy and Natalie jumped onto his lap and started fervently kissing him and each other. Moaning their arousal as their hands caressed and groped each other. He took a few seconds, maybe half a minute, to enjoy it, then he reined in the fear. The pair carried on for a little bit. The girls were naturally vivacious and difficult to stop once they got going, but eventually Alejandro decided the time had come and he separated Roxy and Natalie and told them to stick around.

King Rodriguez was panting like crazy. Alejandro decided it was best not to do it to the poor guy again. He looked almost fifty years old. He'd given heart attacks to people that age. He gave the king a moment to compose himself and laughed with the girls as they watched the eight guards who had run off like children, scamper back once they realized that it was safe again. Several of them had weapons raised which made them laugh even harder. One of them was edging towards him with a broadsword in his hands and murder in his eyes. "Before you take one more step, I could make you piss yourself. Use your head." The soldier stopped in his tracks. "Your highness are you alright?" The king glared at him, then turned his gaze back to Alejandro.

King Rodriguez stared daggers at the psycho across the table from him. "Why did you do that?" He said through gritted teeth, resisting the urge to lunge at him. "To prove a point. These girls, I don't know why but they don't get scared. It turns them on like you would not believe. Isn't that right Roxy." He said to the darker skinned girl as he slapped her rear end. She giggled and then whispered something into Alejandro's eye. He raised his eyebrows and grinned. He stared into her eyes and said something and then they kissed, then kissed again, longer and harder until Alejandro broke it off.

"I wanted you girls to hear the offer, our royal highness just made me. The best whore in the city living full time in a mansion with us, all of it paid for by the crown. What do you think of that?" Roxy grinned and said to the king. "Only one?" Alejandro clicked his fingers. "Exactly what I was thinking. Only one. I'm already living with these two fine ladies. You need to sweeten the pot." King Rodriguez sighed, he just wanted this depraved meeting to be over as soon as possible and this psychopath hunting the man who killed his son.

"Ten whores, full time. You get to pick them." "Yeaaah!" cheered the two whores, he already had, as they high-fived each other. Alejandro nodded, "Alright. They'll need to keep a steady supply of new girls coming in, because unless they're freaks like these two, they won't be able to handle my...charm ." Roxy and Natalie, seemed to enjoy being called freaks, which King Rodriguez would have found disconcerting if he cared in the slightest about them. "Fine, I don't care, work that out with whichever pimps and madams that you come across. I'll pay for all of it." Alejandro slapped the table, "Wonderful. Also, I want this house to have unlimited electricity, a television and complete access to the city's archive of literature, music, television shows and films. And now that I think about it, ten thousand drogons doesn't sound like enough to me. Make it forty thousand."

King Rodriguez bit his lip. He had never met a more greedy man in his life, but money didn't matter, neither did whores or antique entertainment or having to evict one of his friends from their mansion in order to pay this lowlife. All that had ever truly mattered to him in his life had been his son. His purpose had been to love and protect him from the moment that he was born and now that he had been murdered, his mission in life was revenge. Revenge at any cost.

King Rodriguez reached across the table and Alejandro shook his hand. He was smiling openly but on the inside he was laughing his head off. He'd just taken the most powerful person in the world for more than any killer had ever been worth. "I move faster in the wild than anyone else. I'll find him and if it's what you want, I'll stay clear of the hit squad from Dantez. What about the Hell Hunters that Luther is working with? I hear they're good." "Better than you?" "No." "I don't care about Lakeitha and Malek one way or the other. I need you to stay undetected by the team from Dantez to ensure their integrity. They'll be more honest if they think that no one from Alcraze knows what they're doing. Don't interfere with them until after sunrise five days from now. If they can't do it by then, I want you to ensure it gets done." "What if they get in my way?" "Try not to hurt them. None of them are worth starting a war over. But Luther is, so if you have a chance to kill this parasite, then there are no rules." Alejandro laughed, "That's what I like ta hear. I'll set off some time tomorrow." "Why not right now?" "Hey, you can't expect me to risk my life without getting a taste of the payment upfront. It's almost dark already. Tonight, Roxy, Natalie and I will be hitting the brothel. Ay girls." Roxy and Natalie cheered. "We'll send you a bill." said Natalie.

Alejandro got up and took his axe, then he turned back, put a hand on the table and leaned forward. "One last thing. I get paid in full, regardless of who kills Luther. That's non-negotiable." King Rodriguez shrugged, "As long as he dies."

Chapter 61

Sasha's right hand trembled while the rest of her body was frozen in the fetal position. The brothel had been invaded last night. Alejandro had come in; a tall, muscular man, with his black hair, light brown skin and intense brown eyes that you looked into and saw passion and energy and ideas riving around. He'd had his girls with him, Roxy and Natalie, they were gorgeous. And one of the King's enforcers had come with him. The King's man had taken Philip aside and they'd spoken for ten seconds and from twenty meters away Sasha had seen the greedy ecstasy pouring out of Philip as he was told that the King was paying for as many whores as Alejandro wanted, for the whole night.

At first Sasha and her friends had wanted them. A lot of mean, disgusting guys came through here, so whenever she saw someone she actually found attractive she always hoped he'd pick her. Not so much for the business like sex itself, although she did actually enjoy it on rare occasions, but more because the alternatives were so much worse. Jessica, Francesca and a few of the other girls were looking forward to getting close to Roxy and Natalie. She wasn't much one for girls, but she'd never turned down a paying customer.

Then Phillip had told them, that they had to fuck him. That they couldn't drop out once they'd started. This had been really weird. They all knew the rules, none of them had planned on dropping out. This was a long night's pay and three highly fuckable customers; why would any of them want to drop out. She'd been working in this brothel for months, she'd had to fuck some real ugos and never once had she dropped out. Never once had Philip told her that she had to stick in until the customer got what they paid for. They'd all been confused by what Phillip said.

They'd all gone in together. Into the grandest room in the whorehouse. With the nicest bed and old music playing. She'd looked at Alejandro, shirtless, nearly salivating over his rippling muscles and then she got scared.

She couldn't get up from the corner that she lay in. The hallway felt darker than it really was. She knew the light was there. She saw the light through her eyes. But she felt like she was in a dark room. The hall of the brothel, that she had walked through every day for months, was now a cold jagged place. She felt empty.

She didn't know what time it was, but the sun had come up and it shone through the small windows. She wanted to go downstairs. Downstairs, her friends were crying and screaming and cursing Philip and Alejandro and Roxy and Natalie. She still felt like Natalie's tongue was in her vagina, as she shuddered and whimpered and gasped, unsure why she was so scared. She knew that she should be feeling pain soon. That certainty in her mind, trumped everything in the real world. She knew that there was agony to come.

She had realised that Alejandro was doing it. But that didn't make the fear go away. That made the fear worse. She knew that the terror that was cutting into her, was coming from the man in the same bed as her. That this was being done to her by a magic man or a mutant; that he had power over her and he was using that power to frighten her beyond anything she had ever felt. He was destroying her nerves and making her suffer because he enjoyed it.

There were three other girls in the hallway. Elizabeth had fainted. Casey was frozen just like her. She was totally naked and her eyes were set on the stairs. Absolutely desperate but glued to the spot. Fatima was screaming and shaking the banister, she slapped her face and stumbled around, bumping into the walls. She moved with no direction or purpose, just staggering around, screeching and babbling senselessly.

At the end of the hallway was the bedroom, the door was open. She could hear the loud passionate noises of Alejandro, Natalie and Roxy continuing to fuck each other and a few of the other whores. Sasha didn't know who they were. She'd totally lost track of who was still in the room. She had no idea how any of them could still be in there with him, crying and yelling. So many hours had passed by.

She could hear the screams and whimpers from hours ago playing in her head. It wasn't an echo, it was clear and present. After a while she could no longer tell the difference between the scared, anguished noises that she had heard in the room with Natalie and Alejandro's hands all over her, and the noises that her friends were making right at that moment.

She had looked into Alejandro's eyes and saw how he indulged in her panic and her shock, even more than he indulged in her body.

He checked the time. He'd been going for thirteen hours. He wasn't tired. Natalie and Roxy's sweaty bodies, a perfect mix of hard and soft, were laid out on the bed, they were barely able to keep their eyes open. When he wasn't outside the wall, Alejandro did two things. He trained and he fucked. Nonstop. He ran and lifted weights and wielded his weapons like an artist and then he'd go and have mighty sex. He never understood people who got tired from sex. Sex energized him. After a few hours with his girls he'd get right back to training. Outside the wall, there was no sex. Outside the wall it was constant focus, constant fighting and pushing himself as hard as he could. Now that was tiring.

Alcraze was a paradise. No monsters, no threats. Just pleasure and safety. He makes his own day. He sleeps when he wants, he sharpens himself, gets faster and stronger with no risk of getting killed and he's not alone. He always has company when he wants it. In Alcraze, Alejandro wanted for nothing.

But he could never stay permanently. He always had to leave again. Paradise always got boring. Roxy and Natalie were perfect in every way, but they were not enough. He was not going to be fulfilled by a life of fucking the pair of them and marinading whores in fear, until they broke. He missed the sex when he was outside the wall, but when he was inside, he missed the hunt more. He could get faster and stronger inside, but to get fiercer, he had to go outside.

He had a hot bath and then put his clothes back on. He rained the fear back in, dragged it kicking and screaming and corked it inside of him. He poured some water on Natalie and Roxy's naked bodies to snap them awake.

Alejandro led them through the whorehouse. It looked like the aftermath of a battle, only without the blood. There were crying women everywhere, shaking, screaming and zoned into a state of catatonic misery. Looking at the effect he'd had on this entire whorehouse, made Alejandro start to get hard again. Part of him wanted to head back to the room and take a few of the shattered women with him. He could still feel so much fear in the room, it was deliciously pure because he wasn't controlling it.

He didn't go back to the bedroom though, he felt the wild calling him. He walked down the stairs and into the hall where there were more of them sitting around. About seven women scattered when they saw him. He went to the front door and saw that Philip, the owner of the brothel, was hiding behind an overturned table. "You sure know how to run a whorehouse." He said as he opened the door.

He saw two men wearing police uniforms, lying on the ground outside the whorehouse, looking scared. The simplistic uniform of the Alcraze police, a practical brown combat suit with a pattern of thin golden lines crisscrossing the chest and back, could make a tough man look statuesque and intimidating. Unless that tough man was on the floor, smelling of urine. None of the whores had urinated, he supposed that they were made of sturdier stuff.

On their backs were a sword each and one of them had an old revolver in a holster. He looked beyond them at the king's enforcer who had accompanied them to the brothel thirteen hours ago. He was keeping his distance. He looked pissed and he had three more police behind him. Alejandro shrugged, "You send these guys in to get me?" The enforcer looked off to one side for a moment, in a very pissy way. "We called from out here but you didn't answer." "Yeah, the girls were making a lot of noise." he said, slapping Roxy's butt. The three of them laughed.

"The king has ordered you to start your mission at once." he said in a distinctly pissy manner, putting a lot of emphasis on the word 'king' as if the mere mention was going to impress him.

"Alright. I'm going. I had to have a taste of the girls here first. And boy are they honey."

The enforcer nodded and stepped to one side.

Alejandro heard an angry bellowing and feet running towards him. He whirled around and saw Sasha coming at him with a knife in her hand. He thought it was cute. He waited a full second for her to reach him and then he caught her wrist and ripped the kitchen knife from her grip. He tossed it away and then pressed the palm of his hand against her forehead, interlocked his fingers in her hair and held her effortlessly at bay as she furiously pushed against him. Cute.

"This is Sasha guys." He said to the enforcer and the police. "She was great, one of my top five for the night. Natalie, you liked her too didn't you." Natalie stared into Sasha's eyes and made a dirty gesture that Alejandro found very funny.

"Hey Philip, come take Sasha back inside." Philip rushed out from the front door begging for forgiveness. "Oh dear sir, I'm sorry, oh please mister, please. Don't hold her actions against me. I can't believe she'd do this. She's fired, she's gone, you punish her. She needs to be punished. Please, take my knife. It would be an honour for you to kill her with my knife. I'm on your side." "Coward bastard!" yelled Sasha, spitting in Phillip's face. Alejandro shook his head, "No, no, I'm not going to hurt her at all. But I will kill you." Phillip's jaw dropped and his eyes went wide and he started to cry. "Unless, you hire Sasha back. She is an artist, you have to keep her." The look on Philip's face was one of the most relieved that he had ever seen in his life.

"Of course, thank you sir, thank you so much." Alejandro smiled and released Sasha's head, letting Philip hold her back. "I'll be gone a week, maybe longer. When I get back, me and Roxy and Natalie are going to spend a lot of time with your girls." He winked at Sasha, "See you later gorgeous."

Chapter 62

Alejandro crossed The Fucked Pass. It was easy enough. As always it was full of life but all the inhabitants kept their distance from him, so he could focus on avoiding all the sneaky traps. He got to the otherside into a field of tall green grass. He stopped in the middle of the field, turned around and saw a black figure standing in the grass behind him.

It had a big beautiful sword in its hand. It was bigger than him, a lot bigger and it had to be incredibly fast and incredibly quiet to sneak up on him. He gave his pet some slack and it rolled out towards this creature. It didn't move, he didn't even detect a flinch. He amped it up, pushed the fear to scare the stranger away. But still it didn't react. Alejandro was shocked. It was immune, nothing was immune to fear.

It started walking towards him, its long legs taking huge strides. Alejandro licked his lips and tightened his grip on his axe. It may not be scared, but neither was he, he'd take four off it with one swing. Then his hostility started to smooth over and he no longer felt threatened. It stopped in front of him and he knew that it meant him no harm. It wanted him to do something for it. It wanted to die.

The stranger knelt down onto its knees. Its head was just below his. It was asking him to kill it. Alejandro wasn't in the habit of giving out favours for free, but he felt obliged to help it. Holding his axe in both hands, he moved his right foot a step back, raised his weapon and swung at its neck. It was like trying to kill a shadow. The axe head passed from one side to the other, with no sensation. The head didn't drop and he felt this stranger's lament.

Alejandro actually felt sorry for it. He couldn't remember the last time he felt sorry for anyone. It bowed its head lower, it was so disappointed. Alejandro sensed that it wanted to be alone, but just as he was about to leave it had another idea. It held its sword out to him.

Alejandro reached for it and the closer his hand got the more his skin buzzed. He took off his glove, for some reason he wanted to feel it against his bare skin. He was careful not to let his hand touch the hand of this being. As if touching its hand would suck him into a black hole. His hand closed around the handle. He felt a jolt the moment he touched it. It was almost as long as he was, but it felt perfectly balanced to his body.

It yearned for him to end it. He severed its head and it disappeared. The cloak, the body and the sword were gone.

Chapter 63

What a thrill it had been to watch all those warriors from Dantez set up their ambush. He'd practically giggled in his hiding place. What a treat to give his targets a little tingle of fear before they walked into the ambush. And what a show the battle had been.

After that he followed them for two days without them seeing him. They would've been completely unaware of his presence if he hadn't toyed with them, poking them with his magic just to amuse himself. They didn't know why they were scared, he liked that.

All that waiting, the dullness of hiding or following from hours behind over plains of stone and dirt. All the while he was hoping that the death squad from Dantez would fail. He hated the idea of having to turn back without killing anybody. Finally the sun came up on the fifth day of his mission and Luther was still alive.

Chapter 64

Lakeitha's breath rattled through her body as she looked up at Alejandro. He seemed to be savouring his victory and the moment of anticipation before slaughtering the pair of them. They were done, weak and injured, too afraid to stand. She wanted to get up and fight till her last breath, but she buckled in the face of this beast. Her body wouldn't move and the part of her that wanted to was drowned out by all those feelings. Not just the fear, but the tiredness and the pain. **Pick up the sword, you scared fucking bitch, pick up the fucking sword and kill him. Fucking cut him. Stab him and beat him. Get the fuck up! Get the fuck up!** She didn't get up.

Luther felt weak and lonely and small, in a way that adults don't. He was terrified and overwhelmed, but he was still Luther Aprille. He was a winner, a warrior and a survivor and he'd never let fear chase him away from a fight. He rose to his feet, sword in his hand, standing tall and ready. He had so much adrenaline pumping through him that he didn't even feel the fresh hole in his thigh that spilled blood down his leg. He wanted Lakeitha to stand beside him, he was sure she would. But she didn't, it was all on him to fight.

There was a look of shock on Alejandro's face when Luther attacked. He went for the head, Alejandro blocked the sword with his staff, then chopped the axe down at Luther's head. Luther dodged clear and then stabbed at his gut, but Alejandro deflected the sword to the right and then swung the axe at Luther's left knee. Luther couldn't block with the sword so he used his forearm. His forearm guard stopped the axe with a jittery painful block. Luther tried to pull back but Alejandro had already snapped the other end of the staff into his right knee. He limped back, leaning on his left side and keeping his sword up.

Alejandro lifted his axe up over his head with both hands like an executioner. Luther raised his sword horizontality to block it and Alejandro kicked him in the stomach with his long leg. The kick was so powerful that it knocked his legs backwards into the air and made him land on his face. He couldn't breathe but he still managed to roll clear a split second before the axe head would've torn into him.

He got up and went for Alejandro with a torrent of fast, unpredictable sword strikes. Alejandro blocked them all and somewhere in the blur of black metal the pointed back end of the axe cut into Luther's bicep. Luther roared and stabbed his sword into Alejandro's arm. They paused for a moment, stuck together, looking at each other's twisted faces and then they separated, tearing their blades out at the same time. Luther didn't bother checking how badly injured he was, he just attacked, taking two quick steps and jumping, swinging the sword at Alejandro's head. Alejandro blocked it with his axe staff and then punched Luther in the face while he was still in the air. Luther landed on his back this time, he started to get up and then Alejandro grabbed his shoulder with his left hand and kneed him twice in the chest. He stepped back and hit him across the face with the staff.

Lakeitha watched the fight, curled up and frozen by fear; hating herself as she watched Luther get hurt worse and worse.

Luther's head was muddled but he managed to break free and get back on his feet. He realised that he wasn't holding his sword and his jaw had just been broken. He pulled out one of his knives and went for him. He ducked under a two handed axe swing and then stabbed up at Alejandro's throat. Alejandro dropped his axe, caught Luther's wrist and then held him there as he punched down on his face. Luther took the first, he blocked the second, but the third got through, so did the fourth.

Through the haze of getting battered Luther's fighters brain still had some ideas. He stopped trying to block the punches and planted his foot out in front of Alejandro's legs, grabbing his left elbow. He turned and heaved with all his strength, taking him off his feet and flipping him head over heels. The big bastard landed on his back and Luther started stomping on him. He covered his face so Luther stomped on his chest and stomach and balls and back up to the stomach. Luther was still very afraid, he had felt the fear through every attack, every failure and every moment of frenzied stomping. Then the fear disappeared. He wasn't scared and the stomping became about violence and victory and inflicting pain.

Lakeitha felt the fear leave her and she was able to get up to her knees. She watched Luther stomping and kicking, it was beautiful. Then she was terrified again and this time, she got up and screamed and tried desperately to climb over the wall.

It went from zero to a hundred in the blink of an eye. It overwhelmed him and he ran away. He tripped over a dead body, got back up, reached a wall and turned around. Alejandro, the beast, the unbeatable murderer, was back on his feet, holding his axe. His face was covered in blood and looked angry and vengeful. **He's going to kill me! Don't be afraid, you did it before! I can't, I can't!** Luther was trying to hold onto sand as a tidal wave rammed him.

Alejandro blocked the exit, leaving Luther to run back and forth dripping lines of blood on the ground. He could hear Lakeitha screaming but his own mouth was so fucked up that all he could manage was a loud groan.

Lakeitha stole another glance at Alejandro as he approached Luther. Luther had completely lost it and he was about to die. Was she really going to watch her friend die and do nothing? He swept Luther's legs with his axe staff and then kicked Luther in the face. This was it, Luther was dazed and struggling to get from the crawl position to the kneel position. He was going to kill him. Lakeitha found it, a moment of focus and action, removed from her emotions and her pathetic thoughts. She reached down to her hip and drew her World Saver Hand Cannon. She pointed it at Alejandro and they made eye contact just before she fired.

Alejandro brought down his axe, blocking the giant bullet. It hit the axe head, breaking it into flying shards of black alien metal. Two of them went into Alejandro's face. One in the cheek and one in the forehead.

He looked in horror at the twisted headless stump of his axe. Then he drove it through Luther's stomach.

A breath of air was forced from Luther's lungs. Lakeitha's face went slack, her hands went numb.

He was propped up by the broken end of the axe that had gone right through him and lodged in the ground on the other side. It hurt so much. **It's over, this is the thing I die of.** Luther breathed back in, it was gargled, cutting in and out. **I'm not dead yet. Why can't it end? It's already over, why do I have to go through this part?**

Lakeitha was frozen again, she dropped the empty World Saver.

Alejandro ripped out one of the shards, hissing in pain. He stumbled forward a few steps as he fought with the second shard. He came close enough that he brought

Luther back. He had been resigned to death but when Alejandro got close he was given a chance to do one more thing as a living man. He wasn't scared anymore, he was already dead. He drew his knife and stabbed it into Alejandro's leg. Alejandro gasped and tripped, landing at Luther's knees.

Luther grabbed Alejandro by the hair as he pulled the knife out of his leg. Alejandro kicked and pushed and struggled but there was no way that he was letting go. He scrambled his body away from Luther, leaving only his head and neck in reach. He tried to reach his left hand over to his right side but the axe staff was in the way. Alejandro got better leverage, he was pushing harder and Luther was bleeding more and more. Time was running out. He raised the knife up over the staff and then reached down, reached as far as he could, stretching his pinned dying body until he stabbed Alejandro in the throat. He plunged it as deep as it would go and then let go. He leaned back and gave in as he watched his enemy bleed.

When Alejandro died Lakeitha was freed from his magic. She got up and walked over to Luther. His eyes were half open and unresponsive. She got down to her knees so that their heads were level and she spent a moment with him. After a few minutes, she said, "Pretty...Pretty tough for a cage fighter."

Chapter 65

Everybody was dead, there was nobody left hunting her. It was a relief but only a small one. She couldn't go back to Dantez, she didn't know where she would go or what she would do. She wasn't ready to make any decisions about the future, she just focused on the here and now. Water. They'd run out hours ago and she was hurt and exhausted and it was so brutally hot. She checked the canteens of all the bodies and of course they were all empty.

She knew that if she turned back then she'd die before she reached water. But she could climb out of the maze right now and maybe she'd find some. She didn't like the idea of travelling even further away from Dantez but it really was her only hope. There probably were other ways out of the maze, but it was a ridiculous gamble, she'd most likely wander around for a while and then die of dehydration.

She was going over and there was only one way that she could reach the top of that wall. She dragged Alejandro's body under the wall, then she stacked Maximillian's on top and then Renn's. She tested it for wobbliness with her foot, pretty solid all things considered.

She stepped on top of the bodies, raised her hands and jumped. After a couple of attempts she got her hands over the edge and pulled herself up. There were miles of empty dry ground in front of her. But way out in the distance there was snow. A thick white line under the horizon. More water than she could ever drink. She started walking.

Chapter 66

Malek was carried through the gates of Dantez. For hours the parasite inside him had been resting and growing, soon it would be ready to feed again.

They didn't take him to the usual infirmary for Hell Hunters, Grand Scrapers, soldiers and guards. They didn't take him to the public hospital either. They took him to a windowless room in a building he'd never been to before. He was dropped on the only bed in the room and a doctor started looking him over. Malek knew that they must be hiding him so nobody found out that Shante was trying to kill her own Hell Hunters. He still didn't understand why they hadn't killed him. He briefly considered what they would do to him after he was healed, then he brushed the thought aside. He was never going to heal, this parasite was going to kill him. Its instincts and feelings were loud in his mind, louder than his own.

The doctor was cutting off his clothes with a big set of red alien metal scissors, they'd been fused to his skin for days. The white blood stained tendrils stood a few inches above his skin; they wavered in the open air. The doctor looked horrified, he stepped back, turned to the door, then turned back and took a closer look at them. **No, don't come nearer. Don't do it man, go tell the guards.** The doctor seemed to have recovered from his shock and his scientific curiosity was pushing him to examine the tendrils. He tried to warn him, tried to tell him. Spittle and air puffed out of his mouth, but he didn't say a word. **Kill it! Kill it!**

The idiot prodded a tendril with a swab. Malek braced for the tendrils to attack but they didn't, they retreated back inside his body, which was incredibly painful. They weren't ready to eat yet.

The doctor spent ten or fifteen minutes examining the tendrils and then he left the room. The cunt didn't even treat any of his wounds.

Malek was alone and naked except for his filthy underwear. His clothes were still under him, spread open like an empty cocoon. The white tendrils rose up again now that the doctor was gone.

They were going to drain the doctor and absorb him and then this thing was going to spread and devour, growing and growing.

He didn't have much time. He had to stop it and in stopping it he would end his own suffering. It wasn't a conversation, he knew it had to be done and he knew there was no chance of him ever returning to his old life.

There was a table beside him full of medical equipment. There had to be a scalpel or a big needle. He couldn't get up, there was no feeling left in his legs. They might as well have been amputated. His arms were better though and so was his tentacle. He forced it out of his hand. It was slow and weak, but he could still control it, still feel it like it was one of his fingers. It rose over his body in the direction of the table. He tried to raise his head but that seemed to be beyond him right now. He felt around, swinging his tentacle until it bumped into the table leg.

He reached on top of the table, knocking things over until he nicked himself on a blade. He carefully wrapped his tentacle around the scalpel handle and then lifted it up from the table. He fully retracted his tentacle into his arm and gripped the scalpel in his hand. He lifted his arm up above his neck and pointed downwards. He reckoned it would be easier to plunge it down into his throat than it would be to slice across his neck. Otherwise the pain might make him stop halfway through.

He held the scalpel with both hands to make sure it went deep enough. He thought of a happy memory. It's hard to think of a moment happy enough that you don't care you're about to kill yourself. **Enough stalling.** He pushed the scalpel down with all his strength and a jolt of panic shot through him. He felt the panic of the creature inside him and tendrils shot up from all over his body, wrapping around his arms, stopping them six inches above his throat. He fought to push it in lower, he wheezed, his face tensing and twisting, the veins on his arms sticking out. The tendrils fought him, lifted the blade a little higher.

It was stronger than him. Every remaining scrap of muscle and will power was going into this and he was losing. He was about to fail and die a pointless, weak death.

He had an idea. He let go of the scalpel with his right hand, to allow his tentacle to come out through the slit in his palm and quickly loop under his neck. **Shit it won't work, I can't strangle myself because I'll pass out before I die.** A better idea occurred to him. With the tentacle under his neck he sent it up the otherside, wrapping tightly around his left wrist. The red tentacle, surrounded by sloppy white tendrils, was giving him extra leverage. He started to tighten the tentacle, it squeezed the back of his neck. It hurt, he liked that, the pain meant that it was working. The scalpel started to dip lower and lower. It was going to work.

In a flash some of the tendrils unfurled and then stabbed into his right arm. He muffled a scream as the white tendrils dug all the way through his arm, piercing the tentacle. He shivered in agony for ten or twenty seconds, the tentacle getting weaker and weaker. He had no strength to pull the scalpel closer, but he made a futile effort to hold onto it. Then his arm went numb and the tentacle went slack and dropped lifelessly.

Tears ran down his face, stinging as they cut through his burnt skin. After a few minutes the tentacle started moving again, but he wasn't in control. It had grown white spores. His right arm raised without him wanting it to. His own tentacle stabbed into his left arm. His arm fell by the side of the bed and the scalpel clattered to the floor.

Chapter 67

Gradually the air cooled and the wind picked up. Her face stopped burning, her clothes were no longer a sauna, but she wasn't any less thirsty. It took roughly two hours for her to reach the snow. The last fifteen minutes were the worst. She limped towards it, her swollen tongue tingling at the memory of water. She got real dizzy, started swinging her legs in wide, inaccurate steps, stumbling over herself. It got harder to judge the distance to the snow.

She didn't even realise that she'd reached it until she felt it crunching softly under her feet. She fell to the ground and scooped handfuls of snow into her mouth. She chewed it to make it melt faster. More and more and more. She gagged, spat out a stone and then crammed in more snow.

She felt so much better. Water is the best painkiller there is. Now that her thirst had been eased, she was terribly aware once again that Luther was dead.

She took out her canteen and realised for the first time just how dirty the snow was. It was grey, black in patches, icy in patches, there was dirt and grass and stones on it. Further ahead it was fluffy, white and untouched. She crammed her canteen full of snow and started to wonder what she was going to do next.

She had some rations left, what she really needed now was a place to rest. Further ahead the snow grew into an icy mountain. She took out her binoculars and scanned the side of the mountain. She spotted the opening to a cave. She shrugged and started walking, leaving perfect footprints in the snow.

Chapter 68

The doctor came back, he brought two people with him. Malek watched them, feeling miserable and defeated. "How long ago was it first contracted?" asked one doctor, "We don't know. It does appear to have grown since I left." "We need to set up containment measures, it could be infectious." "Is that really necessary? He's already guarded in a secret place. It takes so much longer to get things done once quarantine measures are..." A tendril shot through the doctor's eye. He screamed and a second one went into his mouth. One doctor ran and got three in the back, the other picked up a tool to fight and then got impaled by Malek's own warped tentacle.

The worst part about it for Malek wasn't the death or the suffering. He'd seen plenty of that before. The worst of it was the feeling of blood and nutrients and energy being pumped into his body. It wasn't just feeding off them, it was overtaking them, swelling up inside them until parts of their bodies started bursting. Heads, arms, torsos. Skin and bone peeled and broke open, being replaced by giant grey and white masses. They weren't tendrils anymore, they were blobs that rolled together.

The skin on Malek's own numb legs started to disintegrate and then they popped open and fungus spilled out. It dragged him off the bed and he landed on top of it. It covered most of the floor. It wasn't just the parasite, it wasn't a complete transition. It was a white mass, still covered in live human flesh that pumped blood all over itself.

Chapter 69

Lakeitha walked through the mouth of the cave and into an ice tunnel. The walls, the floor and the ceiling were all made of scuffed transparent ice. The tunnel took a left turn, went on for ten seconds or so, took a right and reached a dead end after twenty metres. She went to the very end and pressed her back against the wall, slowly lowering herself to the ground. She wheezed as she straightened out her legs on the floor. She laid her sword down by her hand. It was very cold, it was a damn ice cave after all, but it was a little warmer than it was outside.

She just needed some sleep, she'd earned that. She wasn't ready to walk back. Would she go back through the maze? If she did she'd have to walk past Luther's body. That was unless some monster had taken it away. She wasn't sure what she would prefer. She was starting to feel unusually squeamish.

She opened her bag and took out her blanket and her towel. As she was rooting around her hand touched the metal disc. She took it out. The glowing red arrow still pointed to Mikey. She wrapped herself up tight and looked at it. What had the last few days been like for him?

The longer she stared at the red arrow the more connected she felt to her brother. This was what she had to live for. No matter how impossible it was, they were family and they owed it to each other to keep their lights burning and follow their arrows until they were together again.

Chapter 70

Malek was dragged through the building at the centre of the fungus as it absorbed everyone it came across. Some of them died instantly but most were trapped like Malek and pushed around by the undulations of this creature as it moved from room to room. The faces of men and women were pressed up against his own. He looked into their bulging eyes and stretched faces; they had an intensity that he was no longer capable of. He felt sorry for them, because their torment was still in its infancy. Those of them that could still scream did so, loudly and pointlessly.

When will I die? had become a lackluster thought for Malek, but he could hear it coming from some of these people as the fungus created a faint link between their minds.

From time to time Malek thought that his nervous system had been damaged to the point that he could no longer feel any pain, but it always came back.

The creature wanted to leave this building. It could sense thousands of lives outside these walls. But it couldn't escape, the doors were too strong, made of metal, designed to keep things in. It couldn't leave yet, so it had to search every room, to find every person and grow stronger until it felt the open air.

Its thoughts blasted through Malek's head, so he knew it wasn't evil, it was just very hungry.

Chapter 71

Mikey woke up and the moment he opened his eyes he thought, **Today is the day that we break into The Guardian's Palace.** He woke Gideon up with a nudge. They ate breakfast in silence. They'd talked about this over and over, there was nothing left to say. They just wanted to act.

They geared up. Gideon had given him a knife and a revolver. He had his own weapons that he'd built, but Gideon still wanted him to carry some old classics. There wasn't much chance of a knife malfunctioning.

Gideon wore his Hell Hunter armoured clothing. Mikey on the other hand wore a suit of lightweight armour that he made for himself six years ago during a paranoid phase. It was about fifty percent harder to cut through than the material used by Hell Hunters and soldiers. He'd only ever made the one suit, then he lost the formula and couldn't for the life of him remember how he'd invented it. It felt loose around his frail body. He used to be so much stronger. Even then he couldn't beat his sister in an arm wrestling contest, but he had been pretty good.

They were both covered in so much weapons and gear that they would draw attention even in this warriors pit of a city. So they covered themselves, Gideon wearing a heavy coat and Mikey dawning a faded red poncho, tucking his long beard underneath. They wore wide brimmed hats to partially cover their faces. Gideon opened the door and joy of joys it was raining. If it had been blistering then their extra clothes would've been just as out of place as their arsenals. He took one last look at the beacon and then tucked it away and went outside.

As soon as Mikey stepped out the door he was shot full of adrenaline. It made his knees shake, yet he felt like he didn't even need his walking staff. Whatever these people on the street were doing today it wasn't as important as what they were doing. Whatever happened, they'd all be talking about it tomorrow. Mikey was taking a lot of deep breaths. This wasn't what he did, Lakeitha went on the adventures, she did the fighting, he stayed home and tinkered and got high.

It was hard to tell with all the extra clothes and the rain but Gideon seemed cool and focused. They reached the square, The Guardians Palace was on the otherside. There were guards everywhere, soldiers too and Blackmasks. More than usual, maybe double the normal number. Alcraze must be about to start a war. They'd have to get in line.

Chapter 72

Shante had changed from her stylish dress into her combat gear. If she was going to war, she wasn't going to did it looking like a fucking doll. It wasn't her official military suit that she wore at ceremonies. This was the suit that she trained in and the public never saw her wear. It was grimy, covered in knives and splattered with dried blood; she absolutely loved it.

She was wearing boots in the throne room. Boots made for running and kicking, not looking slightly taller. She hoped that she'd get to kick somebody.

She'd spent hours looking at profiles of the important people in Alcraze. She knew a lot of them. Some childhood friends, drinking buddies, the second guy she ever had sex with. She hoped they all died. Luther had drained all her regret. She didn't have any emotion left, only a need to keep her tribe alive.

It had been more than twenty four hours since they'd last heard from Akira's team. If she was lucky Dominic just got hit in the head. She hadn't been lucky for a long time. She had no idea if Luther was alive or dead. In spite of how detached she felt, she still loved him. She'd ran out of hate and scorn. She just hoped that he would die quickly and with plenty of fight in him.

Her years of happy memories with Luther threatened to suck her in. She shut them out, they were mushy and fun and powerfully distracting. She wouldn't allow herself to return to them until the war was over.

Bogatar was by her side as always, she wondered how many people they'd kill together in the weeks to come. There were also ten guards, eight soldiers and two Blackmasks in the throne room. They were going to follow her everywhere she went from now on.

She wasn't really doing anything at the moment. The room's only practical use was when she had very official meetings with other important people. But she felt like being there today, because when she sat in her throne she truly felt like the ruler of Dantez. **We're fucked.** She sagged in her throne.

Chapter 73

Mikey and Gideon reached an ordinary looking front door in an ordinary looking house, one street away from The Guardians Palace. Mikey flicked open the concealed panel by the door, revealing the combination lock. He didn't know what the passcode was, but he had been the one to design and install this thing, so it didn't take much effort for him to take it apart and open the door.

The two of them walked down a set of well lit stairs, through the short tunnel and up the otherside. Mikey opened another door and there they were, inside The Guardians Palace. The secret entrance led into a room full of old boxes, which were in turn full of old junk. The door on this side was disguised as a section of wall when it was closed.

Gideon dumped his hat and jacket, Mikey actually quite liked his outfit, so his only change was to unfurl his beard and let it hang out over the front of his poncho. They left the dull little room and stepped into a high ceilinged corridor. Mikey knew every invisible trap in these corridors, he knew how to deactivate them or set them off. They walked along the empty corridor, hoping to be as stealthy as possible for as long as possible. Mikey leaned on his staff for every step he took.

Remaining unseen would take a lot of running and ducking, which Mikey was in no shape for. Gideon could do it, but he couldn't. They were just going to get as far as they could before a guard saw them. About a hundred metres ahead of them, Mikey knew there was an access point for the palace's security system. If they could get to it then he could disable the alarms and the cameras. The chances of them getting there unnoticed were pretty low, he was actually amazed that they hadn't been spotted yet.

A pair of guards walked across the corridor ahead of them. Mikey and Gideon stiffened up as they watched them go from right to left. They were in their cool looking uniforms and had their swords at their hips, all it would take would be a turn of the head. They passed on without noticing anything. Gideon went to the corner first and peeked around it. Then he gestured for Mikey to follow. They kept on going, straight ahead, only three more left to cross.

There were doors up and down the corridor, people could come from any one of them and ruin everything.

A stressed looking woman turned the corner ahead and started walking towards them. She had her head buried in her clipboard. For over ten seconds neither of them breathed. She got closer and closer. The pair of them maintained a slow steady pace and tried their best to look invisible. She never noticed them.

Mikey breathed a sigh of relief that he almost choked on, when ten guards turned the same corner and marched past them in formation. They looked blankly at the two intruders as they passed. They saw Mikey's poncho, his hat, his beard, his staff, not to mention Gideon's many exposed weapons and they didn't think that any of it looked out of the ordinary.

"Well fuck me standing up." said Gideon.

They reached the access point and Mikey got to work. This was a much more advanced system than the lock at the secret entrance. It was a touch sensitive hologram screen powered by electricity and some rare alien mineral. Mikey hadn't been involved in the design of this thing but he still knew how to hack it. He shut down the interior alarms and nodded to Gideon, "It's done."

Alarms started going off. "Mikey" said Gideon. Mikey frowned at the blaring noise. "I turned off the alarm." Gideon shook his head, "No really, this isn't the interior alarm...which means that it's the exterior alarm." "What?" "Oh shit, the exterior alarm only goes off when the city's under attack." "Attack?" They shared a worried look, "Shante" said Gideon. Mikey nodded, "Shante"

A second after it burst through the wall more than a dozen people on the street had already been flattened and submerged. They were stuck, squeezed by the texture of raw chicken and drained of everything they were worth. There were so many people out there that in twenty seconds it had more than doubled in size. The slimy white flooded street after street, each new artery swelled with screams that were instantly smothered. It branched off, knocking through every door and window to devour the people inside.

Malek had no idea how many people had been caught, but he felt every single one of them from the moment that the tentacles punctured their skin, broke through their eye sockets and flooded down their throats. He lost the connection with those that died, they became a part of the mass, their flesh indistinguishable to him from the giant slabs of white fungus.

It sat tall over the city, bigger than any of the buildings in Dantez. The soldiers and Grand Scrapers struggled with artillery designed only to fire outside the wall. They didn't understand what was happening and they didn't need to. A devastating monster was inside the city and every second they spent floundering more people died and more ground was lost. There were five hundred World Saver Turrets on the wall, each one loaded with forty massive bullets, with another two hundred rounds in boxes next to them. The first turret finished turning.

Turrets kicked and boomed for miles along the wall and countless rounds shot deep into the fleshy mass. Before the bullet's momentum was lost and the barbed wire was tangled, the poison was already working. Blood and gunk drained from the entry points and vast areas of it deflated and died. It quivered and strained, but the behemoth had no voice of its own to express its suffering. It screamed only in the minds of Malek and all the other people it had caught. To them it was deafening. But Malek still managed to enjoy its agony.

It was dying but it was also growing and feeding. And it was doing that faster. Tendrils bigger than houses pushed through the poisoned sections and reached out to the wall. The turrets fired on them as they approached, making them falter and whither. But the giant tentacles split into dozens of smaller ones, stretched to the top of the wall and dropped down on it. It swam over the surface of the wall, swallowing up every last soul. It went on for miles and its victims could do nothing more to slow it down.

The poisoned sections fell off as it replenished itself; huge husks crushed houses and people.

It had finally become big enough and strong enough that nothing could kill it. It had achieved domination and there were people everywhere. It flattened more buildings, stampeding and devouring crowds, flesh swelling and bursting all over it as it grew more and more.

Mikey and Gideon managed to get a lot deeper into the palace. They went up stairs and through corridors. Everybody was so focused on the alarm and whatever was happening outside that nobody stopped to check them. It was almost starting to feel like they'd be able to walk right up to Shante without any fuss.

A uniformed soldier passed them and then he grabbed Gideon's arm. Gideon turned his head, trying his best to hide his anxiety and adrenaline and aggression. "You can't be here!" shouted the man, his voice intimidatingly loud even under the alarm. "I'm authorised to be here, sir!" Gideon shouted back. The soldier grinned, his uniform had a lot of stripes and badges on it, he was important enough to know that wasn't true. "Name?" He had a predatory glint in his eyes and he was holding onto Gideon's injured arm awfully tight. **Fuck it, let's get started.**

His knife flashed from its sheath into the soldier's neck and out again. Gideon looked round and made eye contact with a group of soldiers down the corridor, they'd all seen it. No more need for words, he dropped the bleeding officer, sheaved his knife and went to meet the five soldiers. He used his one good arm with a ruthless efficiency. He drew his revolver and shot the first two soldiers in the head up close, one bullet each, flicking back the hammer between shots. They fell and Gideon shifted his aim to the third man, but the soldier knocked his arm aside, making him waste a bullet on the wall. Gideon kicked the soldier away, thumbed back the hammer, shot him in the knee, then hit him in the side of the head with the butt of his gun. Before he'd cleared the third soldier, the fourth was already swinging his sword at Gideon's neck.

He was very close to death when he raised his gun and emptied the last two rounds into the man's chest. He fell hard, dropping his sword before it reached Gideon. The fifth soldier lunged at him with a sword pointed at his belly. Gideon holstered the revolver as he sidestepped the stab and then reached over his shoulder and pulled out his katana.

Their blades clattered, Gideon blocked and deflected several attacks, fitting in a few jabs that didn't land. The soldier slashed at him, Gideon blocked the blade, parried it down to the left and then snapped the front couple inches of his sword up into the man's face, cutting clean through chin, mouth, nose and forehead.

The soldier fell backwards like a wooden plank and Gideon turned around, changed his grip and plunged the sword down into the chest of the third man as he groaned on the floor.

Mikey stared stunned at Gideon, who also seemed surprised by what he'd just down. He looked up at Mikey, slowly shaking his head, he had an electric look in his eyes. "I'm on rare form today."

"Kill them!" shouted a commanding voice from behind Mikey. He shuffled around and saw twenty or so guards and soldiers running towards them from the other side of the corridor.

My turn. Thought Mikey as he reached into the bag under his poncho and took out his sonic gun. He flicked the primer and pointed it at the crowd of able bodied warriors charging towards him. He'd never actually used one of his creations in combat before; it made his hands tingle. He squeezed the trigger and his ears popped. He wouldn't experience anything more than that, but the further it travelled the more it was amplified. All twenty-two of the guards and soldiers stumbled, their faces contorting into wide mouthed grimaces and then blood exploded from their ears. Mikey's confident smirk disappeared. They were all lying still and gushing blood onto the floor. He looked round at Gideon in horror, his jaw shuddering up and down without making any noises. Gideon looked queasy.

Mikey looked back down at the sonic gun. **Crap.** "It was on three!" He shouted to Gideon, his voice sounding strange as his hearing adjusted. "I meant to use one but it was set to three. I was only trying to deafen them." He looked back at all the dead people, then averted his eyes. "Temporarily, it was a temporary deafening."

Gideon choked back some vomit and then said, "Let's just move on. Which way are we going again?" Mikey paused, "That's the quickest route." He said pointing at, but not looking at, all the people he'd just killed.

"Ughhhuckk...let's move." said Gideon. They took up the entire width of the corridor, there was no way to walk around them. They stepped between the bodies, their boots treading on the blood. "You've seen worse right? Out in the wild." asked Mikey. "I have, I'm just struggling to remember when." "But you have?" Gideon took a while to answer, "Sure" Mikey tripped and righted himself by leaning his staff onto the back of a corpse. **That doesn't feel good.**

They made it past the bodies, stamping two sets of red footprints on the clean floor. They turned the corner and carried on. After a few seconds they heard somebody scream. Neither of them acknowledged it.

They took a right turn and a couple of soldiers ran past them. It was a relief not to be noticed. Two seconds later they heard the soldiers stop and turn around. Mikey sighed, took the sonic gun back out, set the dial to one and then turned around. The soldiers were approaching, weapons drawn. He used his gadget and this time they clutched their ears and yelled and kicked around on the floor like they were supposed to. Alive and barely even bleeding from their ears. He looked back to Gideon feeling pleased with himself, "I'd really prefer it if you didn't use that one again." Mikey shrugged, "Charge is only good for two shots anyway, I just wanted to prove to myself that it worked."

They slowed as they approached a corner. Gideon peeked around it, then ducked his head back. "At least ten of them." "Move" "What?" "Move, you're blocking me." Gideon stepped aside and Mikey looked at the black panel on the wall where Gideon had been standing. He took a tool from his bag and turned it on, a narrow laser peeked out two centimetres. He started cutting through the black alien metal with the laser. "Is that a trap station?" asked Gideon. "Yes it is. I need thirty seconds and I can clear the corridor." Gideon peeked around the corner again, none of the guards were moving, they'd been set up in a defensive formation and wouldn't leave that spot until the crisis was over.

Mikey had the panel down and was flicking his fingers through a mess of wires, small screens full of data, power cells and other stuff that Gideon didn't understand. A door ten metres down the corridor opened and a dozen doctors and nurses, with stretchers and equipment, ran out and thankfully headed away from Gideon and Mikey. They were all so focused on their task that none of them looked back and saw the two of them. The doctors turned left at the end of the corridor, on their way to the twenty eight dead bodies they'd left behind. "No way." Said Mikey, "What?" "Years ago as a joke I dared a friend of mine to make a trap that gave people a sort of waking nightmare. They'd all see a vision of their mother telling them that she didn't love them and they were kicked out of the family. It's so powerful that they'll believe it's real." "That's dark man." "I was drunk at the time. Whoops." said Mikey, a mean grin on his face as he cut some wires. Three seconds passed and then every guard started crying.

Mikey walked confidently around the corner and through the devastated men. Gideon started following him, then hesitated. "It's not going to happen to us is it?" "Nah, the trap only lasts a few seconds. But the effect stays longer. Poor little orphans." "You're a lot more evil than people give you credit Mikey." "Thanks pal." "Mummy!" shouted a man with sideburns as Mikey shuffled around him.

"This reaction seems a bit strong. They must be able to figure out that it's not real." He couldn't resist, "Guys it's a trick. Your mums love you." "Don't bother." said Mikey, "They basically lose touch with reality for a couple of hours."

They reached a sturdy black metal door, the throne room was just around the corner on the otherside. The security was only going to get heavier from here. Mikey tried the handle, "Locked, the keys might be on the highest ranked guard." Gideon nodded and started checking the distraught guards weeping at his feet. **At least the dead guys kept their dignity.** He found the cry baby with the fanciest uniform. He was crawling from one bit of floor to another. Gideon used his foot to roll him onto his back like a turtle and took the key ring from his belt.

He'd never seen anyone like Mikey before. He'd spent his life fighting and he'd never come across an unstoppable force like him. But he was still sick, weak and slow. If failing and dying could only be avoided by running, then Mikey would fail and die. They were going to have to plant their feet and fight every time; and nobody wins every time.

Chapter 74

The intruders had been witnessed and calls had been made throughout the palace, until they reached the top. She knew Mikey and Gideon were in the building, but they were the furthest thing from her mind.

The footage was projected thirty feet tall onto a wall of the throne room. She watched her city being destroyed by a giant monster the kind she'd never seen or heard of before. There was no audio. Quentin had pointlessly doubled the number of soldiers and guards in the throne room and all of them were staring at the video, their hearts breaking. So many people were dying, it was torture to watch but she didn't dare look away. Rulers don't get to avert their eyes when their people are massacred. Shante wept.

Chapter 75

They went through the door and right away they were faced by another ten man blockade. Four of them had assault rifles aimed at their heads. Mikey reached inside his bag and held his thumb against the gravity bomb. "Don't move!" shouted the commanding officer, "How did you get past Lieutenant Burgman?" Mikey spoke without thinking, "I'm friends with his mother." Gideon choked on his laughter. They struggled to keep their snickering under control as the guards frowned. "Hands in the air!" Mikey pressed his thumb down on the gravity bomb and started counting down. **Ten, nine.** He took his hand from the bag and took off his poncho. **Seven,** "What's in the bag?" **Six** "Weapons" replied Mikey, **five, four,** "Throw it over here, if you reach inside the bag we will shoot you down." As soon as he heard the word throw, Mikey took off the bag, **two** "Run" he said to Gideon as he threw the bag with all his strength towards the soldiers. **One**, came as the bag was in the air and Mikey and Gideon turned and took their first desperate step towards the open door. Mikey pushed his staff against the ground with all his strength. "Close it!" yelled Mikey as he cleared the threshold. Gideon grabbed the door handle and slammed it shut as the rifles fired and Mikey counted **zero**.

As the bullets passed the bag in the air, they started to bend down to meet it and every guard in the corridor was lifted from his feet and carried to the bag. The first man stuck to it just before it hit the ground, then the second, knocked into the first and then all the rest jammed up against them. The hinges on the door strained and Mikey and Gideon took a couple more steps as the metal door was ripped free and hurried to join the ball of men stuck to the bag. Mikey and Gideon's feet left the ground mid stride, their legs kicking out for the floor. They started going backwards, they passed the threshold and the backs of their feet touched the floor, dragging along it as their bodies bent lower towards the bag. Mikey was consumed with terror, because he knew what came next. They stopped flying and fell, their backs hitting the ground. Mikey hit his head on the hard floor, it was the most wonderful thing he had ever felt.

Gideon rolled over and looked up at the pile of men and the door all stuck together a few metres away from them. They were all groaning and then three spikes shot out from the centre of the pile and pierced through the densely packed bodies. The spikes retracted and those who survived screamed and panicked as they were drenched in blood from the dead bodies they were still stuck to. The spikes shot out again, this time in three different places, they retracted and there were far fewer screams. One more time and there were none at all.

Gideon realised he hadn't breathed since he heard the gunshots. He let out a long shaky breath and took a nervous look at Mikey. "Can you give me a hand?" asked Mikey, Gideon took his hand and helped him to his feet, then handed him his staff.

"Give it a sec." The gravity deactivated and the bodies and the door finally slumped apart, but they were still stacked on top of the bag. Gideon shook his head, the idea of rooting around the corpses made his spit taste like metal. "Sorry Gideon but I really need the bag, don't worry about the poncho." "Ehhghthhhh...I know." But before he had even taken a step towards the bag, a squad of soldiers sprinted in from a side corridor right by where all the men had been standing. They'd seen them get lifted off their feet, but they hadn't seen what happened next. There were eight of them. One fainted, one threw up and the rest charged. Gideon drew his revolver and shot the first guy three times in the torso before he realised that these soldiers were wearing extra heavy armour on top of their suits. He had almost reached Gideon when he put one in his eye.

He fired two shots at the next soldier's head, but he dodged them and they hit the guy behind uselessly in the shoulder. He dropped his gun and went for a knife, it was halfway out the sheath when he was tackled to the ground. He struggled but the guy had him pinned and he knew what he was doing. His limbs were trapped and he could barely breathe against the weight of the man on his chest. The next soldier stood over his head and raised his mace. There was a gunshot, then another. He looked over his shoulder at Mikey and then a bullet tore through his face. He fell hard, his head landing beside Gideon's. His messy, blood covered face convulsed in supreme agony.

This made the soldier pinning Gideon look up at Mikey, giving him a few inches of freedom. Gideon drew his red alien metal knife, slipped it into a chink in his armour and stuck it through the soldier's suit, through his skin, through his ribs and through his lung.

Three soldiers sprinted around the bodies, towards Mikey. Gideon wasn't there to stand in front of him. He had three bullets left, bang, miss, bang, miss, bang, miss. They'd be on him in two seconds. He was out of gadgets, out of traps, out of bullets. They were strong healthy men and when they reached him they'd crush him like a bug. Mikey's heart raced and panic seized him. He looked over to Gideon, who was getting up and then got tackled to the ground by a soldier who had vomit on his uniform.

He wasn't going to get rescued. He dropped the gun and took out the knife that Gideon had given him. A broad shouldered man was about to reach him, he had a furious look on his face, something bloodthirsty and animal, not the least bit squeamish about killing a cripple. Mikey put everything he had into a knife slash and quite by chance it cut across the man's throat and he dropped at Mikey's feet.

The second man reached him, he had a big sword in his hands, he swung it at Mikey and Mikey instinctively raised his staff. The sword embedded halfway through the thick wood, sending a judder up Mikey's arm and through his body. The soldier released his sword and then kicked Mikey's staff out of his hand, sending the sword and the staff clattering across the floor.

Standing still on wobbly legs, Mikey slashed and stabbed at the unarmed soldier who kept trying to catch his arm and take the knife from him. This went on for a couple of seconds, until Mikey accidentally stabbed the man through the hand. They both stared, shocked at the hand and the knife until the third soldier came in and kicked Mikey in the chest. The knife stayed with the hand as he flew off his feet, went horizontal in the air and landed on his back, all the air knocked out of his lungs. To his frail body it was like falling off a three storey building.

Gideon killed the vomity soldier and looked round at his friend, who was empty handed on the floor, with two soldiers about to kill him. He didn't have time to reload his revolver, so he grabbed one of his World Savers, took four steps to the left to get a better angle, aimed for the centre of mass and fired. The bullet buried a big clean hole through the first soldier's torso and then lodged itself inside the second one.

He fell on his back, the poison racing to kill him before he bled to death. Gideon helped Mikey to his feet, then picked up the staff and worked the sword out. There was a deep cut in it but it still supported Mikey's weight. Then Gideon bucked up and stuck his hands into the dead bodies, moving them until his hand closed around the strap of the bag and he lifted it out.

They went to the corner and both peeked around it. Twenty metres ahead of them they saw General Quentin, head of the army, standing with thirty two soldiers in front of the door to the throne room. The front row held big rectangular shields in a tight formation. Behind them there were five guns, three bows, two crossbows and a lot of swords. Gideon immediately ducked back and Mikey shuffled back. Quentin yelled over the alarm, "Gideon Blackwell and Mikey Gleeson. You will not get to The Guardian of Dantez. I will personally oversee your punishment for treason and for the men and women you murdered today!" "Fuck you Quentin!" Gideon shouted back.

"There aren't any traps over there." Mikey told Gideon in a quiet voice. Gideon lost a bit of his vim when he heard that. "Is there anything in the bag you can use?" "No, it's all spent." "How are we going to get through them?" "How many bullets you got left?" "Four" "That's not enough."

Mikey had been feeling such momentum and hope as they fought their way through the palace and now it was gone. Just like that, they'd reached the end of the line without even laying eyes on Shante. "It isn't over." said Mikey through gritted teeth. He wasn't going to admit defeat and he wasn't going to die either. Lakeitha was depending on him and there was no army that could stop him. Mikey's rumbling determination grew into something else. Something he hadn't felt in five years. A charge that his sick body hadn't been capable of holding. At that moment Mikey was whole for the first time in years. Once again he had magic.

Mikey let go of his staff and walked around the corner. "What are you doing!" shouted Gideon. His hands shook, his skin tingled, his eyes locked on Quentin. A bolt of lightning materialised in front of Quentin and shot into his torso and then up through all the holes of his face. It snapped in all directions, shocking through the metal shields and burning up the uniforms. Mikey couldn't remember the last time his senses were this sharp. He felt every movement at the end of the corridor, he knew who was yet to be hit by his lighting and he summoned more bolts to fry them. They screamed and scrambled, some of them flying backwards when they were electrocuted, slamming into each other and the grand metal door.

He had missed this power. He revelled in the familiar ecstasy of his magic. He enjoyed it so much that he continued to fire off lightning bolts for five seconds after the last person had died. Finally he relented, leaving behind thirty two charred bodies, many of them still twitching.

He glanced over his shoulder at Gideon. He was absolutely gobsmacked, "I need my staff." He said, his legs starting to weaken as the energy faded. He wiped some of the heavy sweat from his forehead as he waited. Gideon gave him the staff. Holding it once again felt like a regression but he needed it.

"I thought you weren't magic anymore." "Me too." Mikey swayed and leaned harder on his staff to keep himself from falling. "How are you feeling?" Mikey's heart was beating painfully hard, his head ached, his throat hurt, his bones felt fragile. "Magnificent"

They walked through the dead to get to the obscenely tall and imposing door of the throne room. Killing them had felt extraordinary but stepping over them was disgusting. Mikey took a tool from his dripping, blood soaked bag and got to work. First he dug into the security system from the wall panel and gained control of all the traps inside the throne room. While he was at it he finally shut off that annoying alarm. If King Rodriquez was attacking the city, then he was too slow, because they got to Shante first.

"Gideon come here." He handed his device to Gideon, "They've installed a last resort trap in the throne room that sets the floor on fire. Everyone standing more than five metres away from the throne is gonna burn. You see this green button." He said pointing to the largest button on the device, "Hold this down and don't take your finger off it until I tell you. On my mark, we're gonna clear out every guard that Shante has protecting her." "That's a lot of people." "Not as many as we've already killed. We do this and we have Shante."

Gideon pressed his finger on the button. Mikey and Gideon clasped hands and then Mikey shuffled to the door, took out another pair of tools and started disabling the lock. There were only six people in the world who could break this lock in under two minutes. Mikey did it in seventeen seconds. He took ten steps back as the two doors swung open. There were forty heavily armed guards and soldiers standing in front of him and behind them, sitting in her throne, was Shante. **I'm gonna break you bitch.** "Do it" He said to Gideon. "Kill them" said Shante from her throne, her voice barely audible from this distance. She said it like she was ordering food. The first row took two steps and then they were nothing more than black silhouettes floundering in the fire. A few of them managed to run out of the throne room. They stumbled around, wrapped in yellow flame, then dropped, rolled and stopped rolling.

Shante covered her face against the heat. She closed her eyes and waited for it to end. The fire cut out and when she looked up again they were all dead and the floor was covered in black ash. Then Bogatar stepped out in front of her throne. His face was burnt a little on the right side. He held his kasa in his right hand. It was blackened on top. He put it back on his head and stood between her and the intruders with his sword drawn. He stood still and waited as they walked into the room. Shante noticed that his shoulders were shaking in fury, he was barely restraining himself. Shante herself was bubbling with rage and fear as well, Mikey and Gideon had done an impossible amount of killing for just two men. One of them could barely walk and the other had one arm in a sling. That amount of violence deserved respect. She wanted to hear what they had to say before she set Bogatar on them.

"Call it off. You call them off right now, you leave my sister alone!" shouted Mikey as he limped into the throne room. Shante stood up and walked down from the throne, stopping a few metres behind Bogatar. They faced them, standing five meters away from the bodyguard. Gideon and Bogatar locked eyes. Two big angry men ready to tear each other apart. Gideon quite liked the idea of firing all his remaining bullets into Shante's kneecaps, then making her crawl to the nearest sensitive to call of the attack.

"Mikey Gleeson, I never had a problem with your sister or with Malek. I had to kill Luther Aprille to prevent a war and the two of them were with him. It had to be done. You both understand that don't you, I did my duty as a leader, there was no other option." "I don't care. Call them off." "I can't" said Shante. "Yes you fucking can." spat Gideon. Bogatar inched forward, his upper lip rising, almost like a dog. Gideon kept his hand on the grip of his World Saver, still in its holster.

"No I can't. We lost contact with our sensitive yesterday. He's almost definitely dead and we have no other way of reaching them." "You're lying." said Mikey, his voice full of venom, "You betrayed my sister, your word means nothing. I'm going to torture you, until you bring Lakeitha back." Gideon thought that Bogatar was going to lunge at Mikey when he mentioned torture. But he didn't, this was a man who truly wanted to fight, but he wasn't going to make a move until he got the order.

Shante sighed, "I'm sick of lying, holding things back. None of it matters anymore, the city is being destroyed as we speak. Did you know that? There's a giant monster outside, killing everyone, it'll be here in a few minutes. Our defences can't stop it." "Don't try to change the subject bitch." "I'd show you, but I'm pretty sure that fire ruined the projector. Anyway...Me and Luther were in love. You didn't know that, did you? He used to be my bodyguard and he meant everything to me. But he was stupid one night. He got hit in the head a lot, got drunk and fucked the hottest woman he could find. She turned out to be Princess Eleanor. I loved him, but I still had to kill him to save my city and now I can't even do that. Right now your sister is actually safer in the wild than in Dantez."

Mikey didn't give a fuck about her broken heart. He wasn't going to let Shante talk her way out of this, whether or not the city was being destroyed. "Just do it." "If Dominic, the sensitive, was still alive, I still wouldn't. Luther and Malek and Lakeitha are all probably dead right now. The four of us are definitely dying today. All that matters now, is that I'm not gonna let you beat me. Bogatar." Bogatar covered four out of five meters before Gideon blew his head off with the World Saver. The kasa fell to the floor with a big hole in it.

Shante drew a small black knife in each hand and went for Mikey, Mikey took a hurried step back as he fumbled with his own knife. Gideon darted to intercept Shante, dropping the World Saver and grabbing his katana. He swung at her head and she ducked under, carving both blades across his torso, piercing his armour and his skin. He turned as she came flying at him, slashing him twice across the chest before he kicked her in the head. She fell hard, rolled, came up and threw both knives at Gideon's head. Gideon deflected them with his sword and then Shante was on him with two new knives. She lightly stabbed him three times down the legs and then he cut her across the chest and she gasped and backed off.

Mikey watched them fight. Shante was fast, even faster than Gideon. Mikey would be useless unless he found his magic again. He focused on the feeling of power and all the hatred he felt, not just towards Shante, but also towards this whole fucked up, doomed world. Shante had said that he'd never see his sister again. He felt the magic.

Gideon had bleeding cuts all over, but he still felt deadly. He took a swing at Shante and she cut him across the wrist, then broke away, out of range of his last swing.

Blood spilled painlessly down his wrist and he became very weak. He locked eyes with Mikey, his new best friend.

Mikey was overflowing with power as he watched Gideon fall. He turned his head to Shante as she ran at him and he annihilated her.

And that was it. Everybody was dead and Lakeitha was still being hunted. His magic waned and he reached inside his bag. He took out the beacon and looked at the little arrow. It was still red. He gasped happily and tears started to dribble from his eyes. She was alive and he wished her the best.

A sloppy mass of white tendrils, stretched skin, jellied blood and writhing bodies ripped around the corner. Mikey heard it coming but didn't bother to look up from the little red arrow.

Chapter 76

Lakeitha woke up from her shallow sleep. The cold stang her face. Her blanket and towel had been turned stiff by the frost. She reached into her bag and took out some dry meat and nuts. She chewed it slowly. Shivers crawled up and down her body.

She picked up her beacon and looked down at the black arrow. Panic snatched her as she felt the briefest moment of horrible shock. Her brother was dead. Mikey was dead. She couldn't breathe, she gagged on the cold air over and over. Then she managed to suck in a breath and as she let it out she started sobbing. Tears fell into her mouth and snot dribbled from her nose. She felt the worst pain of her life squeezing her soul.

She bent over, putting her face into her blanket. Her mouth opened wide and she released many strange aching noises as grief twisted her lungs and shook her throat.

She tried to sink into happy memories of her brother but her misery blocked them off. She couldn't think of any words or any location or any warm feelings. All she could reach was a shifting image of his face. Him as an eight year old, a twelve year old, a seventeen year old. With a black and grey beard, a black beard or no beard at all. Going through so many facial expressions but with no context to give them meaning.

She couldn't escape into the past, she was stuck in this ice cave. Ice on her right and her left, behind her and down the tunnel ahead. This was more vivid than the special moments that she spent with her brother. She could feel the cold and see her steamy breath and hear the gentle echoes as she cried.

"Mikey, Mikee, Mikey, Mika...a ooo, Mikey, Mi...Mikey ack Ma, oh Mikey no no no Mikey, Mikey, Mikey uh huhuhhuhhhhhhhi wa no oh Mikey...Mi Ma Ma Mooo Mikey."

She cried past the point that the skin on her face warmed and the muscles in her face ached.

Taking care of Mikey, bringing him medicine and raising his spirits had become her purpose in life. It had brought them closer as siblings than ever before. She had been tough before but taking on that responsibility had raised her endurance for pain and her drive to win. Without it she never would have survived so many years in the jungle.

It had felt like the love she had for her brother was an immortal, invincible bond that would always bring them back together, overcoming everything. But in reality it wasn't an untouchable force of the universe, it was a very small and very vulnerable thing. That family bond was always going to be tainted by his death, until the day she died, then it wouldn't exist at all.

How had Mikey died? Did his illness kill him or was he murdered on orders from Shante? Did he go sniffing around asking questions after she turned on the distress signal? Would he still be alive if she hadn't? Did he suffer or did he go quickly? Did he wish that she was there with him?

She ran out of tears, her eyes were sore. She continued to gag, gasp, shake and call his name.

She drank some water and looked at her hazy reflection in the ice. She was so very cold.

When she had sat down on this spot, she'd had every intention of getting back up after some sleep and walking right out of the tunnel. She had had no choice in the matter, she had to find her way back to Mikey. Now the very idea of walking, even to the end of the short tunnel, seemed so difficult.

"What am I going to do now?" **Doesn't matter.** Her brain answered her mouth. **I can't change anything.**

Lakeitha was so buried in grief that she wasn't sure if it had been minutes or hours since she saw that the beacon's light had gone out.

He was her big brother. Seven years older.

Finally she was able to embrace her memories of Mikey. She closed her eyes and did her best to relive all those precious moments since they were little kids playing together, right up until the last time she saw him. She left behind a sad mark on every memory she touched.

She heard footsteps coming around the corner, from the entrance to the tunnel. She didn't have much interest in the noise, she kept on crying. A flickering orange reflection shone against the ice at the other end of the tunnel. She started hearing a dripping noise that got faster and heavier. Akira walked around the corner, his body engulfed by a raging fire.

He's still alive. Thought Lakeitha, **I shoulda checked**. He held a club in his left hand, keeping his right empty. Through the fire she could see the hatred in his eyes. The surface of the dense ice above him and below him, melted. Droplets hissed when they hit the flames. Lakeitha pushed off the frozen blanket and towel and rose to her feet, sword in her right hand.

They stared at each other.

She charged him. Akira hit her in the face with a stream of fire. She did her best to cover her face and continued charging as her skin burned. She lunged to the left, breaking from the fire and then she clattered into the ball of flames. He held his ground, grabbing her, turning and carrying her momentum into a wall of ice. Her face was a horrible crisp mess of black and red, but her eyes were well enough to see his club coming for her head. She blocked it with her sword and then stabbed at his face. He sidestepped away but she caught him in the shoulder. She withdrew the blade, was about to swing for his head but then she saw him splaying his palm and ducked under another blast of fire.

She jumped up and kicked him in the stomach, making him slip on the ice and his back hit a wall. She went for him and he knocked the sword from her hands with his club. She closed in empty handed, pushed his bat down with her right forearm as she hit him in the face with a left jab. The ice wall hissed louder the longer he spent pressed up against it. Right hook, left hook, left jab, the metal studs on her gloves cracked into his skull. As her blows rocked his brain the flames started to die down.

His bat hit her in the knee and she buckled, wide open for him to punch her across the face. She lost some teeth and her knee bent to the left as the punch carried her to the right. She struggled to stand and then his bat shattered her cheekbone and she fell, dropping her sword. He pulled out a knife and jumped on her. She moved her head and raised her hands as he landed on her, the knife digging into the ice beside her head and his knees crushing the air from her lungs. Most of the fire had died out, but some flames still shot out at random. She bucked, trying to shake him off while doing her best to block his stabs. One hit the ice, two scraped against her forearm guards and one cut her cheek and her ear. Then she managed to get a leg out from under him. She grabbed his arm and did a kick and roll, pushing him off her.

She tried to scramble up but Akira was on his feet impossibly fast and he kicked her in the head. She blacked out, then came too before she'd even finished falling. She landed beside her sword, grabbed it and rolled to her left instinctively just before a jet of flame cut across the ice where she'd landed.

Fuck my face hurts. She got up, turned and saw him rushing towards her, club drawn back. Just before he reached her he slipped on the ice and his head hit her in the stomach. They both went down, and Lakeitha drew one of her stilettos. Lying on the ice beside her Akira let out a hate filled roar and swung the club down towards her head. Lakeitha's upper body lurched towards Akira and she took the club in the shoulder as she reached her knife up into his bicep, using all her strength to push the steel blade through his armour. **My burning skin smells horrible.**

He kicked her in the face again, and she rolled away, leaving the knife dangling from his arm. She jumped up and grabbed her sword. She slashed down at Akira but he wasn't there anymore, he was on his feet, with a metal club in each hand. They went at it, Lakeitha holding her sword with both hands to strengthen her blocks against the thicker and heavier weapons. Akira was so fast and strong that he was as quick with the extra weight as she was with her sword.

Lakeitha blocked the first three attacks, then slashed him across the chest. He blocked her attempt to stab him through the heart and then he took a swing at her head. She ducked under it and the club cracked into the ice wall. She tried to cut his head off but he disarmed her on the backswing. Suddenly they were standing face to face and Lakeitha was empty handed. He smashed a club into her face and broke her jaw. She fell sideways and hit her head on the ice. She spat out some teeth and bled heavily from her mouth. She was so dizzy.

Akira crouched over her and put his clubs away. He seemed to think she was finished, he had a toothy grin on his face. She had a devious idea and started curling up into a ball, looking very scared and making some pathetic noises. He smiled wider. One of his eyes had turned fully bloodshot, but both of them were wet with joy. **You enjoy your revenge.** He leaned closer and punched her in the face. It hurt but her whole head was a clusterfuck of overwhelmed pain receptors, so another punch didn't make much difference. He hit again and again, turning her vision red.

Then she drew her boot knife and stabbed up into Akira's side. She pierced the suit and the skin, but the knife was too short to cut between the ribs and into his heart. He gasped as the blade scraped against his ribs, then he pulled his own knife and stabbed her in the gut.

They both held onto their knives for a few seconds struggling to breathe. Then Lakeitha let go and reached for her largest knife and Akira did the same. They swung and slashed at each other in a wounded frenzy on the ground, sometimes scraping each other's clothes and even breaking the skin, but not doing any lethal damage. Lakeitha kicked him in the chest to get some space between them, then got to her feet. As an afterthought she pulled the knife out of her stomach. She was losing quite a lot of blood but this wasn't a fatal injury. Well it was, but not for a while.

Akira raised his hand as sparks started spitting out and a small flame formed. Lakeitha lunged a step forward and cut off four of his fingers with her knife. He gasped and she stabbed at his head but he blocked it with his forearm guard and then slashed his knife at her neck. She jumped back clear of the blade, raised her knee, chambering her leg and hit him with a double kick. First to the groin, second to the stomach. He doubled over and she grabbed his ear in her left hand, yanked his head up and stabbed her knife into the base of his chin, pushing it as deep as it would go.

For the briefest moment they locked eyes, he knew he was dead but he still looked so determined. His knife scraped against her armour, he frantically tried to stab her as he made a wet choking noise. She removed the knife and stepped back. Without her holding him up Akira fell on his face and his blood started overflowing the little puddles that his fire had left in the ice.

She didn't feel like staying in this tunnel with Akira's dead body. She picked up her sword and her boot knife and slid them back into their sheaths. Then she walked slowly out of the tunnel and into the open snow. She could see two sets of footprints in the snow, leading off towards dry ground. She followed them for thirty seconds, just wanting to get some space between her and the cave. It was a very clear day, she could see the maze and the hills beyond it, but no trees, they were too far away.

She took a swig of water and spat it out right away. Her mouth couldn't take it. She stopped walking and stood looking over the ground she had covered and doing her best to ignore the extraordinary pain in her stomach and her face and some other places.

A portal opened. It was a shiny circle of creamy blue light, darker around the edges. It was less than a hundred metres away from her. It was small at first, appearing out of nothing and it grew steadily, stretching towards the sky. Lakeitha watched it, swaying gently from side to side, curious about what would happen next. She hadn't seen a portal in over two years. Every time she saw them she would always be careful, running or hiding. This time she just wanted to look at it, there was another dimension on the other side of it, absolutely anything could come through.

It grew over a hundred metres tall, then twice that. It wasn't facing directly towards her, more pointed to her left. It was only about a metre wide and she could see the empty space on either side of it.

A foot stepped through the portal, the foot was about twice as tall as she was. It was followed by a shin and a knee and then a whole body. A giant stepped out in front of her, it stood and looked around, scanning its new surroundings for miles. The giant cast a huge shadow behind it. The portal shrank down to nothing in an instant, the giant reached for it but it was already gone.

Lakeitha stared up at it, entranced by the creature. It was the biggest thing she'd ever seen. It had two arms, two legs, a head with a mouth, a nose, two eyes and two ears. It had skin and was wearing clothes made from tattered brown cloth. Yet it didn't look human, because no human had ever had a face like that. It was hard to explain why; it had a narrow face, a bald head and sunken yellow eyes. It was still turning to look at the new landscape. It was fascinating watching how its massive body shifted, even though it was so similar to how humans moved.

It looked right at her and she gasped as it bent down to look closer. Its head was a stone's throw away from her own. She could see a lot more detail, see the subtle grey brown tinge to its skin that was so different from any human beings. It had a curious expression on its face, it opened its mouth a crack and she saw that it had three rows of crooked teeth.

It leaned even closer and the breath from its nose felt like the wind. She looked directly into one of its huge yellow eyes. "What are you looking at." She croaked. It moved one of its hands in front of her and curled its index finger into its thumb. It flicked her away and she died in the air.